JEFF, KARMA, AND ME

Jere' M. Fishback

A NineStar Press Publication

Published by NineStar Press
P.O. Box 91792,
Albuquerque, New Mexico, 87199 USA.
www.ninestarpress.com

Jeff, Karma, and Me

Printed in the USA
First Edition
February, 2020

Print ISBN: 978-1-951880-55-2

Also available in eBook, ISBN: 978-1-951880-53-8

Warning: This book contains sexually explicit content, which may only be suitable for mature readers, suicidal ideation, suicide, homophobia, deceased family member, drug use, drinking and driving, child abuse, cancer, death of a prominent character, and infidelity.

Twenty-year-old college student, Jakub Mazur, is a loner consumed by feelings of helplessness due to his mother's unexplained disappearance many years before. He feels he's not in charge of his own life, that forces beyond his control will always determine his destiny. But when a summer affair ignites between Jakub and Jeff Brucelli, Jakub tastes both romantic love and self-empowerment.

After returning to school for his third year of college, Jakub suffers another tragic loss; it shakes his faith in his ability to navigate life's challenges. Is he doomed to suffer at the hand of fate forever?

When Jeff is diagnosed with Hodgkin's Lymphoma, a potentially fatal cancer of the lymphatic system, Jeff's oncologist says he must endure debilitating chemotherapy cycles, then radiation treatments. Jakub is devastated when he learns of this, but decides, for once, he will take control of his future instead of behaving like a helpless bystander.

The Twelve Laws of Karma

1. The Great Law

Whatever we put into the universe will come back to us.

2. The Law of Creation

Life does not happen by itself, we have to make it happen.

3. The Law of Humility

We must accept something before we can change it.

4. The Law of Growth

By changing ourselves, we change our lives.

5. The Law of Responsibility

We are responsible for what happens in our lives.

6. The Law of Connection

The past, the present, and the future are all connected.

7. The Law of Focus

We cannot think of two different things at the same time.

8. The Law of Giving and Hospitality

Our behavior should match our thoughts and actions.

9. The Law of Here and Now

We cannot be present if we are looking backward.

10. The Law of Change
History repeats itself until we learn from it and change our path.
11. The Law of Patience and Reward
The most valuable rewards require persistence.
12. The Law of Significance and Inspiration
Rewards are a result of the effort and energy we put into it.

CHAPTER ONE

I was twenty years old when Jeff Brucelli walked into my life and turned it upside down. I had just finished my sophomore year of college and was home for summer break, to live with my dad in the head ranger's residence in Fort De Soto Park, a county facility fronting Tampa Bay and the Gulf of Mexico. Dad oversaw the park's campground, as well as the picnic areas, boat ramps, piers, and beaches. Our house was a two-bedroom, wood frame structure seated on nine-foot pilings, with a screened porch overlooking a placid bayou. The floors were polished oak, and the wood burning fireplace was built of local limestone. A wooden dock and covered boat slip extended into the bayou, where Dad kept a sixteen-foot Carolina Skiff with a forty-horsepower outboard.

My first morning home, I gobbled a bowlful of cornflakes and chugged OJ from a carton. Then I took a bike ride through the RV section of the campground. The sun had risen two hours before and already the day heated up. Dampness gathered in my armpits while I pedaled along the crushed shell road. Most campsites I passed were waterfront, shaded by live oaks and sabal palms. Native foliage grew between them: sea grape, hibiscus, turkey oaks, and flame of the woods.

Many sites were empty, but at one near the eastern tip of the campground, an RV the size of a city bus hulked. A guy my age sat there at a picnic table, strumming an acoustic guitar. Shirtless and wearing cutoff denim shorts, he was slender and fair-skinned, and his cola-colored eyes narrowed when I approached on my bike.

"Are you staying here?" I asked.

Sunlight reflected in his mop of dark and wavy hair when he nodded and answered in a scratchy tenor. "My folks are serving as campground hosts the next few months. They're both schoolteachers and have the summer free, so we'll be here through August."

I dismounted and lowered my kickstand. Then I pointed my chin at the RV. "That's a nice ride."

"It belongs to my mom's parents. Grandma's not well these days, and they don't use it much, so they lent it to us for this trip. We're from Indiana."

I extended a hand. "I'm Jakub Mazur."

Jeff told me his name while we shook. His palm felt warm, his grip firm.

I explained how I was home for the summer from Florida State University and living inside the park.

"I just finished my second year at IU," Jeff said. "I'm a journalism major."

Jeff glanced here and there before he spoke again, this time in almost a whisper. "We've only been here a few days, but I get the impression most people in the campground are older—retirees and the like."

I rolled my eyes. "You won't find many college kids here, but we can hang out if you'd like. Got a bicycle?"

Jeff jerked a thumb toward a ten-speed Schwinn chained to a sabal palm.

"Let's take a cruise," I said, "and I'll show you my house."

Minutes later we rolled westward, side by side, while our tires ground against the road. We passed beneath limbs of ancient live oaks draped in Spanish moss. Up ahead, at an empty campsite, a great grey heron stood on a seawall, studying a canal in hopes of finding breakfast.

"How long have you lived in the park?" Jeff asked.

"Since I was eight, when my dad was promoted to head ranger. The residence comes with the position."

"Must be nice."

I rocked my head from side to side. "The park's pretty, and fishing here is good, but I never had other kids to do things with. It could get lonely, especially during summer when I wasn't in school. The days dragged by, if you know what I mean."

Jeff grimaced. "I spent a summer on my uncle's dairy farm, when I was thirteen. The nearest kid my age was three miles away, and I thought I'd go crazy from boredom."

When we reached the house, I pulled two Cokes from the fridge, and we sat on a glider sofa on the screened porch. Above us, a ceiling fan clacked and stirred the air. Out on the bayou's placid surface, a half dozen brown pelicans floated while an osprey chattered in a nearby long leaf pine.

"This is sweet," Jeff said while his gaze traveled here and there. "We don't have such places back home. Indiana's nothing but prairie."

Jeff talked about his hometown of Peru.

"We have about ten thousand people. There's a courthouse and high school, and it's only a three-hour drive from Bloomington, so I can come home on weekends if I choose to, but I don't often. There's not much going on in Peru."

I asked Jeff about his family.

"My dad's a middle school shop instructor, and Mom teaches freshman English at Peru High. They come from large families, so I have aunts and uncles all over Miami County, loads of cousins as well."

I shook my head.

"What is it?" Jeff asked.

"My parents were both only children, so I have no extended family or siblings. It's just me and my dad."

"Where's your mom?"

I kept my gaze fixed on the bayou while my stomach knotted like it always did when I had to explain. "She has...mental health issues. About eleven years ago, she disappeared—just packed up her belongings and left. We haven't heard from her since."

"Damn, that had to be rough."

"My dad nearly lost his mind. Even today, I don't think he's fully recovered from the situation."

We rocked on the glider for a bit without saying anything more until Jeff rose.

"I need to help my folks with servicing restrooms, but after lunch why don't we do something together, maybe go to the beach and take a swim?"

"Sounds good," I said while following Jeff out of the front door.

After he climbed aboard his Schwinn, he raked a hand through his hair, and I noticed his slightly oversized nose had a few freckles on it. Then, while he pedaled away, I wondered if I'd found someone I could share my summer with.

*

Jeff and I stood waist deep in Mullet Key Bay, about forty yards from the campground's grassy shore, with a view of Bunce's Pass and, beyond it, the shimmering Gulf of Mexico. Jeff used a spinning reel and rod I'd lent him to cast a greenback southward. His bait hit the water with a splash and quickly sank beneath the surface.

The morning was humid, and sweat beaded on my upper lip. Jeff and I both wore swim trunks and broad-brimmed straw hats. The sky was cloudless, and by noon the temperature would likely reach the low nineties.

Five days had passed since I'd first met Jeff, and each of those we'd spent together, once we finished whatever chores we needed to complete. Jeff always appeared on his Schwinn, and we'd sit on the screened porch while discussing what we might do.

Jeff had never fished before meeting me, but he quickly grew to like it. Angling in the grass flats north of the campground produced a variety of catch: redfish, flounder, speckled trout, and Spanish mackerel. For bait, I always used a cast net to gather greenbacks in the shallows, and we placed these in a floating bucket I tied to a loop on my swim trunks.

Jeff also liked exploring Fort De Soto, a shell-and-concrete edifice built in 1900 by the United States Army, to provide defense against naval invasions of Tampa Bay. One day, we spent two hours visiting every part of the fort and then reading its history from a pictorial display located in a former powder magazine. According to the display, the two enormous mortars mounted on turntables at the fort's center were intended for firing at enemy warships trying to enter the mouth of Tampa Bay, but had never been used in hostilities.

When we climbed a stairway to the fort's roof, we had a view of the mouth of Tampa Bay and the Gulf of Mexico. On the other side of the bay's mouth was Egmont Key, where another fort, not quite as large as De Soto, had been built to house a second battery. A lighthouse winked at us from one edge of the island.

Late afternoons, when the sun descended toward the western horizon and the day's heat had lessened, Jeff and I rode our bikes to North Beach to swim in the Gulf. We stood chest deep in warm and placid water and talked about our lives at school.

At IU, Jeff shared an off-campus house with two other students from Peru, guys he knew from his high school days. He worked part-time at a Bloomington supermarket and played basketball with his roomies. On weekends, he drank beer or smoked marijuana at parties.

I explained to Jeff how I'd dwelled in a campus dormitory my freshman and sophomore years, and how raucous the place was, with all the partying and loud music blaring from guys' sound systems.

"My grades suffered, and Dad wasn't happy, so this fall, I'll share an apartment near campus with a guy from Fort Lauderdale. He's a good student, and hopefully his study habits will rub off on me."

What I *didn't* tell Jeff was my future roommate, a boy named Brian Keene, wasn't just a friend. We were, as Brian had termed it, "sex buddies." The relationship had started somewhat by accident, the previous fall, during an alcohol infused Friday night in Brian's room at the dormitory. His roommate was gone for the weekend, and we had the place to ourselves.

I had no previous sexual experience, and it came as a shock when Brian put his hand on my crotch. But I didn't resist his advances—I didn't want to. I quickly learned male/male sex techniques from Brian and soon became adept at pleasuring both him and myself.

Brian was good-looking, with a slender build, chestnut hair, and a dazzling smile. And when it came to sex, I couldn't have asked for a better partner. Throughout the school year, we paired up on a regular basis, whenever we found privacy, and though I felt no emotional attachment to Brian, I sure enjoyed the intimacies, especially when Brian let me take him in the butt. The warmth of his body and the clench of his muscle drove me crazy with lust, plus I loved gazing into his cobalt eyes when I thrust inside him.

Now, at Mullet Key Bay, while I fished alongside Jeff, I wondered how he'd react if I told him about my activities with Brian. Homosexuality was pretty well accepted in Florida, but I wasn't sure the same was true in Indiana, and I thought it best if I kept my sex life with Brian to myself. I enjoyed Jeff's daily company and wanted to keep our friendship going all summer long.

Why risk spoiling that?

CHAPTER TWO

Ten days into my summer break, Jeff and I anchored my dad's boat in Bunce's Pass, a good place to fish on an outgoing tide. The time was around 4:00 p.m. on a Wednesday, and few boaters bobbed on the water. The sky was overcast, and the afternoon breeze tickled my cheeks. To the east, charcoal-colored clouds boiled. Thunder rumbled, and lightning bolts skittered across the sky.

Jeff studied a section of the *Tampa Bay Times* while the boat rocked. The handle of his fishing rod rested in a PVC tube bolted to the skiff's gunwale. On my portable radio, a country station played a Toby Keith tune.

Fishing at Bunce's always made me a bit nervous. A pass is a gap appearing between two barrier islands, allowing water to flow from the Gulf of Mexico into various bays and inlets along Florida's west coast, then back out. Bunce's Pass bisected Shell Key and the northern end of Fort De Soto Park, and at certain times of day the flow of water was swift, often dangerously so.

More than once since my family had moved into the ranger's residence, a foolhardy swimmer drowned in or around Bunce's Pass when caught by the powerful tidal currents. I still remember when I was twelve and the body of an unlucky tourist, a middle-aged man with a Navy tattoo on his chest, washed up on the campground's shoreline, pale and bloated. My dad and I found him right after daybreak, and I couldn't help myself; I puked up my breakfast while the sun crested the tree line to the east. Dad sent me to the house to fetch a tarp to cover the body until an ambulance could take the guy away.

Now, in the Carolina Skiff, Jeff looked up from his reading.

"You know, this is a first-rate newspaper—well edited and left-leaning politically. I'm impressed."

I nodded. "Conservatives in Pinellas County used to call it *The St. Petersburg Pravda.*"

Jeff laughed. His lips folded back into a smile and his big teeth gleamed. After spending two weeks in Florida, his skin had darkened to a light-brown shade, so the freckles on his nose had disappeared. And his hair looked wavier, probably from constant exposure to the park's salt-laden air and the Florida sunshine.

My thoughts turned to the previous evening, when Jeff and I had viewed a DVD on his laptop computer, a classic musical film released in 1972 called *Cabaret,* starring Liza Minelli and Joel Grey. It wasn't the sort of movie I'd normally see, but Jeff had expressed an interest, so we watched it in his room in the RV.

I was glad we did.

First of all, the music was stellar, the acting as well. But the most interesting part of the film was a homosexual affair between the two male stars in the film, both of whom had also slept with Minelli's character, Sally Bowles. One of those men was played by Michael York, a good-looking guy with a British accent. His big blue eyes and craggy cheekbones gave him a sexy aura, and I liked the way his blond bangs fell across his forehead at a jaunty angle. He appeared shirtless in a couple of scenes, and I couldn't help it; I grew stiff between my legs while gazing at his smooth and slender physique.

After the film ended, Jeff asked at what point I'd first suspected York's character, Brian, and the other guy, Max, had fooled around behind Sally Bowles's back.

"I honestly didn't know until Brian told Sally about it. I guess I'm a bit clueless about such things, but how about you? When did you realize something was up?"

Jeff shrugged. "When Brian and Fritz went to the beer garden by themselves. The way they looked at each other said it all."

Now, while we rocked in the boat, more thunder rumbled and another lightning bolt snaked across the sky, this one looking far larger than the ones before. Wind gusts created little whitecaps in normally calm Mullet Key Bay.

I pointed eastward. "That storm is headed our way. We should pull up anchors and head for the house."

Unfortunately, I had misjudged the speed at which the gale approached. We weren't even halfway home before rain pelted us and the bow of the skiff hopped on the bay's churning surface. By the time we reached the boat slip, both Jeff and I were drenched. Our wet clothing clung to us, and our hair was plastered our skulls.

After I secured the boat's bow and stern lines to cleats on the dock, Jeff and I bolted for the house, dodging rain puddles as best we could while thunder rumbled and shook the ground.

The temperature must've dropped ten degrees; both of us shivered when we entered the house. I grabbed two towels from the linen closet and led Jeff into my bedroom, where we both peeled off our clothing, even our briefs, and for the first time I saw Jeff naked. While he toweled himself, I studied the bulge of his genitals and the curve of his ass, and my mouth grew sticky at the view.

I lent Jeff dry clothing—briefs, denim shorts, and a T-shirt—and we sat on the porch glider, watching rain sheet off the eaves. Thunder roared and lightning crackled while mangrove trees flanking the house thrashed about like frenzied dancers in a tribal rite.

"Does it storm here like this often?" Jeff asked.

"In summer, always. During daytime, heat builds up in farmlands east of Tampa Bay. The warmth rises and forms thunderheads by late afternoon. Then a land breeze kicks up and blows the clouds westward to the Gulf, almost like clockwork."

Jeff looked at me with his eyebrows gathered. "It never gets cold here, does it?"

"Not really."

"I can't imagine. In Peru, it seems like winter lasts forever, and the wind never stops blowing. Lousy weather starts in mid-November and lasts till April. Sometimes you don't see the sun for weeks at a time."

We rocked in silence for a minute or so. The only sounds were the glider sofa's creaking and rain clattering in puddles beyond the screens.

"I've thought about something you shared with me," Jeff said.

"What's that?"

"The situation with your mom seems so sad. Do you think you'll ever hear from her again?"

Like always, the mention of my mother made my stomach muscles clench.

"I have no idea. The first year or so, after she left us, I felt certain she'd return. Every day when I came home from school, I expected she'd be here at the house and things would get back to normal. But then I came to realize it wasn't going to happen, that maybe she didn't want me and my dad in her life any longer. And for some reason—I'm not sure why—I convinced myself the whole thing was my fault."

I kept my gaze fixed on the bayou while the glider ticked.

"I went through something similar," Jeff said, "my first year of college."

"What happened?"

"I fell in love with someone who rejected me, and it hurt so badly I wanted to cut my wrists. For many months, I couldn't think of a single reason to live."

"But you're okay now?"

He tilted his head toward a shoulder. "Passage of time has helped, but I'm not sure I'll ever be the same. I think love can damage you like nothing else."

"Are you still in touch with this girl?"

Jeff gazed at me and crinkled his forehead. "Who said it was a girl?"

Oh...

I lowered my chin and cleared my throat. "Sorry, I just assumed—"

"Does it surprise you I like boys?"

I brought my gaze back to Jeff's and shook my head. Then I spent the next five minutes describing my activities with Brian. "I'm not in love with him, we're only fooling around."

"But don't you want something more than that?"

I shrugged. "I'm not sure it's possible for two guys to love each other."

Jeff dipped his chin while keeping his gaze fixed on mine. "*I* think it is."

I looked at the bayou. The storm's intensity had lessened, but rain continued to trouble the bayou's surface and drip off the roof eaves.

"Look," Jeff said, "if this conversation is making you uncomfortable, we can talk about something else."

I swung my gaze to his.

"I'm not uncomfortable, but you took me by surprise. I guess we have more in common than I knew."

Jeff nodded. He reached for my cheek to stroke it with a fingertip, and right away my pulse galloped. His voice sounded seductive when he spoke.

"What should we do, Jakub, now that we know?"

CHAPTER THREE

On a Wednesday afternoon, Jeff's mom, Catherine, chuckled while she sat at the Brucellis' picnic table, chopping a purple onion. Her hearty laughter echoed through the live oaks shading the campsite. A big-boned woman, she wore Bermuda shorts and a sleeveless blouse. Her onyx hair was gathered into a pony tail extending halfway down her back.

Jeff's dad, Mario, stood at the campsite's charcoal grill. He tended speckled trout fillets, bounty Jeff and I had caught earlier in the afternoon at Fort De Soto's bay pier. Mario was a slender, fair-skinned man with dark hair, acne scars on his cheeks, and a perpetual five o'clock shadow. He never seemed to sit still. If he wasn't raking a campsite or trimming shrubbery, he'd weave a broad-brimmed hat out of strands stripped from a sabal palm frond.

Now, at the Brucellis' campsite, Jeff and I tossed a football back and forth, both of us shirtless and suntanned, wearing only khaki shorts and leather sandals.

Three weeks into the Brucellis' stay, I already felt like a member of their family.

My dad worked long hours, often not arriving home until seven in the evening, and his idea of dinner was usually a bologna sandwich or a can of beef stew warmed up on the stove. I was left to forage our barren cupboards and fridge for whatever I could find, and if Dad visited the supermarket once a week, I was lucky.

The Brucellis, on the other hand, took food seriously. They prepared elaborate meals: lasagna, white clam sauce over linguini, veal scaloppini or antipasto, always accompanied by a fresh garden salad and a crusty loaf, all washed down by bottles of Chianti and cold Soave wine I quickly came to appreciate.

I'd taken to dining with Jeff's family most nights, which they didn't seem to mind, and to show my appreciation, I did my best to contribute fresh fish whenever Jeff and I got lucky, like we had been that day. The four speckled trout we caught were beauties, each about three pounds and fleshy. Catherine would team the grilled and seasoned fish with new potatoes and fresh asparagus spears slathered in butter and parsley.

Jeff's parents were devout Catholics. Every Sunday morning, they attended mass at St. John's on St. Pete Beach, and before every meal I shared with them, Jeff's dad said a prayer, thanking God for the Brucellis' many blessings.

In private, Jeff told me he was not a believer and had no interest in religion of any kind. He said his parents weren't happy with his lack of devotion, but did not insist he join them on their visits to St. John's.

As campground hosts, the Brucellis received a free site in the park in exchange for tending campsites, restrooms, and picnic areas. They kept their campground section as neat as a surgical room. No litter or overflowing trash bins. The sinks and showers in the restrooms gleamed, and the paper dispensers were always full.

"I'm dreading their departure in August," Dad told me one morning while we shared a breakfast of cold cereal and orange juice. "How will I find replacements as responsible as them?"

I wasn't looking forward to the Brucellis leaving myself, but for reasons far more important than neat campsites.

Jeff had become the center of my world.

Every afternoon, right around one, he arrived at my house on his Schwinn. Within minutes, we writhed naked on the mattress in my bedroom, pawing each other's limbs and caressing tender flesh while our tongues dueled and our lips smacked. I craved Jeff's stringy muscles, his smooth skin, and wavy hair. And I loved gazing into his dark eyes while I fingered his earlobe.

Whenever I penetrated Jeff and worked my hips, I felt as if I'd entered an alternate universe, one where only Jeff and I dwelled. Our sighs chorused while the bedsprings twanged, and my orgasms were unlike any I'd experienced with Brian. Each time, it seemed as if Jeff and I had melted into each other.

I had never felt so close to another person.

And I also came to realize how, prior to meeting Jeff, I had walked around with a huge hole in my heart, a deep sadness resulting from my mother's departure from my life. Sure, my dad was a great guy, someone I could always count on, but he wasn't one to talk about feelings or show me any physical affection. Our conversations weren't personal, and he *never* mentioned my mom or how badly he missed her presence.

With Jeff it was different. He encouraged me to talk about my emotions and spoke freely about his own.

"I was always a clumsy kid," he told me while we wade fished in the bayou on a high tide. "I was terribly shy and couldn't play sports worth a shit, so I got teased a lot by my classmates and neighborhood kids."

"I tended to be a loner," I told Jeff one afternoon, right after we made love in my room. "In school, I never joined a club or played a sport. I didn't feel confident enough to do something like that. And then I'd come home to my empty house and feel so depressed I went to my room and hid under the bedcovers. I thought about my mom and wondered where she was, and why she cared so little about me."

I lay on the glider sofa when I spoke, with my head resting in Jeff's lap. The air was warm and humid, and the ceiling fan clacked above us. The sofa's hinges squeaked while we rocked.

"When I think of how much pain you've gone through," Jeff said, "it makes me sad. I hope having me here makes things a little better for you."

I fingered the back of Jeff's wrist. "Up in Tallahassee, I wasn't looking forward to this summer, but with you here, I'm loving life in the park."

Then, without thinking, I blurted something childish from the depths of my heart.

"I wish it could last forever."

*

Near the mangrove forest at the park's East Beach, Jeff and I took turns swinging a sledgehammer, dismantling a plywood equipment shed where lifeguards had stowed their equipment for many years. A new aluminum shed had been delivered, and now my dad was paying Jeff and me to destroy the old one. After crushing the shed into pieces, we'd haul the refuse to the county dump in the park's pickup truck.

The day was warm, and we sweated like farm animals, smashing the little building apart. Both of us were shirtless, wearing only shorts, work boots, and leather gloves. Every time the sledge connected with wood, a sound erupted like a pistol shot. The structure was termite infested and offered little resistance to our assault.

"This is almost fun," Jeff hollered when he swung the hammer and a section of plywood caved into pieces. "I've never done something like this before."

I grinned while sweat rolled down my cheeks. "I guess there's a certain pleasure in destruction, but I'm not sure why."

"Maybe because it seems like a forbidden activity."

I looked at Jeff and winked. "I think we both like that sort of thing."

Jeff reached for my shoulder to flick off a splinter that clung to me, and the touch of his fingertip sent a jolt of sexual tension through me.

The fourth week of June had arrived, and by then it seemed I'd known Jeff all my life. The previous day, with my dad gone to Orlando for a park ranger conference, Jeff had slept at my house—it was the first time I'd shared a bed all night with another guy—and I liked falling asleep in his arms while a ceiling fan hummed above us. In the morning, I woke to find Jeff snoring softly on his back, so I turned toward him and bent an elbow. I rested my cheek against the palm of my hand and watched Jeff breathe. His hair was tangled, but he still looked beautiful to me. His facial features seemed as delicate as flower petals, especially his thick eyebrows and curvy lips.

After a few minutes, I woke him by running my fingers through his hair, and when his eyes fluttered open, a bewildered expression crossed his face. But then his gaze met mine, and he flashed his amazing smile.

"Morning, sexy."

We used the toilet and then returned to my bedroom for a sweet half hour of lovemaking, and when it was over, we lay side by side on our backs, holding hands and not saying a word, just listening to each other breathe. I could have stayed in my room the entire day, touching Jeff and gazing into his eyes. But we had work to do, so we dragged ourselves out of bed and tended to the business of everyday life.

Now, when we tossed pieces of busted-up plywood and lumber into the pickup's bed, we caused quite a racket, but the good kind that made me feel we'd accomplished something useful.

An assistant park ranger driving a golf cart arrived. His name was Ned, and I'd known him for many years, a middle-aged guy with an easy manner and an endless collection of jokes. He handed both of us cold cans of soda he pulled from a small ice cooler in the cart's storage basket.

"It's hot as hell out here, and I figured you boys could use a drink."

After we thanked Ned, we both guzzled our sodas while Ned surveyed the damage we had wrought with the sledgehammer. Little was left of the building besides debris and floor joists resting on cinder blocks.

"About time that shed came down," Ned told us, "the darn thing was falling apart." He opened a can of soda for himself, took a gulp and swallowed before licking his lips and looking at me with his eyebrows raised.

"Hey, Jakub, do you know how to fit four gay men on a barstool?"

Heat rose in my cheeks while I shook my head.

"Turn it upside down."

Ned burst into laughter, and his beer belly jiggled. Then he drove off toward the ranger's station at the entrance to the campground, waving a hand.

Jeff shook his head and scowled. "Imagine what he'd have thought if he'd seen us in bed earlier."

I turned down one corner of my mouth and rolled my eyes. What was there to say? Guys like Ned would never change.

Once we'd fully loaded the pickup's bed with debris, we climbed into the cab and drove onto the roadway. In moments we had crossed the bridge to Tierra Verde, an island community of condos, custom-built homes, and strip centers.

Wind rushed through the windows, tossing Jeff's bangs about, and when I looked at him, a glow emerged inside my chest, as if my heart were afire.

It doesn't get any better than this, does it?

CHAPTER FOUR

The day after Fourth of July—a Wednesday—Jeff and I drove my dad's Jeep Cherokee one hundred and forty miles northward to Chiefland, a two-and-a-half-hour trip. We had reserved a campsite in Manatee Springs State Park, and now the car was crammed with gear: a nylon tent, sleeping bags, cooking equipment, two ice coolers, and our clothing. We would stay two nights, returning to Fort De Soto on Friday.

The night before, we had attended a firework display in St. Pete Beach, and on the way, we smoked marijuana in the station wagon, passing a joint back and forth. We sat on a blanket at the shore, watching rockets ignite and giggling like schoolgirls. Like always, the weed made me feel a bit removed from everything around me, as if I viewed the world through plate glass. The display lasted about forty-five minutes, and afterward we devoured ice cream sandwiches purchased at a convenience store.

Back at Fort De Soto Park, we found a picnic table in the North Beach recreation area. No one else was around. A three-quarter moon shone, and thousands of stars twinkled in the sky's blackness. We sat on a bench, pawing each other while our lips smacked and our tongues dueled. I was still high from the grass we'd smoked, and when I unzipped Jeff's shorts, I trembled. I brought him to orgasm with my hand—he did the same for me—and the whole thing felt amazing.

Now, while we roared up US 19, we passed through the town of Homosassa, a collection of strip centers, a Walmart, supermarkets, gasoline retailers, and a few cheesy motels.

"I wonder if any gay men live here?" Jeff said. "The name of the town suggests so."

I chuckled. "It's a Native American word, stupid; it means 'place of many peppers.'"

"How do you *know* that?"

"In Florida, every fifth grader studies the state's history and geography. It's required. Many towns here have Indian names: Tallahassee, Kissimmee, and Apalachicola, to name a few."

"Where are all the Native Americans today?"

I gazed at the dashboard before looking back at the road.

"It's a sad story. Andrew Jackson drove the natives from their lands. Most were forced to move out west, to places like Oklahoma, but a few hundred Seminoles fled to the Everglades, where their descendants live today."

Jeff rested his forearm on the passenger door sill while wind rushed through the car. "It doesn't seem fair, does it? After all, they were here first."

I nodded. "But Jackson thought—and this was true of most white folks back then—the Native Americans were an inferior race, just as the Nazis believed Jews and Gypsies were. Looking back, the Native Americans were treated horribly."

Jeff shook his head. Then we rode in silence for a good five minutes before he spoke again.

"Let me ask you something—if you told your friends from the dorm you're gay, how do you think they'd react?"

"They'd probably treat me like Jackson did the Native Americans."

"Do you really think so?"

I looked at Jeff and nodded.

Jeff turned down one corner of his mouth. "You know, up until now, I never thought of myself as part of a persecuted minority, but I guess it's what we are in many places, even though gay marriage is legal now. How do you feel about that?"

I wasn't quite sure how to answer Jeff's question, so I turned my gaze to the windshield while my brain churned.

Until the day Jeff had first touched my cheek, I didn't think of myself as gay. I figured Brian and I only fooled around because we didn't have girlfriends. But the intensity of my feelings toward Jeff had dispelled any doubt in me about my sexual orientation. I was queer, and that would never change. The same was certainly true for Jeff, and what did that portend for our futures?

*

Manatee Springs State Park was six miles west of Chiefland, only a short distance from the Suwannee River. The Magnolia One campground, where we pitched our tent, was shaded by towering red oaks keeping the site comfortable, even in the afternoon's muggy heat.

Our site had a fire pit, water tap, picnic table, and barbecue grill, and was only a five-minute stroll from the park's main spring. According to a leaflet provided us by a park ranger, the spring pumped out one hundred million gallons of fresh water every day.

Right after we set up camp, Jeff and I slipped into our swimsuits. Then we swam in the spring, a crystalline beauty the size of a baseball diamond. And because the spring's water had just emerged from Florida's aquifer, its temperature was a consistent seventy-two degrees, chilly but refreshing. The spring's color was an unearthly aquamarine. We stood in a shallow area, on a sandy bottom as white as table sugar, shivering while sunlight reflected in water droplets dotting our shoulders.

Jeff shook his head when his gaze traveled to the tops of cypress trees on the spring's far bank.

"I've never seen any place like this. It's so beautiful."

"Welcome to the *real* Florida. Most people who visit our state never see things like this. Instead they go to Disney World or Miami Beach and think they had a real Florida experience, when they haven't."

"You know," Jeff said, "this has to be the best summer I've ever spent, and it's all thanks to you. Not just because, you know..." Jeff glanced at a pair of middle-aged women sunning themselves on the spring's bank before continuing. "We've done so many things I'd never dreamed of. I have never seen a natural spring until now, and what a beautiful sight it is."

A half hour later, Jeff and I followed a four hundred-yard boardwalk passing through a grove of bald cypress trees with trunks so thick I couldn't encircle them with my arms. The trees' broad bases made them resemble candlesticks. The boardwalk ran alongside a creek flowing from the main spring to the Suwannee.

Dappled sunlight reflected in Jeff's dark hair. Neither of us wore shirts, just our swim trunks and leather sandals, and I let my gaze travel over Jeff's sleek frame while we ambled along.

The Suwannee is one of Florida's larger rivers, maybe three hundred yards wide, with coffee-colored water and a sandy bottom. When Jeff and I reached the boardwalk's terminus, we sat on a dock and studied the river with our knees touching. An alligator cruised by with only its snout and eyes visible, while overhead an osprey soared in a cloudless sky. A group of boys wearing life jackets, accompanied by two men, paddled past us in fiberglass canoes, all of them chattering away. Their laughter boomed across the water and echoed in the trees.

"Ever been in a canoe?" I asked Jeff.

He shook his head.

"The park's concessionaire rents them and offers a shuttle service. I thought tomorrow we'd spend the day paddling."

"Sounds great," Jeff said. "But right now..."

"What?"

Jeff rubbed his knee against mine and our leg hairs commingled. When I turned my head to meet Jeff's gaze, he waggled his eyebrows.

"Let's go back to the campsite and climb inside our tent."

I leaped to my feet. "I'll race you there," I cried before breaking into a run. The soles of my sandals pounded the boardwalk while sweat broke out on my forehead, and I chugged my arms.

I was never too swift in the running department and wasn't halfway back to the campsite before Jeff caught up and passed me. He ran fluidly. His hips didn't rock from side to side and his sandals barely kissed the planks.

I felt weightless and blissful. All I thought about was holding Jeff in my arms and feeling his fingers caress my body in all the right places. If I could have frozen things in time—right there in the park—I would have. Then I could live forever with Jeff, and the two of us would enjoy the simple joys Florida offered: sunshine, a spring, cypress trees, and a river.

*

Midmorning the next day, Jeff and I clambered into the concessionaire's van along with six other folks who intended to paddle the Suwannee. Our driver wasn't much older than me and Jeff. He towed a trailer with canoe racks holding four canoes. In the back of the van was a gaggle of paddles, seat cushions, and life vests.

Like our fellow paddlers, Jeff and I had packed sandwiches and sodas in a small cooler I held in my lap when we rumbled out of the park.

We drove northward on Highway 207. Already the day was warming up. Heat shimmered over the asphalt, and I was glad Jeff and I had brought our straw fishing hats to shield our heads and shoulders from the sun's relentless glare. We wore swim trunks, T-shirts, and sandals.

When the driver spoke, he had to raise his voice to be heard over the roar of the engine and the wind rushing into the van's interior.

"I'm taking you to a boat ramp west of the river. It's about ten miles north of the park, so you'll need about four hours to get back there. On the way, you'll find plenty of sandy river banks where you can go ashore to stretch your legs or enjoy your lunches."

"What about alligators?" a woman in a tennis visor asked.

"You'll see a few for certain, but trust me, they're timid creatures and won't approach you. Just the same, don't go near them. Play it smart and keep your distance."

"Is the river deep?" Jeff asked.

"In certain places, yes. So, always wear your life vest when you paddle. Even if you're a good swimmer, it pays to be safe."

Our drop-off point was little more than a concrete embankment. Jeff and I helped the driver unload canoes from the trailer, and minutes later we paddled in the river's tannin-stained water. Jeff was forward and I sat at the stern, which meant I steered. Sunshine beat on my shoulders and the tops of my thighs, and I was glad Jeff and I had applied sunscreen before we left our campsite.

Canoeing the Suwannee was not arduous. The river flowed at a lazy speed of maybe one mile per hour. No rapids or sudden turns, no obstacles like fallen trees or rocks. Most of the land we passed was undeveloped and heavily forested with cypress trees, live oaks, and long leaf pines. An osprey's cry echoed in the wilderness, while a seven-foot alligator, looking like a fire-charred log, sunned itself on a river bank.

Our fellow paddlers weren't quite as energetic as me and Jeff, and we quickly left them behind. Then the only sound was the swishing of our paddles in the water. Both of us had already shed our shirts, and I loved watching Jeff's back muscles move under his skin when he stroked.

"I can't believe a month of my summer has already passed," he said. "Next thing you know I'll sit in Memorial Stadium watching a Hoosiers football game."

"Do you like it up there?"

Jeff shrugged. "Until we drove down here, Indiana was all I knew. I'd always thought Peru and Bloomington were kind of cool, but now..."

"What?"

"I won't be happy when I leave Florida, not only because I'll miss this kind of natural beauty, but I also won't have you to hold in my arms every afternoon."

I tried to imagine Jeff trudging across the IU campus under gray skies with his breath steaming in the chilly air and his backpack bulging.

"You don't think it's possible you'll find some guy up there to get close with?"

"At IU? No goddamned way. Like I told you, I fell for a classmate during my freshman year; he lived on my floor in the dormitory. For a few months, we were inseparable. We did everything together: studying, eating in the cafeteria, playing basketball, you name it. I suspected he had feelings for me, the same kind I had for him. But then I made the mistake of telling him, and he didn't react well."

"What did he say?"

Jeff twisted at his waist and brought his gaze to mine.

"Are you sure you want to hear this?"

I nodded.

Jeff lowered his eyes before returning them to mine.

"He called me a pervert and told me to stay away from him. After that, we never spoke to each other again. He wouldn't even look at me when we passed in the dorm hallway, like I was invisible."

Jeff turned back toward the canoe's bow and paddled while he continued talking.

"I felt the worst I had in my entire life. My interest in food plunged; I lost ten pounds. I forgot to bathe or brush my teeth, and my skin broke out in zits. I couldn't concentrate on my studies either. After a month or so, I asked my parents' permission to take a leave of absence from school. I moved back to Peru and spent much of the next two months lying in bed just staring at the ceiling."

"Did you tell your folks what happened?"

"How could I? They would have flipped."

I stroked my paddle and tried to put myself in Jeff's position when he went through the crisis he'd just described. I, of course, had never experienced such an event, but it sounded awful.

"How long did it take before you started feeling better?"

"Several months. I returned to IU in the fall, but still felt lousy, as if a part of me was dead. I sleepwalked through campus, and my grades weren't what they should have been. Then, every once in a while, I'd see the boy I'd fallen in love with, and all those feelings I had for him came rushing right back. Honestly, I thought I'd never get him out of my head."

A short distance ahead of us an enormous fish leaped from the water. Sunlight reflected in its coppery flanks when it soared several feet into the air before diving back into the river, making a huge splash that sprayed Jeff and me.

"What *was* that thing?" Jeff hollered.

I chuckled while wiping droplets from my nose and cheeks. "A Gulf sturgeon. Tons live in this river. They grow as long as eight feet and sometimes weigh two hundred pounds; they've existed since prehistoric times."

"Are they dangerous?"

"Nah, they just *look* scary."

We paddled in silence for a bit. I savored a light breeze tickling my cheeks while a cormorant surfaced from the river with a slithering fish in its beak. I gazed skyward to watch an American bald eagle soar above a stand of cypress trees. The eagle's chalk-white head and yellow talons made splashes of color in the cloudless sky.

Jeff finally ended the silence.

"You know something? I feel better right now than I have since that guy called me a perv, and that was almost two years ago." He turned to look at me with a smile on his lips. "I have *you* to thank for that, Jakub."

CHAPTER FIVE

We returned to the Fort De Soto campground on Friday afternoon, and when we arrived at the Brucellis' campsite, I immediately knew something was wrong. Normally, swimsuits hung from a clothesline, bicycles were chained to sabal palms, and the picnic table was stacked with books, magazines, and a propane lantern. But now, aside from the RV parked there, the site looked deserted.

I looked at Jeff and crinkled my forehead. "What's going on?"

Jeff's mom answered my question moments later when she emerged from the RV toting a bulging plastic trash bag.

"Your grandmother's taken a turn for the worse," she told Jeff. "She's in the hospital, and my dad's an emotional wreck. He needs us there for support."

Jeff's voice had a tremble in it when he spoke. "We're going back to Peru?"

His mom nodded. "We'll hit the road in less than an hour, so you need to put your things in order. There's no time to waste."

Had someone just punched me in the stomach? My vision blurred and my knees wobbled so badly I thought I might fall down.

Jeff's going to leave me?

While Jeff's mom carried the trash bag to a disposal bin, the two of us stood there looking at each other in disbelief. Jeff clenched and unclenched his fingers at his hips while his chest rose and fell with his breathing.

"I'm sorry," he whispered before turning to his mom. "I have belongings at Jakub's, I'll come back in just a bit."

"Fine, but make it quick. We need to beat rush hour traffic in Tampa."

I drove the station wagon down the crushed shell road, and neither of us spoke. I think we both felt too stunned to say anything coherent. The moment we entered my house, we headed for my room. Then we lay in each other's arms on the bed with tears rolling down our cheeks.

"I can't believe it's over," Jeff said, sniffling. "I thought we had another seven weeks together."

"Why don't you stay here with us? My dad wouldn't mind, and you could take the bus up to Peru in late August."

Jeff puckered one side of his face and shook his head. "We're in family crisis mode, and my parents will want me with them—it's how things work with us."

We lay there holding each other for fifteen minutes or so before Jeff spoke again.

"Promise you won't forget me, even though I'm a thousand miles away from you."

"I will always love you," I said. "You can count on that."

*

I won't ever forget the moment I watched the Brucellis drive off in their RV with the muffler growling and the tires grinding on the campground road. I leaned against the Jeep's fender with my arms crossed on my chest, feeling as though the life had drained from my body. I barely had the energy to breathe.

Even though the day was warm and humid, a shiver ran through me.

Jeff was gone, and how could that be? Within a day or so he'd live a thousand miles away from me. No more afternoon sex in my bedroom, no more fishing excursions, and no more meals to enjoy with the Brucellis at their campsite.

When I returned to my empty house, I strode to my room and collapsed onto the bed. I wept like a five-year-old, and my sobs echoed off the pine-paneled walls. I hadn't felt so lonely since the day my mom had disappeared, eleven years before.

Would I always lose the people I loved?

I thought of a loaded .38 revolver my dad kept in his bureau, and for a fleeting moment I considered sticking the barrel in my mouth and pulling the trigger. At least if I were dead, I wouldn't feel the agonizing pain gnawing at my stomach. I wouldn't have to endure the incessant pounding in my head.

But no.

I'd have to deal with the misery and loneliness, just as I had when Mom left us. So, now, I did what I had back then to assuage my pain. I shed my clothes and climbed into my bed. I pulled the bedcovers over my head and lay in darkness.

I listened to my nightstand clock tick.

CHAPTER SIX

"Do you know how to work this thing?" Brian asked.

We stood in the kitchen of our apartment, preparing our first dinner after our arrival in Tallahassee earlier in the day. Brian clutched a manual can opener in one hand and a can of peas in his other.

I squinted. "You've never used one before?"

"My mom does all the cooking at our house. When would I learn?"

I shook my head while demonstrating the workings of the can opener. I showed Brian how to position the blade on the can's lid and then how to squeeze the grips to pierce the lid's surface before rotating the bar. Already I found myself wondering if I'd made a mistake by rooming with Brian. Sure, he was sexy and self-disciplined, but I wasn't going to nanny him for nine months.

Our apartment wasn't much, just a one bedroom, one bath unit in a cinder block building a few blocks from campus. Brian's great aunt had recently passed away and Brian's dad inherited her estate, including a collection of high-end Louis XV-style furniture. Brian brought a load of the pieces to Tallahassee in a U-Haul van: two beds, a mirrored double bureau, a nightstand, a sofa, two armchairs, and a pair of ottomans. The furniture looked ridiculous with its red brocade upholstery and curvy wooden frames painted gold, but at least it was free. Brian also brought a Formica dining table and three metal chairs his mom had bought at a garage sale, so the place was fully furnished. The apartment had a mini-split air conditioner, so we wouldn't sweat in our beds at night, and we could walk to campus in five minutes.

What more could a couple of twenty-year-olds ask for?

Now, while a shirtless Brian worked on opening a can of new potatoes, a tingle arose between my legs when I studied his lean torso and the trail of dark hair spilling from his navel. Seven weeks had passed since I'd last touched Jeff Brucelli, and I hadn't thought much about sex since his departure for Indiana.

Would that change, since Brian and I would enjoy complete privacy any time we wanted it?

While pre-heating the oven, I basted two chicken breasts with olive oil and seasoned them with salt, pepper, and rosemary leaves. I thought about my latest phone conversation with Jeff, several days before.

"I'm already back in Bloomington," Jeff told me. "I felt bad about leaving my folks, especially my mom. She's been so sad since my grandma passed."

Back in early August, I had made a proposal to Jeff: I would take a bus from St. Petersburg to Peru. But then his grandmother died, and Jeff told me my proposed visit wouldn't be a good idea.

"I'd love to see you, but it's too depressing around here right now. Plus, we wouldn't have any privacy. My folks are at the house all day and night, so we couldn't...you know."

So, I had lived the last seven weeks *sans* Jeff, walking through my days like a guy in a trance. In my mind, I kept replaying the times I'd spent with Jeff and the things we did. I often lay on my bed, staring at the ceiling and recalling our sex, and—I swear—I smelled the musky aroma of his groin and the scent of his hair.

Every time I heard his voice over the phone, my belly muscles knotted and I flexed my toes because I craved his touch so badly. But now he was at IU, and I was in Tallahassee, and I doubted I would see Jeff anytime soon.

Shit...

*

A month into fall semester, Brian and I had fallen into a comfortable routine. Weekdays we rose at 7:00 a.m. While Brian showered and shaved, I brewed coffee and wolfed down a bowlful of Cheerios and milk. Then I took my turn in the bathroom. Just before 8:00 a.m., we walked to campus for our first classes of the day, or to study in library carrels.

At noon, we returned to the apartment for a quick lunch, and then it was back to campus for afternoon classes and more studying. We both arrived home around 4:00 p.m., and maybe once a week, we devoted an hour to sex. I always took Brian on his back with his legs slung over my shoulders, his preferred position. Squeaks from his bedsprings filled the room while I thrust my hips and gazed at the upholstered headboard behind him.

Sex with Brian was something I always looked forward to, but it wasn't the same as with Jeff, because I felt no deep emotional connection with Brian. And I often thought of something Jeff had said to me when I told him about my sessions with Brian.

"Don't you want something more than that?"

But having Brian was certainly better than having no one.

Weekday evenings, following dinner, Brian and I studied for a while. Then we watched movies or sports on a TV I'd bought from home. Brian liked watching reruns of *Friends*, while I preferred cop shows like *CSI:NY*. And we both enjoyed watching *Monday Night Football*.

Weekends, we spent our days shooting baskets or tossing a baseball back and forth on Landis Green at FSU. We visited the campus swimming pool and sunned ourselves on chaises. Friday and Saturday nights a party happened somewhere, and certain weekends the Seminoles played football games at Doak Campbell Stadium.

Although I'd initially doubted the wisdom of rooming with Brian, my decision turned out to be the right one. Brian exercised self-discipline when it came to his studies, and his habits quickly became mine. We didn't let anything get in the way of school, and I was pretty sure my grades would dramatically improve over the mediocre marks I'd earned the previous school year.

Brian was a neatnik. He made his bed each morning before leaving the apartment. He kept his toothpaste tube capped and all his belongings organized. We took turns doing the daily dishes, and once a week we cleaned our bathroom from top to bottom, scrubbing the sink and tub with cleanser till they sparkled, and brushing the toilet bowl.

A couple of guys from our old dorm visited our apartment and gave us shit about the Louis XV pieces—they called them "faggot furniture"—but I didn't care and neither did Brian. The sofa was a nice place for taking a nap, and the chairs and ottomans were super comfortable for studying or watching TV.

Jeff and I continued to speak by phone a couple of times each week, but the conversations grew shorter as the weeks passed, I suppose because the intensity of our summer relationship had lessened. We spoke about classes and our respective schools' football games, but not anything personal.

When Jeff asked if I were still having sex with Brian, I took a few seconds before I answered.

"I am, but it's not the same as with you."

Jeff cleared his throat. "Is it okay if I tell you I feel a bit jealous about you and Brian doing that sort of thing?"

"Should I stop? I will if you want me to, I mean it."

Jeff let out his breath.

"No, don't—at least *you're* getting laid."

CHAPTER SEVEN

Christmas break arrived, and right after we took final exams for the fall semester, I rode a Greyhound bus to St. Petersburg, a miserable seven-hour drive with multiple stops along the way. My dad picked me and my suitcase up at the bus station and then we rode to Fort De Soto. I was so exhausted from exams and the bus ride, I made a beeline for my room, where I collapsed onto the bed and slept for ten hours.

The next morning, while I read the *Tampa Bay Times* on our living room sofa, Jeff called, and the sound of his voice made my heart skip a beat.

"I have an idea," he said.

"What's that?"

"My grandpa's moving into a retirement home. He won't need a car anymore, so he's giving me his Chevy Impala for Christmas. If it's okay with you and your dad, I thought I'd drive down to Florida on December 26. I can spend a week with you."

My pulse raced at the thought of spending time with Jeff again.

"Of *course*, it's okay."

"If I leave Peru early and drive straight through, I should make it to your place before midnight."

When my dad came home for lunch that day, I told him about Jeff's proposal.

"It's fine with me," Dad said, "but where will he sleep?"

I lowered my gaze and rubbed my lips together. Then I raised my chin. "Jeff can share my bed with me. There's enough room for two guys, no problem."

Dad shrugged.

The days leading up to Christmas dragged by. With my dad at work all day, and no young people staying in the park, I didn't have someone to spend time with. So, I fished for Spanish mackerel at the Gulf pier. I took long bike rides from one end of the park to the other. I hiked trails winding through groves of sabal palms and Australian pines. I borrowed my dad's car to Christmas shop for him and Jeff at a sporting goods store in St. Petersburg, where I bought Dad a new tackle box and Jeff a Swiss Army knife.

Christmas morning wasn't much at our house.

My dad gave me a $400 gift certificate from an online retailer.

"I know it seems impersonal, but I'd rather you bought a few things you really want instead of the stupid stuff I'd pick out."

"It's fine. I need a few clothing items, and this will more than cover them."

Dad liked the tackle box, and he certainly enjoyed the pancake breakfast I prepared. Odors of fried bacon wafted through the house while we savored our food at the kitchen table.

After our meal, we took coffee mugs to the screened porch and sat on the glider, staring at the bayou. The day was sunny, still and cool. A school of mullet swam past our dock, and occasionally a fish would leap from the water in an arc before crashing back into the bayou.

My thoughts wandered to my mother. I was nine the last Christmas she had spent with us. Dad and I pooled our money to buy her a chenille robe and house slippers, and she seemed happy with her gifts. A petite woman with auburn hair, her ivory skin quickly burned if she spent more than an hour in the Florida sun.

Now, on the porch, I asked my dad, "I wonder where Mom is today?"

Dad's face clouded when he turned to look at me. "God only knows; let's just hope she's safe, wherever she is."

My voice sounded strangled when I spoke.

"I still miss her. Do you?"

Dad looked at the bayou and didn't answer.

*

Around noon on December 26, Jeff phoned. "I'm in Tennessee. At this rate, I should make it to your place by midnight."

Already I had cleared out a bureau drawer in my room for Jeff's folding clothes and made space in my closet for his hang-up items and shoes. I laundered the bed linens too. I wanted Jeff to feel at home with us and enjoy his stay, so things needed to be just right.

The hours dragged by.

Every time I looked at a clock, the hands seemed mired in muck. A cold front had swept into central Florida Christmas night, and I had a blaze going in our fireplace. The pine logs snapped and crackled as they burned; occasionally a sap jet ignited, hissing a blue flame. Outside, the sky was the color of dishwater, and a chilly wind stirred the fronds on sabal palms.

For dinner, I made spaghetti with meatballs, a tossed salad, and garlic bread, knowing I'd have plenty of leftovers if Jeff were hungry when he arrived. Then Dad and I watched Clint Eastwood's film, *Gran Torino*, on cable TV. When the movie ended, the time was 10:00 p.m., and my father went to bed.

I paced the living room floor like a madman. I had not touched Jeff in nearly half a year, and the thought I'd soon hold him in my arms had me bouncing my heels.

By 11:15, I was going nuts. Had Jeff's car broken down? Was he involved in an accident? Or maybe he was stuck in a traffic snarl someplace. But then a car engine roared out front, and the glow from a pair of headlights lit up our house. I flew out of the front door and raced toward our driveway with my arms chugging and my heart pumping.

Jeff stepped from the driver's side of a 2014 Impala with sleek lines and brushed chrome wheels. He wore an IU hoodie, blue jeans, and sneakers, and his hair was in tangles.

Since I knew Dad was already asleep, I didn't hesitate to embrace Jeff, right there on the driveway. I wrapped my arms around his waist and kissed his cheek, while he did the same to me.

"God, it's good to see you. The traffic in Atlanta was terrible; I thought I'd never get here."

"But you did."

After I released Jeff from my arms, I stepped back to study him. He'd put on a little muscle since July, and I told him the extra weight looked good on his frame.

"You're looking pretty sexy yourself," he said while he reached into the Impala's back seat to retrieve his suitcase and another pair of shoes.

I led Jeff into the house. In my room, he tossed the suitcase on the bed while glancing here and there. He looked at me and knitted his eyebrows.

"Where will I sleep?"

I pointed to the bed.

Jeff flickered his eyebrows. "Sounds good, but I'm exhausted and stinky. Can I grab a shower? Then I'll be ready for dreamland."

"You're not hungry?"

"I grabbed a burger in Valdosta."

A half hour later, we lay face to face in the darkness, wearing only our briefs and holding each other. Dad had the heat running, but my room was still a bit chilly, and Jeff's warm skin soothed me. He smelled of soap, shampoo, and toothpaste, and his hair was damp. I stroked his smooth cheek while we spoke in whispers.

"I've missed you so badly," Jeff said. "Up in Bloomington, you're on my mind constantly. I keep thinking of all the things we did down here last summer: fishing, camping, and canoeing, to name a few. But what I miss the most is touching you and hearing your voice like I am right now. This is...amazing."

I kissed Jeff's forehead, the tip of his nose, and his lips. I ran my fingers through his hair while my pulse galloped. How had I managed to live without him the past five months? I thought of my sex sessions with Brian and how they *paled* in comparison to the simple joy of holding Jeff in my arms. And it occurred to me that sex was one thing, love another entirely. Jeff had become an inseparable part of me, despite the fact he lived a thousand miles away.

I reached between Jeff's legs and gave him a squeeze. "Do you want to...?"

"Let's wait till tomorrow when your dad's at work. After that long drive, I'm really tired. Do you mind?"

*

Two days after Jeff's arrival, we sat at a picnic table in the Arrowhead recreation area of the park, a shady expanse overlooking Mullet Key Bay and Bunce's Pass. We dined on ham and cheese sandwiches, potato chips, and pickles. The day was cool, calm, and sunny. We both wore blue jeans and sweatshirts, and sunlight glistened in Jeff's dark hair while he spoke.

"It's *so* dreary in Indiana this time of year. During exam week, the sun didn't shine a single time, and the temperature went below twenty every day. I had to wear gloves, scarf, and a beanie to keep warm."

I took a bite from a pickle while trying to imagine Jeff living in such dismal conditions up at IU, and the thought made me wince.

"Would you consider moving to Florida after you graduate?" I asked.

"Definitely, but I won't finish at IU for another eighteen months, and I'm not sure I want to live apart from you for that long. Wasn't this morning wonderful?"

Jeff referred to our lovemaking earlier in the day, not long after sunrise. Right after my dad left the house, we both visited the bathroom before returning to my room and peeling off our briefs. Then we sank to the mattress to pleasure each other.

Now, at Arrowhead, I looked left and right and saw no one. I stroked the back of Jeff's forearm, using my fingertips to tease the fine hairs there. "It *was* amazing—maybe the best ever."

Jeff gazed into my eyes and grinned. "It's so great, being here with you again. I can't tell you how many times I've thought about all we did here last summer. It seems like a dream but it wasn't. What we had back then—and what we have right now—is real, and I don't want to live without it any longer."

"What are you saying?"

Jeff rubbed the tip of his nose with a knuckle. "I'm thinking of transferring to FSU. It has a communications college, and I can complete my degree requirements there."

Already my pulse pounded. "When would you do this?"

Jeff shrugged. "It's too late to transfer this school year, but if I could spend the summer here with you, then we could both move up to Tallahassee in the fall. What do you think?"

For a moment, I was speechless. Jeff and I sharing a summer at Fort De Soto and rooming together at FSU in the fall?

"That would be...amazing," I finally managed to say.

"I'll catch some flak from my parents—they won't like the fact I'm so far away—but I'm legally an adult, so there's nothing they can do to stop me if I choose to relocate." Jeff reached under the table and stroked my knee with his fingers. "Do you think your dad would let me spend the summer at your house? I'd kick in on the food bill and help with chores."

"I'm sure he wouldn't mind."

Jeff's hand traveled up my thigh. "Just think, we'd wake up next to each other every morning and fall asleep in each other's arms every night."

"It sounds wonderful," I said.

But will it really happen?

CHAPTER EIGHT

Thursday night, Jeff and I visited the Sundial AMC cineplex in St. Petersburg to see a Spiderman film that left me with jangled nerves and a slight headache, so when we arrived home, I suggested we take a walk through the campground.

"I need some fresh air."

Because it was holiday season, very few campsites in the park were occupied, and we had a measure of privacy. Our shoe soles scraped the crushed shell road, and crickets chirped in the trees while we strolled. A close-to-full moon bathed us in silvery light. I held Jeff's hand in mine, and right away I relaxed.

"I'm dreading the moment you'll leave on Sunday. Can't you stay a few more days?"

"I wish I could, but classes start at IU on January third. I have to be back in Bloomington by then."

We walked past a shiny silver Airstream travel trailer with a Michigan license plate on its rear bumper. The trailer's interior lights revealed a gray-haired couple playing cards at their dining table.

"I'll bet they aren't missing the winter weather up north," Jeff said. "I know *I'm* not."

I squeezed Jeff's hand. "I think I've turned you into a Floridian."

"Hey, this place doesn't even give you a choice. How can you *not* love it?"

We came to the east end of the campground, where we sat on a bench overlooking the Intracoastal Waterway. Hundreds of stars twinkled above us, while somewhere in the distance an outboard engine hummed. The glow of the campground streetlights reflected in the Intracoastal's surface.

Jeff put his arm around my shoulders, and the warmth of his body was delicious. He kept his gaze fixed on the water when he spoke.

"Will you continue having sex with Brian when you're back in Tallahassee?"

"Only if you're okay with it. I already told you, if you want me to stop, I will."

"I'm not asking you to do that. I'll be a long way from Florida, and you're a horny twenty-year-old; you're entitled to animal pleasures. It's just..."

"What?"

"Promise me Brian won't ever come between you and me."

*

Saturday night, my dad grilled steaks over charcoal while Jeff and I sat in camp chairs, sipping from bottles of beer. The night was cool and still, and smoke from the grill hung in the air above us. An exterior wall fixture cast a cone of yellow light; its glow reflected in Jeff's dark eyes.

The evening before, while Jeff had showered, I spoke with my dad about Jeff living with us for the summer. "He'd contribute to the food bills and help out around the house too."

We sat in our living room, me on the sofa and dad on his Barcalounger with a *Field & Stream* issue resting in his lap. Dad crinkled his forehead and moved his jaw from side to side before he looked at me.

"It's one thing for you to share your bed with Jeff for a week—it's a short-term situation—but for three months? That doesn't sound too comfortable to me."

I lowered my gaze and rubbed the back of my neck, sensing discomfort was not the true source of Dad's concern. Had he figured out what was going on between me and Jeff?

I returned my gaze to Dad. "I mean, I guess Jeff could crash on the living room sofa. But honestly, I'm okay sleeping next to him. There's plenty of room."

Dad lowered his gaze and nodded. "We'll see" was all he said.

Dinner was delicious: steak, baked potatoes slathered in butter and sour cream, and a fruit salad Jeff and I prepared—a mixture of orange sections, strawberries, grapes, and banana slices, all doused in freshly squeezed orange juice.

After Jeff and I cleaned up the kitchen, we took a walk through the silent campground, holding hands and listening to the breeze stir shrubs and tree branches. The sky was cloudy, so we weren't able to see the moon or the stars like we normally could, but streetlamps provided puddles of light that allowed us to view our surroundings. We strolled in silence for a few minutes before Jeff finally spoke.

"I'll need to get up early tomorrow morning, right after daybreak, so I can reach Peru before eleven tomorrow night. It's going to be a long day, especially since I don't have anything to look forward to, only cold weather and packing for school."

I imagined Jeff driving a thousand miles on his own, most of it through the rural south, and the thought made me cringe. I would have taken the trip with him, but then I'd have to turn right around and take a Greyhound bus back to Florida. And that didn't make any sense, did it?

*

I woke to the sound of my cell phone's alarm chirping.

Jeff groaned when I turned off the alarm and fell back onto the mattress, face up. Sunrise approached, and already I could make out shapes of trees and shrubs when I gazed out of the windows. Somewhere a blue jay tootled its morning tune.

"Let's sleep another half hour," I said.

Jeff's morning voice sounded husky. "I can't, I need to hit the road by seven."

While Jeff grabbed a quick shower, I brewed coffee and prepared breakfast for our household—scrambled eggs, bacon, toast, and boiled grits.

My dad joined me in the kitchen with a newspaper under his arm. He hadn't shaved yet, and his stubble gave him a swarthy appearance. After he poured himself a mug of coffee, he studied the sports page for a minute or two before setting it aside and clearing his throat.

"I guess this isn't a very happy day for you and Jeff, is it?"

I looked at him and shook my head before returning my gaze to the stove.

"I know you boys have a friendship unlike any I had at your age. You're lucky to have each other."

Right away my scalp prickled at Dad's remark.

"If Jeff wants to share your bed with you this summer, it's fine with me. And I'll have projects the two of you can work on together, here in the park. I'll pay minimum wage—that's all I have budgeted—but at least you'll each have spending money and maybe some savings by the end of August."

While I whisked eggs in a bowl, I glanced over my shoulder.

"Dad?"

His gaze met mine and he raised his eyebrows.

"Thanks," I said, "for everything."

*

An hour after Jeff's departure, I sat on the screened porch, staring at the bayou while the glider rocked back and forth, making its peculiar squeaking sound. I tried to remember the feel of Jeff's lips pressed to mine when we'd said our goodbyes in the privacy of my bedroom. Both of us got a little teary before it was over, and we had to compose ourselves before we left the room.

When I watched Jeff drive away, I listened to the growl of his muffler and it was all I could do to keep myself from chasing after him before he reached the county road. I wanted to ask him to stay, or to take me with him, but, of course, I didn't. I only stood there and watched him disappear from view while feeling as if my heart were breaking in two.

CHAPTER NINE

The Tallahassee winter I returned to was brutally cold. Temperatures often dipped below freezing and sometimes the sun would not shine for a week. I shivered in my North Face jacket, and my breath steamed in the frigid air when Brian and I walked to campus each morning. Heavy rains fell, and dampness seemed to cling to everything: trees, clothing, and even my hair.

Our apartment's mini-split heater was less than effective, and within a week after Brian and I returned to school, we moved our beds together. We slept skin to skin at night, not for romantic reasons, but because it kept us warmer. And it felt nice falling asleep with Brian's arm draped across my chest and his hips pressed against my butt cheeks. Each night, after we switched off the nightstand light, Brian snuggled up to me and kissed the back of my neck.

"Sleep well, Jakub."

As time passed, Brian opened up a little about his feelings, and he got a bit emotional at times, especially when talking about his family life, down in Fort Lauderdale. His dad, it seemed, had a drinking problem; it had caused constant strife in their household when Brian grew up.

"The bastard was always roughing up my mom and making her cry. Sometimes, when he'd pass out in his Barcalounger, I honestly thought about stabbing him with a butcher knife. We'd have been better off without him in our lives."

Also, Brian had lost a younger sister to leukemia, several years before. One night, when we shared a six-pack at the apartment, his eyes glistened and his voice quivered when he talked about her death.

"Lisa was only nine when it struck. She battled it two years before it took her. I was in high school at the time and had no social life because I was constantly at the children's hospital, trying to cheer her up. I kept saying, 'You have to be strong. I couldn't stand it if you gave up and left us.'"

Brian whimpered for a few moments. Then he sniffled and wiped snot from his upper lip with the back of his wrist.

"Toward the end, she was nothing but skin and bones. She'd lost all her hair and these dark circles grew around her eyes—she looked like a spook. Honestly, I think it was a blessing when she finally died. At least she didn't have to suffer anymore."

I didn't know what to say when Brian spoke of these things, so I only put my hand on his shoulder and squeezed.

Who could ask for a better roommate?

*

Because of the self-discipline I'd exercised last school term, my fall quarter grades soared to a level I'd never before achieved: three As and one B. My dad was so elated he sent me a check for $300, along with a note.

> *Buy yourself whatever you want, even if it's silly.*

I took the practical approach and purchased a new ten-speed bike to glide around campus on. Of course, due to the cold weather, I had to wear gloves when I rode so my hands wouldn't turn into blocks of ice, but still it was nice not to walk everywhere.

At my academic adviser's urging, I declared a major—education. I'd always liked my teachers when growing up and considered theirs a noble profession. So now I took two of my classes at the Education College. Three-quarters of the students there were women, which I was fine with. One course dealt with childhood development, the other focused on classroom management.

Brian and I strictly kept to our study schedules, and we added an exercise regimen to our lives. Three days a week we worked out with weights at the campus gym for an hour, and other days we ran three miles at the FSU track. In short order, the muscles in my shoulders, arms, and chest beefed up, and I slept more soundly, too, I guess due to the distance running.

Of course, my private life with Brian continued. By now, I knew exactly what got his motor racing. And we often gave each other full-body massages before sex, something I found delicious whenever Brian kneaded my flesh.

Sunday nights, Jeff always phoned me from Bloomington, and we talked for a half hour or so.

"It's *so* damned cold up here," Jeff told me one evening. "Friday morning, the temperature was five degrees when I walked to my first class, and the wind blew, which only made things worse. What I'd give to be with you in Florida right now."

Another night, he told me, "I met with my academic adviser Thursday. We talked about my transfer to FSU, and he'll check into things. It's probably doable without me losing any credit hours from my IU classes."

Whenever I thought about Jeff moving to Florida, my pulse quickened. Not only would we spend our entire summer together, but when fall arrived, we'd share an apartment just as Brian and I did now, and how great would that be?

CHAPTER TEN

"My cousin Mason will visit this weekend," Brian told me on a Thursday afternoon. "He's a cool guy, and I *know* you'll like him."

I crinkled my forehead. "I don't understand."

"He's the one who turned me on to gay sex, when I was fifteen."

"Your *cousin*?"

Brian nodded. "My parents and I visited his family in Jacksonville Beach. I shared Mason's bed with him a few nights and...you know."

I glanced toward the bedroom. "Where will he sleep when he's here?"

Brian shrugged. "We'll move the beds apart. He can have mine, and I'll crash in the living room."

The next afternoon, when I arrived home from my last class of the day, a guy a little older than me sat alongside Brian on the Louis XV sofa.

Brian pointed a thumb at our guest, "Jakub, meet Mason."

When Mason rose, he stood half a head taller than me. His cobalt eyes were the same color as

Brian's; they gazed into mine while we shook hands. Mason's palm was warm and his teeth gleamed when he smiled at me. A riot of copper-colored freckles danced across his nose and cheeks. His rust-red hair grew in ringlets to his shoulders, and he spoke with a syrupy north Florida drawl.

"Thanks for letting me stay here. I have a job interview with DOT Monday morning. Their offices are just down the road, so I thought I'd pay Cousin Brian a visit while I'm in Tallahassee."

We made small talk.

Mason had a degree in structural engineering from University of Florida. For the past two years, he'd hitchhiked his way around Europe, then Australia, before returning to Florida and waiting tables in Jacksonville Beach for a spell.

"I wouldn't trade those travels for anything, but I guess it's time I started acting like an adult. The first step is finding a real job with decent pay and benefits."

While Mason talked, I studied his clothing. He wore blue jeans with holes in the knees, Converse sneakers, and a T-shirt with the sleeves hacked off. The tee showed off his biceps and shoulder muscles. A silver bracelet with a single opal mounted on its plateau encircled one wrist, and his leather jacket draped the coffee table.

Mason stretched his limbs like a housecat and groaned. "After that three-hour drive, I need fresh air. Let's do something outdoors."

Moments later, the three of us tossed a Frisbee back and forth in our building's parking lot. The sky was overcast, the afternoon air chilly.

Mason spoke about his visit to Sydney, Australia, several months before. "I stayed in a youth hostel in a community called Manly Beach. You would not believe the surfing conditions there."

"Good?" Brian asked.

"The best. The water's clear as gin and the waves are twice the size of those we get in Jacksonville Beach. I bought a used board as soon as I got there and hit the water every day. The bottom's even sandy so you don't have to worry about bailing into rocks or coral."

"How'd you support yourself?" I asked while tossing Mason the Frisbee.

Brian hissed. "His parents spoil him."

When I swung my gaze to Mason, he shrugged.

"They let me take two years off as my college graduation present, but don't think for a minute I lived in luxury. I had a backpack, a tent, and a sleeping bag. Most nights I slept outdoors, and I found odd jobs most everywhere I went; chopping wood, raking leaves, whatever. The work helped keep food in my belly."

I narrowed my eyes. "You did all this travel by yourself?"

Mason nodded.

"Didn't you feel lonely?"

Mason lunged to his left to catch an errant Frisbee toss from Brian. His movements were fluid and quick, those of a natural athlete.

"Sometimes, sure. But I met all kinds of folks along the way, ones I could talk with. And I can't tell you how many times someone bought me a meal or let me sleep in their home for a night or two."

"Europe gets cold in winter, right?" Brian asked.

"In certain areas, yeah, so I made sure I spent my winter months in southern Italy."

We kept tossing the Frisbee for a short while longer before Mason pointed to Brian's wristwatch. "What time do you have?"

"Five-thirty, why?"

"Let me buy us a twelve-pack. I don't know about you guys, but I'm ready to relax."

We all piled into Mason's pickup truck, a ten-year-old Chevy Silverado with dented bumpers, oxidized paint, and cracked vinyl upholstery. Mason turned the ignition key three times before the engine finally sputtered to life. I sat between Mason and Brian, and our shoulders, hips, and knees rubbed when Mason backed into the road.

Brian fiddled with the passenger sideview mirror. "I'm surprised this piece of junk still runs. How many miles does she have on her?"

Mason squinted while he studied the car's odometer. "A hundred seventy thousand and change, so don't make fun of this baby, she's served me well."

From the corner of my eye, I studied the typhoon of Mason's hair. Afternoon sunlight reflected in golden strands interweaving his curls. He turned onto Tennessee Street, and the muscle in his shoulder bulged while he worked the steering wheel. He seemed almost hyper-masculine, and I found it hard to believe he had once shared sex with Brian.

Mason pulled into the parking lot of a liquor store across the street from campus, and moments later emerged from the store with a twelve-pack of Pabst Blue Ribbon under his arm. Once he'd started the truck's cranky engine, he tore open the twelve-pack and handed both me and Brian a can. Then he opened one for himself.

"Got an idea," he said, crossing two lanes of westbound traffic and steering us eastward. "I hear Miccosukee Road's real pretty. Why don't we have a look-see?"

I sipped from my can, enjoying the beer's crisp taste on the tip of my tongue. Wind rushed through the car, and I zipped up my jacket to stay warm.

Mason turned left onto Capital Circle. Then, a few minutes later, he turned right onto two-lane Miccosukee Road, and within minutes we had left the city behind us.

"This is one of Tallahassee's canopy trails," Mason said when we entered a natural tunnel created by live oaks. Drainage ditches had been dug out of the burnt-orange soil on either side of the asphalt ribbon we cruised. The land we passed was deeply forested with long leaf pines, magnolias, and a variety of oaks. Rusty fences built with hog wire and twisted tree limbs undulated with the rolling terrain.

Brian turned to gaze at me with a grin on his handsome face. "We've lived in Tallahassee over two years but never saw this place. Why is that?"

Mason cuffed the back of Brian's head. "You need to get out of the city once in a while. Life's not all about dorm parties and books. Do either of you guys own a tent?"

"No, cousin, we don't."

"Well, *I* do, so if I get this DOT position we'll have to put it to use. I hear the campground at St. George Island—"

"Saint what?"

Mason shook his head and his curls danced from side to side.

"St. George Island, fool. It's mostly a state park, right on the Gulf of Mexico, only about two hours from here. I hear the sand there looks like table sugar, and the Gulf water's crystal clear. We should spend a weekend there, the three of us. I know you'll both like it."

Mason drained his beer, crushed the can in his fist, and opened another. Then Brian and I followed suit. Already I felt a bond forming between the three of us.

"Do you guys know we're only twenty miles from the Georgia state line?" Mason said.

Brian raised his eyebrows. "Are you serious?"

"Hell, yeah. You're not in Fort Lauderdale, this is the Deep South."

When we reached an intersection with another two-lane road, Mason executed a three-point turn and reversed our direction. "I'm taking us home, fellas. It's getting dark, and I don't know about you two, but I'm hungry. What kind of grub do you have at the apartment?"

"Jakub's the household cook, ask him."

I spoke up. "I can make spaghetti with hamburger and marinara sauce. And we have stuff for a salad, I think."

"Sorry," Mason said, "but I don't eat meat of any kind."

"What?" Brian cried.

"I mean it. I turned vegetarian while I lived in Europe. It's a healthy way to eat and cheaper too."

Brian shook his head. "I'll bet if I tossed burgers on a charcoal grille, you'd devour two of them in nothing flat. I've seen you do that in the past."

"But not anymore. I won't pollute my body with animal flesh, there's no need to. I get my protein from nuts, soy beans, and dairy products, and do just fine. You guys should give it a try."

I crinkled my forehead while I sipped from my beer. Already I felt light-headed from the alcohol I'd consumed.

Me give up meat? No way....

On our way home, Mason stopped at a food co-op where he purchased a bag of short-grain brown rice, a variety of vegetables, a loaf of whole wheat bread, and a block of cheddar cheese. He bought a blue bottle of German Liebfraumilch too.

"*That's* going to be our dinner?" Brian asked when we left the co-op. "It's nothing more than rabbit food."

"Give it a chance; you might like it."

Brian hissed.

I, on the other hand, was intrigued. If Mason hadn't eaten meat in over a year, his diet certainly hadn't detracted from his athleticism. He moved like a jaguar you might see in the zoo, and I liked the way his muscles flexed in his arms and shoulders.

At home, in our cramped kitchen, Brian and I watched Mason chop yellow squash, Vidalia onion, a tomato, and a bell pepper while a pot of brown rice simmered on a burner. Mason cubed the cheese and placed the squares on a plate along with bread slices. Then he sautéed the veggies in a frying pan coated with olive oil.

The food smelled tasty, and my stomach growled in anticipation of our meal. "Who taught you how to cook like this?" I asked.

"A university student I met in a bar in Marseille. We talked over a drink—her English was pretty good—and she invited me to her apartment. We got along well, so I ended up living with her for almost a month before I went to Italy."

"She was vegetarian?"

Mason nodded. "And a hell of a sweet girl. I hated leaving her, but had to move on."

Brian clucked his tongue. "Sounds like you and Frenchie enjoyed your stay a *whole* lot, cousin."

A grin crossed Mason's face, but he didn't respond verbally to Brian's teasing. He only stirred the vegetables sizzling in the frying pan. After he'd seasoned them with soy sauce, he served them over the rice on three plates.

The food was delicious; even Brian said so in between forkfuls. Coupled with the bread, cheese, and a glass of wine, the meal satisfied me entirely.

"Notice how you don't feel bloated after you eat this way," Mason said when we'd all cleaned our plates. "I honestly don't think humans were meant to consume meat; it's too damned hard to digest."

I nodded.

After Brian and I cleaned up the kitchen, the three of us watched a DVD rental, a film called *Hell or High Water* starring Jeff Bridges. The movie was pretty good, but by 11:00 p.m., all three of us were yawning.

"Don't know about you guys," Mason said, "but I got up early this morning and I'm ready for some shut-eye." He looked at Brian. "Got a spare pillow and blanket? I'll sleep on this couch if it's okay."

Brian's gaze swung to me, then Mason. "You're our guest this weekend, cousin. You take my bed, and I'll surf the sofa. I don't mind."

"You're okay with that?"

"Of course."

Minutes later, Mason and I undressed in the bedroom. Mason wasn't wearing briefs, and when he shucked his jeans, I couldn't help myself. I stole glances at him while my pulse accelerated. His chest looked like it was carved from marble, and his belly muscles rippled like a washboard.

I pondered whether or not I should ditch my boxers and sleep naked, too, but I wasn't quite as immodest as Mason, so I left them on and climbed under my bedcovers. After I switched off the nightstand lamp, we lay in darkness, and even though the windows were closed, I still heard crickets chirp in trees outdoors.

Mason cleared his throat.

"This bed may look kind of sissy, but it's real comfortable. As much as I enjoyed my travels, I sure don't miss sleeping on the ground."

I turned onto my side, facing Mason. "I can't imagine spending two years on the road, especially in foreign countries. Hell, the farthest I've ever traveled was Key West."

Glow from a nearby streetlamp entered the room, enough so I could make out Mason's facial features: his straight nose that came to a point, his square chin, and full lips. He crooked an arm behind his head and gazed at the ceiling.

"I think travel, especially abroad, enriches your life like nothing else can. It makes you realize there are other ways to live than how we do in the States. I believe Americans are too obsessed with convenience and comfort. And there's a conformity in the way we think, whether you're in Florida or Ohio. We watch the same movies and TV shows, eat the same types of food, and wear the same kinds of clothing."

Mason thrust his free arm beneath his covers to scratch himself, and the sound of his fingernails raking tender skin made my mouth grow sticky.

"Your friend in Marseilles," I said, "do you stay in touch with her?"

"We trade e-mails and texts. She may visit me this summer when her classes are out."

"What's her name?"

Mason turned his head to look at me. "Babette, why?"

"Just curious."

"Brian tells me you have a buddy up north you're pretty tight with."

My belly quivered. "You mean Jeff?"

"Is that his name?"

"Yeah, he lives in Indiana and attends the university in Bloomington, but he may transfer to FSU next school year. If he does, we'll probably share a place."

"Sounds nice," Mason said. "I loved living with Babette; she made every day special, if you know what I mean."

I didn't say anything, but already I knew Babette had been more than a friend to Mason. And I was pretty certain Mason knew exactly what sort of relationship I had with Jeff. The two of us were dancing around the obvious, and why?

I pondered whether or not I should talk more openly about Jeff, but then Mason yawned and flipped onto his stomach.

"I need some rest, Jakub; I'll see you tomorrow."

CHAPTER ELEVEN

Sunlight poured through the bedroom windows when I woke on Saturday morning. The light was so bright it made Mason's mop of hair look like it was on fire. He had flipped onto his back during the night and his ribcage rose and fell beneath his blanket. I studied his face in profile while recalling the moment he'd taken his pants off the night before, and the memory caused a stirring inside my boxers.

I headed for the bathroom before returning to the bedroom to get dressed. Then I put on a T-shirt, a flannel shirt, and blue jeans. I was tying the laces on my sneakers when Mason's eyelids fluttered open.

"Hey, there," he said, his morning voice throaty.

"How'd you sleep?" I asked.

"Like a dead man. Did I snore last night?"

"A little, yeah."

Actually, I'd had a difficult time falling asleep the previous evening because Mason sounded like a cement mixer. I'd never heard anything like it, but didn't want to offend him by saying so.

"Babette used to give me shit about the noise I made when I lived with her."

My gaze met Mason's. *Go ahead, ask...*

"You guys shared a bed?"

Mason nodded. "Does it surprise you?"

"Not really."

Mason bent his arms at the elbows and tucked his hands behind his head on the pillow. The hair under his arms was also bright red. "I'd had girlfriends before, but never lived with one."

"How was it?"

"Amazing—that's the only way I can describe it. I'd wake up in the morning, feeling her skin pressed against mine and smelling her hair, and I couldn't believe how lucky I was to have her in my life."

"Is she pretty?"

Mason tossed his bedcovers aside and brought his feet to the floor, and right away my mouth went dry. He reached for his blue jeans, and after fishing a black-and-white photograph from his wallet, he handed the photo to me.

"That's Babette."

The girl looked to be twenty or so, slender, with dark hair and eyes and a sensual mouth.

"Nice," I said before handing the photo back to Mason.

"*More* than nice, actually."

After Mason placed the photo back in his wallet, he made no attempt to get dressed, but only scratched the side of his head and yawned.

"I've never met anyone like Babette. She's bright and funny, and she's a wild woman in bed—I had a hard time keeping up with her."

Sounds of stirring came from the living room and Brian called out to us in falsetto.

"Good morning, girls. Did you two sleep well?"

"Just fine," Mason said. "This bed's great."

Mason's knees crackled when he rose. He ambled toward the bathroom with his cock wagging and his beefy butt twitching, and I had no doubt the French girl had enjoyed a pleasant month with Mason as her companion in Marseilles.

Moments later, the shower ran and steam billowed from the open bathroom door. Mason sang a Kenny Chesney number, "When the Sun Goes Down," and his baritone voice sounded pretty good.

After I made my bed, I went to the kitchen, where I cracked open a half dozen eggs and whisked them in a bowl. Then I got the coffeemaker gurgling.

Mason joined me in the kitchen, smelling of soap and shampoo and wearing his jeans. He toasted and buttered bread slices while I scrambled the eggs in a frying pan. Brian took his turn in the shower, but his singing wasn't nearly as melodic as his cousin's.

Mason shook his head. "He sounds like a cat squealing in there."

I chuckled while I worked the eggs with a spatula. "In the dorm, every time Brian sang in the shower, guys threw shampoo bottles at him till he stopped."

Mason cackled.

When the food was ready, the three of us gathered at the dining table. Brian wore a towel wrapped around his waist. His hair was damp and water droplets glistened on his shoulders. His gaze traveled from me to Mason.

"Saturdays, Jakub and I don't study. It's our day for fun, so what do you guys suggest we do with ourselves?"

Mason looked up from his food. "You two ever hear of Ochlocknee River State Park?"

Brian and I shook our heads.

"It's a forty-five-minute drive south of here, not far from Sopchoppy. I'm told it's a real pretty spot, and we can rent kayaks from the park, maybe do a little exploring."

I thought of me and Jeff paddling the Suwanee, back in July. "I've canoed before, but never used a kayak. Is it hard?"

Mason shook his head. "You'll pick it up quickly. The hardest part's getting in and out of the kayak without tipping it over."

"Sounds like fun," Brian said.

Mason looked at me. "Is there a newspaper box close by? I'd like to read one before we leave for the river."

"Just down the street," I said. "After breakfast, I'll go get one while you guys clean up the kitchen."

Several minutes later, when I strolled down a sidewalk, a mockingbird whistled in a live oak I passed beneath. The sky was clear and the temperature was warming up.

I paid four quarters for that day's edition of the *Tallahassee Democrat* and stuck the paper under my arm. While I strolled back to my apartment, I pondered my earlier discussion with Mason about his friend Babette and how he had talked about the whole thing so blithely. Then I thought about Mason's bringing up Jeff in our earlier conversation. Clearly, Brian had told Mason I had a boyfriend, but Mason didn't seem the least offended by the situation, and how cool was that?

Back at the apartment, I found Brian lying on the sofa with his head resting in Mason's lap. Mason twirled a lock of Brian's hair around his finger when I came through the door, and he didn't cease when I sat in an armchair and studied the two. He kept on twirling.

Brian's gaze was fixed on the ceiling. He wore a pair of briefs—nothing else—and he looked utterly comfortable with Mason's attentions.

I knitted my eyebrows while moving my gaze from Mason to Brian and back.

"Were you guys *doing* something while I was gone?"

"Nothing tawdry," Mason said. "We've always been affectionate with each other, but don't make any more of it than it is."

I tossed Mason the newspaper. Then I checked the Sopchoppy weather forecast on my cell phone.

"Sunny and still, with a high of seventy-two degrees."

"Sounds perfect," Mason said before looking down at Brian. "What do you say, cousin?"

"I'm in."

"I'll make us ham and cheese sandwiches," I said.

"Hold the ham on mine," Mason told me. "Just give me extra cheese."

I got busy in the kitchen, slathering bread slices with mayonnaise and mustard, while Brian and Mason remained on the sofa. Mason had ceased twirling Brian's hair. Instead, he entwined the fingers on his right hand with the fingers on Brian's left and stroked the back of Brian's hand with his thumb.

"I hope you get the DOT job," Brian said. "It's nice having you here."

"It *is*, and I missed seeing you these past two years."

"Did you?"

"Of course. Why wouldn't I?"

Brian shifted his hips. "You never even sent me an e-mail or text."

"I know, and it wasn't nice of me. I'm sorry."

Mason brought Brian's hand to his lips; he kissed Brian's wrist two or three times.

I didn't know what to make of the situation on the sofa. Of course, I knew Mason and Brian had been always been close. "He's like a brother to me," Brian had said of Mason. And though I knew the two had enjoyed bedroom romps in their younger days, their actions on the sofa didn't smack of lust at all. I figured they were simply sharing a physical closeness they'd been deprived of for a long while, a special brand of familial love that made me jealous as hell.

*

The drive to the park was a pretty one, especially after we passed through Crawfordville, and the terrain turned from small town to rural. The roadsides were heavily wooded with slash pines, live oaks, magnolias, and sabal palms. Wind rushed through the truck's cab, fluttering my hair and tickling my cheeks.

At the park's entrance, we paid a ranger our admission fee, along with rental charges for three kayaks. He gave us a map of the area and suggested we paddle an eleven-mile trail on the meandering Ochlocknee.

"It'll take you fellows a good four hours to complete the loop," he said. "The weather's calm right now, so you won't have wind to contend with, but often the breeze kicks up in midafternoon. If it does, stick to the banks so you're not fighting chop."

He provided us with life jackets and paddles and pointed down a road leading to the river.

"The kayaks are stored on a rack, down by the boat ramp. You boys have a safe trip."

Mason had been right—climbing into a kayak was tricky if you hadn't done it before. I almost tipped mine over before Mason grabbed the stern and held it steady while I lowered myself into the seat. My legs were fully extended in the direction of the bow. After Mason helped Brian into his kayak, he launched us both into the river. Then he followed behind us, looking as comfortable in his kayak as he might be sitting on our living room sofa.

We paddled past the park's eastern tip, where the banks were high and shaded by live oaks. Then the river curved in a northeasterly direction and the banks quickly turned to nothing more than swaths of sawgrass. The sawgrass reminded me of a wheat field with its green and gold stalks that waved whenever the slightest breeze moved. Off in the distance, stands of long leaf pines thrust skyward.

Just like the Suwannee, the Ochlocknee's water was coffee-colored, stained by tannins leaching into the river upstream.

I studied a great white heron perched in a sabal palm, one of the few trees growing on the banks around us. The lanky bird didn't seem disturbed by our presence. It busied itself by peering into the shallows, searching for its lunch, and the heron's snowy feathers contrasted starkly with our surroundings.

A half hour into our paddle, I realized no one among our trio had spoken a word. Each guy seemed absorbed in his own thoughts, and that was particularly odd behavior from Brian, who was normally a chatterbox. Each time I looked at him, his gaze was either fixed on the sky or the river banks. The only sound was the swish of our paddles in the dark and placid water.

After another half hour passed, Mason finally broke the silence when we approached a sandy river bank. He pointed with a paddle blade. "It's close to noon, and that looks like a good spot to have lunch. You fellas hungry?"

Minutes later, we beached our kayaks and dined on the sandwiches I'd made, washing them down with sodas kept cold in a small ice cooler we had brought along. We sat on the soft, ecru-colored sand, and I don't think I'd felt so relaxed since Jeff's Christmas visit to Fort De Soto. My breathing was rhythmic and my limbs were like jelly.

Two men in a bass boat motored past us, both dressed in flannel shirts, work pants, and ball caps. They waved hello, and we waved back. They were the first people we'd seen since leaving the park's boat ramp.

Mason pointed at the water before us.

"This river flows in a southeasterly direction till it empties into Ochlocknee Bay. Then the bay dumps into the Gulf of Mexico, just about five miles from here. I'll bet the fishing's good in this area, especially where the water's brackish."

I raised my eyebrows. "You fish?"

Mason looked at me like I was nuts. "Back home, I visited the Intracoastal Waterway most every weekend as a kid. I know spots that *always* produce—redfish, flounder, specks, and sheepshead."

I spoke of my angling days at Fort De Soto. "It's what I miss the most when I'm living in Tallahassee— no salt water."

Brian made a face. "I've never understood the whole fishing thing. Every time I tried it with my friends, I only felt bored."

Mason shook his head. "Fishing's a sport for the patient, cousin, and *you* are the least patient person I know."

I took a sip from my soda and smacked my lips.

I told Mason, "If you move to Tallahassee, bring your fishing gear. I have a pole and tackle box in a closet at the apartment. We can visit Alligator Point, just south of here, and maybe do some wade fishing once the weather warms up."

"I'd like that," Mason said. "It'll be nice having a fishing buddy up here."

"What about me?" Brian cried.

Mason looked at Brian and raised his eyebrows. "You just said you don't like to fish."

Brian shrugged. "I can learn to like anything if it keeps me involved in the fun."

Mason placed a hand on Brian's shoulder. "You can come with us, cousin. I'll lend you one of my poles, and you'll have a good time, I guarantee it."

Brian beamed like a kid on Christmas morning.

*

Darkness came early in the panhandle during winter. By the time we'd completed our paddle, the shadows grew long, and a crisp breeze tickled the river's surface when we disembarked at the park's boat ramp. We placed our kayaks on the rack, clambered into the truck, and after we returned our paddles and life jackets to the ranger station, we cruised northward on Highway 319.

With the sun rapidly descending behind the tree line to the west, the air rushing into the truck cab turned chilly, and we rolled up the windows to keep ourselves warm. Mason flicked on the radio and tuned it to a Tallahassee country western station. While the DJ played a Brad Paisley tune, all three of us sang along.

Brian, of course, sounded worse than a howling mutt.

In Crawfordville, Mason pulled into a gas station/convenience mart, where he purchased a six-pack of Budweiser and a bag of potato chips. After we popped open our cans, Mason raised his beer toward the ripped headliner.

"To a successful adventure, fellas. That sure was fun."

Brian and I raised our cans.

By the time we reached our Tallahassee apartment, stars had emerged in the eastern sky and the western horizon glowed in muted colors of orange, pink, and green. Streetlamps flickered on. I shivered in my flannel shirt when I exited the truck. Already I felt a bit tipsy from the two beers I'd consumed, and I looked forward to drinking more while the evening unfolded.

Inside the apartment, Mason sat next to Brian on the sofa and leafed through the *Tallahassee*

Democrat I'd purchased that morning. "You fellas know of any vegetarian restaurants in town?"

"I'm clueless," Brian said.

Moments later, Mason clucked his tongue. "Here's an ad for a place on College Avenue called 'Nature's Bounty.' What do you say we check it out?"

"Can't we just get burgers?" Brian said in a whiny tone.

"I am *not* eating meat, cousin. Come on, be adventurous. This place sounds nice, and I'm sure you'll find *something* on the menu to satisfy your hunger. I'll even pick up the tab."

"It sounds good to me," I said, glancing between Brian and Mason.

Brian looked at me and turned down one corner of his mouth. "You're a traitor, you know that?"

"Jakub's *not* being disloyal. He's willing to try new things, and you should do the same."

Brian rolled his eyes. "Okay, cousin, whatever..."

We took turns showering before leaving for the restaurant, and once again I viewed Mason in his birthday suit, a sight I couldn't get enough of. His body was perfectly proportioned, and the movement of his limbs seemed synchronized.

Amazing...

*

Nature's Bounty occupied a two-story brick structure with heart-of-pine flooring and a storefront window. Ferns and philodendrons grew in hanging baskets.

The dozen or so tables were draped with red-and-white checkered tablecloths, and the day's menu appeared on a chalkboard. Our server, a girl in denim overalls and a bandanna, smiled when she placed a basket of bread slices and a bowl of butter pats on our table.

"How are you guys this evening?"

Mason chuckled. "We spent the day outdoors, so we couldn't be better. What's good for dinner?"

The girl placed a hand on her hip while she answered. "Our special tonight is vegetarian lasagna. It's yummy and comes with a tossed salad."

Brian squinted. "What's in the lasagna?"

"Three kinds of cheese, whole wheat noodles, spinach, onions, carrots, and tofu."

"What's tofu?"

The girl giggled. "You must be new to this."

"Tofu's curdled milk made from soy beans," Mason said. "It's a good source of protein."

Brian made a face like he'd swallowed medicine.

"It doesn't have any taste, really," the girl said. "You won't even know it's in the lasagna."

"Okay, I guess I'll give it a try, but do you at least serve beer in this place?"

The girl laughed. "Of course. It's locally brewed using grain and hops grown organically—no pesticides or chemical fertilizers. It's tasty and has a kick to it. I can't drink more than two bottles or...*adios* reality."

"We'll take a round," Mason said.

After the girl headed for the kitchen, I glanced about the room. Most of the patrons looked to be college students. A lot of the guys had bushy beards and there wasn't a fraternity jersey or sorority pin in sight. Old Crow Medicine Band's song, "Wagon Wheel," played on the sound system.

"You know," Brian said to Mason, "you're *not* going to convert me to this vegetarian nonsense. I'm only eating here because you wanted to."

Mason squeezed Brian's shoulder. "I understand, and I *do* appreciate it. Look, I don't expect you to like everything I do, but at least give this a chance. It's all I'm asking."

The food was excellent. Even the homemade bread had a unique flavor to it. Brian gobbled his lasagna like he hadn't eaten in a week. And the server was right about the beer—after I drank two bottles, the whole room seemed to glow. I was a bit unsteady on my feet when we walked down College Avenue toward our apartment. The night had turned chilly and our breaths steamed in the air.

On our way, Mason ducked into a liquor store on Tennessee Street to purchase a bottle of Spätlese, a sweet white wine from Germany.

"I developed a taste for this stuff when I visited Bavaria. It goes well with weed."

My scalp prickled at the mention of marijuana. I hadn't used any since Jeff and I had shared a smoke on the Fourth of July, and I recalled how we had pawed each other in the darkness at a Fort De Soto picnic shelter, with the taste of ice cream sandwiches on our lips.

"We don't keep any grass in the apartment," Brian said. "I'm scared of getting busted."

Mason grinned and shook his head. "Not a problem, Mr. Eagle Scout. I brought a couple of joints from Jacksonville Beach, good shit that'll make you feel *fine*."

Back at the apartment, I brought out an ashtray and cigarette lighter while Brian put a CD by The Chainsmokers on the stereo. Mason uncorked the wine and we gathered around the coffee table. We passed a pungent-smelling joint and washed the smoke down with sips from the wine bottle. Very quickly, objects in the room took on a two-dimensional appearance, and the glow from our floor lamp seemed brighter than normal.

"Let me give you guys a shotgun," Mason said. He turned to Brian, who sat next to Mason on the sofa. After placing the lit end of the joint inside his mouth, Mason brought his lips to Brian's and blew a jet of smoke into Brian's mouth. When Brian exhaled moments later, a cloud of smoke billowed into the room.

Brian coughed a couple of times while beating his chest with a fist.

"Jesus, that stuff's *strong*. I feel like I'm floating."

Mason repeated the shotgun process with me, and I shivered when he knelt before me and brought his lips to mine. After I exhaled my own cloud of smoke, I took a gulp from the wine bottle. Then I closed my eyes and rested my spine against the armchair's back cushion.

Someone's knees crackled when they rose to put another CD on the stereo, this one a Taylor Swift album titled *Reputation,* and while I listened to the lyrics, a vision of afternoon sunlight reflecting off the Ochlocknee River's surface stole into my mind. And then the great white heron I'd seen perched in a sabal palm entered my thoughts. It seemed as if I were bobbing in my kayak and dipping my paddle blades into the coffee-colored water.

When the CD eventually ended, someone rose and switched off the sound system. The room fell utterly silent. Far later, when I opened my eyes, the floor lamp was extinguished, and the only light in the apartment came from a candle flickering in the bedroom.

Brian lay fast asleep on the sofa, covered by a blanket.

I rubbed the flat of my hand against my cheek and shook my head to clear out the cobwebs. My knees wobbled when I rose. I shuffled into the bathroom and used the toilet before finding Mason in the bedroom. He lay on Brian's bed, shirtless and barefooted and staring up at the ceiling with one arm crooked behind his head. The candlelight reflected in his hair and eyes.

"You okay?" I asked.

"I'm fine. How about you?"

I sat on my bed and unlaced a shoe. "I think I lost contact with reality for a while; I'm not sure how long."

"I'd say ninety minutes or so. You zoned out right after I shotgunned you."

I nodded while unlacing my other shoe. "What time is it?"

"Close to eleven. Are you tired?"

I shrugged while unbuttoning my flannel shirt.

Mason moved to a sitting position, and the bedsprings beneath him squeaked. He rested his forearms on his knees and let his hands hang.

"I want something from you, Jakub."

"What's that?"

"I think you know."

"Sorry, but I don't understand."

Mason rose. He crossed the space between the beds and sat down next to me. His skin smelled gamey when his shoulder and hip touched mine. He nuzzled my ear for a long moment before kissing my temple, and right away I grew as stiff as a peg.

Okay, I was stoned as shit and ready to do just about anything Mason asked of me. I turned my face toward him and brought my lips to his. Our mouths opened and our tongues rubbed. Mason placed his hand on my nape and squeezed while his tongue explored my teeth and gums.

Meanwhile, my thoughts spun.

Until then, I'd thought Mason was totally straight, and nothing he'd said or done since his arrival on Friday indicated any sexual interest in me. Was he only doing this because he was high, or maybe because he missed the French girl so badly, he planned to use me as a surrogate?

Mason's mouth left mine. He pulled my shirt off my shoulders and arms. Then he teased my nipple with a fingernail while I gazed into my lap.

"Is something wrong?" Mason said.

"I'm not sure we should do this."

"Why?"

"Brian might—"

"He's asleep."

"Yeah, but…"

Mason stroked my cheek with a thumb. "It'll be okay. I like you, and I *know* you like me."

"What makes you say that?"

"Last night, I saw the way you stared at me when I took my jeans off."

I lowered my gaze and swallowed while my cheeks flamed. Had I been so obvious? I licked my lips while a vision of Mason walking naked toward the bathroom that morning filled my head.

Go ahead, idiot. He's sexy as hell, and this might be your only chance.

Again, I brought my gaze to Mason's.

"All right, let's do it."

After we shucked our clothes, we left the candle burning. I lay on my back, and Mason climbed on top of me. Our chests, hips, and thighs met; our erections rubbed. Mason's skin was warm and smooth. While we kissed, I let my hand travel down his spine to squeeze his butt cheeks.

I had never made love with a guy so muscular. His body had a power to it neither Brian's nor Jeff's possessed, and Mason's strength overwhelmed me a bit, so I let him take the lead. His big hands gripped my shoulders while he rubbed his stubble against my cheek and twirled his tongue inside my ear.

I ran my fingers through his shiny hair, marveling at its thickness.

He seized my wrists and pinned both to the mattress before licking my armpits and chewing on my nipples till they swelled and grew tender. He speared my navel with his tongue. Then he released my wrists and brought his lips to my groin. He took me inside his mouth and I moaned at the feel of his tongue caressing me. I gasped when he explored the cleft of my butt with a finger.

After he let my erection pop free from his mouth, he looked up at me and winked.

"Ever bottomed before?"

I shook my head.

"Will you do it for me?"

I'd never dreamed I would let another guy take me. After all, I was always top man with both Brian and Jeff—it was my role. But now Mason had asked for my submission, and what should I say? Resistance seemed out of the question, not if I wanted things to continue.

"All right, but take it slowly."

I won't say the next half hour was entirely pleasurable, not at first anyway. Twice I asked Mason to withdraw because the pain down there was too much for me to handle. But after I relaxed and adjusted to the feel of Mason's invasion, a glow arose in my entire body, even in my scalp and the soles of my feet.

I grunted each time Mason worked his hips. I lay with the backs of my knees resting on his muscular shoulders while he pounded away and his breath huffed. When he came inside me, he let out a spooky wail, one more animal than human, almost like a coyote's howl.

I came seconds later. My chest heaved and my spine tingled. I touched myself only once before scattering my chest and belly with sticky pools of semen Mason quickly lapped up. Then he rested his cheek on my chest while our breathing slowed.

"You okay?" he whispered.

"I'm fine."

"Did you like it?"

"Oh, yes."

Mason chuckled while he withdrew. After kneeling on the mattress and straddling my waist, he ran his fingers through my damp hair. Glow from the flickering candle revealed the contours of his face.

I licked my lips. "Do you think we should tell Brian about this?"

Mason glanced into the living room and blinked a few times before returning his gaze to me.

"Let's keep it to ourselves, okay?"

I nodded.

Mason kissed me on the mouth before rising to his feet. "I'll take a quick shower. Should I leave the water running for you when I'm done?"

CHAPTER TWELVE

During the second week in February, Mason called Brian from Jacksonville Beach, and after Brian and I sat on the sofa, Brian switched their conversation to speaker so I could overhear.

"Good news," Mason said. "I got the DOT job and start in two weeks."

Right away, the sound of Mason's drawly voice made my pulse quicken. I had not seen him since the morning after our sexual encounter, almost a month before, and memories of the experience flooded my brain. I recalled the way candlelight played on Mason's body. I remembered the sensation of his hot breath sweeping my face when he worked his hips and my muscle gripped him like a vise.

Now, Brian sounded eager. "That's great. Any idea where you'll live?"

"Not sure, but I hope to find a place near you and Jakub."

Brian grew so excited he bounced his heels. "You damn sure *better* find a place close by. We can share dinners together some nights, and I'll even eat your wimpy vegetarian meals if I have to."

Once Mason rang off, Brian slapped my knee and squeezed it. "It'll be so cool having Mason in town. Think of all the mischief the three of us will get into."

I gazed into my lap.

Mischief indeed.

Per Mason's request, I had not told Brian about the sex I'd shared with Mason, but I felt guilty about the secrecy. After all, I had known Brian for over two years, but had only met Mason in January. Brian was my closest friend in Tallahassee. We studied and exercised together, had sex a time or two each week, and slept beside each other every night. So, was it fair to keep him in the dark?

Go ahead, you need to do this.

I turned my gaze to Brian's. "There's something I need to tell you."

"What?"

The words tumbled from my lips so fast I could barely breathe. I explained everything—I didn't leave out a single detail—and while I spoke, Brian lowered his gaze. He worked his jaw from side to side while his bottom lip quivered.

"You were asleep, and I was stoned. When Mason asked me for sex, I couldn't say no, although I'm not sure why. I let him have me, and I hope you're okay with it."

When Brian's gaze met mine, his eyes gleamed and his voice trembled.

"I'm *not* okay with it, and I'll tell you why."

Brian rose from the sofa and paced the living room floor while running his fingers through his hair.

"The summer after my senior year of high school, I spent three months in Jacksonville Beach with Mason and his parents. Mason had just finished his third year at UF. Of course, we fooled around whenever his folks were away, and for Mason it was no big deal, but for me, the sex was something more."

"In what way?"

"I grew infatuated with Mason, so badly it made my stomach ache. I wanted us to run away someplace and live together. But when I told him how I felt, he only laughed at me and told me I was acting stupid. His words hurt me so badly I cried—right in front of him—and after that he never let me touch him again, not in that way."

I scrunched up one side of my face. "I watched you guys on the sofa the day we kayaked the river. You seemed awfully close right then."

"We are, and I still have strong feelings for Mason, but when it comes to sex, he's off-limits, at least to me."

"Says who?"

"Mason."

I shook my head. Now, I understood why Mason had asked me to keep my encounter with him a secret. He didn't want to make Brian jealous and create problems between the three of us, but I wasn't sure how to feel about the whole thing.

"Look," I said, "I used poor judgment when I let Mason have me. I'm sorry if I hurt you."

Brian stopped pacing. He returned to the sofa to lay his head against my shoulder, and we sat together silently for the longest time.

*

On a rainy Saturday morning in early February, Brian and I helped Mason unload household furnishings from a U-Haul trailer attached to Mason's rust-ridden truck. The temperature hovered somewhere in the high thirties, and I shivered while toting a cardboard box filled with dishes up a flight of exterior stairs.

Mason had rented an apartment only a few blocks from the building Brian and I dwelled in. Mason's one-bedroom unit looked much like ours: cinder block walls, linoleum floors, venetian blinds, and casement windows. Most of the trees in the area had lost their leaves, and patches of ice appeared in the building's crabgrass yard.

"I start work Monday," Mason told us. "I'll design highway overpasses, small bridges, and similar structures. It should be interesting, and the pay is decent. I think I'll like the job."

I still wasn't sure how I felt about his move to Tallahassee, especially to a dwelling so close to mine and Brian's. Things had gone well between me and Brian, ever since fall term began. Our grades were stellar, and our bodies were fit from our exercise regimen. I'd never felt so robust, physically or mentally. My cooking skills were honed to the point where most every meal I prepared for Brian and myself tasted great.

Would Mason screw all that up?

*

Hours after we'd helped Mason move into his apartment, I lay next to Brian in our bedroom, listening to him breathe. Beyond the windows, rain dripped off the eaves of our building and the sky was cheerless. Our ceiling fixture wasn't switched on, so the room looked as dismal as a prison cell.

The odor of our recent sex hung in the air.

I turned my head to gaze at Brian in profile. His hair was damp at the temples and his lips were parted so his teeth were exposed. He had not shaved that morning, so stubble dusted his chin and cheeks.

I reached for his chest and fingered a nipple, causing him to swing his gaze to mine.

"What is it?" he said.

"Nothing, it's just…"

"What?"

I turned my head. "You won't like what I'm about to say, but I need to."

"Go ahead."

"I don't want Mason disrupting what we have here. Sure, he's older than us, but that doesn't give him the right to tell us how to live."

Brian shifted his hips on the mattress. "I've always let him call the shots, ever since we were kids. It's a hard habit to break."

Hours before, when we had finished helping Mason move in, he made a proposal.

"Why don't you fellas let me fix dinner for us tonight? I'll make spaghetti with tofu and marinara sauce."

I looked at Brian and turned down one corner of my mouth. We had planned on dining at our favorite fried chicken joint before visiting the bowling alley at the student union to roll a few games, a ritual we often enjoyed on weekends.

Brian shoved his hands inside the back pockets of his jeans. He lowered his chin and studied his shoes before looking at Mason.

"Jakub and I made plans for this evening, but you're welcome to join us if you'd like."

After Brian explained our intentions, Mason frowned. "You know I don't eat chicken, and bowling's not really my thing. You guys should have dinner with me instead. Afterward, we can find a bar with a pool table. It'll be fun."

Brian's gaze flitted between me and Mason. "We'll think about it."

Mason squinted. "It's my first night in Tallahassee. Are you guys really going to make me spend it alone?"

Brian looked at me and raised his eyebrows as if to say, "Well?"

I shrugged.

Brian shifted his weight from one leg to the other. "I guess we can change our plans, cousin. What time should we come over tonight?"

Now, in our shadowy bedroom, I turned onto my side to face Brian. I bent an elbow and rested my jaw against the palm of my hand.

"You're twenty years old and entitled to make your own choices—so am I."

Brian puckered one side of his face. "I know, but I'd feel bad if Mason spent this evening alone; he just got here."

"You invited him to join us. He could have come along, even if he only ate French fries and coleslaw for dinner. But what we planned wasn't to his liking, so he bullied you into doing something *he* wanted to, and that's not fair."

Brian nodded. "If you want, I'll walk over to Mason's right now and tell him we'll stick to our original plans. He'll understand...I guess."

I was tempted to ask Brian to do exactly what he'd suggested, but I knew it would make him feel guilty, and then our evening wouldn't go very well.

"Don't do that," I said. "But from now on, we both need to make it clear to Mason we'll make our own decisions. Agreed?"

*

Ten days after Mason's arrival in Tallahassee, he phoned me on a Wednesday evening. "Where's Brian? I rang him, but he didn't answer."

"He's attending a concert. The university orchestra's performing a Mahler piece at Ruby Diamond Hall, and Brian has to be there for his Humanities class."

Mason grunted. "*That* sounds boring as hell. What're you up to?"

"Not much. Why?"

"Thought I'd come over and pay a visit."

I tapped a toe while fingering my cell phone. Did I really want to see Mason again? Over the past week, he'd visited our place or we'd been to his several times, to share meals, play cards, or watch movies on cable television.

"Well?" he asked.

Hell, what does it matter?

Fifteen minutes later, Mason appeared at our door clutching a bottle of Zeller Schwarze Katz, a German white wine he liked to drink at room temperature. He was freshly showered and his hair was damp. After tossing his leather jacket onto an armchair, he plopped on the sofa. He wore a cotton sweater, tight-fitting blue jeans, and leather cowboy boots.

I uncorked the bottle in the kitchen. Then I grabbed two jelly glasses from the cupboard, and we sat side by side on the sofa. While we sipped the wine, Mason talked about his DOT job, and I spoke of my afternoon workout with Brian where we'd lifted weights and performed calisthenics until our muscles turned into noodles.

"I've noticed the extra bulk on Brian," Mason said. "He's never looked so good, and you're pretty toned yourself. I saw that when..."

"What?"

Mason pointed his chin toward the bedroom before his gaze met mine. "I know you haven't forgotten."

My stomach flip-flopped, and I swallowed hard while keeping my gaze fixed on Mason's. This was the first time we had discussed our January encounter, and it made me uneasy. He reached for my temple and stroked it with a fingertip, and I knew another request for sex was imminent.

When Mason spoke, his voice sounded seductive. "Every time I think about that night, I get stiff. You were something else."

"As good as Babette?"

"Maybe better."

Aye-yi-yi.

I backed away from Mason, so he couldn't touch my face again. "Look," I said, "you need to know something."

"What's that?"

"Not long after you and I got together, I told Brian about it."

Mason winced while I continued.

"He told me about the months he spent at your house, after he graduated from high school. I guess he cared a lot for you back then—and still does—but he said you rejected him. Is that true?"

Mason blinked his eyes a few times before he answered.

"You have to understand; Brian was a kid at the time and acting crazy. He threatened to jump off the Dames Point Bridge if we couldn't be boyfriends, and I had to put a stop to things before they got out of control. I love Brian—I really do—but as a cousin and that's all. He needs to accept that."

"I'm not sure he can. He grew terribly jealous over what you and I did that night, and I don't want to hurt his feelings again."

Mason scooted toward me and laid a hand on my knee. "He won't get hurt if he doesn't know what we do when he's not around."

I grew so angry, my vision blurred. I shook off Mason's grip and stood. Then I looked down at him with my hands resting on my hips.

"First of all, don't assume you can have me whenever you feel like it because—"

"You didn't enjoy that night?"

"You *know* I did, but pleasure's not the point. Brian is my best friend. We trust each other completely, and I won't sneak around behind his back, not with you or anyone else. I'm not that sort of person."

Mason looked up at me and shook his head. "I think you're acting foolishly. But if that's how you want things between us, I'll keep my distance. I certainly don't want to hurt Brian's feelings, and as for you and me..."

"What?"
"I'm fine with being just friends."

CHAPTER THIRTEEN

On Valentine's Day, I woke to a cloudless sky. Sunlight poured into the bedroom through our venetian blinds. Brian's arm was draped over my belly and his soft breathing tickled my nape.

I studied a greeting card on the window sill, one I'd received from Jeff Brucelli two days before. The card's face bore shiny hearts and confetti. Inside, beneath the printed words saying, *You're my Valentine and don't forget it*, Jeff had scribbled a message.

Thinking of you every minute of the day. I love you and always will.

My eyes had fogged when I first opened the card. I thought of Jeff, shivering in the cold up in Bloomington while he walked across the IU campus bundled up like an Eskimo. And then I remembered all those easy afternoons at Fort De Soto when we lay in my bed and held each other.

Oh, Jeff...

I peered out of a window to gaze at an oriole's brilliant breast feathers. The bird bounced around the branches of a laurel oak, looking so innocent and guileless I shook my head in disgust, because neither of those two adjectives described me. Not only was I screwing Brian on a regular basis, but I'd also let Mason have me, and what did that say about my character?

Again, I studied Jeff's greeting card while my stomach muscles clenched. If I were a decent sort, I would cut things off with Brian. I'd swear fealty to Jeff and keep my sex drive assuaged with a tube of jelly and my fist.

I thought of Jeff's slender frame and his wavy black hair. I recalled his cola-colored eyes and slightly oversized nose I thought lent him a touch of nobility. And when I closed my eyes, I heard his scratchy tenor voice inside my head, telling me how much he loved me.

Jeff.

Behind me, Brian stirred. He buried the tip of his nose in my hair and smooched my neck.

"Good morning, roomie. Happy Valentine's Day."

*

Jeff phoned me on a Sunday evening in mid-February, just after Brian and I had dined and cleaned the kitchen.

"I checked the IU academic calendar. Our spring break runs from March seventeenth through the twenty-fifth. When's yours?"

"The same."

"Do you want me to drive down to Florida? I could stay a week if your dad won't mind."

A shiver ran through me when I thought of spending so much time with Jeff at Fort De Soto. "Perfect, and Dad will be glad to see you. The weather in March is sunny and cool, so we can spend a lot of time outdoors, maybe even camp a few days."

Jeff chuckled.

"What's so funny?"

"I don't give a shit *what* we do. It's been forever since we touched each other, and I'm starving for it."

A twinge of guilt traveled through me, as I knew Jeff had gone without sex since he'd left for Indiana, while I had enjoyed Brian's affections any time I wanted to.

I cleared my throat. "Believe me, I'll give you all the attention you can handle when you come to Florida."

Our talk moved on to other matters: our classes at school, the IU basketball team, and Bloomington's crappy weather. In truth, I didn't care what we discussed, I just loved the sound of Jeff's voice. In my mind's eye, I saw him sitting on a sofa and fingering his cell phone, just as I did.

My heart ached for Jeff's presence. He was, of course, my first boyfriend, but so much more than that. I thought back to the previous summer, when I had felt Jeff and I were one person instead of two. We were so close at the time, and I wanted to get that feeling back.

After Jeff rang off, Brian and I kicked off our shoes and lay at opposite ends of the sofa with our legs bent and our knees raised. To me it felt like a typical Sunday evening when we might watch a little television, but no.

"How's Jeff doing?" Brian asked while his gaze traveled about the room.

"He's lonely up there."

"I guess he misses you?"

I nodded.

"Do you miss *him*?"

"Of course. Why would you ask me something like that?"

Brian rubbed his foot against mine while his gaze drilled into mine. "Aren't I giving you everything you need?"

Huh?

Immediately, I knew something important stirred inside Brian's head—they were thoughts he had not shared with me, and I was pretty sure what they involved.

"Look," I said, "the sex you and I have is fine, and sharing a bed with you when the weather's cold is great. But we're just friends. What I have with Jeff is something else entirely. You understand that, right?"

"Not really. I mean, think about it: Most days we're inseparable, and every night I fall asleep holding you. That's not a friendship—it's something more—and to be honest, the way you feel about Jeff makes me jealous."

My pulse pounded so hard it echoed inside my head. I rose to a sitting position and rubbed my temples with my fingertips. Then I turned my gaze back to Brian.

"Are you telling me you consider us *boyfriends*?"

"What if I say yes? How would you feel about that?"

I didn't want to hurt Brian's feelings, but also didn't want to mislead him into thinking we had more between us than we did. I rested my elbows on my knees and spoke as honestly as I could.

"You're my best friend—I couldn't ask for a better guy to spend time with—but there's a big difference between friendship and love. And as much as I like you, I don't love you the way I do Jeff. Sorry, but it's true."

Brian sat up, and when he looked at me, a vertical crease appeared between his eyebrows.

"I don't understand. What does Jeff offer you I don't? Is he smarter than me or better looking?"

I shook my head.

"What, then?"

"Remember when you had a crush on Mason?"

Brian snorted. "It was a lot more than a crush."

"Then you know exactly how I feel about Jeff. He means everything to me—that's the only way I can describe it—and I can't let you or anyone else come between me and him."

Brian stood and walked to a window. His hands hung at his hips while he flexed his fingers.

"Why doesn't life ever work for me? I loved my sister more than anyone in the world, but she died anyway. Then I loved Mason, and he blew me off like I was a pest. Now, I love you—a lot more than you know—but it doesn't matter. You have Jeff, and I'm nothing more than a convenience."

I went to Brian and wrapped my arms around his waist. I kissed his neck. "You're *not* a convenience; don't think that."

"Then why do I feel like one?"

I rested my chin on Brian's shoulder. "One day you'll meet someone who will love you like I do Jeff. You're nice-looking and smart as hell, and you're a sweet guy too."

"But I'm not good enough for Jakub Mazur."

I recalled how guilty I'd felt on Valentine's Day morning, when I stared at the card Jeff had sent me and realized what a selfish person I'd been by crawling into bed, not only with Brian, but also Mason. Wasn't it time I respected my relationship with Jeff?

I let go of Brian and took a step backward. Then I stuffed my hands into my hip pockets.

"You know, both of us might be better off if we separated our beds and quit swapping fluids. We're acting like teenagers, and maybe it's time we behaved like adults. What do you think?"

Brian turned on his heel to look at me. His eyes had a stricken look to them, but his voice did not waver when he answered my question.

"If that's what you want, Jakub, fine. Let's do it."

CHAPTER FOURTEEN

Brian and I moved our beds to the opposite walls of the bedroom. We ceased touching each other, and though our new protocol felt odd at first, after a week it seemed like things were fairly normal. We continued our study and exercise routines and shared our meals. We conversed, as always, and if Brian harbored any resentment toward me, he didn't let it show.

I thought all between us was fine—I believed everything was copacetic—but I was terribly wrong.

*

On a Friday afternoon, when I returned home from my final class of the day, I tossed my backpack onto our dining table. I whistled a tune when I entered the bathroom, but then my heart leaped into my throat.

Oh, Jesus, no.

In our bathtub, Brian dangled from the shower nozzle on a hangman's noose he'd fashioned from a leather belt. He did not breathe. Claw marks appeared on his neck, his eyes were bloodshot, and his tongue stuck out of his mouth. His clothing was disheveled, as if he'd struggled to free himself from his predicament at some point.

My vision blurred and my knees wobbled, but at least I had enough sense to act.

I raced to the kitchen to grab a carving knife, and after I sliced the noose in two, Brian collapsed onto the tub floor. He had soiled himself and smelled awful, but I didn't care. I tried performing CPR on him, but his teeth were clenched so tightly against his tongue, I couldn't pry his mouth open. So, I called the fire department and begged them to come as quickly as they could.

After the phone call, I returned to the bathroom and climbed into the tub with Brian. I lay beside him and wrapped my arms around his scraped-up neck. Then I rested my cheek against his shoulder and wept so hard I could barely breathe. Already, Brian's skin felt cold when I kissed his cheek.

"I'm sorry for everything," I whispered. "Please don't hate me."

Time seemed to stand still, but finally I heard a siren's wail. Two EMTs in navy-blue uniforms entered the apartment. They told me to let go of Brian and get out of the tub, and though I didn't want to, I did. One EMT pressed a stethoscope to Brian's chest and shone a pen light into his eyes, then he looked at the other EMT and shook his head.

I trembled so hard I could barely talk. I did my best to explain how I'd found Brian when I arrived home, and how I tried to revive him.

"You were too late," one EMT said. "Nothing you could have done would have helped."

After the EMTs brought a gurney up the stairs, they placed Brian on it and covered his body with a sheet while I watched in disbelief.

He's dead and gone forever?

How can it be?

A police cruiser pulled to the curb out front. By now a crowd of a dozen people, mostly students, had gathered on the lawn, and they gazed up at my door with puzzled expressions on their faces while whispering to one another.

A Tallahassee cop with a gun belt and nightstick arrived with a grim expression on his face and a tablet computer in his hand. Though the size of a linebacker, he spoke as softly as a priest. After he conversed briefly with the EMTs, he motioned me to the sofa while the EMTs carried Brian down the stairs.

"I know you're upset, but I'll need to ask you some questions."

He tapped on the tablet while I gave him basic information on me and Brian. I provided Brian's parents' phone number in Fort Lauderdale. My voice shook and tears leaked from the corners of my eyes, and eventually the cop gave me his handkerchief so I could blot my face while I spoke.

"We ate lunch together today; he seemed fine."

The cop nodded. "Any idea what might have brought this on?"

Go ahead...

I gazed into the cop's ruddy face. "He fell in love with someone who didn't love him back."

"Do you know who that someone was?"

I nodded and poked my sternum with a fingertip.

The cop lowered his gaze for a moment before returning it to me. "I know you're blaming yourself for what happened here, but don't. He made the decision, and nothing you might have done would have stopped him."

I gazed into my lap and worked my jaw from side to side.

The cop cleared his throat. "Do you have any family in Tallahassee?"

I shook my head.

"How about a close friend, someone who could stay with you tonight?"

I couldn't think of a single soul. Brian had been my best buddy and constant companion since the school year began. And I'd pretty much lost touch with my friends from the dorm, now I didn't live there, so none of those guys would be of much help.

Then I thought of Mason.

I sniffled and dabbed at my leaky eyes. "Brian has a cousin who lives in town; I know him pretty well."

"Would you like me to call him?"

I glanced at my wristwatch. The time was 5:30 p.m., and I figured Mason was home from work.

"I'll phone him myself. He should learn of this from me instead of someone he doesn't know."

The cop nodded and rose to his feet.

"I'll notify Brian's parents as soon as I reach the station, but I won't tell them what happened between the two of you. It would only make them feel even worse if I did."

The cop walked out of the door and descended the stairs while I stood at a window watching. He started his cruiser's engine and roared away while the crowd on the lawn kept staring at my apartment like I lived in a haunted house.

I returned to the sofa, so despondent I didn't know what to do. I stared into space while scenes of all I'd done with Brian in recent months passed through my head: our study sessions and exercise regimens, sharing meals together and, of course, our intimacies.

It was all over.

Despite what the cop had told me, I believed Brian's death was my fault. He had confessed his love for me unequivocally, and I spurned him as if he wasn't worthy. Shouldn't I have reached a middle ground with Brian? Instead, I'd placed an emotional barrier between us—one he wasn't able to cope with. Now, he was gone, and I'd have to explain everything to Mason, a task I didn't look forward to.

But what other choice did I have?

*

I lay in my bed, listening to Mason snore on the other side of the room.

He had come as soon as I called him, and after he arrived, we sat together on the sofa and held each other while tears streamed down our cheeks. Mason wailed like an abandoned child, and his shoulders shook like a sapling in a gale.

He's not even trying *to be tough, is he?*

When we both calmed down and composed ourselves, I explained how, several days before, Brian had told me he was in love with me and wanted me for his boyfriend.

"He took me by surprise—I had no idea he felt that way—and looking back, I think I behaved badly in the situation. I cut him off—gave him no hope we'd ever be anything more than friends. He couldn't handle it, I guess."

Mason sniffled while wiping his upper lip with the back of his hand.

"God *damn* it, I should have known something like this would happen. I told you he threatened to take his life before, right?"

I nodded, then Mason continued.

"Brian always put on a good front—he came across as a carefree person to most people, but wasn't that way at all. In truth, he was a fragile guy who couldn't stand it when life disappointed him."

"But I can't help feeling this is my fault."

Mason looked at me and shook his head. "You only spoke honestly to Brian, and what other option did you have? If you had lied and said you loved him, it only would have made matters worse."

When I asked Mason if he'd spend the night with me, he readily agreed.

"You don't need to be alone right now, and neither do I. I'll run home and throw some things into my truck. Then I'll stay here till the situation calms down."

When he returned, he carried a twelve-pack of beer in one hand and a bulging paper sack in the other. "I figured we could both use a beer to drink, and I picked up Chinese takeout. It's important to eat in situations like this."

Despite the day's dreadful events, I was hungry and grateful for the meal. We sat at the little dining table and gobbled the food. Then we washed it down with beer. After I drank three cans, the alcohol dulled my senses, putting a little distance between me and the afternoon's horrid events.

When it came time for sleep, Mason undressed and crawled into Brian's bed. I got into mine and switched off the nightstand lamp. After I laid my head on the pillow, a vision of Brian's body, lying on the EMTs' gurney and covered by a sheet, entered my head. I still couldn't comprehend the fact I would never see him again, nor would I hear his voice. The whole situation seemed surreal.

"You okay?" Mason said.

"Not really, but having you here sure helps."

Mason's sheets rustled when he rearranged his limbs.

"I'll stay for as long as you want me to, Jakub, and we will get through this craziness together."

*

The next several days passed in a blur.

A dean in student affairs gave me permission to skip classes for a week. In my condition, I couldn't face crowded classrooms, and my brain wasn't working as it normally did either. When I tried reading a magazine or newspaper, I found it hard to concentrate on the words.

All I wanted to do was sleep.

Brian's parents came up to Tallahassee to claim his body. They also retrieved the Louis XV furniture and Brian's personal belongings. Mason and I helped load those into a U-Haul trailer hooked onto the Keenes' shiny Escalade.

Mr. Keene was a florid faced guy with a raspy voice, a beer gut, and shoulders so broad they brushed against the jambs of my front door whenever he passed through it. He wore blue jeans and a chambray shirt, and his gold wristwatch glittered with diamonds. When Mason introduced him to me, he seized my hand in his massive paw and squeezed my fingers so tightly I feared he might break a bone or two.

"Call me Stan," he said while he looked into my face with his piercing, onyx-colored eyes, as if he could read my inner thoughts.

Brian's mom, Laura, was a petite woman with graying hair, a pinched voice, and a careworn face. She avoided eye contact and had very little to say. Mr. Keene ordered her around like a drill sergeant while they gathered Brian's clothing and shoes and stuffed them into cardboard boxes they'd brought with them.

Of course, I didn't tell them about my personal relationship with Brian or why he'd taken his life. How could I? But I found it hard to keep my voice steady when I told them how sorry I was about everything. In truth, I couldn't wait for them to go. After the last of the Louis XV pieces went into the trailer, I sighed with relief when they told Mason and me goodbye and drove away.

The only furniture remaining in the apartment was the dinette set and a floor lamp. The place looked almost abandoned, and even the slightest of noises echoed off the walls and linoleum floor.

"I'll bring a few things over," Mason said. "I have a queen bed we can share till you get another."

My dad came to Tallahassee in the park's pickup truck. He rented a hotel room for a few days and did his best to console me while I wallowed in grief. We ate meals in restaurants and took long walks through campus, and during one of those, Dad talked to me about my mom's disappearance, for the first time ever.

"The loss hurt me like nothing had before. For months, I didn't want to go on living, but I had to be strong for you, so I toughed it out, and the pain grew less after months passed. I think you'll find the same will be true with Brian."

We visited thrift shops to buy used furniture—a bed, a bureau, a coffee table, and a battered Naugahyde sofa—to replace the things Brian's parents had taken with them.

Of course, I often spoke on the phone at night with Jeff because I needed to hear his voice.

"I wish I could be there to hold you," he said one evening, "but right now I can't. Try to be strong. I'll be there soon, and everything will be okay."

One afternoon, right after my dad left Tallahassee, I took a long walk. The day was bright and cool, and a light breeze tickled Spanish moss beards dangling from the limbs of live oaks I passed beneath. I ambled down Park Avenue and turned onto Duval Street before reaching Trinity United Methodist Church, a stately brick structure with a soaring white steeple and columned portico.

After ascending the church's concrete stairs, I found the front doors unlocked, so I entered the sanctuary, a high-ceilinged room capable of seating six hundred people with ease. Above a raised altar, three stained glass windows admitted diffused light into the quiet and empty space.

My footfalls on the parquet floor echoed off the walls.

I sat on a pew up front and studied the altar with its brass cross and vases holding gladioli arrangements. After a few minutes, I removed my jacket and folded my hands in my lap. Then I closed my eyes and tried to surrender to the beliefs of my childhood—I fashioned a silent prayer.

God, I don't even know if you exist, but if you are there, please forgive me for the pain I caused Brian. I didn't mean to hurt him, and I know I acted stupidly. Why didn't I think before speaking? And now look what's happened.

If Brian is with you right now, please tell him I love him and miss him so, his laughter and tenderness. His quirky personality too.

In the future, please help me make better choices so something like this never happens again. I couldn't stand it if I caused another person to take his life. If so, I'd probably take mine as well.

I sniffled while tears rolled down my cheeks.

Thank you for giving me Jeff. I love him so much, and I promise to always treat him with care. I'll think about his feelings before I consider my own; I'll put him first. Maybe if I'd done that with Brian, he would still be here today, I don't know. But help me learn from what's happened. Show me how to become a better person, not just for Jeff but for everyone else in my life.

I sure hope you don't hate me, God.

CHAPTER FIFTEEN

Mason remained in my apartment, and his companionship during those awful days made a huge difference while I struggled to cope with Brian's death. Each night, we shared vegetarian meals. We ate a lot of brown rice and vegetables and a fair amount of whole wheat spaghetti with tofu and red sauce. We even dined on omelets and toast, a decent combination for dinner.

Mason slept in his bed; I slept in mine. Every time Mason undressed, I viewed his athletic physique but felt no desire for him as I had before. I didn't touch him, and he made no attempt to get intimate with me. I think Brian's suicide had left us too stunned to engage in something as inconsequential as sex.

Most nights, Mason brought home a bottle of wine for us to share, and while we sipped from our glasses, we spoke of Brian, of his personal tics and the good times we had shared with him. Sometimes we even laughed, but I still found it hard to adjust to Brian's absence and wondered if I ever would.

My opinion of Mason changed as days passed. Before, I'd considered him overbearing in his dealings with me and Brian. But now, when we shared our evenings together, I found him more sensitive than I'd earlier thought. Brian's death had clearly hurt him, perhaps more so than it had me.

One evening, he and I took a stroll through my neighborhood. A three-quarter moon cast shadows onto sidewalks we trod, and the cool night air chafed my cheeks. We both kept our hands in our jacket pockets and walked in silence for a long time. Each guy seemed immersed in his own thoughts until Mason finally spoke.

"Would you consider letting me live in your apartment? I'd pay half the rent and utilities."

"What about your lease?"

"I'm on a month-to-month."

What should I do? On the one hand, letting Mason move in would offer benefits, and not just the financial kind. With him in residence, I wouldn't come home to an empty place every day. But...

"Tell me *why* you want to live with me."

"I'm lonely in my apartment, and I feel terrible about what's happened with Brian; it's killing me. Spending time with you will help me survive this insanity."

H-m-m-m.

"Let me think things over. I can't make a decision on something like that right away. But while I'm deciding please continue living at my place. I'm really shook up about Brian, and it's nice having you around."

Mason bobbed his chin. "I had a weird dream about Brian two nights ago. You and I sat on the sofa in your apartment, and Brian walked out of the bathroom with a belt hanging around his neck. He pointed at me and started babbling stuff about you and me having sex behind his back. Then he started *crying*."

"That sounds scary as shit."

"It was. His face turned beet red, and snot poured out of his nose. I wanted to console him—you did too—but it seemed we were glued to the sofa. So, we had to sit there and listen to Brian sob. It seemed to go on forever before I finally woke up, and when I did, my sheets were damp."

"Jesus…"

"That's a nightmare I hope I'll never have again. It left me feeling weird and guilty, and I couldn't shake my mood for the rest of the day. I kept closing my eyes and watching Brian weep like a little kid." He put his hand on my shoulder and squeezed. "It helps when I talk with you about these things. I know they're disturbing, but—"

"Mason, talk to me about Brian anytime you want."

CHAPTER SIXTEEN

On the first Friday in March, Mason drove us southward on the Florida Turnpike to attend Brian's funeral the next day. The afternoon was cool and sunny, and we kept the windows rolled up to stay warm. While in Fort Lauderdale, we would stay at the Keenes' home, and I wanted to know what I should expect, so I asked Mason to fill me in.

He grimaced and shook his head.

"Brian's mom is my mother's older sister, and I can't say I'm a fan. She was never the parent she should have been for Brian. And Mr. Keene is a total bastard. The last time I saw him down in Fort Lauderdale, he was stinking drunk in the middle of the day and grouchy as a bear."

I winced. "Brian once told me his dad got rough with his mom at times. Is that true?"

"Absolutely, and he slapped Brian around as well. I saw that kind of thing way too often when we were younger. I can't tell you how many times my mom tried convincing my aunt to divorce the asshole. But aunt Laura was scared of him, plus she didn't want to give up their swanky standard of living."

Envisioning a turbulent household like Brian's wasn't easy for me. Sure, my family wasn't perfect, with my disappearing mom and all, but at least I'd never dealt with domestic violence or drunkenness. My dad was as reliable as the sunrise, and he'd never once hit me.

No *wonder* Brian had been an emotional house of cards.

By the time we reached Fort Lauderdale, shadows had grown long, and the sun was low in the western horizon. The temperature was almost balmy compared to Tallahassee's. The Keenes' one-story home was located in Las Olas, a tony suburb not far from downtown. Sailing yachts and powerboats floated alongside docks in the Intracoastal Waterway. Coconut palms abounded and foliage was lush: hibiscuses, crotons, bottlebrush shrubs, bougainvillea, and firecracker plants, to name a few. Lawns were trimmed and edged as neatly as pie slices.

Brian's mom, Laura, greeted us when we rang the doorbell. She wore a sleeveless blouse, culottes, and white leather sandals. She hugged Mason for at least thirty seconds before letting him go. Then she shook my hand.

"I'm so glad you boys could come," she said while wiping a tear from her cheek with a knuckle. "Brian would be pleased if he knew you made the trip. You'll share Brian's bedroom," she told us when we followed her through the living room. My shoes sank into cut pile carpet. The furniture looked like something out of *Architectural Digest*, and framed watercolors with tropical themes adorned the cream-colored walls. Yellow roses in a crystal vase scented the air.

Brian's room was furnished with two full beds, a mirrored bureau, a desk and chair, and a bookcase filled with sports trophies. The tartan plaid drapes matched the bedspreads. The room's windows overlooked a kidney-shaped swimming pool and a concrete deck with cushioned chaises and a glass-topped table shaded by an umbrella.

"I'm sure you're both hungry after your drive," Laura said. "We'll have dinner as soon as Stan gets home from work, but in the meantime make yourselves comfortable."

As soon as Laura left us, I whistled while my gaze traveled around the room.

"I feel like we're staying at a country club."

Mason rolled his eyes. "Stan may be a drunk and a jerk, but he earns big money selling life insurance to rich folks."

After we stowed our bags in the room's walk-in closet, Mason and I visited the kitchen, where the scent of roasting meat made my stomach growl. Laura used a masher to crush a bowlful of steaming potatoes. We plucked two beers from the refrigerator and then strolled to the pool deck. The sun had already disappeared behind the house to the west of us, and the sky in that direction glowed in shades of pink, orange, and green. Swayback coconut palms grew at the edges of the pool deck, and hibiscus shrubs with chunky yellow blossoms hedged the white vinyl fence.

Studying our surroundings, I sensed why Brian had been such a perfectionist. Nothing inside the house, or even in the backyard, seemed out of place. The swimming pool sparkled, and not a single leaf floated on its surface or rested on the pool's marcite bottom. We sat at the glass-topped table and opened our beers. Then I took a sip while watching an iguana do push-ups on a palm's banded trunk.

I swallowed and shook my head. "This place is so different from Tallahassee or even St. Petersburg. I feel like we're at a swanky Caribbean resort."

Mason raised his upper lip. "I don't like it here. Too much money gets thrown around, and everybody's a phony. It's all about image and what you own."

"But I never thought Brian was that way."

"He wasn't. That's why he came to live with my family in Jacksonville Beach right after he finished high school. He wanted to get away from all this pretension and his miserable home life."

Fifteen minutes later, Mr. Keene emerged from the house, dressed in a business suit, a regimental necktie, and a pair of wingtip shoes that shone like mirrors. He had already drained half the highball glass he held.

"Hello, Uncle Stan," Mason said while we rose. "You remember Jakub, don't you?"

Stan nodded when he shook my hand, and I suffered his crushing grip. Then he shook Mason's hand as well.

"Thanks for being here, fellas. Laura says dinner will go on the table in fifteen minutes, so you might want to go inside and wash up."

The Keenes' dining room was almost as large as my Tallahassee apartment. The lacquered pecan wood table had seating for ten. A matching china hutch held a fancy-looking service with all sorts of bowls and platters, and a silver tea set rested atop a pecan sideboard with multiple drawers.

Above us, a cut-glass chandelier cast a gentle glow.

We dined on roast beef, the potatoes Mrs. Keene had mashed, and sweet peas, all of it smothered in a brown gravy. A straw basket held fresh-baked rolls, and I ate like I hadn't seen food in a week.

Mason, of course, eschewed the beef, drawing a grunt from Stan.

"No meat?" he said to Mason after draining his second highball. "Are you turning into a flake?"

Mason shrugged. "I don't think eating animal flesh is healthy."

As soon as Stan handed his empty glass to his wife, she rose and darted through a swinging door. Moments later, the sounds of ice cubes tinkling sounded from the kitchen.

Stan drummed his fingers on the table while keeping his gaze fixed on Mason. "There's a barber shop on Seabreeze Boulevard, just about a mile from here. The funeral's not till one tomorrow, so you'll have time for a trim in the morning."

Mason looked up from his plate and glared at Stan. "I don't *need* a haircut."

"You look like somebody's sister."

Mason lowered his gaze while his cheeks colored. He shoved a forkful of peas into his mouth and chewed while Stan kept on.

"You shouldn't come to the funeral home with all that hair. Show a little respect for Brian, will you?"

"I'm showing respect by making the trip down here. Isn't that enough?"

"Not if you show up tomorrow looking like some sort of circus clown."

I cleared my throat and looked at Stan. "A lot of guys up at school have long hair. It's popular again, like it was in the 1960s."

Stan shook his head, just as Brian's mom entered the room with a fresh highball. He took a sip and swallowed before returning his gaze to Mason. "I'm surprised the DOT hired you with all that hair. Don't they have grooming standards up there?"

Mason's face turned as red as a stop sign. He laid his fork on his plate and rose before tossing his napkin onto the table.

"I didn't come down here to listen to your criticism. Have you forgotten I'm twenty-three years old? I'll make my own decisions about the length of my hair and the clothes I wear and everything else. And if you don't approve of my choices, I don't really care."

Stan opened his mouth to say something, but before he could, Mason turned on his heel and strode from the room. I stared into my plate and worked my jaw from side to side, listening to the tinkle of ice while Stan guzzled his highball.

When I finally looked up, Stan's gaze was fixed on me.

"I sure hope you're not as disrespectful to your elders as Mason is. His folks never disciplined him when he was a kid—they let him do whatever he pleased—and look how he's turned out. He'll never go anywhere in life with that attitude."

I didn't know what to say, so I kept quiet and worked on my food. The Keenes did the same, and for the next few minutes no one said anything, until Stan broke the silence.

"Jakub?"

I looked up and raised my eyebrows.

"Laura and I know you were Brian's closest friend. From what he told us, the two of you did everything together."

I lowered my gaze and nodded.

"We're hoping you might shed some light on what happened up there. We are completely bewildered by what Brian did. It seems...out of character."

I flexed my toes while I let my gaze travel to Brian's mom, then Stan, and I tried to keep my voice from cracking when I spoke.

"I wish I could help you out, but I have no idea why Brian took his life. I saw him only hours before it happened, and he seemed fine, so it's a mystery to me."

Laura dabbed at the corners of her mouth with a napkin. "Was he dating someone in Tallahassee? Was there a breakup of some kind?"

I shook my head.

"Was he having trouble with school?" Stan asked.

"No, his grades were excellent."

Stan puckered one side of his face. "You were with him every day, Jakub. Surely you must have some suspicions."

Shit.

"I'm sorry, but I really don't."

Laura brought her knuckles to her teeth. She whimpered a time or two and then straightened her spine and looked at me with watery eyes.

"You see, Brian was quite skilled at hiding his true feelings. I worry he might have been a sad person, and I wonder if Stan and I are to blame for that. Perhaps we raised him the wrong way. Maybe we should have been better parents and—"

Stan pounded his fist on the table so hard my fork rattled on my plate.

"Shut up, will you? This is *not* our fault. If anything, we were too lenient with Brian. After we lost Lisa, I think we tried to make up for her death by giving him whatever he wanted. Hell, we could have sold Aunt Jean's stupid French furniture for a nice chunk of change. Instead we lent it to Brian so he'd be comfortable up at school. He couldn't have asked for better parents."

I didn't know how to react. Part of me wanted to do what Mason had—leave the room. But another side of me said, *these people are hurting terribly. Say something to make them feel better.*

I turned my gaze to Laura. "Brian always said nice things about both of you. He described his childhood as wonderful."

Laura frowned and shook her head. "Are you aware Brian moved in with Mason's family right after graduating from high school?"

I nodded.

"He told us he hated Fort Lauderdale and this house. He also said if he never saw us again, he'd be fine with it."

I lowered my gaze and stirred a dollop of mashed potatoes with my fork.

"Laura, will you make me another highball?"

As soon as his wife left the room, Stan rested his elbows on the table. He raised his forearms and formed a steeple with his hands while his gaze drilled into mine.

"You think I'm an absolute bastard, don't you?"

"No, sir. I barely know you, so why would I think something like that?"

"Because no doubt Mason's filled your head with a lot of nonsense about Brian's upbringing. Sure, I was stern when I had to be, I ran a tight ship. But that's a father's responsibility, to keep order. Does this house look like a terrible place to grow up in?"

I shook my head while Stan continued.

"When Brian was ten, we hosted a birthday party for him and his friends, kids from the neighborhood, his Little League teammates, and some boys from his fifth-grade class. There must've been twenty of them. They swam in the pool, ate hot dogs, and played on a Slip 'N Slide. You never saw so many grins as I did that day.

"I remember this one boy from Brian's school, a kid with red hair and buck teeth, a regular Opie from Mayberry with a southern accent and all. I heard him tell Brian, 'You're the luckiest dog in town. You've got everything a guy could possibly want.'"

Laura returned with highball in hand. After she handed the drink to Stan, she sat and placed her hands in her lap.

Stan turned to her. "I was telling Jakub about Brian's tenth birthday party. Remember how happy everyone was?"

Laura glanced at me for a moment before turning her gaze to Stan. "What I remember most about that day wasn't the party, but what happened afterward."

Stan narrowed his eyes. "Jakub doesn't need to hear about that, it's a private matter."

Laura looked at me again. "Did your father beat you when you were a boy?"

"No, ma'am."

"Well, Brian wasn't so lucky."

"That's enough," Stan cried. He stormed from the room with the ice in his highball tinkling.

Laura shifted her weight in her chair.

"It's difficult to explain to a boy why his father treats him harshly. How can you rationalize violence? I tried telling Brian discipline was a form of love, that Stan was only trying to prepare him for the tough world he would face as an adult. But I don't think Brian believed what I said. I think he detested his dad, and maybe me too."

"He never said anything like that to me."

But then I recalled how Brian once told me he hated his father so badly he wanted to sink a knife into Stan's chest.

After I thanked Laura for my meal, I took my empty plate to the kitchen. Then I found Mason by the swimming pool. He lay on a chaise longue with his hands folded on his stomach and his gaze fixed on the night sky. A thousand stars twinkled above us, looking like so many loose diamonds scattered onto a jeweler's cloth.

I took a chair from the table with the umbrella and placed it facing Mason. Then I sat and listened to traffic pass on nearby Las Olas Boulevard. I wasn't quite sure what to say, so I didn't say anything. The pool light was illuminated and the pump ran while I gazed into the swirling water.

Mason crossed his ankles, weaved his fingers behind his neck, and drew a breath.

"Did things settle down in there?"

"Not really."

Mason hissed. "What a fucked-up situation. I can't wait to get out of here."

"I know—I feel the same—but we need to be here for Brian."

"Do we? I'm not sure he'd even care if we no-showed tomorrow, and I'm tempted to do just that. You know, they say funerals aren't about the departed, instead they're supposed to bring closure for the dead person's loved ones. But I'm not interested in Stan's feelings and don't much care about Laura's either. They were selfish, crappy parents. Brian deserved better."

I chewed a hangnail while a jetliner's engines roared above us and the plane's position lights glowed. "Do you think we should tell them?"

"What?"

"The reason Brian killed himself. At least then they'd know it was my fault, not theirs."

Mason swung his feet to the ground and faced me; he pointed at my nose.

"I told you before—you are not to blame. Brian's troubles stemmed from the way he was raised. If he hadn't met you, he'd have fallen in love with someone else who didn't want him, and then the same result would have happened. His suicide was inevitable."

"You really think so?"

Mason nodded. "The people responsible for Brian's death dwell on this property, and I won't hesitate to remind Stan of the fact if he keeps after me like he did tonight. He can stuff the haircut suggestion up his fat ass."

We sat in silence for a bit before Mason spoke again.

"I don't want to spend another night here unless you do."

I shook my head.

"Then tomorrow, right after the funeral, I say we head back to Tallahassee. If traffic's not bad, we should get there by ten."

*

Attendance at Brian's funeral was sparse. Several relatives, including Mason's parents, appeared, along with perhaps a dozen kids Brian's age who I presumed were friends he'd known during his high school days. A stoop-shouldered mortuary attendant wearing a cheap suit handed Mason and me little pamphlets with Brian's photo on the front. Inside was a brief biography, including the dates of Brian's birth and his christening in the Episcopal church.

Brian's closed casket, resting on a bier at the head of the room, was draped in a Boy Scout flag. An organist played mournful-sounding music while people took their seats, and then a preacher spoke about how tragic it was when a youth like Brian, so full of promise, is taken from us.

"I know this moment is difficult for every person in this room. Your hearts are filled with sadness and disillusionment, and you may find yourselves wondering how a loving God could possibly let this happen. But remember, God has a plan for each of us. Brian may have been unhappy on this Earth, but I feel certain he's at peace now, because he dwells with our Lord."

The preacher read a passage from the Bible, where St. John quoted Christ:

"Let not your hearts be troubled. Believe in God; believe also in me. In my Father's house are many rooms. If it were not so, would I have told you that I go to prepare a place for you? And if I go and prepare a place for you, I will come again and will take you to myself, that where I am you may be also."

I fidgeted on a pew, seated alongside Mason. Every time I looked at Brian's casket, I thought of our conversation, days before his death, when I'd told him I didn't love him and never would. I recalled the stricken expression on his face.

My eyes fogged and a tear rolled down my cheek.
Brian, I'm so sorry.
Will you please forgive me?

*

The drive back to Tallahassee seemed endless. We passed cow pastures and slash pine forests and the occasional trailer park. But the trip gave me time to think about Mason's dwelling with me. When we reached my apartment, I opened two beers and asked him to join me on the sofa in the living room. After I sipped from my beer and swallowed, I cleared my throat.

"I'm fine with you living with me here. I think we're good for each other, especially with Brian gone. But you need to understand something."

"What?"

"We'll be friends and roommates, but that's all."

Mason looked at the bubbles rising in his beer bottle before returning his gaze to me.

"I already told you—it's understood."

CHAPTER SEVENTEEN

In the days following our return from Fort Lauderdale, Mason and I developed a routine. Weekdays, of course, I attended classes and studied in a carrel at the library, while Mason worked his DOT job. He normally arrived home around 5:30 p.m. Often, we changed into gym clothes and athletic shoes to work out with weights at Tully Gym. Or we ran three miles at the FSU track.

I ate vegetarian like Mason. Some nights he cooked, others I did. We always shared a bottle of wine with our meals, and afterward took a walk through our neighborhood if weather permitted. I talked about my studies, Mason discussed his job, and sometimes we spoke of Brian.

"Are you religious?" Mason asked one night while we passed beneath a streetlamp.

I rocked my head from side to side. "I was raised Lutheran and went to Sunday School as a kid. But I haven't attended since I was nine or so."

Off in the distance, a transfer truck driver shifted gears on Tennessee Street. Early March was upon us, and though we still wore jackets to keep ourselves warm, at least our breaths did not steam in the cool air while we ambled along.

Mason rubbed the tip of his nose with a knuckle.

"I keep thinking about what the preacher said at Brian's funeral—how Brian's up in Heaven with Jesus and feeling just fine—and I can't buy into it. To me, religion's nothing more than a fantasy."

"But if it makes people feel better about life and death, whom does it harm?"

Mason shrugged before turning his gaze to me. "Do you believe God exists? And if so, why did he take Brian? Does God get a thrill out of making us sad?"

I clenched my jaw and ground my molars before I answered.

"Honestly, I don't know *what* to think. A lot of intelligent people attend church. They pray every night and teach their children to love Jesus, so I guess religion's not only for the gullible."

"Do *you* pray sometimes?"

I described my visit to the Methodist church, not long after Brian's death, when I'd done my best to speak to God.

Meanwhile, a battered pickup truck with three high school boys in the cab and four more seated in the bed cruised past us with a growling muffler. They all wore red and white football jackets with the letter "L" stitched onto the chests.

We walked in silence for a bit, until Mason cleared his throat.

"If I share something personal with you, will you keep it to yourself?"

"Of course."

"Last week at work, I sat at my drafting table, next to a window overlooking a parking lot. I gazed outside and saw a guy walk toward his car. I could have sworn it was Brian—same age, same build and hair, everything. Right away I started trembling, all the way from my feet to my shoulders. I must've looked like I'd been stuck with a cattle prod."

"What did you do?"

Mason hissed. "I managed to get myself to a toilet stall in the men's room down the corridor, and thankfully no one was around."

"Why, what happened?"

Mason stopped walking and turned his gaze to me.

"I sat on the john and bawled like a kindergartner. I don't think I've ever shed so many tears."

We came to an intersection with a traffic light, and after we crossed Tennessee Street, we entered the Old City Cemetery on Macomb Street where members of Tallahassee's oldest families rested. We passed by once-elegant mausoleums and marble tombstones, most of them mildew-stained, with indistinct engravings, many more than a century old. Confederate battle flags decorated a squatty monument honoring the lives of unknown rebel soldiers buried in the cemetery. Many had died in the 1864 Battle of Olustee, west of Jacksonville.

"I wonder if anyone ever visits the graves here?" I said.

"I would doubt it. I mean, look around us, I don't even see any *plastic* flowers. It's almost as though the people buried here never existed."

I nodded. "I read somewhere we have two deaths. The second is when no one speaks your name anymore, because all the people who knew you are gone."

We walked on while Mason spoke.

"You and I will outlive Brian's parents by a long shot, so I think it's likely one of us will be the last person to utter Brian's name."

I knew what Mason said was true. He and I would be Brian's final survivors, and in time might my memories of Brian fade? I didn't even own a photograph of him, so would I eventually forget what he looked like?

"Let's make an agreement," I said.

"What kind?"

"You and I were closer to Brian than anyone else in his life—we knew him best—and I think we should honor his memory for as long as we can. He died on February 23, so every year on that date, no matter where we are, we should get on the phone and talk to each other about Brian for a while.

"That way his memory will survive as long as we do."

*

Dear Mr. & Mrs. Keene:

I'm writing to say thanks for hosting Mason and me when we attended Brian's funeral. I'm sorry we didn't stay in Fort Lauderdale longer, but midterm exams approach, and I need to spend as much time as possible with my studies.

Anyway, can I ask a favor?

I don't have any photographs of Brian. If you have one taken in the not-too-distant past, will you send it to me? Ten years from now, I don't want to forget Brian's face.

Thanks so much.

Jakub Mazur

CHAPTER EIGHTEEN

On the second Sunday in March, Jeff called me from Bloomington, and like always the sound of his voice made my pulse quicken.

"I have an idea. My last midterm's Thursday afternoon. Friday, I can drive the Impala down to Tallahassee and spend the night with you. Then we'll travel to Fort De Soto Park on Saturday."

My spirits soared, and not just because I wouldn't have to make a miserable seven-hour Greyhound bus trip to St. Pete. The thought of me and Jeff cruising down US 19 and likely holding hands the whole way, seemed too good to be true.

"That would be wonderful," I said.

"If I leave Bloomington by nine in the morning, I should reach Tallahassee before ten p.m., if traffic's not bad."

After Jeff rang off, I sat at our dining table and paged through my Sociology text book, scanning passages I had highlighted with a felt-tipped pen earlier in the quarter. I faced four midterm exams during the week ahead of me and knew they'd be tough. But all semester I had kept up with my reading and taken careful notes during each class period. I was well-prepared and ready to get things over with, so I could relax with Jeff at Fort De Soto.

Nothing would get in the way of our week together.

Mason lay on the living room sofa with his nose buried in a book. Now that we cohabitated, he spent every evening with me. Weekdays, while I studied, he read from a lengthy biography of Andrew Jackson or sometimes a Thomas Wolfe novel, *You Can't Go Home Again*. He subscribed to the *Tallahassee Democrat*, and after devouring the sports and news sections, he solved the daily crossword puzzle.

"I can't abide the crap on television," he'd told me. "Why even watch it?"

So far, we seemed to get along well as roommates. Of course, I had to adjust to Mason's freight train snoring, and the fact he wasn't a neatnik like Brian. His clothing and shoes were strewn about the apartment as if they'd been tossed about by a tornado. He had a habit of leaving half-empty glasses of water in various places—the coffee table, the toilet tank, atop the refrigerator—and he also disliked daily bathing.

"Soap dries out my skin."

So, I had to put up with his gamey scent until he chose to shower.

As requested, Mason had not laid a hand on me since our return from Fort Lauderdale, nor had he made any suggestive remarks. We were as virtuous as monks, and I was fine with it. I would save my sexual energy for Jeff's visit, and if I needed relief, I could take care of business alone.

Brian's death still disturbed me, but focusing on my studies kept me from dwelling on the tragedy. And schoolwork kept my feelings of guilt at bay when I prepared for my midterms.

By Friday night, I was both exhausted and exhilarated—burned out because I hadn't gotten much sleep during the week, and excited about Jeff's impending arrival in Tallahassee. Hours before, he had called me to let me know he was running on schedule, that he'd just passed Birmingham and would likely arrive in Tallahassee right around ten.

Since then, it felt like someone had poured glue into the works of my wristwatch.

I paced the living room and kitchen floors like a caged animal, while Mason sat shirtless at the dining table with his brow furrowed and a pencil stuck sideways in his mouth. He was preparing his federal income tax return using forms and a manual he'd picked up at the post office.

"You're as nervous as a tomcat," he finally told me. "Have a beer and settle down; you're making it hard for me to concentrate."

I uncapped a chilled bottle and plopped onto the sofa. After I took a gulp of beer, I seized the newspaper and tried to focus on events of the day, but found it hard to stay interested in matters that didn't impact me directly. Did I really care about Donald Trump's latest rants?

"This is *such* a pain in the ass," Mason groused while drumming his pencil eraser against the table. "I haven't filed a return before—I never needed to—but if I want my tax refund from waiting tables, it's necessary."

I shrugged. "Wish I could help you, but I've never filed one either."

Mason scowled and shook his head. "I think I'll take a walk to clear my head. Care to join me?"

"I can't. It's past 9:30, and Jeff should be here any time now."

Mason rose and slipped into his jacket. "I'll be back in a bit."

I drained my beer bottle and opened a second. My first sip was so cold it numbed the back of my throat when I swallowed, but in a good way. Then I let my gaze travel about the living room. A poster of Bob Marley hung on one wall, a former possession of Brian's that his parents had shown no interest in taking back to Fort Lauderdale. A Salvador Dali print titled "The Persistence of Memory," the one with melting clocks and a dead tree, hung on another wall. I'd bought the print at the campus bookstore, and now I recalled how Brian had laughed at me when I brought it home.

"Were you tripping on LSD when you purchased that ugly thing?"

Brian's ghost seemed to haunt all four rooms of the apartment. I heard his throaty laughter inside my head when I recalled how our dorm friends had called our Louis XV decor "faggot furniture."

"You're just jealous," Brian told them. "These pieces cost more than a brand-new Harley."

I remembered how, on our first day in residence at the apartment, I had shown Brian how to use a can opener in our little kitchen and wondered if I'd made a mistake in rooming with him.

My lease on the apartment would expire on May 31, and I hadn't given much thought to whether or not I'd renew it for next school year. Perhaps if Jeff and I moved to another place in the fall, I wouldn't be reminded of Brian so frequently. Maybe I could put his death behind me and focus on my future. Maybe—

A knock sounded on my front door, and my heart skipped a beat. I leaped to my feet while my pulse accelerated. I flung the door open to find Jeff standing in the corridor. He held the handle of a rolling suitcase in one hand while running the fingers of the other through his unruly hair. A smile crept onto his lips when his gaze met mine.

"Hey, sexy. Mind if I come in?"

As soon as he passed through the door, I closed it behind him. Then I threw my arms around his neck and pulled him to me. Our sternums and hips met while I inhaled the familiar scents of Jeff's skin and hair. He dropped his suitcase to the floor with a bang.

Then we kissed, and our tongues dueled. The smacking of our lips was the only sound in the room, and I was already stiff between my legs.

When I finally tore my mouth from Jeff's and asked about his drive, he grimaced and shook his head. "Twelve and a half hours, and I only stopped twice to buy gas. It seemed to take forever to get here."

I reached for Jeff's cheek and stroked it with my thumb. "It's so good to see you."

His gaze traveled around the living room. "I've always wondered what this place looks like—not too bad."

I fetched two bottles of beer while Jeff stowed his suitcase in the bedroom and hung his jacket in the closet. Then we plopped onto the sofa and sipped from our beers with our knees and shoulders touching.

"You must be tired from all that driving."

Jeff blew air out his nose. "I'll sleep well tonight, but where is Mason?"

I explained.

"Are you guys getting along okay?"

"He's a bit sloppy—it seems I'm always tripping over his shoes—but other than that and his snoring, he's fine."

Jeff brushed my bangs from my forehead with his fingertips, and I thought of the many days we had shared at Fort De Soto Park, the fishing excursions, the walks on the beach, and our lovemaking.

"How about you?" Jeff asked. "Are you all right?"

I drew a breath and released it while I rocked my head from side to side. "Some days are okay, others aren't. It's only been three weeks since..."

Jeff squeezed my knee. "What an awful thing. I—"

"Can we not talk about Brian?"

Jeff let go of my knee and scooted halfway across the sofa. He placed his palms on the tops of his thighs and stared into my face. "I know you're upset by what happened, but you don't have to snap at me like that."

Shit.

"I'm sorry. It's just...my feelings are raw. I do best when I don't think about Brian, understand?"

Jeff nodded.

I patted the sofa cushion. "Move back over here, please."

After Jeff did, I took his hand in both of mine.

"I haven't felt this bad since the weeks after my mom disappeared. It's like someone's cut out my heart and fed it to a dog. Everyone keeps telling me what happened wasn't my fault, but I know better. I was a jerk and only thought of my own needs."

Jeff squeezed my fingers and kissed my cheek.

"Let's make an agreement: We have an entire week to spend together, and we should make the most of it. So, let's not mention Brian again while I'm here. This should be about us and our future, and we'll focus on that. Deal?"

I stared into my lap and nodded.

"I need a shower," Jeff said. "I probably smell like a farm animal."

"You *are* a bit ripe. Mind if I join you?"

Moments later, we stood beneath the shower nozzle while the air in the bathroom steamed. I soaped up a washcloth and took my time scrubbing Jeff front and back. Then I shampooed his hair, using my fingertips to massage his scalp while he sighed.

"Man, that feels good," he whispered.

After he'd rinsed himself clean, I turned off the flow of water. Then I dried him with a fresh bath towel.

"You're spoiling me," he said while I dabbed water droplets off his shoulders.

"Hey, you're the guy who spent twelve hours in the car. This is the least I can do."

When I'd finished drying him, Jeff wrapped the towel about his waist and combed his hair while I rubbed myself with another towel.

"I can't believe how warm it is down here," Jeff said, gazing into the mirror above the sink. "When I climbed out of my car, I felt like I'd arrived on another planet. And what's that sweet smell in the air?"

"Shrubs are blooming, magnolia trees too. Spring's the best time of year in Tallahassee."

In the bedroom, we both slipped into fresh pairs of boxer briefs, just as Mason walked into the apartment, toting a twelve-pack of Budweiser and a bag of potato chips.

After I made introductions, Mason and Jeff shook hands.

"You must be exhausted from your drive," Mason said. "How about a beer?"

Jeff and I sat on the sofa, Mason in an armchair. All three of us sipped from a can while we chatted. The beer was cold and crisp—it tasted just right—and after I'd drained half a can, my limbs relaxed. Jeff and I hadn't bothered to dress, and when my knee pressed against his, a jolt of sexual energy passed between us.

"I guess you fellas will leave for St. Pete in the morning?" Mason asked.

I nodded, then looked at Jeff. "It's only a five-hour drive, so we don't have to get up early tomorrow. You could probably use some rest."

Jeff yawned. "I'm beat. Where do I sleep—on this sofa?"

I glanced at Mason before looking at Jeff again. "My bed's big enough we can share."

After we drank another round of beers, the three of us took turns in the bathroom, using the toilet and brushing our teeth. I killed the lights in the kitchen and living room, and we all entered the bedroom.

I was curious to see Jeff's reaction when Mason undressed for bed. When I looked at Jeff, his gaze was lowered, his cheeks flushed.

"Don't mind nature boy there," I said. "He always sleeps bare assed."

"Hey, why not?" Mason said. "You guys should give it a try."

Jeff looked up at Mason. "We already have—several times in fact—down at Fort De Soto, and also when we camped. Does that surprise you?"

Mason looked at me and raised his eyebrows.

"It's true," I said.

"Well, feel free to get naked tonight if you want. It won't make me uncomfortable in the least."

Jeff didn't hesitate. He rose and hooked his thumbs inside the waistband of his boxer briefs before peeling them to his ankles and kicking them aside. Then he placed his hands on his hips and smirked at me.

"Well?"

I shrugged and ditched my briefs as well while Mason giggled like a schoolgirl.

"We got us a damned nudist colony here tonight," he cried.

*

The drive to St. Petersburg felt dreamlike when we rolled down US 19 in bright sunshine. I listened to the rise and fall of Jeff's voice and couldn't stop touching him. I stroked his forearm, his thigh as well. I wove my fingers through his and squeezed his knuckles. And when we hit a patch of empty road, I kissed his cheek and nuzzled his ear.

All those feelings Jeff had evoked in me the previous summer came roaring back, and it seemed as if we'd seen each other only yesterday. Whatever distance I'd felt from him in the months we were apart simply evaporated, chased away by Jeff's beauty and, more importantly, his tenderness. In a town called Perry, we ate lunch at a McDonald's, surrounded by men in ball caps, flannel shirts, and work pants. Their clothing gave off a sewer-like aroma, because they worked in paper mills anchoring the area's economy.

Back in the Impala, and an hour farther south, we passed a county road leading to Manatee Springs State Park, and Jeff reminded me of our camping trip we'd taken there.

"What a pretty place it was, especially the spring and the river. And remember the cypress trees surrounding the boardwalk? I felt like I was inside a cathedral."

By the time we reached Fort De Soto Park, the sun was already low, and shadows had grown long. We visited my dad at the ranger's station, where he mussed my hair before shaking Jeff's hand.

"Good to have you boys here. There's beer in the fridge at the house, and snacks in the cupboard, so make yourselves comfortable. I'll be home around six, then we'll get the charcoal grill fired up."

Minutes later, we occupied the porch at my home, rocking on the glider sofa, sipping from bottles of Miller High Life and munching on pretzels with our shoulders, hips, and knees touching. The afternoon air was cool and still. A mullet jumped in the bayou and hit the water's surface with a splash, while a cormorant alit on a mangrove tree and spread its wings to dry them in the fading sunlight.

"It's so beautiful here," Jeff said. "This is the first time I haven't worn a jacket since October."

I raked my fingers through Jeff's wavy hair. "Thanks for making the drive from Bloomington. I know it was a journey."

Jeff shrugged. "The trip's worth it just to be with you, and especially here. I feel like the park is our special place. After all, it's where we first met, remember?"

"How could I forget?"

I teased his earlobe with a fingertip. "Dad won't be home for at least an hour. Do you want to…?"

When Jeff and I entwined on my bed, I felt like a starving man who'd wandered into a banquet hall. I dragged my fingers over Jeff's warm flesh, and rubbed my tongue against his while I caressed his private places. I was licking Jeff's neck and listening to him sigh, when I noticed a swelling under his skin, just beneath his ear, and I nudged it with a fingertip.

"You have a bump here. Is it sore?"

"Nah. It's been there a few weeks, but I'm sure it's nothing. Get to work, boyfriend."

Our orgasms came quickly, and mine was intense. I cried out Jeff's name so loudly, I spooked an osprey perched in a sabal palm outside my bedroom window. Afterward, we lay in each other's arms while our breathing relaxed and our pulses slowed. I stroked Jeff's shoulder and bicep, admiring his muscles.

"Feeling good?" Jeff asked.

I nodded. "Better than I have since…"

"When?"

I cleared my throat. "Last night we agreed we wouldn't talk about Brian while you're here, remember?"

"Sure, but maybe we need to."

I rearranged my limbs so I sat facing Jeff in the lotus position with my hands resting on my knees. And, for the first time in weeks, a vision of Brian hanging from the shower nozzle stole into my head. A shiver ran through me when I recalled all the ghastly details, and I couldn't help myself. My face crumpled, and I wept so hard the bed shook.

"I'm sorry," I cried. "I don't want to ruin your visit."

Jeff took me in his arms and rubbed his chin against my tear-stained cheek. "It's okay, Jakub. You don't have to apologize for feeling sad."

In a quivering voice, I described for Jeff how I'd cut Brian down from the noose and held him in my arms while waiting for the ambulance to arrive.

"I wanted to die myself. And when they took him away, draped in a bedsheet, it seemed like I was sinking in quicksand. I *still* feel that way, whenever I think about finding Brian that afternoon. Sometimes I fear I'll never be myself again."

Jeff stroked my temple with his thumb. "You can't recover from something like that overnight. You'll need time to heal. But you shouldn't bottle up your grief; it'll only make you feel worse. *Let* yourself be sad, and don't be afraid to cry."

I dabbed my dripping eyes with a corner of my bedsheet.

"When I told the cop why Brian killed himself, he said it wasn't my fault. And I wanted to believe him, I really did. But I knew he only wanted to make me feel better, especially when he said he wouldn't share what I'd told him with Brian's parents. He said the truth would only make them feel worse."

"So, they don't know?"

I shook my head. "When Mason and I stayed with them in Fort Lauderdale, they pried about things in Tallahassee, but I played dumb. I couldn't bear to tell them what went on between me and Brian, 'cause I knew they'd hate me if I did."

I sniffled while continuing.

"I never should have let Brian touch me, even when we lived in the dorm, and I shouldn't have moved into that apartment with him either. Why didn't I keep my distance? But I was too goddamned selfish, and when Brian told me he loved me, my response couldn't have been more callous. Why didn't I—"

"Just a minute, look at me."

I brought my gaze to Jeff's.

"You were honest with Brian. What other choice did you have?"

"That's the same thing Mason told me, but..."

"There *was* no other option. Can't you see that?"

I wiped snot from my upper lip with the back of my hand. "Then, why do I feel so damned *guilty*?"

"You shouldn't. Brian must've had major emotional issues unconnected to you."

I looked into my lap and nodded before gazing into Jeff's eyes. "Thanks for telling me that, and I hope I'm not depressing you by discussing the way I feel."

"It's fine, but let's talk about something else now."

*

Sunday morning, we rose with the sun. After slipping into blue jeans, sneakers, and flannel shirts, and following a quick breakfast, we fished for flounder in a campground canal. Conditions were cool, dry, and utterly still.

Saturday night, we had gone to sleep not long after cleaning up the kitchen. Both of us seemed weary from our drive and it felt nice snuggling next to Jeff under a blanket while cool air poured through my bedroom windows. I think I fell asleep three minutes after my head hit the pillow.

Now, at the canal, a group of great grey herons passed above us, flying in V formation with their broad wings fully extended. I loved the park, where shrubs blossomed and the air smelled both salty and sweet. As much as I liked Tallahassee, with its towering live oaks, Fort De Soto was my home.

Jeff kept his gaze fixed on the bobber attached to his line while he talked. "You're still okay with me spending summer here?"

"Sure, things'll be great."

"And you're positive your dad's all right with it?"

"Of course, and I should tell you something."

Jeff looked at me and raised an eyebrow.

"I'm pretty sure he knows we're more than just friends."

"You're kidding?"

I described my conversation with my dad, back in December, when I had asked if Jeff could spend summer with us. I recounted how Dad and I discussed where Jeff would sleep.

Jeff chuckled and shook his head. "I guess we're not too subtle, are we?"

"And maybe we shouldn't be—at least around my dad. I honestly don't think he cares."

Jeff reeled in his bait to be sure it still existed. Then he cast it into the canal again, where the shrimp hit the water with a splash and sank.

"I keep wondering what *my* folks would say if I told them about us. Maybe they wouldn't care, but then again, they might freak out. I've never talked about homosexuality with them, so I'm not familiar with their views on the subject."

The bobber on my fishing line dipped beneath the water's surface for a moment before reappearing, and I cursed after I reeled in my line to find my shrimp missing.

I grumbled while placing a new shrimp on my hook and casting it to the canal's center, where the depth was greatest. Then we fished in silence for several minutes before Jeff asked about my Tallahassee apartment.

"Will Mason continue living there when summer arrives, or will he look for something else?"

"We haven't discussed that yet. It would be nice if he stayed on until you and I come up in the fall. That way, I wouldn't have to put all my furniture and kitchen stuff in storage."

"Have you told him we plan on living together next school year?"

I nodded. "He knows you're transferring from IU."

Jeff shifted his weight from one leg to the other. "Mason's a good-looking guy—anyone can see that. Have you ever thought about...?"

I glanced here and there to be sure no one else was within earshot. "Before Brian died, Mason and I got together once."

Jeff looked at me with his forehead crinkled. "Exactly what did you guys do?"

I explained.

"You let him *screw* you?"

I nodded.

"How was it?"

"It hurt at first, until I finally relaxed. Then I enjoyed it."

Jeff rubbed his chin with a knuckle. "I'll keep that in mind next time we're between the sheets. Variety's nice, you know."

Jeff's bobber disappeared beneath the water's surface, and his rod bent into a "J" shape while the fish pulled line from his spinning reel. He jerked his rod toward his shoulder and cranked in a bit of line.

"Flounder don't fight like that," I told Jeff. "You've caught something else."

"What?"

"It could be a sail catfish, or maybe something edible. We'll see."

A few minutes passed before Jeff finally brought his catch to the surface and I scooped it up in my dip net. A five-pound redfish, almost two feet long, thrashed about, all silver, gold, and gray, with several dime-sized spots on either side of its tail.

"That's a beauty," I said.

Jeff looked like a kid with a birthday cake. "I haven't caught a fish since last July. This is great."

I smiled while I lowered the fish onto the crabgrass next to the seawall. Then I used pliers to work the hook out of the fish's jaw while it continued to thrash and thump. Finally, I picked it up by its gills and dropped it into a five-gallon bucket full of seawater.

I told Jeff, "I guess you know what we're having for dinner tonight?"

He grinned and nodded. Then, after baiting his hook again, he cast into the canal, not far from where my bobber floated.

I rubbed my jaw while fixing my gaze on Jeff.

"I hope you're not angry about the business with Mason; it just kind of *happened*. But after Brian died, and Mason moved in with me, I made it clear to him nothing will occur between him and me again. No more promiscuity for Jakub Mazur."

Jeff crinkled his brow. "Why the change?"

I had to think for a few seconds before I decided exactly what to say.

"When sex occurs solely for pleasure, it can end up hurting someone. That's what happened with Brian, and I don't ever want to cause a person pain like that again."

Jeff turned down one corner of his mouth. "Are you telling me we'll be monogamous from now on?"

"If you're okay with that."

"I'd like nothing better. Sex is something we should save for each other. No one else should touch you but me, and vice versa. I'm willing to make that commitment if you are."

I reached for Jeff's shoulder and gave it a squeeze. "I am, Brucelli. You can count on that."

CHAPTER NINETEEN

Monday morning, we drove Dad's Jeep eastward on State Road 64 in Manatee County, south of Tampa Bay, passing by cow pastures, citrus groves, and slash pine forests. The rear compartment of the car groaned with camping paraphernalia: tent, sleeping bags and pads, ice cooler, cook stove, propane lantern, a cardboard box containing dry food, and a duffel bag full of clothing.

We would spend two days paddling the Peace River and two nights camping on its sandy banks. I had last canoed the Peace with my dad when I was twelve and still had vivid memories of the three-day excursion we took. At the time, the river's banks were entirely undeveloped, and now I recalled how, on the last day of our journey, we did not encounter a single human being until we reached the conclusion of our thirty-three-mile journey in Arcadia.

The Peace flows in a southeasterly direction. Jeff and I would leave the Jeep with the folks at Arcadia Canoe Outpost. Then an outpost staffer would drive Jeff and me northward, along with our gear and a rental canoe, to our jump-off point at a boat ramp at Zolfo Springs.

The day was sunny and cool, so we rolled the windows down. We both wore flannel shirts and blue jeans to keep ourselves warm. Jeff hadn't shaved in a couple of days. Dark stubble dusted his chin and cheeks, and when I stroked his temple, I told him his unkempt appearance looked sexy.

He looked at me with a one-hundred-watt grin on his face. "Should I grow a beard?"

"You're far too pretty for that, but a few days' growth looks good on you."

Jeff seized my forearm and kissed the back of my wrist. "You're looking handsome yourself, Mazur, and I have plans for you once we pitch camp."

"Oh, *really*?"

Jeff let go of my forearm before his hand traveled between my thighs. He gave me a squeeze and waggled his eyebrows. "You're all mine for the next two days, and I intend to make the most of it."

A jolt of excitement ran through me, as if I'd received a mild electric shock, and I was pretty sure I understood why.

The pledge of fidelity I'd given Jeff the previous morning had altered my relationship with him. He wasn't just my boyfriend now; he was my *partner*. I belonged to him completely—I was off-limits to everyone else—and I liked the idea. Instead of feeling restricted, I felt liberated.

Was this how married couples felt after they tied the knot?

Jeff's hand remained between my thighs, and I rested my hand on top of his wrist, savoring the warmth of his skin.

"You make me happy," I said while keeping my gaze fixed on the highway before us. "I want this day to last forever."

Jeff chuckled. "Be patient, lover boy. Nine weeks from now, I'll live fulltime with you at Fort De Soto. Then we can have each other whenever we want, and think how amazing *that* will be."

In my mind's eye, I envisioned Jeff's clothes hanging in my closet, his briefs and socks mingling with mine in my bureau, and his toothbrush resting alongside mine on the bathroom sink. Every night, we would crawl beneath the covers and hold each other while the ceiling fan above my bed hummed.

When we reached Arcadia, the time was close to 11:00 a.m., and sunlight reflected off eddies swirling on the river's surface while we transferred our gear to a pickup truck with a canoe trailer attached to it.

"You'll have good weather today and tomorrow," an outpost agent told us while we signed a rental agreement, and he furnished us with paddles and life jackets. "No rain or wind, and a high of seventy-five or so. You can't ask for better than that."

I asked where we should pitch our tent, that night and the next.

"Most of the land along the river is privately owned, primarily by cattle ranchers. But they don't mind if you camp on their property, as long as you stick to the river banks and don't cut down any trees for firewood."

An hour later, Jeff and I paddled our eighteen-foot aluminum canoe in the Peace's coffee-colored water, with all our gear and provisions stacked between me and Jeff. I sat aft and steered. At that point, the river was perhaps forty feet wide and no more than five feet deep in the channel. Beyond its sandy banks grew a tangle of vegetation: paw-paw, gopher apple, Cherokee bean, wax myrtle, turkey oak, and scrub palmetto, all shaded by slash pines, moss-laden live oaks, and bald cypress trees soaring forty feet into the air. Clumps of sabal palms abounded.

"It's so quiet out here," Jeff said.

And it was true. The only sounds were the swishing of our paddles and an occasional osprey's cry echoing through the forest. Above us, the sun had reached its zenith, and the day was warming up. We soon shed our flannel shirts, but left our undershirts on. Jeff wore a clingy wifebeater that showed off his shoulder and arm muscles, and his dark armpit hair as well, the same hair I had licked during our lovemaking the previous afternoon. I recalled the piney scent of Jeff's sweat, and the remembrance caused a stirring in my jeans.

"Weekend before last," Jeff said, "I drove the Impala to Peru so I could talk to my folks about transferring to FSU."

"How did that go?"

Jeff shook his head and the coils of hair on the crown of his head swayed. "Not well. They can't understand why I want to make the change this fall, when I'll only have one year of school left."

"What did you say?"

"I couldn't very well tell them the *real* reason I'm transferring, so I talked about the nice weather in Florida, and how much I like outdoor activities like this. I told them what a good school FSU is, and how job opportunities for journalists are better in Florida.

"My mom got all weepy. She said, 'We'll only see you at Christmas if you move down there.' Then my dad made noise about not helping me financially if I transfer."

"Do you think he was serious?"

"Probably not, but the rest of the weekend, both of them walked around with frowns on their faces. Honestly, I couldn't wait to leave on Sunday."

"Maybe if you tell them what's really going on—that we're going to live together as a couple—they might understand why the move's so important to you."

Jeff shrugged. "If I did that, it might make the situation worse. They might totally freak out."

We paddled in silence for a half hour or so, until I suggested we dine on the turkey and cheese sandwiches I'd prepared earlier in the day. After we beached the canoe at a sandy river bank, we pulled the sandwiches and two cans of soda from our ice cooler. Then we sat on a fallen tree trunk, enjoying our lunch and bathing in the sun's warm rays. Near the river's opposite bank, a half dozen painter turtles sunned themselves single file on a half-submerged tree.

"This place is beautiful," Jeff said. "I'm glad you thought of making the trip."

"I figured after five months of cold weather in Bloomington, you'd be ready for some fresh air and sunshine."

Once Jeff had finished his sandwich, he balled up the plastic baggie I'd sealed it in. Then he rose and tossed the ball into our canoe, following suit with his empty soda can. He stretched his limbs like a housecat.

"How far will we paddle today?" he asked.

"Maybe another four hours—that'll take us halfway to Gardner. We'll find a comfortable site to pitch the tent and have everything situated before sunset."

"Can I take a swim before we launch the canoe?"

I made a face. "That water's as cold as ice."

"Not to me, it isn't."

Within moments, Jeff was naked. He waded into the river till he was knee-deep, then dove toward the channel with a splash. When he surfaced, he shook water from his hair and wiped it from his face while he treaded.

"It feels great," he cried.

"I'll take your word for it. Floridians don't swim in rivers or the Gulf until May."

"Pussy," Jeff cried in falsetto.

"I plead guilty."

When Jeff came ashore, water glittered in his hair and on the tops of his shoulders. It streamed down his limbs when he plucked a towel from our duffel bag and commenced drying himself. Meanwhile, I feasted my eyes on his lean body, already looking forward to the moment when we'd crawl inside our tent.

"You're getting me horny, running around in your birthday suit like that."

"I like it when you're horny."

"Do you?"

Jeff nodded.

I rose and approached him. After glancing here and there, I seized the back of his neck and brought my mouth to his. Our lips parted and our tongues writhed while Jeff's breath steamed my upper lip. Then, after only a few moments, Jeff pushed me away.

"Calm down, Romeo. Someone might see us, and I don't care to get acquainted with a redneck's shotgun."

*

Shortly before sunset, we pitched our tent on a grassy bluff overlooking the river. We gathered firewood in the nearby forest and lit our lantern. Already, stars had appeared in the eastern sky, and the temperature was dropping.

"What's for dinner?" Jeff asked while I unfolded the propane cookstove.

"Nothing fancy—beef stew and green beans, *and* I brought chocolate chip cookies for dessert."

Jeff rubbed the palms of his hands together while his gaze turned here and there. Then he looked back at me.

"Before you start cooking…"

"What?"

He jerked a thumb in the direction of the tent while a mischievous grin spread on his face.

"Get in there, Mazur."

A shiver ran through my limbs when I rose and made my way to the tent. I pulled aside a flap and scooted inside on my hands and knees. Jeff followed me, and we went about kicking off shoes and shucking our clothing. Already, my pulse galloped.

"Leave your briefs on," Jeff told me. "I'll take those off myself when the time's right."

"Yes, *Daddy*," I trilled.

Jeff pushed me onto my back and crawled atop me so our hips and sternums met. His skin was warm and smooth. I ran my fingers through his wavy hair while we slobbered. I grew as stiff as rebar, and so did Jeff while we panted like dogs in heat.

I slipped my hand inside the seat of Jeff's briefs and squeezed his buttocks, marveling at their firmness. But when I tickled the crevice between them, Jeff reached behind his waist and pulled my hand away.

I crinkled my forehead. "What's wrong?"

"I'm not getting poked today. Mason may have stolen your cherry, but your ass belongs to me tonight, and I'm taking what's mine."

Aggression wasn't something Jeff normally exhibited when we made love; he tended to be the passive guy when we were together. But there in the tent, he wasn't the least bit shy about taking charge of things. When he yanked my briefs off, my thoughts spun and my heart thumped. He took me on my back, easing inside me while he bared his teeth and his eyes gleamed. He thrust his hips and warmth flowed into my limbs.

Jeff lifted his chin and shouted like a savage when he came. Meanwhile, I felt as though I sat atop a rocket hurtling through outer space. And when I squirted, my cries echoed in the nearby forest. Jeff collapsed on top of me like a sack of grain. We lay with our sweaty skins stuck together and our breaths chugging while, outside the tent, crickets chorused and the river gurgled. Ten minutes must have passed before Jeff finally spoke.

"That was...amazing."

I kissed his temple and rubbed my cheek stubble against his, making little scratching sounds.

"Did you like it?" he asked. "Because—"

"It was great, I mean it."

Jeff withdrew and lay beside me on top of his sleeping bag. He weaved his fingers together behind his neck and stared at the tent ceiling. Dusk was upon us, and light from our lantern stole into the tent, enough so I saw the contours of Jeff's face—his beautiful nose, thick eyebrows, and craggy cheekbones.

"I hope it's always like this between us," he said.

"What do you mean?"

"As if we're a single person. When I was inside you, just a few minutes ago, I felt I'd become a part of your body. Does that sound weird?"

"No, I felt much the same."

When Jeff had thrust inside me, I felt subsumed within him, much as I had when Mason took me up in Tallahassee, only this was somehow different. Like Mason, Jeff had taken control of my body and bent it to his will. But more importantly, Jeff stroked each of my senses—sight, touch, smell, taste, and hearing—and used them to create a sort of sexual symphony within me. And, of course, per our agreement I belonged only to Jeff now.

At Jeff's suggestion, we bathed in the river's chilly water. Goose bumps sprang up on my body when I lathered myself and shampooed my hair. I rinsed off by immersing myself and then dried my shivering flesh with a towel on the river bank. The air temperature had dipped considerably since sunset, and my teeth chattered, but I still enjoyed getting clean and smelling fresh.

After we dressed, I went about building a campfire, stacking tree branches into a pyramid over a pile of twigs and cardboard scraps I ignited with a butane lighter. Flames quickly rose inside the pyramid, illuminating our campsite and the shallows of the river. The glowing branches crackled and hissed.

Jeff stood watching me with his hands stuffed into the hip pockets of his blue jeans. The flames reflected in his damp hair. "You're good at that," he said. "Were you ever a Boy Scout?"

"Nah, my dad taught me everything I needed to know about the outdoors."

Jeff rubbed the tip of his nose with a knuckle. "Do you think he likes me?"

"I believe he does. Like I said, I'm pretty sure he knows what's up between you and me, and he seems fine with it. Plus..."

"What?"

I looked up at Jeff before returning my gaze to the fire.

"Dad remembers how badly I got hurt when my mom disappeared. He also knows I was never involved with someone romantically until I met you. I'm sure he worried I might be emotionally damaged, so he's probably relieved I can open my heart to someone."

Jeff dragged an ice cooler over and sat on it. He crossed his legs at the ankles while gazing into the flames.

"The same might be true for my folks, if I told them about us. They know I've never had a girlfriend or even dated, and I imagine it concerns them. When it comes to love, they probably think I'm stunted."

"Then maybe you *should* tell them, and not just because it will stop their worrying. They'll also understand why you're so damned eager to move to Florida."

Jeff gazed into the flames and didn't respond to my suggestion.

*

"Jakub, wake up."

When I opened my eyes, I was in the tent with Jeff on the second night of our Peace River trip. My chest heaved, and the inside of my sleeping bag felt damp.

"Are you okay?" Jeff asked. "You were talking in your sleep and rolling around like a crazy person."

Then I remembered the dream I'd just experienced. In it, I stood in the living room at my Tallahassee apartment, along with Brian, who stared out of the front window with his back turned to me. I kept asking him to talk to me, but he wouldn't respond, as if he couldn't hear me.

I finally approached Brian and squeezed his shoulder. "Please, say something."

Brian turned to look at me, but he wasn't the handsome Brian I'd lived with for many months. Instead he was the guy I found hanging in the shower: red face, buggy eyes, scratched-up neck, and tongue sticking out. He stood there staring at me for the longest time before he finally spoke.

"Look what you've done to me, Jakub. Are you happy now?"

Now, in the tent, I ran my fingers through my damp hair. "I had a nightmare, a bad one. Sorry if I woke you."

Jeff stroked my sweaty cheek with his thumb. "Do you want to tell me about it?"

I explained, in detail, and when I'd finished, Jeff left his sleeping bag. He crawled into mine and held me. "How awful," he said. "You know, I think you're carrying a huge load of guilt about Brian; that's probably why you had the dream."

"Really?"

"Yeah, and it's not good. I think you should see a counselor, somebody who can help you work through your feelings. You can't keep walking around with that kind of burden eating at you."

I rubbed my cheek against Jeff's chest, savoring the warmth of his skin. I felt so safe, lying in his arms and listening to his voice, while the terror of the nightmare receded.

"Do you think one day I'll recover from what happened?"

"I hope so, but you can't do it on your own. I'll be here for you, of course, but you need the kind of help I can't give you."

CHAPTER TWENTY

Spring Break ended far too quickly. Jeff would depart for Bloomington Saturday morning, and on Friday afternoon, my dad handed me seventy dollars.

"Take Jeff out for a nice dinner."

I chose a restaurant on the top floor of a twenty-story office building in downtown St. Petersburg, a place where many of my high school buddies had taken their dates for a meal, prior to attending the prom. Jeff borrowed clothing items from me, and we both looked like Ivy League boys in our oxford cloth shirts and dress slacks.

I made sure the hostess seated us at a window table with a view to the west, where the setting sun gilded the tops of the city's multitude of trees—oaks, pines, and magnolias, mostly. Clouds at the western horizon glowed in shades of pink, tangerine, green, and gold.

Florida's drinking age was twenty-one, so we ordered iced tea from our server.

Nearly every table in the room was occupied, mostly by middle-aged couples. Men wore sports jackets while their wives dressed in smart outfits and heels. A sound system played elevator music, but a crush of conversation around us muted the tunes.

Jeff and I raised our glasses and clicked them together before taking healthy gulps. I gazed into Jeff's eyes, and his masculine beauty made me dizzy. He looked like a prince, and when I told him so, a grin crossed his handsome face.

"You're looking pretty sharp yourself. I have a mind to kiss you in front of this whole restaurant."

I feigned a scowl. "You might cause a scene if you did."

Jeff let his gaze travel around the room before returning it to me. "I wish I wasn't leaving tomorrow. The weather's been beautiful all week, and spending time with you is the best. I can't *wait* for summer to get here."

"I know; it seems so unfair you have to return to Bloomington. But come June, we won't let anything separate us. Agreed?"

"You bet."

Our waiter approached with his digital tablet. I ordered chicken cordon bleu while Jeff chose prime rib, and in minutes our waiter brought us garden salads drenched in blue cheese dressing, along with more tea. We dug into our salads, and the sharp taste of the dressing was so pleasurable, I groaned.

"I could eat here every night," I said.

Jeff nodded, then shifted his jaw. "I've given a lot of thought to what we discussed on the river."

"Explain, please."

"I think maybe you're right: I should tell my folks about us and our future plans."

I turned my gaze to the window beside us. By now, the sun had disappeared behind the western tree line and the sky had darkened. Streetlamps flickered on below us. I tried to imagine the new world Jeff and I would create, once our parents knew. We could live as a couple, without shame or guilt. I would become part of Jeff's family and he a part of mine, as tiny as it was. And when autumn arrived, we would establish our own household in Tallahassee.

"Jakub?"

I turned my gaze back to Jeff and raised my eyebrows.

"You got quiet all of a sudden. Is something wrong?"

I shook my head.

"Everything's just right."

*

Dad and I sat on the glider sofa, both of us clutching beer bottles and gazing at the bayou, where a school of mullet stirred the water's surface. The afternoon air was still, and the fronds on our sabal palms hung as limp as dishrags. The only sound I heard was the creaking of the sofa's hinges while we rocked. Dad still wore his ranger's uniform and scuffed work boots, and he smelled of pipe tobacco.

Jeff had departed many hours before, and since then I seemed like a lost child. Most of the day, I lay in my bed with the covers pulled over my head. I felt hollow inside, as though all my organs had been sucked from my body. I hadn't eaten a thing all day—food didn't interest me—and every time I tried to leave the bed, it was as if I were glued to the mattress.

When Dad came home from work, that's where he found me, under the covers.

"Jakub, I know you're feeling badly, but you can't stay in bed forever. Go wash your face and come to the porch."

I nodded and hit the bathroom. Then I joined him on the glider sofa, wearing nothing but a T-shirt and a pair of boxer shorts. Dad handed me a cold bottle of beer, and after I took a few sips, the alcohol stole through my limbs, helping me relax for the first time all day.

"I guess Jeff left on time?"

I nodded.

"It's always hard for you when he goes, isn't it?"

I didn't say anything; I only watched bubbles rise in my beer bottle.

Dad crossed a knee with his ankle; he kept his gaze fixed on the bayou when he spoke.

"You know I'm not very good at talking about personal matters. I wasn't raised in a household where people did. My folks kept their feelings to themselves, and I followed suit because I figured that's how things should be, but maybe you and I *should* talk about private things."

I licked my lips and stayed quiet.

"Like I told you in Tallahassee, when your mother left us, I thought it would kill me. For months, I walked around like a dead man. In fact, to this day I still don't remember much about that period. I forced myself to get out of bed every morning and go to work, but I didn't help *you* cope with the situation, and I'm sorry. You were hurting, and I should have been a better father."

"It's okay."

"No, I'm the only family you have, and we should talk about anything—no matter how personal it is—and I will listen and try to understand as best I can. That's what a father should do."

I gazed into my lap and rubbed my lips together.

"You know about me and Jeff, don't you?"

"Of course."

I turned my gaze to Dad's. "How do you feel about it?"

Dad shrugged. "If he makes you happy, it's all that matters. He's a fine boy from a good family, and he certainly cares a lot for you—it's easy to see. I'd say you're one lucky guy."

The combination of Jeff's departure and Dad's acceptance overwhelmed me. I let out a wail that echoed in the mangroves. Then I lowered my head onto my father's lap and wept.

Dad sifted his fingers through my hair; he patted my shoulder while I blubbered.

"S-h-h-h, I know it hurts. But Jeff will be back soon, and the three of us will have a fine summer, you'll see."

After a few minutes, I managed to calm down, enough so I could speak coherently.

"You're not disappointed in me, are you?"

"Of course not."

"I'll never have a wife or give you grandchildren. You know that, right?"

Dad kissed my cheek, the first time he'd done so in many years. "I'm not worried about grandchildren, and marriage isn't always a good thing—look how mine ended up. What's important is you're happy."

I rose to a sitting position and wiped snot from my upper lip. "I'm sorry for getting upset. It's just—"

"You don't have to apologize. I know you're in pain, but at least you know where Jeff is, and soon the two of you will be together again. Be grateful for that."

CHAPTER TWENTY-ONE

April in Tallahassee was a wonder. Azaleas bloomed in a variety of colors: pink, white, purple, yellow, and red. Wisteria vines exploded in purple blossom clusters resembling grape bunches. Camellias produced showy red and white blossoms as big as a man's fist, while dew glistened in the grass at FSU's Landis Green.

Most nights, Mason and I slept with our windows open to enjoy the temperate evening air, and I loved nestling under my bedcovers while flowery scents drifted through the screens, lulling me to sleep.

I tried to stick to the routines Brian and I had followed when Brian was still alive, determined to keep my grades up and my physical condition in top form. I rose every morning at seven and made it to campus on my bicycle by eight, to attend class or study at a library carrel.

Mason and I resumed our afternoon exercise regimens, working out with weights at the gym and running laps at the FSU track, and as the first weekend after Spring Break approached, we took an evening walk through our neighborhood, inhaling the sweet aromas hanging in the air.

"There's a girl at work, her name's Jessica," Mason said while we strolled. "She's cute and pretty darned smart as well. If you don't mind, I'll invite her over for dinner Saturday."

"Not a problem, but…"

"What?"

"Don't take this the wrong way, but I'm confused about your sexual persuasion. I know you lived with that French girl, but then you had me once and wanted more. Which do you like better, girls or boys?"

Mason snickered and shook his head. "What does it matter? All I know is, I find Jessica interesting. Not too many women study engineering, so she's unique. Plus, she's easy to talk with—no coyness or game playing—and that's a rarity."

"Do you want me to make myself scarce Saturday? I can find something to do."

"Please don't. I want you to meet Jessica, plus conversation's easier between three people instead of just two. Stick around and share a meal with us; I'll cook something you'll like."

*

Friday afternoon, I arrived home to find an eight-by-ten manila envelope addressed to me, propped against our front door, left there by the post office because the envelope was too large to fit in our mailbox downstairs. The return address was the Keene residence in Fort Lauderdale.

Once inside, I slit the envelope's flap and removed the contents, which included a studio portrait of Brian in his Eagle Scout uniform. He must have been seventeen or so when the picture was taken. Also included was a note from Brian's mom.

Dear Jakub:

Enclosed is a photograph you can keep to remember Brian by. I'm sorry I don't have anything more recent, but Brian wasn't fond of having his picture taken; I don't know why.

All the best,

Laura Keene.

I gazed into Brian's cobalt eyes and shook my head.

Oh, how I miss you, buddy.

*

I met Mason's friend, Jessica, on Saturday when he brought her over for dinner in his pickup truck. A tall, large-breasted girl with a ready smile and hair growing in waves to her shoulders, she talked with me on the living room sofa while Mason busied himself in the kitchen, preparing eggplant parmesan. Scents of garlic and oregano wafted through the apartment.

"I come from a family of engineers," Jessica told me. "My dad and two brothers have a firm in Tampa—they wanted me to come to work for them—but I wasn't ready for that. I needed freedom, so I took a job with DOT right after I graduated. I've been there almost a year."

I explained how I majored in Education and planned to teach, down in Pinellas County, after earning my bachelor's degree.

Jessica nodded. "My roommate, Katie, is an elementary school teacher, and she looks forward to work every day. The kids love her. She makes them want to please her, and I think that's a real gift if you're going to teach—getting the kids on your side."

After Mason brought us bottles of beer, we sipped from them while we continued chatting.

"Mason told me you grew up in a county park," Jessica said. "That must've been interesting."

I shrugged. "It could get lonely at times."

Jessica shook her head. "I can't imagine. I grew up in a neighborhood full of children, so I always found someone to do something with. I'm still in touch with several people I've known since I was five or six."

"I don't have any long-term friendships. In fact, you might say I'm kind of a loner."

"Well, at least you have Mason. What's it like sharing a place with him anyway?"

"We get along okay," I said, choosing not to mention Mason's infrequent bathing, his snoring, or his habit of strewing the apartment with his belongings. "And he's converted me to vegetarianism, at least when we share meals together."

Jessica toyed with her hair while she glanced toward the kitchen. "I'm not sure I could give up meat—I'm a steak and potatoes kind of gal—but whatever he's doing in there smells pretty good."

"You're going to love it," Mason bellowed while he shoved a baking dish into the oven. "This is one of my premier recipes."

Jessica smiled. "I can't wait," she told Mason before returning her gaze to me. "So, Mason tells me you have a boyfriend up in Indiana."

My cheeks flamed while I lowered my gaze to my lap.

Thanks a lot, Mason. Maybe I should tell her about us *fucking.*

"Don't be embarrassed," Jessica said, placing her hand on my knee. "One of my brothers is gay. I've spent a lot of time with him and his partner, so I'm used to men getting affectionate with each other."

I cleared my throat and brought my gaze back to Jessica.

"My sexuality isn't something I'm used to discussing with people. But, yeah, my boyfriend's name is Jeff. He's moving to Florida this summer, and we'll room together in Tallahassee come August."

Jessica glanced toward the kitchen again. "What about poor Mason? Who will he live with?"

Mason stuck his head into the living room.

"Maybe I can move into your place. Just think how much fun we'd have."

*

Hours later, after Mason drove Jessica home, he and I sat at our dining table, playing gin rummy with a dog-eared deck of cards that had once belonged to my parents. We both sipped from glasses of room-temperature Liebfraumilch.

"What did you think?" Mason asked while he drew from the deck.

"About what?"

"Jessica," Mason said before discarding a four of clubs.

I shrugged and snatched up Mason's discard. Then I laid down a three, four, and five of clubs. "She seems nice enough, and you're right, she's very direct. No use playing games with her, is there?"

Mason shook his head. "And she's a pretty good kisser too."

I took another sip from my glass and swished the sweet liquid around in my mouth before swallowing. "Were you serious about moving in with her?"

"I was mostly joking, but while we're on the subject of living arrangements..."

"What?"

"How would you feel about me keeping this apartment until you and Jeff move up here in the fall?"

I fanned my cards and studied the discard pile while I pondered Mason's proposal. Then I drew a nine of spades from the deck, which wasn't going to help me at all, so I discarded it.

"If you stay here over summer, you'll really help me out. I won't have to put all my stuff in storage—a real pain in the ass and expensive. So, it's fine if you want to stay here. I'll even kick in on the rent."

Mason picked up my nine of spades and laid down a trick of three nines. Then he discarded a seven of hearts. "You don't need to contribute anything. I make good money at DOT and my expenses aren't much, so I'll be good."

I nodded my thanks, and we played a few minutes in silence. Our windows were open, and down the street a group of college boys sang a drinking song on the front porch of their fraternity house. Horns honked and transfer trucks roared on Tennessee Street.

I thought about the photo and note I'd received from Laura Keene the day before. Should I share them with Mason or keep them to myself? After all, Mason harbored his own guilty feelings about the way he'd treated Brian.

Go on, he's entitled.

I pushed my chair back from the table.

"I have something to show you; I'll be right back."

Ten minutes later, we sat on the sofa with Laura's letter and Brian's photo resting on the coffee table.

Mason's hands hung between his knees while he stared at the items as if I'd found them in a spook house.

"I've made a decision," I said. "Tomorrow afternoon, I'll visit the University Counseling Center to ask for help. I can't shake this feeling I'm responsible for Brian's death, and I shouldn't keep walking around with that kind of guilt hanging over my head."

"Would you like me to go with you?"

"Thanks for offering," I said, "but this is something I need to do on my own."

CHAPTER TWENTY-TWO

Late morning sunlight entered the windows of Patricia Bigelow's office in the counseling center. We sat in leather upholstered chairs, facing each other. This was my second visit with her, and already I felt I could trust her with any confidence, no matter how personal or embarrassing.

A petite woman with graying hair and minimal makeup, Patricia wore a pleated wool skirt and a silk blouse. A thin gold necklace gleamed at her throat, and a writing pen and note pad rested in her lap.

On my first visit, after I'd explained the circumstances of Brian's death, she asked me to describe my childhood and family life, and when I talked about my mother's disappearance, tears glistened in her dark eyes.

"How sad for you and your father. It had to be painful."

I talked about my boyhood habit of coming home from school to hide under my bedcovers every afternoon. I explained how I savored the darkness and solitude my room offered.

"Sometimes when we grieve," Patricia said, "it helps to spend time alone, just staying quiet and keeping the world at bay. Our hearts and minds need time to heal from a loss like you suffered."

I nodded. "To this day, whenever I think of her, my stomach feels funny and my head hurts."

"I'm not surprised. It sounds to me like you've never fully recovered from her departure, and that's understandable. Our childhood losses are always the hardest to face, and the emotional scars they leave are tough to resolve."

Now, on my second visit, Patricia focused on my relationship with Brian.

"Be specific, and tell me everything that happened between you two."

I spent ten minutes describing how I'd become Brian's sexual partner, back at the dormitory. I spoke of our apartment and the daily routines Brian and I had followed, and I talked about how we slept together every night.

Patricia made a face. "It sounds like a marriage."

"But it wasn't, because I already had Jeff."

"Who is Jeff?"

After I explained, Patricia shook her head. "You led a complicated life back then; you know that, don't you?"

I lowered my gaze.

"Look," Patricia said, "I'm not trying to judge your actions—it's not my place to do so—but the situation with Brian was bound to implode. Was he an emotionally stable person?"

I shook my head. Then I talked about Brian's childhood and his lousy relationship with his parents, especially his dad. "I think I was the first person to ever treat him affectionately."

"It's no wonder he grew so attached to you."

"But he never *told* me he felt that way. I thought we were just friends."

Patricia drew a breath and let it out. She rose and strolled to her office windows to gaze at the brightness of the day with her arms crossed under her breasts. On West Tennessee Street, the Presbyterian church's bell tolled.

"Did I say something wrong?" I asked.

Patricia glanced at me from over her shoulder. "Not really. I'm taking a minute to gather my thoughts. You've shared a whole lot of information with me today and also during our last session. When you leave here, I want to give you something constructive to think about before we meet again."

"All right."

Patricia returned to her chair. She leaned toward me and rested her forearms on her knees. "Between now and our meeting next week, I want you to write a letter to your mother. Tell her how you felt when she abandoned you."

"How will that help me deal with Brian's suicide?"

Patricia patted the back of my wrist. "You've never learned how to deal with loss, Jakub. Your typical reaction is to hide beneath your bedcovers and blame yourself for what's happened, even when it wasn't your fault. And that sort of behavior doesn't work. You'll have to come to terms with your losses, and recognize who is truly responsible for them."

Minutes later, while I rode my ten-speed across campus, I studied faces of students I passed on sidewalks. They seemed so carefree and spirited, while I felt like I toted a pair of cinder blocks in my backpack. Just thinking about writing a letter to my mother made me feel weary. Exactly what should I say to her? And was Patricia right? Had I spent the last eleven years of my life blaming myself for Mom's departure when it wasn't at all my fault?

Was I doing the same thing now regarding Brian's death?

*

"This place is pretty," Mason said. "I heard about it from the guy I bought bait from last night. He told me redfish feed on the grass flats here, just after daylight."

We stood waist deep in Ochlocknee Bay, about a half-mile west of the US 98 bridge. The time was 7:30 a.m., and the sun had just risen in a cloudless April sky. We fished with live shrimp kept frisky in a floating bait bucket tied to a belt loop on Mason's denim shorts. The water was chilly, the air temperature cool.

We had driven down to the coast in darkness, listening to Mason's dashboard radio. The only station we found played gospel, which was pretty good. I liked the harmonizing and the rhythm of the music. But now, on the grass flat, everything was quiet, save for an occasional rumble from a transfer truck crossing the bridge.

I hadn't used my spinning reel and rod since my last outing with Jeff down at Fort De Soto and thinking about Jeff gave me a warm feeling inside my chest. I tried to imagine what he might be doing at the moment, and I figured because it was a Saturday, he was probably sleeping in. How I wished I could lie beside him under the bedcovers and run my fingers through his dark hair. But I would have to satisfy myself with a telephone conversation, perhaps that night.

I swung my gaze to Mason to view him in profile. Morning sunlight reflected in his fiery-red hair and in the tangerine stubble on his cleft chin.

The previous night, I had accompanied Mason and Jessica to a screening of a movie at the FSU campus theater. Prior to the movie, the three of us dined on vegetarian fare at Nature's Table, and at one point during the meal, Jessica let it be known she'd have preferred a cheeseburger for dinner instead of the spinach souffle on her plate.

For the rest of the evening, Mason said little, and as soon as the movie was over, he dropped Jessica at her apartment without even walking her to her door. As soon as we arrived at our place, Mason muttered something about rising early the next morning to fish. Then he climbed into bed, leaving me in the living room, watching Jimmy Fallon's monologue on *The Tonight Show.*

Now, at the bay, I asked Mason, "What happened between you and Jessica last night?"

He shrugged. "At work on Friday, when I invited her out for Saturday night, I asked if I could spend the night at her place after the movie."

"And?"

"You'd have thought I asked her to chop off her hand. She said something like, 'Katie wouldn't like it.' And I said, 'You each have your own bedrooms. Why should she care?' Then Jessica said, 'I'm not sure I'd like it either. You're pushing things too fast, and I'm not comfortable with it.'"

"Maybe you *are* rushing things."

Mason hissed. "Come on, this isn't high school. We're adults, and I don't think asking Jessica to share sex with me was out of line. Last night was our third date, so I'd say it's about time we got closer. What do you think?"

"You're asking the wrong guy. I've never dated a woman, so I don't know how they feel about sex."

Mason reeled in his line to check on his bait, only to find it was gone. "Damned trash fish took my shrimp," he said before fishing into the bait bucket. After he skewered a shrimp on his hook, he cast it into the bay's greenish water. Then he looked at me and shook his head. "I can't believe a good-looking guy like you has never been in bed with a female. How can that be?"

I rocked my head from side to side. "You don't understand what it's like to be 100 percent gay. I feel no attraction to girls, so why would I date one, much less have sex with her?"

"Maybe you should give it a try; you might like it. I could set you up with somebody from work if you'd like."

"Thanks, but I'll save myself for Jeff—he's all I need."

"But Jeff's a thousand miles from here. Don't you ever get horny?"

"Of course, and when it happens, I get out the jelly tube."

Mason made a face. "Next time you get the urge, let me know, and I'll help you out."

I turned down one corner of my mouth and shook my head. "I made a deal with Jeff: From now on, he's the only guy who gets to touch me, and vice versa. We're a couple, and that's how it's going to be."

The tip of my rod dipped and bent. My reel hummed as a fish took line and ran with my bait.

"Oh, you've got one," Mason hollered while the fish kept taking line. "You might want to tighten your drag a bit to slow him up."

I did as Mason suggested, turning the little knob on my spinning reel clockwise, but only a tad. I didn't want to put too much strain on the line and possibly cause it to break. My maneuver did the trick, and the fish took no more line; it only tugged every few seconds, causing the tip of my rod to twitch.

I used a pumping motion with my rod, bringing it toward my shoulder and reeling in line, then lowering the rod a little and letting the fish rest momentarily before raising the rod and bringing in more line until the fish finally came to the surface, a short distance from me.

"That's a red, all right," Mason cried while he pulled his dip net from the back pocket of his shorts. "Bring him a little closer if you can, and I'll nab him."

I took in more line and soon the fish was less than six feet from us, creating eddies on the water's surface. Mason stepped toward it, submerged the net, and scooped up the fish, a beauty almost two feet long, with silvery scales and multiple spots near its tailfin.

"He's probably five or six pounds," Mason said while the fish thrashed around in the net. "Why don't you wade to shore and put him in the cooler while I try to catch another."

Mason passed the net handle to me, and I sloshed toward the grassy shoreline with the net in one hand and my pole in the other. The fish continued to thrash about, and I was thrilled about catching him, but despite my excitement, I couldn't help but ponder Mason's proposal. Clearly, he wanted to have sex with me again, and I certainly found him attractive. I knew he was a tiger in bed, but then I recalled my discussion with Jeff at Fort De Soto when we'd made our pledge.

I left the water shivering in my wet shorts. The grass was chilly on my bare feet while I trod toward the truck bed with the fish still wriggling in the net. After I opened the cooler's lid, I emptied the fish onto a pile of crushed ice and watched its gills flex.

"Don't worry," I whispered to Jeff. "I'll be a good boy."

CHAPTER TWENTY-THREE

Sunday evening, Jeff phoned me at exactly eight o'clock, and right away I knew something was wrong because his voice had a quiver to it when he asked how I was doing.

"Okay," I said, "but you don't sound too good. What's going on up there?"

Jeff cleared his throat. "I visited Peru this weekend, and..."

"What?"

"Saturday night, at the dinner table, I told my parents about us."

I fingered my cell phone. "Tell me what happened."

"Things didn't go as smoothly as I'd hoped. My dad got quiet, and my mom *cried*."

"Holy shit, Jeff."

"After I finished cleaning the kitchen, I found them sitting on our porch swing, and the three of us talked for over an hour. They asked tough questions. They wanted to know what we do together in bed, and who plays a passive role. They also asked about STDs and whether we're both healthy."

"Oh, for Christ's sake."

"It's true, and there's more. They're terrified people will learn I'm queer."

"Why?"

"You have to understand; Peru is not St. Petersburg. It's a small town, and everybody knows one another. Folks gossip like crazy—it's a favorite pastime—and if people found out about me, it wouldn't be good. At best, my relatives and friends would shun me. At worst, I'd get pummeled in an alley by some farm boy."

I shook my head. "How were things left at the end of your talk?"

"They told me they still love me. But it may take some time before they accept us as a couple."

After Jeff rang off, I stared out of the kitchen window. I thought of how rotten Jeff's weekend had turned out, while anger boiled inside me. For a fleeting moment, I considered phoning the Brucellis. Maybe I could convince them my relationship with Jeff wasn't something to fear or be ashamed of. I would explain how my father had accepted me without hesitation.

But then I decided maybe the phone call might only make things worse.

Fuck.

*

Days later, I sat in Patricia's office again, reading aloud to her from a letter I'd revised at least a dozen times, before it said exactly what I wished it to.

Dear Mom,

Where do I begin?

I will never forget the day I came home from school to find our house empty. I was nine. I remember walking from room to room. I even looked in the attic, hoping maybe you were playing a joke on me, but soon I realized you weren't. Your clothes, shoes, and jewelry were missing along with your toothbrush.

I remember going to the porch and sitting on the glider sofa. I looked out at the bayou and told myself, "This can't be happening; maybe she went to visit someone." But you didn't have anyone to visit, not that I knew of anyway. I sat there on the glider, listening to the hinges creak and wondering what would become of me and Dad.

Because it was February, the sky was almost dark when Dad arrived home. He found me on the glider because I hadn't moved from there for several hours. When Dad asked me where you were, I explained how your things were gone and so were you. Then I asked Dad if we should call the police.

When he sat down beside me, he had the strangest expression on his face, like he'd seen a ghost. We must've stayed there for a half hour or longer, listening to seagulls cry. Neither of us said a single word. Then, Dad finally looked at me and said, "Your mother is mentally ill, Jakub. She suffers from schizophrenia. I've done my best to hide it from you, but maybe I shouldn't have."

I asked Dad, "Where do you think she is right now?"

He shook his head and said maybe you were in a motel in St. Petersburg, but it was quite possible you'd ridden a bus to New York City or California. He said, once before, not long after he'd married you, you disappeared someplace and didn't come home for three months. No letters or phone calls—nothing. Then, one day you returned, and everything got back to normal. But he never found out where you went or why you left, because you wouldn't say.

I remember, while we sat there on the glider, I asked Dad if he thought you'd come home again, if your absence was something temporary, and he said he didn't know.

"Maybe," he said, "but don't count on it."

Dad heated up frozen dinners in the microwave oven for our evening meal, while I stayed on the glider in the dark, wondering what my life was going to be like without you in it.

Well, here's how it was, Mom: For months after you disappeared, I walked around in a daze. I grew dark circles under my eyes, in spite of sleeping ten hours every night. I lost weight because I didn't care to eat. A couple of my teachers phoned Dad to say they were worried about me because my grades were suffering, and I guess he had to explain to them what had happened in our family.

Every day, when I came home from school, I undressed in my room and climbed into bed. Then I pulled the covers over my head and lay there in the darkness—my only escape.

Sometimes when I lay in bed, I talked to you, even though you weren't there. I said things like, "Mom, where are you? How could you leave me like this? Don't you love me? Do you know how sad I am about you leaving? Do you know how worried I am about you? And will you ever come home to me? Can't you at least give me a phone call?"

But, of course, I never got an answer to any of those questions. All I heard was the clock ticking on my nightstand. And I know it seems strange, but the ticking sounded as loud as a pile driver.

As months passed, and you didn't return, the reality of the situation began to sink in, and finally I knew you weren't coming back, that I'd probably never hear from you again. Mom, you cannot imagine how badly it hurt, so much I made myself stop thinking about you altogether, as if you'd never existed, so I wouldn't feel the pain anymore. The only time you came to mind was when some unsuspecting person asked me why my mother didn't live with me, and thankfully that didn't happen too often.

For many years after you disappeared, I was probably the loneliest person on the planet. I had no friends at school, and none at the park. I spent my free time fishing or reading or riding my bike, always by myself. In fact, I never grew close to another person until last summer, when I met a boy named Jeff. He's the best thing that ever happened to me. He helped me let down my defenses, and I fell in love with him. Having him in my life has made all the difference. For the first time since you left, I'm happy.

If you wonder what I think about you today, I can only say this: It's hard not to hate you for what you've done. You abandoned your only son when you knew how much I loved you and depended on you. How could you be so cruel? You only thought of your own selfish needs, instead of putting mine first like a decent mother would.

I can't forgive you for that. And to be honest, I hope wherever you are today, you are lonely and friendless and utterly miserable, because that's what you deserve after what you've done to me.

I used to fantasize you'd return home one day and everything would be okay—that you, me, and Dad would live as a family again—but your neglect and selfishness have beaten my love for you to death. I went to hell and back because of you, and I sincerely hope I won't ever hear from you again. That's the god's honest truth.

Fuck you, Mom,

Jakub.

When I looked up from the letter, Patricia's eyes had reddened.

"It took a lot of courage to write that letter; I'm proud of you for doing so."

"Do you think I'm being fair, feeling the way I do about her?"

Patricia rocked her head from side to side. "This is not about fairness. It's about releasing the anger you feel toward her and facing it. She caused you a good deal of emotional pain, and you're entitled to be bitter. After all, you were only a child when she disappeared."

"But she was mentally ill. Maybe she didn't even realize what she was doing."

"Perhaps, but it still doesn't diminish your pain, nor does it invalidate your anger toward her. You have every right to the feelings expressed in your letter."

I scratched the side of my jaw. "What should I do with my hostility? Walk around with it for the rest of my life?"

Patricia shook her head. "Your anger toward your mother is an albatross you'll need to rid yourself of, the sooner the better."

"And how do I do that?"

"By forgiving your mother for what she's done."

I looked at the carpet and swallowed before returning my gaze to Patricia. "I don't know if I can."

Patricia nodded. "It won't be easy, but forgiveness is the key to walking away from your pain. Once you let go of the hate expressed in your letter, the process of healing will begin. A wise man named Paul Boese once said, 'Forgiveness does not change the past, but it does enlarge the future.' You need to think about those words, Jakub."

CHAPTER TWENTY-FOUR

On the fourth Sunday in April, Jeff phoned me from Bloomington, and like always the sound of his voice made my heart skip a beat.

Initially, we spoke about our classes at school and what we'd done since we last talked. I told Jeff about the redfish I'd caught in Ochlocknee Bay, and how Mason had even dined on the fillets with me, eschewing for once his vegetarian diet. Jeff reminded me of the fish he'd caught down at Fort De Soto, back in March. Then we talked about my counseling sessions with Patricia Bigelow and the letter I'd written to my mother.

"I'd like to read it sometime," Jeff said, "if you wouldn't mind."

"Of course, you can. In fact, I *want* you to."

"Do you think the counseling helps?"

"I do. Of course, I'm still hurting about Brian. It's only been a couple of months since he...you know. But I'm not feeling quite as sad as I did back in March. Talking about my feelings with Patricia eases things, but what about *you*? Have you spoken to your parents since last Sunday?"

"Actually, I called them last night, but we didn't talk about the gay business. I had something more important to discuss with them."

"What was that?"

Jeff cleared his throat. "I saw a doctor at the IU infirmary on Thursday."

"What for?"

"Ever since I returned from Florida, I've felt tired no matter how much I sleep. A couple of times, I woke up in the middle of the night all sweaty. And remember that bump on my neck, the one you noticed down in Florida?"

"Yeah, why?"

"Now I have bumps in my armpits too."

Uh-oh.

"Are you sick?"

"Maybe. The doctor I saw at the infirmary didn't know, but he referred me to a specialist at the IU teaching hospital in Indianapolis. I have an appointment there next Thursday afternoon."

"What kind of specialist?"

"An oncologist—a cancer doctor."

My stomach clenched. "Cancer?"

"Don't worry, it might be something as simple as an infection they can clear up with antibiotics. Or it could be mononucleosis—a lot of guys our age come down with it."

"But why a cancer doctor? I don't understand."

"There's a possibility it could be something worse, a disease called Hodgkin's lymphoma."

I fingered my phone while my brain buzzed like a hornet's nest. Jeff might have *cancer*? How could it be? He already had enough trouble on his plate, dealing with his parents' reaction to his sexuality. The last thing he needed was a health crisis.

"Don't panic," Jeff said. "Like I told you, it's probably something less serious, but they need to rule out Hodgkin's as a part of diagnosing what's wrong with me. Understand?"

Aye-yi-yi...

"I guess," I said, "but promise you'll call me after your appointment. I want to know what's going on as soon as you do."

CHAPTER TWENTY-FIVE

Patricia Bigelow handed me a box of tissues to wipe my dripping eyes. Outside her windows, an afternoon storm raged. Lightning flashed, and thunder rumbled so loudly the building shook. Brian's photo and his mom's letter rested in my lap.

Patricia brought the tip of her index finger to her temple while she gazed into my eyes.

"I know people have told you not to feel guilty about Brian's suicide, that it wasn't your fault. And I'm sure they were trying to be helpful, but you need to understand something: It's quite normal to feel guilty when we grieve over the loss of someone we cared for."

I lowered my gaze and nodded.

"But just because you *feel* guilty about Brian's death doesn't mean you *are* guilty of causing it. From what you've told me, Brian was an emotional mess even before you two met, so don't assume your withdrawal from him was the sole reason he killed himself. It may have been a factor, but I suspect a group of issues led him to take his life."

I sniffled and squirmed in my chair. "Maybe if I'd been kinder to Brian when he told me he loved me, this wouldn't have happened."

Patricia grimaced.

"You're making a mistake in thinking you could have prevented Brian's suicide. We experience guilt and blame in deaths like his because we want to believe there's a rational order to life, that we can control what happens to us and others around us. But in reality, we don't. I know that's a scary concept, but it's true."

I shook my head. "I can't help but believe Brian would be alive today if I'd offered him some sort of compromise. Why did I have to be so rigid?"

Patricia crossed her knee with an ankle.

"Let's talk about the difference between guilt and regret. Guilt occurs when we commit an act we know is wrong *while* we do it, like shoplifting or telling a lie. Regret, on the other hand, is an emotion we experience when we look back and feel we should have behaved differently. Regret differs from guilt in that we didn't know or feel at the time what we did was wrong.

"In the situation with Brian, when you deprived him of your affection, you had no idea your action might trigger his suicide. You thought you'd simply corrected a misconception on Brian's part and were right to do so. You'd have been terribly cruel had you pretended to love him when you didn't."

I blinked a time or two while I pondered all Patricia had told me. "I hear what you're saying, but how do I deal with these feelings? I don't care whether you call them guilt or regret, they still gnaw at me."

Patricia leaned toward me and gripped the back of my wrist.

"Remember when we talked about forgiving your mother?"

"Of course."

"When it comes to Brian's death, you have to forgive yourself."

*

On a Wednesday afternoon, a few days after my fourth meeting with Patricia Bigelow, Mason and I sat on a blanket by the shore of Silver Lake, west of Tallahassee. We had just run three miles on a trail winding through a palmetto and pine forest, and now our T-shirts were damp with sweat. We both swigged from bottles of apple juice while watching shadows grow long as the sun began its descent behind the western tree line. A team of wood ducks bobbed on the lake's placid surface.

In recent days, my brain had churned nonstop, as well as my stomach, partly because of my meeting with Patricia, but also because of my last phone call with Jeff. His appointment with the specialist in Indianapolis would be the next day, and though I hoped for the best, I also feared the worst might occur, and the possibility Jeff might have cancer had torn me up inside.

Even the run I'd taken with Mason failed to calm my nerves, and now I chewed a hangnail while listening to him talk about his workday. He described a small bridge he was designing when I interrupted him midsentence.

"There's something important I have to tell you."

"What?"

After I described my phone call from Jeff, Mason frowned and shook his head.

"I'm sorry, Jakub. I know how close you guys are, and I sure hope he'll be okay. You must be going nuts."

I nodded. "I feel like some creature's chewing on my guts. Between classes today, I made a sandwich for my lunch but couldn't eat it. If I'd taken a bite and swallowed, I probably would have spit it back up."

Mason brought his hand to the back of my neck and squeezed. "Life's tossed a ton of shit your way lately, hasn't it? Between Jeff's situation and the whole business with Brian, I'm surprised you haven't lost your mind."

I lowered my gaze to the blanket while my stomach roiled.

"How's your counseling going?" Mason asked. "Is it helping?"

"I think so," I said, before describing my sessions with Patricia in detail. I had never told Mason about my mother's disappearance, but now I explained what had happened and how badly I suffered as a boy. I talked about the letter I'd written to my mother, and how good it felt to express my anger toward her. And then I talked about Brian's suicide and how Patricia said it was perfectly normal for me to feel guilty, but I shouldn't blame myself for Brian's death.

Mason kept his hand on my neck. "We've talked about this before: Brian was a train wreck looking for a place to happen. You happened to stand in the spot he chose."

Mason's knees crackled when he rose and extended a hand to me. "Come on, roomie, let's go home. I know you said food doesn't interest you right now, but tonight I'll make us cheese omelets stuffed with veggies. I'll dash a little hot sauce on them, and they'll taste so good you won't be able to resist."

*

Thursday afternoon, when I returned home from classes, I pulled my phone from my pocket and called Jeff's number, but he didn't answer. I ran my fingers through my hair while pacing the living room floor, wondering where Jeff was and what the Indianapolis specialist might have said.

Maybe, as Jeff had suggested, the swollen lymph nodes in his body were the result of an infection like mononucleosis. I recalled when one of my friends in high school had contracted mono, and how his lymph nodes grew to the size of Ping-Pong balls. Maybe all

Jeff needed was bed rest and antibiotics to shake off his illness. But what if he didn't have mono? If he had Hodgkin's lymphoma, was it treatable? And if so, how?

Despite my Lutheran upbringing, I was not a religious person. I had long ago abandoned my belief in God. But I'd heard the concept of "karma" discussed by my Philosophy professor, and I knew millions of Hindus and Buddhists believed our actions determine how our futures unfold. If we treated others badly, negative things would eventually happen to us. And then I wondered if Jeff's illness—if it turned out to be serious—was karma's payback for how I had wronged Brian.

Okay, perhaps Patricia was right, maybe I wasn't to *blame* for Brian's suicide. But that still didn't mean my callousness toward him was defensible, and now karma might make me pay the most unbearable price I could imagine for my behavior—losing Jeff.

I went to the bedroom and pulled Brian's photo from the manila envelope in my bureau drawer. Then I lay on my bed with my back resting against the headboard. I gazed at Brian's handsome face and studied the merit badges on his Eagle Scout sash— there were dozens of them—and I noticed how the photographer's butterfly lighting had reflected in Brian's eyes.

"Forgive me," I whispered.

I closed my eyes and hoped I might hear Brian's voice, telling me he would grant my plea, but of course I heard nothing other than traffic passing on Tennessee Street. So, I put Brian's photo away. I lay flat on my mattress with my face buried in a pillow, and within minutes, I fell asleep.

When I woke, the sky had darkened, and the bedroom door was shut. In the living room, I found Mason reading a newspaper on the sofa with the aid of our floor lamp. He still wore his office attire, but had kicked off his shoes.

"Hey," he said when he looked up. "I tried to be quiet so I wouldn't disturb you."

I pointed to my phone on the coffee table. "Did anyone call me while I was asleep?"

"Not since I got home, and that was forty-five minutes ago."

I nodded and yawned. "I'm not a nap-taker, but I've been so stressed out lately, I must've worn myself out."

"Any word from Jeff?"

I shook my head. "I guess I'll try phoning him again."

Mason set aside his newspaper. "Do you want me to go for a walk or something? I don't mind if you want to be alone when you make the call."

"No, stay where you are."

My hand trembled when I called Jeff's number, but again he did not answer. Then I stared out of the bedroom window and rubbed my jaw with the flat of my hand. *Where are you, and what did the doctor say?*

In the kitchen, I pulled a can of beer from the fridge and peeled off the pop top. I took a sip and swished the cold liquid around the inside of my mouth.

"Hey, bubba," Mason called from the sofa. "Grab a beer for me and come sit on the sofa."

I did as he'd requested, and after he took a gulp of beer, he reached for my shoulder and squeezed. Then he made a face.

"You're as tense as a treed raccoon; no wonder you needed a nap."

I shrugged. "How can I relax when I can't find out what's going on with Jeff?"

"I know what you need," Mason said.

"What's that?"

"A back rub." Mason tugged at my shirt collar. "Take this off and lie face down. I'll get you loosened up in no time."

Moments later, Mason knelt astride me on the sofa. He had removed his own shirt, and now I smelled his body odor while he kneaded the back of my neck with his fingers.

"That feels great," I said.

Mason worked on my left trapezius. "I took classes in massage when I was in Gainesville. I never got my license, but my technique's pretty good. It's all about pinpointing areas of tension and making them relax."

"I've felt distracted and nervous all day long," I said while Mason moved to my right trapezius and squeezed it. "When I rode my bike home for lunch, I nearly ran into a parked car. I'm lucky I didn't split my skull open."

Mason hissed. "You'd better settle down before you hurt yourself."

I groaned when Mason pressed his thumb into a particular spot just above my shoulder blade.

"That feel good?" he asked.

"Wonderful, actually. I could do this for hours."

Mason chuckled.

"Let me ask you something," I said. "If you told your folks you've had sex with guys, how do you think they'd react?"

Mason stopped rubbing for a moment. "I don't really know, why?"

I explained the situation with Jeff's parents while Mason massaged my temples with his fingertips. "Peru's a conservative place—I get that. And the Brucellis are devout Catholics. But I've spent a lot of time around Jeff's mom and dad—I know them pretty well—and I never thought they'd react the way they did."

"He's their only child, right?"

"Yeah."

"If Jeff spends his life with you, they'll never have grandchildren. I'm sure it's a big disappointment for them."

"It wasn't for *my* dad when I told him."

Mason massaged the crown of my head, sending tendrils of pleasure down my spine and into my limbs. "Consider yourself lucky," he said. "Like Jeff's hometown, Jacksonville Beach is an intolerant place. Folks there still think homosexuality's something to be ashamed of."

"But *you* don't feel that way, do you?"

"Of course not, but I've never been a conformist. I don't give a rat's ass what people think about my private life. I'll do as I please, and if they don't like my choices, *they* have a problem, not me."

Mason lifted his beer from the coffee table and took a sip. Then he commenced kneading either side of my spine, using his thumbs and the flats of his hands, producing little grunts from me. Already I felt more relaxed than I had in many days. The tension inside me had melted under Mason's attentions.

"Would you have the balls to live as an openly gay man?" I asked him.

"That would depend on where I'm living. In Jacksonville Beach? No way. But in most American cities, people don't even *care* if you're gay. It's like having freckles on your nose."

While Mason worked my spine, I closed my eyes and tried to imagine sharing an apartment in St. Petersburg with Jeff, one with a view of the Sunshine Skyway Bridge and Tampa Bay. We'd have flower boxes on our balcony and a comfortable sofa where we could hold each other while we watched TV in the evening. Every Christmas, we would send out cards signed by both of us, and—

My phone chimed.

"You want to get that?" Mason asked. He climbed from atop me and the sofa springs creaked.

My heart banged against my rib cage while I brought the phone to my lips.

"Jeff?"

"Hi, Jakub."

"How was your appointment? What did the doctor say?"

Jeff cleared his throat. "He doesn't know what's wrong with me yet, but he took a biopsy from one of the nodes in my neck; he's sending it to a pathology lab for examination. I have a follow-up appointment next Wednesday; he should know something by then."

"What else did he say?"

"Not a whole lot, just Hodgkin's is often seen in males my age."

I squeezed my phone so hard I thought it might shatter. "Do you think this doctor knows what he's doing?"

"Of course. IU's teaching hospital is the best in the state."

I shifted my weight from one leg to the other while I chewed my lips. "I wish I were there in Bloomington so I could hold you."

"I'd like that too."

"Have you called your parents yet?"

"I will as soon as we're done talking. I wanted to fill you in first, because I knew you'd be waiting for my call."

We chatted for a few more minutes before Jeff told me he had to go. Then I stood there in the living room, staring out of the window and feeling as if all the energy had drained from my body. What would happen if Jeff's doctor discovered he had cancer?

"What did he say?" Mason asked.

I returned to the sofa and described the phone conversation.

Mason grimaced. "That doesn't sound too good."

"No, and I'm so shook up, I'm about to jump out of my skin."

Mason wrapped an arm around my shoulders and pulled me to him. I felt the bulk of his muscles while I trembled.

"What'll I do if I lose Jeff? I won't ever find another guy like him."

"Don't be so pessimistic," Mason said. "Maybe it's not cancer, and even if it is, Jeff's doctor can probably help him lick it."

For a moment, I considered taking a bus trip to Bloomington, even if it meant I had to sleep on Jeff's sofa a few nights. But then I thought about the fact Jeff's roommates didn't know he was gay, and they'd probably wonder who the hell I was, and why I was there. The whole situation would be uncomfortable, plus Jeff and I would have no privacy.

I would have to remain in Tallahassee and fret.

CHAPTER TWENTY-SIX

The days following Jeff's phone call crawled by. I attended my classes and studied, and Mason and I kept up our exercise regimen, but I felt as if I were only going through the motions of living without feeling much. At least once an hour, I'd pull my cell phone out of my pocket and stare at a photo of Jeff I kept there, a shot I'd taken at Manatee Springs State Park. In the photo, a shirtless Jeff was laughing at something I'd said, and his beautiful smile engulfed me.

Sunday night, when Jeff phoned me again, he sounded listless and didn't have much to say. He told me the weather had warmed up in Bloomington, and flowers were blossoming on campus. He talked about his studies, and I spoke of mine, but we didn't discuss the most important topic occupying our thoughts—Jeff's health.

At the end of our conversation, Jeff said, "My appointment on Wednesday is at two p.m., so I should be on the road back to Bloomington by three. I'll call you then and let you know what the doctor said."

Now, early on Tuesday night, Mason and I played Twenty-One on a campus basketball court. The sun had set minutes before. The evening air felt cool, and we both wore sweatshirts.

Mason, of course, was a far better athlete than I, and he quickly took a lead I knew I'd never catch up to, but I didn't care. At least the game kept my mind off Jeff and his appointment the next day. The *thunk-thunk* of the basketball against concrete pretty much drove any complex thoughts from my head, and I focused only on defending Mason's attempts at making layups. His mop of curly hair bounced about his shoulders while he dribbled here and there, and I marveled at his agility.

When our game ended, with a score of twenty-one to nine, we played another, which I also lost badly, but all the running about got my cardiovascular system pumping, and by the end of the second game, I had relaxed somewhat. We lay down on the spongy turf at the edge of the court and stared up at the darkening sky while our breathing slowed.

"You kicked my ass," I told Mason. "You're too damned good to play someone as slow and uncoordinated as me."

"You're not so bad. It's just I'm really good."

"And so *humble*."

Mason chuckled. "I played point guard in high school, my junior and senior years. Our coach was amazing; he taught me all kinds of moves."

I shook my head. "I never had the confidence to try out for a team sport in school. I don't have any natural athletic ability—absolutely none. As a kid, when I played Little League, I had to work twice as hard to be half as good as the next guy."

Mason turned his head and looked at me with his forehead crinkled. "Are you feeling sorry for yourself? If so, you should cut it out. You have a lot going for you—you're smart and good-looking, and people like you as soon as they meet you."

"Who does?"

"Me, for one, and Jessica thinks you're sweet. Jeff's obviously crazy about you, so don't run yourself down."

He's right, Mazur. Dump the pity party.

"Speaking of Jessica," I said, "will you continue seeing her?"

"Why not? She's pretty, and I like her personality, but when it comes to sex, I'll just have to be patient. In the meantime..."

"What?"

Mason's gaze drilled into mine. "I know you and Jeff have an agreement, but can't you make an exception once in a while?"

I thought of Jeff, and how badly he'd feel if he learned Mason and I were having sex. I had a pact with Jeff, one I considered sacred. And Jeff had troubles enough without worrying about my commitment to him.

"I can't do that," I told Mason.

He shook his head, but then a grin crept across his face when he ruffled my hair with his fingertips.

"All right, Saint Mazur, but if you should happen to change your mind, let me know."

*

Wednesday afternoon, I arrived home from classes a little before three. After I locked up my bike at the rack under my building's stairwell, I bounded up the steps and entered the apartment, anxious about Jeff's impending phone call. I guzzled apple juice from a bottle I kept in the fridge and then I paced here and there, wondering exactly what Jeff's doctor had told him. I kept telling myself, *it'll all be okay, you're probably worrying for no reason.* But I couldn't help but stew.

For almost a year, Jeff had been the center of my world, and I had assumed he would always be there for me. But would he?

I tried to focus on a reading assignment for my Behavioral Psychology class, but every time I gazed at the text, the words on the page seemed to blur. I tossed the book aside and strode back and forth between the front door and the bedroom, cracking my knuckles and raking my fingers through my hair. I thought about drinking a beer to calm my nerves, but decided against it because I wanted to be sober when I received the news, whatever it would be.

I walked to the front windows and stared into the street, where a pair of students, a boy and girl, leaned against a car fender. The boy had his arm across the girl's shoulders and the two looked awfully happy while they conversed, about what I couldn't hear. But they seemed as if they didn't have a worry in the world.

Why couldn't *my* life be like theirs?

My phone chimed at a quarter till four, and my heart leaped into my throat when I answered, but the caller was only a rental agent who handled my apartment lease, wanting to know if I intended to renew when it expired at the end of May.

"I probably will," I told her, "but give me a week to get back to you with a definite answer."

"That's fine, but you should know there's a waiting list for units in your building. If you don't renew, someone else will snap it up in a heartbeat, and I doubt you'll find as good a deal in any other complex near campus."

After I rang off, I made a mental note to discuss the situation with Mason over dinner that night. If I renewed the lease, he could stay in the apartment until Jeff and I came to Tallahassee in the fall. Then Mason could move elsewhere.

I glanced at the wall clock in the living room. Now the time was approaching 3:30, and I was close to going nuts. My T-shirt was damp in the armpits, and my pulse galloped. I dropped to the floor and performed twenty push-ups, the muscles in my shoulders and back flexing. I counted the push-ups out loud and my voice sounded pinched when I did so.

Come on, Jeff. Where are you, and what do you know?

He finally called at ten till four, and when I heard his voice, I immediately knew something wasn't right. Jeff sounded as though he hadn't slept in days.

"Bad news—the laboratory found cancer cells in my biopsy."

Oh, shit.

"How serious is it?"

"It's hard for the doctor to tell how far the cancer may have spread. He took more biopsies, from both sides of my neck and my armpits. The lab will examine those for cancer cells too. But even if the cancer's not present in those places, I'll have to start treatment real soon."

"What *kind* of treatment?"

"A combination of chemotherapy and radiation." Jeff whimpered for a few moments before he continued in a shaky voice. "It's going to be rough, Jakub. And to be honest, I'm frightened out of my wits."

I slammed my fist against a wall, so hard it hurt. "God, I'm so sorry. Is there anything I can do? I mean, I'll come up there tomorrow if it'll make you feel better. I can miss classes for a few days."

"Don't do that. The doctor said I should plan on moving back to Peru when the treatments start. My folks will have to drive me to and from the Indy hospital, because I'll be too weak to drive myself. And I'll need looked after constantly."

"What about your classes at IU?"

"I start treatment after my final exams, in early May."

I asked Jeff how long the treatments would last.

"At least four months, maybe more."

"Four *months*? Why so long?"

"They'll have to make sure they've rid me of all the cancer cells in my lymphatic system, and that will require multiple visits to Indianapolis for chemo and radiation."

Was I sinking in a bog? How could this have happened? Jeff had seemed so healthy when he visited in Florida in March. We had made so many plans for our summer and next school year, but now it seemed Jeff would fight for his life instead.

I was so light-headed, I sat on the living room floor. I rested my back against the wall behind me, and my voice trembled when I spoke.

"Are you going to be okay? Are *we* going to be okay?"

Jeff let out his breath. "I sure hope so—only time will tell—but right now I need to call my folks. They're waiting to hear from me, and I know they're worried sick."

Moments later, after Jeff told me goodbye, I remained on the floor, clasping my biceps in my hands while I blubbered and tears streamed down my cheeks. Jeff was the most important person in the world to me. How would I go on living if I lost him? And why had fate chosen Jeff to plague with such an awful disease? Why not somebody else?

I pounded my fist on the linoleum.

All right, Mazur, get a grip on yourself. For once, do something. You are not helpless in this situation.

I rose to my feet, still feeling a bit wobbly, but not as badly as before. I wiped my dripping eyes and blew my nose into a paper towel. Then I reached for my phone and looked up the number for the Greyhound station, already knowing what I needed to do.

Despite Jeff's protestations, the next day I would take a bus to Bloomington. I'd hold Jeff in my arms and tell him I loved him. And I would stand at his side when he underwent his treatments. Weren't those my responsibilities as his partner in life? And if Jeff's parents didn't approve of my presence, too damned bad.

God or karma, or whatever deity's running this crazy world I live in, you robbed me of my mother, and then took my best friend, but you will not steal my lover.

Not if I have a say in the matter.

CHAPTER TWENTY-SEVEN

The bus left Tallahassee at 6:00 a.m., heading first to Montgomery, then Birmingham, and on to Nashville. We rode in darkness for an hour or so before the sun crested the eastern horizon. The bus was half empty, occupied mostly by older folks traveling in couples. I sat alone in a window seat, feeling half asleep while we cruised northward on US Highway 231.

I had spent the previous evening packing a suitcase, my backpack, and a duffel bag, all now stowed in the bus's luggage compartment. I made phone calls to Jeff and my dad, and though Jeff still thought I should stay in Tallahassee, he caved to my insistence.

"In Bloomington, you can crash on our living room sofa," he told me. "My roomies won't mind. And I'll let my folks know you'll stay with us in Peru this summer. They might not like it, now they know we're gay, but I'll handle things."

The end of spring semester was only two weeks off, and I assured my dad I would return to Tallahassee to sit for final exams when the time came. "I'm taking my books and lecture notes with me, and I'll have plenty of time to study. Plus, right now in classes we're only reviewing materials I've already read. Don't worry, I'll be prepared."

Mason had driven me to the bus station in the darkness, and after we unloaded my bags from his truck bed, he gave me a hug and kissed my cheek, right in the middle of the station's parking lot, which I thought was awfully sweet.

"Tell Jeff I said best of luck, and you take care of yourself up there."

Mason and I had agreed I would renew my present lease on the apartment. He'd occupy the place and pay the rent during my absence in Peru, and depending on how things worked out up there, perhaps I'd return with Jeff in the fall or, God forbid, if I came back to Tallahassee by myself, I'd share the apartment with Mason.

Now, on the bus, the terrain we passed was little more than pine forests and farmlands where cotton, soybeans, and corn grew. Occasionally, we stopped in a small town to drop off or pick up passengers, and the bus's air brakes would screech. In Birmingham, I grabbed a grilled cheese sandwich in the station's café, and then napped all the way to Nashville with my cheek resting against the window.

At the Nashville station, a curious art deco structure painted electric blue, I switched my luggage to a bus bound for Bloomington and boarded right around 2:00 p.m. The bus was crowded, and I sat next to a chubby girl close to my age, with acne and hairy forearms. She spoke with a drawl so thick I had a hard time understanding some of her words, and I resisted her repeated attempts to draw me into conversation. Instead, I studied from a textbook, using a yellow highlighting pen to mark passages I thought might be important for my exam.

We made stops in Evansville and a few other smaller towns. The trip seemed endless, and when we visited a town called Washington, I asked the bus driver how long it might be until we reached Bloomington.

"Less than an hour; we'll be there by seven."

I phoned Jeff to let him know when to pick me up, and I sent my dad a text message, letting him know where I was and how smoothly everything had gone.

"Good luck up there," he texted back. "And give Jeff my best. I'll think of you both in the days ahead."

Good old Dad.

Bloomington's downtown was low slung, with leafy streets and two or three-story brick structures dating to the Nineteenth Century. But the bus terminal looked brand new, a sleek stone and glass building.

Jeff waited for me when my bus ground to a halt in a covered berth. He wore a light jacket and blue jeans, and though he appeared weary, I still thought he looked handsome as hell. I didn't hesitate to wrap my arms around his neck and pull him close to me while passengers milled around us. The evening air was cool, and I shivered in my T-shirt.

"It means so much to have you here," Jeff whispered.

After I collected my bags from the bus's luggage compartment, I tossed them into the Impala's back seat, and we cruised toward the university, passing through a neighborhood of modest homes with mature trees and well-tended yards. I held Jeff's right hand while he steered with his left.

"How was the bus trip?"

"Long and none-too-memorable. We must've made twenty stops along the way, and somewhere around Evansville, my legs went numb because I'd sat for so long."

Jeff shared a two-bedroom house with two roommates, Craig and Tyler, both Peru natives. The dwelling had a covered front porch, asbestos shingle siding, a few spindly shrubs, and a weed-and-dirt lawn. Jeff had the smaller bedroom to himself, while his roommates shared the larger one.

Craig was blond and bearded and looked like he might have played linebacker in high school. His voice was a booming baritone.

Tyler reminded me of Brian with his handsome face and slender build. He was preparing a meal of spaghetti and garlic bread, and the smell of cooking food made my stomach growl. My grilled cheese sandwich had long ago lost its punch.

"There's plenty of food," Tyler told me. "So, if you're hungry, please join us. We'll eat in about fifteen minutes."

I stowed my bags in Jeff's room, a cramped space furnished with a double bed and a bureau.

Jeff pointed to a folding aluminum cot with a thin mattress leaning against one wall. "I bought it at a thrift shop this afternoon, so you wouldn't have to sleep on the sofa. We'll set it up with sheets and a blanket later tonight. I know it's nothing fancy, but we can close the door and have a bit of privacy."

The four of us gathered around a porcelain-topped table, and the food was pretty tasty. I shoveled forkfuls of noodles and meat sauce into my mouth, while offering descriptions of my trip.

"Thirteen hours?" Tyler said, while tearing a slice of garlic bread in two. "That's a lot of bus riding."

I shrugged. "Exams at FSU are two weeks from now, so it gave me plenty of time to study."

"Yeah," Tyler said, "with exams coming so soon, why'd you decide to take a break from classes?"

I shrugged. "I needed a change of atmosphere."

Craig stirred the food on his plate with a fork. "Indiana women tend to be on the hefty side, but I hear the girls down in Florida are slinky. Is it true?"

I nodded. "FSU's full of babes. You'd like it there, I think."

"Do you have a girl?" Tyler asked.

I lowered my gaze. "No one special."

"But you date?"

"Stop asking him so many questions," Jeff interjected. "The guy just spent a whole day traveling."

Tyler shrank back and scowled at Jeff. "Whoa, buddy, I'm only trying to be sociable."

"He's tired," Jeff said. "Let him enjoy his dinner."

When I looked up from my plate, both Tyler and Craig stared at Jeff with narrowed eyes.

"Is something wrong with you tonight?" Craig asked Jeff. "You seem kind of cranky."

Jeff lowered his gaze. He fiddled with a slice of garlic bread for a moment and then looked up at me before turning his gaze to Craig. "I need to tell you guys something—there's a reason Jakub is here, and it's not for a vacation."

Uh, oh...

"I'm sick; I have Hodgkin's lymphoma. Do you know what that is?"

Craig and Tyler shook their heads.

"It's cancer in my lymphatic system. I'll receive treatments for it at the IU teaching hospital this summer, and Jakub will look after me until I'm better."

The faces of Jeff's roommates turned as pale as eggshells. Both of them stared at Jeff as if he were a specter.

"It's going to be rough," Jeff said. "The doctor said I won't have much energy. I'll be able to read and watch TV, but that's about all."

"Are you going to be okay?" Tyler asked in a squeaky voice.

"I sure hope so."

Craig rubbed the side of his face with the flat of his hand. "Do your folks know about this?"

Jeff nodded.

"They must be going nuts," Craig said. "I know *my* parents would be."

"Mom's taking it pretty hard," Jeff said. "She lost her mother last summer, and now she has to deal with this. They wanted me to come home right away, but I insisted on staying here till I take my finals. Then I'll move home, and Jakub will join me there, once his exams are finished."

Tyler looked at me with a puzzled expression. "Are you taking nursing courses down in Florida?"

I looked at my plate while my pulse quickened. What should I say? In desperation, I turned to Jeff, and when his gaze met mine, he turned down one corner of his mouth. Then he looked at his roommates.

"As long as we're getting things out in the open, I need to tell you guys something else."

"What's that?" Tyler asked.

"Jakub and I are gay. We've been boyfriends since last summer, when I lived in Florida, and he wants to be with me when I go through this illness. I know you are both surprised, but I want you to treat him with respect while he's here."

Craig put his fork on his plate and licked his lips.

"What is it?" Jeff asked.

"Next, you're going to tell us you're a Martian, right?"

Laughter erupted around the table, and the tension in the room disappeared like a puff of smoke from a campfire.

"Seriously, man," Craig said to Jeff. "We've been friends forever, and the fact you're gay...well, it doesn't change anything between us."

"Ditto here," Tyler added, "and now I don't have to keep trying to set you up with women."

*

Hours later, Jeff and I lay in his bed in the darkness, holding each other. My head rested on Jeff's sternum and I listened to his heartbeat.

"Craig and Tyler took things pretty well, I think," I whispered.

"They did. I hadn't planned on telling them, but it seemed the right time. With what I'm facing, I can't hide things. I just hope it didn't make you uncomfortable."

"I was fine. And you know, I think the more people we tell, the easier it'll be."

Jeff stroked my cheek with his thumb. "You're probably right. Once the words left my mouth at the dinner table, I felt a huge sense of relief, like I'd put down a fifty-pound dumbbell I'd carried around for the longest time. Why didn't I tell them sooner?"

*

Three days after my arrival in Bloomington, I had fallen into a comfortable routine. Jeff and his roommates always left for classes first thing in the morning, leaving me alone in the house. After a simple breakfast, I brewed a cup of instant coffee and plopped onto the living room sofa with my books and notes. Around noon, Jeff returned to the house and we shared lunch, usually soup and sandwiches with a glass of milk. Then Jeff returned to campus while I got back to studying. Around 4:00 p.m., I slipped into my gym clothes and took a half-hour run on the IU campus track.

Evenings, someone volunteered to cook dinner, and someone else offered to clean up. I gave Jeff money for my share of the food, and his roommates seemed fine with the arrangement. And I tried to be as helpful as I could, cleaning the bathroom fixtures, taking out the trash, and vacuuming the rugs.

My second day in residence, Tyler came home midafternoon, and after he grabbed a bag of potato chips from a kitchen cupboard, he sat beside me on the sofa.

"How do you like Bloomington so far?" he asked, in between munches.

"It's a nice town. People seem friendly, and the campus is beautiful. What kind of stone are the buildings made from?"

"Mostly granite. Huge quarries are right outside the city limits. Stonecutting was a major industry here for many years, but not so much now."

Tyler told me his parents owned a dairy farm, and he was the first in his family to attend college.

"Will you work in your parents' business after you graduate?"

He shrugged. "I think they expect it, but I'm not sure I'll want to. Living in Bloomington has changed my world view. It's not all about cows and drinking beer in cornfields."

He asked about Fort De Soto Park, and after I described it for him, he said, "It sounds like a magical place. Maybe one day I'll pay a visit."

"Ever been to Florida?"

He shook his head. "My family doesn't travel, because a dairy farm requires constant attention. I once visited Chicago for a long weekend on a school trip, and that's about it. Compared to you, I'm probably a rube."

"Hey, my bus ride up here's the longest journey I've ever made, so we're in the same boat when it comes to seeing the country."

Tyler lowered his gaze and fiddled with the edge of his potato chip bag before returning his gaze to me. "Mind if I ask you something personal?"

"What's that?"

"When did you first suspect you were gay?"

I rubbed my chin with a knuckle while I pondered Tyler's question.

"I think in sixth grade, my first year in middle school. We had to dress for PE in the boys' locker room, and I grew excited watching other guys change."

"Until Jeff told me and Craig, I'd never have guessed he was gay. All the time we were growing up, he never did or said anything that made me suspect he liked guys. But he sure seems to care about you."

I nodded. "We're pretty tight. Jeff's more important to me than anyone else in the world—it's why I'm here. I couldn't stand the thought of losing him."

"This Hodgkin's disease...it's serious stuff?"

I nodded.

"Well," Tyler said, "I'm spending this summer with my folks in Peru, so I'll be around if you need help with anything. And look, there's not much to do in our town, but you can always hang out with me if Jeff's resting or whatever. We'll drink beer and cruise in my dad's pickup truck."

I chuckled and shook my head. "*That* sounds exciting."

"Hey, in a town like Peru, you make your own fun. It's either that or watch TV till your brain rots. But tell me, how bad do you think this illness will be for Jeff? Can he stay active this summer?"

"Before I left Tallahassee, I did Internet research on treatments for Hodgkin's. The chemotherapy's taxing, and I don't think Jeff will do cartwheels while it's going on."

Tyler wiped his fingers on one leg of his blue jeans. "What are his chances? Do you think he'll...?"

I drew a breath and let it out. "From what I've read, the survival rates for guys Jeff's age are decent.

It varies from patient to patient, of course, so there's no way to tell for certain. But I think it's important we give him all the emotional support we can in the months ahead."

"Have you met Jeff's parents?"

"Down in Florida, yeah, when they were campground hosts in the park. We got along pretty well, but at the time, they didn't know Jeff and I were boyfriends."

"Do they now?"

I nodded.

"Are they okay with it?"

I explained how Jeff had broken the news two weeks before. "He thinks they'll accept things eventually, but it'll take a while. They're deeply religious, and I doubt Catholic dogma approves of two guys loving each other. Plus, I'm not sure how they'll feel about me living under their roof either."

"They don't know you're coming?"

"Not yet."

Tyler rearranged his limbs while rubbing his lips together. "I've known the Brucellis all my life. They're kind people, and I can't imagine them saying you can't stay with them. But if they say no, what'll you do?"

CHAPTER TWENTY-EIGHT

The last week of April passed quickly. It seemed I had only arrived in Bloomington when the month came to an end, and I had to pack for my bus trip back to Tallahassee. The thought of leaving Jeff made my stomach hurt, but I had no choice. I needed to sit for my exams, or the entire spring semester would be a waste, something too nonsensical to even consider.

The afternoon before I left, Jeff and I made love in his bedroom while his roommates weren't home. Then, after we cleaned ourselves up, we took a long walk through the IU campus, where red and white tulips blossomed at the school's main gate. All around us, students wearing backpacks on their shoulders scurried along sidewalks, passing between the university's Gothic stone buildings. The sun shone in a cloudless sky, and the afternoon air smelled fragrant. Both of us wore T-shirts; we strolled with our hands in the hip pockets of our blue jeans.

"Are you going to be okay while I'm gone?" I asked Jeff.

"I'll survive, but I sure hate to see you go."

"I know; I don't want to leave, but..."

"Don't apologize; your exams are important, so go down there and take care of business. Then get your ass back to Bloomington."

"Yes, boyfriend."

Jeff smiled while keeping his gaze on the sidewalk before us. "I know you're disappointed we can't spend summer at Fort De Soto. I'd like nothing better."

"Hey, we'll be together in Peru, and we'll find stuff to do in between your treatments. I'll have all summer to kick your butt in Scrabble and gin rummy, and I'm already making a list of movies I want to watch on your laptop. We'll make things work."

We encountered a girl Jeff knew from the journalism college, and after Jeff introduced her, the two of them talked about upcoming exams and what they'd do with their summers. Jeff did not mention his illness or the treatments he'd undergo in Indianapolis, he only said he'd spend his summer in Peru.

"Maybe I'll get a job flipping burgers at a fast food joint," he joked.

After the girl went on her way, and we resumed our walk, I asked Jeff, "How many people do you plan to tell about your cancer?"

"As few as possible. Why?"

"You're not ashamed of being sick, are you?"

"No, but I don't want people dumping pity on me. Can you understand that?"

"Of course."

Jeff pointed to a bench. "Let's sit a few minutes."

After we did, Jeff rested his forearms on his knees and stared at his shoes for the longest time, and I could almost hear his brain fluids churn. When he finally turned his gaze to me, his voice quivered when he spoke.

"These cancer treatments are going to be rough, and I need to know something: Do you promise you'll be there with me every day? Because I don't know if I can survive this shit without you."

"I'll be there every step of the way," I said. "You can count on that."

*

My bus ride back to Tallahassee was monotonous and never-ending. I did my best to pass the time by studying, but found it hard to concentrate on my books. My thoughts kept returning to my last glimpse of Jeff, at the Bloomington station, where he stood by himself in the early morning darkness, waving to me while my bus backed out of its berth. His face looked so forlorn it made me want to weep, but instead I forced myself to smile and wave through the window. I even blew Jeff a kiss.

By the time I made it to Tallahassee, the sun had already set, and Mason met me inside the terminal. He greeted me with a hug and insisted on carrying my duffel bag while we strolled to his truck. The early evening air felt far warmer than Bloomington's, and sweat beaded on my upper lip while we tossed my luggage into the truck's bed.

"It was boring as hell," I told Mason when he asked how my bus ride had gone. "But I'm really glad I made the visit to Bloomington."

"How's Jeff doing?"

"He's scared shitless, and I don't blame him. The next few months are going to be awful."

"I guess you'll go back up there, once your exams are finished?"

I nodded. "I may spend all summer in Peru, depending on how things go."

"Well, I have news," Mason said while he steered us down Monroe Street. "Jessica spent the night with me Saturday."

"How did you make *that* happen?"

"A smooth approach and two bottles of Spätlese."

I shook my head. "You're a crafty dog. Was the sex what you'd hoped for?"

"Pretty damned good, actually. I didn't know this till Saturday, but she had a long-term boyfriend during college, a guy ten years older than her, an FSU faculty member. Seems he gave Jessica quite the bedroom education before she found out he was married and had two kids."

I winced. "No *wonder* she was skittish about having sex with you."

"Well, not anymore, *compadre*. I think we may become a steady item. Hell, we even talked about living together in the future, if things go well between us."

When we reached our apartment, I tossed my bags in the bedroom and kicked off my shoes. I changed into khaki shorts and a T-shirt and then raided the refrigerator and cupboards. I sat at our little dining table, munching on corn chips and chasing them with cold beer, while Mason lay on the sofa, perusing an atlas.

"What are you looking at?" I asked.

"A map of the Appalachian Trail. If my boss will give me a week off this summer, even if it's without pay, I want to hike a section in Tennessee and Virginia. I hear it's pretty there."

"Would you do this alone?"

Mason set the atlas aside and folded his arms at his chest. "I was hoping you could join me, but I guess you'll be busy?"

I nodded. "Jeff has to come first."

Hours later, I lay in my bed, bathed in silvery moonlight, while Mason snored away. I tried to imagine myself ascending a mountain trail, gazing at streams and wildflowers and maybe encountering a deer. I pictured Mason and myself sitting by a campfire in the evening and sharing a tent each night. The whole idea seemed tantalizing, but like the dashed plans I'd made with Jeff to spend our summer at Fort De Soto, the hiking trip with Mason would not happen.

Jeff's cancer had taken center stage.

CHAPTER TWENTY-NINE

Despite the fact I'd missed the last two weeks of classes, I breezed through my exams. All the self-discipline I'd exercised during the semester paid off, and when I finished my last final, I was sure I'd done well in each of my classes. My dad would be pleased, and now I could forget about school and concentrate solely on Jeff.

I spent a day doing laundry and packing my suitcase, duffel, and backpack. Mason took me out for dinner at a vegan restaurant, where we dined on sweet potato and black bean burgers that were pretty damned flavorful, and the next morning, I was back on a Greyhound, riding northward on U.S. 231 with my hands in my lap, my headphones playing Kenny Chesney's "I Go Back," and my cheek pressed against the window beside me.

I had no idea what would happen in the weeks ahead. How would Jeff's chemotherapy and radiation treatments affect him physically and mentally? How would his parents react to my presence in their daily lives? And how would it feel to live in a small Midwestern town like Peru?

*

Jeff's roommate, Craig, laid a large pot on the dining table in Bloomington, where Jeff, Tyler, and I sat.

"Dig in, boys, it's *real* tasty."

Craig had prepared a dish he'd nicknamed "dogfood", a mixture of mac and cheese, ground beef, and sautéed veggies. He served it with a dish of frozen green beans he'd zapped in the microwave and slathered with margarine. The stuff was tasty, and I piled my plate high, but Jeff served himself less than half of what I did.

I nudged his shoulder. "You're not eating much. Are you feeling okay?"

He shrugged. "I'm just tired, and not particularly hungry. Exams were tough—I didn't get a lot of sleep during the last week—so it'll be an early bedtime for me tonight."

Jeff didn't need to tell me he was weary. When he'd picked me up at the bus station an hour before, his hair was in tangles, his shoulders were slumped, and he moved sluggishly when we carried my bags and backpack to the Impala.

On the ride to Jeff's house, he held my hand in his while we talked.

"I spoke with my parents yesterday afternoon, after my last exam. I told them you'd stay with us in Peru this summer, to help out with things."

"What did they say?"

"They weren't thrilled with the idea. I had to do some bargaining in order to bring them around."

"Explain, please."

"You can't sleep in my room; you'll stay in the guest bedroom. And no open displays of affection in their presence, or when we're out in public either. When I introduce you to friends or relatives, we're just pals. And I have to go to mass every Sunday; that's the deal."

"It's not so bad, really."

Jeff looked at me and turned down one corner of his mouth. "They're treating us like second-class citizens, as though we're doing something shameful, and it pisses me off."

"At least we'll be together every day, and..."

"What?"

I gave Jeff's hand a firm squeeze. "We can sneak in quickies when they're not around. It'll be fun."

A smile crept onto Jeff's lips while he executed a left turn at a traffic light, and we entered his leafy neighborhood. "How can you be such a 'glass-is-half-full' guy? How come you're not as angry as me about the situation?"

"Look," I said, "in the weeks ahead, I'm sure we'll have to make compromises, lots of them. But your parents are making a huge concession by letting me live under their roof, so let's be grateful for that. And you won't have to deal with me hogging the covers in bed."

Jeff chuckled and shook his head.

Now, at the dinner table, Jeff's roommates talked about their summer plans.

"I'm staying here and taking classes full-time," Craig said. Then he looked at me. "My freshman year, I fell off a ladder while repairing the roof on my folks' house. I was in the hospital for weeks and had three surgeries. I missed spring semester, so now I need to play catch-up."

"I'm working the dairy farm all summer," Tyler said. "I'll be up to my knees in cow shit. But how about you guys?" he asked, looking first at Jeff, then me.

Jeff stirred the uneaten food on his plate. "I'm not sure how much I'll be able to do. I asked my folks to open a Netflix account so we can stream content through my laptop. We'll watch movies and play cards, those sorts of things. But I doubt I'll play one-on-one with Jakub in the driveway."

Everyone fell silent and worked on their food for a minute or two, until Tyler looked up from his plate and spoke to Jeff.

"You need to eat your meal, whether you're hungry or not. You know that, right?"

Jeff narrowed his eyes when he returned Tyler's gaze. "I'm not a child."

"Then don't act like one. I'll bet you've already lost all the weight you gained this school year, and the last thing you need to do is to get skinnier."

Jeff pushed his chair back from the table and rose.

"I already *have* a mother in Peru, and I don't need another in Bloomington. Mind your own fucking business, why don't you?"

Before Tyler could respond, Jeff turned on his heel and stormed into his bedroom. He slammed the door behind him, leaving the three of us looking at each other.

"What was *that* all about?" Craig asked.

I looked at Tyler. "I'm sorry he snapped at you—I know you meant well—but he's tired from cramming for his finals and worried about the treatments he's facing. I think his nerves are shot."

Tyler lowered his gaze and nodded.

Moments later, I knocked on Jeff's bedroom door. When he didn't answer, I entered and found him lying in bed with his face buried in a pillow. After I sat beside him on the mattress, I placed a hand on his shoulder.

"Are you okay?"

Jeff turned his head to the side and sniffled. His face was flushed and his eyes were swollen and bloodshot. When he spoke, he sounded congested.

"I don't want people babying me. And I don't want them feeling sorry for me either. Why can't they just leave me alone?"

I gripped my knees with my hands and studied the floor while rubbing my lips together. What exactly should I say?

"In the months ahead, a whole lot of folks will want to do whatever they can to help you deal with your illness. And you can't get angry at them for caring; it's what friends and family are for."

"I'm not helpless; I can look after myself."

"Not right now you can't. So, you'd better get used to people fretting about you, including me. Don't fight it, be grateful instead."

*

The next morning, a Friday, the sky was overcast, the air damp and cool. After Jeff and I loaded our possessions into the Impala's trunk and rear seat, Craig and Tyler joined us on the driveway, both wearing somber expressions.

"Tell your folks I said hi," Craig said to Jeff while they shook hands.

Jeff turned to Tyler and extended his hand. "I'm sorry about last night, man. I'm not myself right now."

Tyler shoved Jeff's hand aside. Then he took Jeff in his arms and held him. "I should be in Peru in about a week; I'll stop in and check on you first thing. And take care of yourself—remember to eat, goddammit."

"I'll be fine," Jeff said, patting Tyler's shoulder. "I'm tougher than you think."

The drive to Peru only took two-and-one-half hours, but seemed longer. Indiana was, as Jeff had once told me, an endless prairie, most of it farms and pastureland, punctuated by small towns that all looked the same: brick storefronts, fast food joints, churches, and strip malls.

Jeff kept his gaze fixed on the windshield while we talked.

"I meet with my oncologist, Dr. Mashburn, on Monday morning. He seems like a decent guy; I think you'll like him."

"I'm going with you?"

"Of course."

"I don't know if your parents will like it; they might feel I'm intruding."

Jeff kneaded the steering wheel while he worked his jaw from side to side. "We'll have to make it clear to them, right from the start, that you will always be involved in my treatments. The medical people need to understand that too—doctors and nurses, everyone."

"They'll all know we're a couple?"

Jeff looked at me and nodded. "I don't see there's any other way to handle things. Do you?"

I shook my head. I knew Jeff was right, but declaring myself an openly gay man to strangers would be a new experience for me. Could I handle it deftly?

Jeff turned his gaze back to the highway. "Like I said, in Peru we'll have to act as though we're just buddies. Tyler and my folks will be the only people in town who'll know we're boyfriends. But once we arrive at the hospital, all that changes."

We reached Peru right around noon, and my spirits plunged when we crossed the Wabash River and entered the town's core via Main Street. Downtown was little more than a collection of two and three-story brick or frame buildings, many badly in need of paint, some vacant and cordoned off by chain-link fences. The Miami County Courthouse was the town's most prominent structure, a domed sandstone building in good repair. And we passed an ornate Presbyterian church sporting plenty of stained glass, but otherwise the town's architecture was unimpressive.

Jeff's family home was a red brick, ranch-style residence shaded by a pair of elm trees, and surrounded by houses almost identical to the Brucellis'. A plexiglass backboard and basketball hoop stood at the edge of the driveway. The RV Jeff's family had driven to Florida was parked in the side yard, and I was reminded of the day I'd first met Jeff, in the Fort De Soto campground. How long ago it seemed, and back then who would have believed our lives—mine and Jeff's—would lead us to this moment?

"School's still in session in Miami County," Jeff told me when he let us into the house with a key. "My folks won't be home till late this afternoon."

Inside, we passed through a comfortably furnished living room, then into a hallway leading to a pair of bedrooms and a tiled bath. Jeff showed me his room, where he tossed one of his bags on the floor. Then he led me to the room I would occupy, a space furnished with a queen-size bed, a nightstand and lamp, a bureau and a ladder-back chair. The windows offered a view of the Brucellis' backyard, a treeless expanse with a redwood picnic table, a rusty swing set and a jungle gym.

"This house has a split-plan design," Jeff explained. "The master bedroom and bath are on the opposite end from our rooms, so if we decide to get frisky after lights out, my folks won't even hear us."

Jeff's room looked pretty much like mine, except for a collection of sports trophies and photographs displayed in a bookcase. Jeff's framed diploma from Peru High School hung on a wall.

"Let's fix some lunch," he said. "Then we can unpack our things."

Jeff cooked up grilled cheese sandwiches, and we dined in the Brucellis' kitchen. The appliances and linoleum floor gleamed, and the countertops were not cluttered like those at my home in Florida.

I fidgeted while my gaze traveled about the room. "I don't mind telling you, I'm feeling nervous about seeing your parents."

"Why?"

"When they were in Florida, they didn't know we were boyfriends. But now..."

After Jeff took a sip from his glass of milk, he licked his lips.

"It'll feel awkward at first, for everyone, but we'll get through it. My parents will have to adapt to the situation, then we can relax and feel comfortable sharing this house with them."

Jeff and I spent an hour unpacking our clothing, shoes, and personal items, and stowing them in our closets and bureaus. I placed two framed photos on my nightstand—one of Jeff I'd taken at Fort De Soto's

Gulf fishing pier, and another of my dad in his uniform, standing in front of the park ranger's residence.

I called out to Jeff while I stuffed socks and underwear into a drawer. "What's a guy do for fun here on a Saturday?"

In his room, Jeff snickered. "You drive to Fort Wayne and either hang out at the shopping mall or see a movie at the cineplex."

"That's it?"

"I'm afraid so, Dorothy. You're not in Florida anymore."

Once we'd finished unpacking, we took a stroll through Jeff's neighborhood, passing houses with neat yards and late model vehicles parked in the driveways. A woman in a housedress planted zinnias in her home's window boxes, and when she spotted Jeff, she smiled and waved.

"Hi, Mrs. Dockery," Jeff called out. "How's Biff doing?"

"He finished his tour of duty in Afghanistan six weeks ago, and came home in one piece, thank the Lord. Now he's stationed at Camp Lejeune."

In the course of our thirty-minute walk, we encountered several other people who greeted Jeff by his name: an electrician in a panel van, a pair of high school girls on bicycles with backpacks hanging from their shoulders, a gray-haired gentleman walking his schnauzer, and a postal worker in her Jeep who waved and smiled.

"You're a popular guy around here," I said.

Jeff shrugged. "Welcome to life in a small Midwestern town. Everyone knows everyone else, and there are *no* secrets. It's also a conservative place, which is why my folks want us to act discreetly whenever we're here."

Back at the Brucellis', two more cars occupied the driveway, along with Jeff's Impala. Right away, my pulse raced and sweat gathered in my armpits. I felt like a kid about to try out for a role in a school play. When we entered the house, we found Jeff's dad reading the Fort Wayne newspaper, the *Journal Gazette*, on the living room sofa. He wore dress slacks and a piqué polo shirt, and when he saw me, he rose and extended his hand.

"Hello, Jakub. Welcome to Peru."

I said thanks while we shook firmly. Then Mr. Brucelli turned to Jeff.

"Your mother's in the kitchen, grading spelling tests. Why don't you let her know you guys are here?"

Mrs. Brucelli sat at the kitchen table wielding a red pen, with two stacks of paper before her. She wore a silk blouse and a pleated skirt, which took me by surprise because, at Fort De Soto, all she'd worn were shorts, T-shirts, and flip-flops.

She rose to give Jeff a hug before shaking my hand. Then she pointed to the papers on the table.

"I'll be done here in twenty minutes tops. Make yourselves comfortable till I'm done, then the four of us can talk."

Jeff and I passed the time by sitting on his bed and leafing through his yearbook from Peru High School. Jeff had been active in extracurriculars: track team, student government, and thespian society.

"God, you were skinny," I said while gazing at Jeff in his cross-country singlet and shorts. His limbs looked like toothpicks.

Jeff smiled. "Back then, my grandma used to say, 'When you turn sideways, I can't see you anymore.'"

Jeff showed me Tyler and Craig's senior photos, both taken by a professional photographer who'd posed them in outdoor settings wearing casual clothing. Even back then, Tyler had been a looker with his handsome face, slender frame, and wavy brown hair, while Craig appeared as he did now—a guy who could work as a bouncer at a strip club.

"He dated a girl in our class named Sarah, and she was so tiny she barely reached his shoulder. They made for a funny sight at school dances, but were crazy about each other. Everyone thought they'd get married one day."

"But they didn't?"

Jeff pursed his lips. "Sarah didn't go to college. She stayed in Peru and worked as a cashier at the Save-a-Lot. She eloped with the store's assistant manager."

Jeff's mom rapped on the door jamb. "You guys ready to talk?"

In the living room, afternoon sunlight entered through a trio of double-hung windows. Jeff's parents sat side by side on the sofa, while Jeff and I faced them, both of us seated in upholstered armchairs.

I crossed my knee with an ankle while Jeff's dad spoke to me.

"When Jeff told us you and he were...together, I'll have to admit, we were shocked. We had never suspected Jeff was gay, and the same went for you. We figured you guys were just friends, but now we know otherwise.

"I'll be honest with you. I'm a small-town type of guy. I've never had a gay friend or relative, save for a nephew in Chicago. It's not something you encounter in a place like Peru, and our gravest concern is, someone might say or do something unkind if your relationship became known to local people."

"Yes," Jeff's mom said to me, "our first concern is for Jeff's safety, and yours as well. Also, if our priest learns you and Jeff are a couple, Jeff won't be permitted to receive communion at mass, and that worries us greatly, especially with the troubles Jeff faces. In our view, he'll need God's help to get through it."

I licked my lips. "Mrs. Brucelli, I—"

"You're old enough to call me Catherine."

"And call me Mario," Jeff's dad said. "No reason to stand on formalities around here."

I nodded. "Thanks, to both of you, for letting me live here. First of all, I understand the need for my relationship with Jeff to remain private while we're in Peru. We'll be careful what we say and do. As to church matters, Jeff's told me he's agreed to attend mass, and I'm fine with that. But I'm not a religious person and won't join you on Sundays."

"Understood," Mario said, still looking at me. "Now, as to personal matters between you two...Catherine and I are not stupid. We know guys your age are sexually active, and that's to be expected. But please keep your hands to yourselves when we are present. We're trying hard to be accepting, but give us a break and save it for when you're behind closed doors."

Catherine rearranged her limbs on the sofa while keeping her gaze fixed on me. "We, of course, are familiar with your father from our days at Fort De Soto. Does he know about you and Jeff?"

I nodded.

"What does he think?"

"It's not a problem for him; he's just glad Jeff makes me happy."

Catherine and Mario exchanged glances before returning their gazes to me. "He's not concerned you won't give him grandchildren?" Catherine asked.

I shook my head.

Mario cleared his throat. "Let's change the subject. As Jeff's parents, we want to know what your expectations are while you're living here. Exactly how do you plan on spending your time?"

I leaned forward and rested my forearms on my knees.

"I'm here for one reason—to do everything I can to help Jeff get through his treatments. I know it's going to be rough for him, and many days he'll feel lousy. I'll do whatever it takes to make his days easier, and yours too. I can perform housework, and I don't mind mowing the grass or whatever. But mainly I want to focus on caring for Jeff."

Catherine looked at Jeff, then me. "We're driving Jeff to Indianapolis Monday morning, to meet with his oncologist. What'll you do while we're gone?"

"He's going with us," Jeff said. "I want him next to me, every time I go over there."

Catherine looked at Mario and raised her eyebrows. Then she returned her gaze to Jeff.

"Who will you say Jakub *is*, if someone asks?"

"I'll tell them he's my partner, Mom. This is 2018, and I don't think the people treating me will care if I'm gay or that Jakub's my boyfriend. We'll keep things private in Peru but not over there, and that *isn't* negotiable."

Jeff's parents lowered their gazes, and no one spoke again until Jeff did.

"I know you never expected me to turn out queer—I'm sure you're disappointed—but I am who I am, and Jakub's my partner. I'm not going through life pretending otherwise, so if we're going to keep our family together, you'll need to accept Jakub as a permanent part of our lives."

Chapter Thirty

Indianapolis is eighty miles due south of Peru, and on Monday morning I sat in the back seat of Mario's SUV, alongside Jeff, while we made the trip to the teaching hospital. The sky was overcast and a steady breeze stirred prairie grasses growing on the road shoulders. In the passenger seat up front, Catherine worked on a cross-stitching project, while Jeff and I read sections of the Fort Wayne newspaper and sipped from insulated coffee tumblers. Very little was said during the ninety-minute journey, and soon we entered downtown Indianapolis, passing by Monument Circle, the state capitol building, and the Pacers' basketball arena. People in business attire hustled through crosswalks whenever we halted at stoplights. Horns honked and sirens yowled.

The teaching hospital was a massive contemporary structure, with much steel and glass, connected to several other health care facilities and occupying many acres. We parked in a multi-level garage and used a skywalk to access the Simon Cancer Center, a free-standing building on the medical campus.

We first met with an intake specialist, a smartly dressed woman who didn't flinch when Jeff introduced me as his partner. She gathered basic information from Jeff about his medical history, insurance coverage, and so forth and then assigned Jeff a cancer center patient number and provided him with a diagram of the facility. She also provided Jeff with a thick patient brochure full of information about the Simon Center and its offerings, and also about the nature of chemotherapy and radiation treatments.

"Chemotherapy's provided on the fourth floor, while radiation treatments are given on the fifth. Dr. Mashburn's office is on level six, in room 617." She glanced at her wristwatch. "He's expecting you there in about fifteen minutes, so let's wrap things up."

She looked at Jeff.

"Have you executed a Medical Power of Attorney?"

"A what?"

"It's a legal document appointing someone to make health care decisions for you, in the event you're unable to make them for yourself. If you're mentally impaired at any time, the POA takes effect until you've recovered. It also authorizes your appointee to terminate life support measures if it's clear you will never recover from your illness."

"I don't have one of those, but I'd like to sign one."

After the woman handed Jeff a form, he studied it a moment before asking for a pen.

"Does the person I appoint have to be a blood relative?"

"No, it can be anyone you choose, as long as they're an adult and mentally competent."

Jeff looked at me and his parents before scribbling on the document. "I'm appointing Jakub to make my decisions in case I can't. He'll know best what I'd want done."

"Honey," Catherine said, "are you sure that's a wise idea? Maybe—"

"I'm a grown-up, Mom. It's my choice, and Jakub is it."

After Jeff handed the intake specialist the signed document, she witnessed and notarized it before placing it in Jeff's file folder. Then Jeff, his parents, and I headed for the elevator. Nobody spoke, and tension crackled between the four of us.

Wiley Mashburn, MD looked like a doctor in a television soap opera. Tall and slender, with a full head of prematurely gray hair. His gaze met mine and he shook my hand firmly when Jeff introduced me. The five of us sat in Mashburn's private office, the doctor behind his desk, the rest of us in leather-upholstered armchairs, while morning sunlight entered the room through plate glass windows.

Mashburn had attended IU's medical schhool and also performed a residency at Sloan Kettering Cancer Center in New York City, according to framed certificates hanging on one wall.

"First of all," he told us, "I know a cancer diagnosis is frightening, but it's certainly not a death sentence, especially in Jeff's case. Yes, we found cancer cells in the nodes in Jeff's neck and armpits, but the good news is, all his swollen nodes are above his diaphragm. That means the cancer hasn't spread very far.

"Also, Jeff's young and otherwise healthy, so he's better able than many patients to tolerate chemotherapy and radiation treatments."

"Yes," Catherine said, "but we've heard stories about the side effects—hair and weight loss, nausea, those sorts of things."

Mashburn nodded. "Jeff may suffer from some, if not all of those. They're unavoidable, I'm afraid. And he'll have to sign an informed consent document, acknowledging I've warned him about the risks involved in his treatment plan. But they're temporary risks."

"Exactly what is your treatment plan for Jeff?" Mario asked.

The doctor rested his elbows on his desktop.

"We'll do four cycles of chemotherapy, with a three-week gap between each cycle, to allow Jeff to recover his strength. Chemo, of course, affects every patient differently. Some tolerate the cycles without much problem. Others have a rougher time. In any case, a person must transport Jeff to and from his appointments; he'll likely feel too weak to drive himself."

I raised my hand. "That'll be me."

The doctor continued.

"The biggest risk from chemotherapy is infection, because Jeff's immune system will be suppressed by the treatments. He should limit his contact with others, and most certainly can't be around anyone with a head cold or the flu. He should not eat at restaurants or consume uncooked food, and he must wash his hands with hot water and soap, before eating and always after using the toilet. Prevention is everything, and if Jeff develops even the slightest fever, he should immediately visit the Emergency Room at your local hospital."

Jeff stirred in his chair. "When do I receive the radiation treatments, and what's involved?"

"We begin radiation treatments three weeks after your last chemo cycle, so you'll have time to recover. You'll be under the care of a radiation oncologist who will work closely with me. You will come here five times a week for seven weeks. Each treatment will last about twenty minutes and will target the lymph nodes in your neck and armpits."

"Is radiation painful?" I asked.

Mashburn shook his head. "The only side effects are mild skin burns in the areas treated, and those we can often prevent with application of specialized skin cream before and after each treatment." He pointed to the brochure resting in Jeff's lap. "I want each of you to read it from cover to cover. It'll answer most every question you'll have about Jeff's therapies, and also the many services we offer patients undergoing cancer treatment. It's not just about chemo and radiation. We offer nutritional advice, mental health counseling, relaxation therapies, and even a wig salon for those suffering from hair loss."

Jeff looked at me and smirked. "I've always wondered what I'd look like as a blond. Now, maybe I'll find out."

"I'd rather see you with red curls like Mason's."

"This isn't funny," Catherine cried, rising to her feet and scowling. "Stop it, both of you."

"Mom, a little humor isn't going to hurt."

Catherine's eyes glistened. "You're my only child, and I don't want to lose you. This is no time for joking around."

"Of course, it's a serious situation," Mashburn said to Catherine, "but please sit down and try to remain calm. While Jeff's going through this, he must not feel stressed. Emotional pressure weakens a patient who undergoes cancer treatment, and Jeff will need all the strength he can muster in the months ahead. If he wants to laugh—I don't care for what reason—let him."

After Catherine sat, Mario patted her wrist. "It's going to be okay, sweetheart. We need to trust Dr. Mashburn's judgment."

Catherine turned her teary gaze to Mashburn.

"Is my son going to live, doctor?"

Mashburn rocked backward in his swivel chair while his gaze traveled from face to face in the room. "Jeff's a Stage IA HL patient, and our success rate with that group is quite favorable. I have every reason to believe Jeff will make a full recovery." He turned his gaze back to Jeff. "We have your first chemo cycle scheduled a week from today, at nine a.m. When you arrive, go to the center's fourth floor. A phlebotomist will draw blood samples from you so we can check your white blood cell and platelet counts. Assuming the lab finds everything satisfactory, you'll receive an anti-nausea drug by IV drip, followed by ABVD, a combination of chemotherapy drugs: doxorubicin, bleomycin, vinblastine, and acarbazine."

"How long will each cycle take?" I asked.

"Less than three hours; you'll be out of here before lunchtime."

Jeff stirred in his chair. "These side effects we talked about...how soon after the chemo session will they kick in?"

"It's different with every patient, but you'll be ready for bedrest by the time you get back to Peru. The ABVD is highly toxic, and you should expect nausea and fatigue to appear within hours after treatment."

Jeff's face grew pale. "This stuff you're putting in me is poison?"

Mashburn shrugged. "That's one way to put it, but the toxin doesn't attack your entire body. Instead, it primarily targets the type of cancer cells we found in your biopsies."

"And you're quite certain," Catherine said, "this is the best course of treatment for Jeff?"

"Absolutely."

Jeff looked at me and raised his eyebrows. "What do you think, Jakub?"

Don't let him know how scared you are.

I lowered my gaze for a moment before returning it to Jeff's.

"I say let's do it."

*

Wednesday afternoon, Jeff and I worked on his parents' flower beds, where tulip bulbs had sprouted weeks before. After carefully removing last year's mulch from the beds and stuffing it into plastic garbage sacks, we scattered granulated fertilizer among the tulips and worked the granules into the soil using hand rakes.

I was content to simply breathe fresh air and do something useful, rather than slouching around inside the house.

Since our visit to Simon Cancer Center, what little conversation I'd engaged in with Jeff's parents seemed stilted, and I sensed resentment bubbling beneath the surface of their attitudes toward me. I didn't know whether this stemmed from Jeff's granting me his Medical Power of Attorney, or the fact they viewed me as an interloper in their family's dynamic.

Evening meals were especially awkward, as no one seemed to have much to say. Jeff's parents talked about the school year's winding down, and what they'd do with their summers. Catherine would teach remedial classes at the high school, helping students who'd failed to pass standardized tests required by the State of Indiana to advance a grade.

"It's so depressing," she told us. "Some of these fifteen-year-olds can't read at a sixth-grade level. How they got promoted to high school I'll never understand."

Mario would work in sales at a local hardware store, wearing an apron and headset. "Summer's always a busy time for them, so I'll be on the move constantly, selling everything from PVC pipe to mailboxes."

Tuesday night, at the dinner table, I made a suggestion to Jeff's parents.

"It seems Jeff and I will have a good deal of time to fill this summer. I don't want to lie around watching television all day, and I'm sure Jeff doesn't either. If there are tasks needing done around here—yardwork, cleaning, car washing or whatever—let us know and we'll take care of them. Just make up a list."

Now, Jeff and I were on our hands and knees, working in the flower beds. The sun shone in a cloudless sky, and a light breeze tickled the bangs on Jeff's forehead while he scattered handfuls of fertilizer.

"I'm sure," he said, "you'd be having a much better time spending your summer at Fort De Soto. I'll bet it's nice down there right now."

I nodded. "May's a great time of year in Florida, but if I were at the park, I wouldn't be with you. So, here is where I want to be."

"Feeding tulips?"

"Why not? It beats doing nothing, plus landscaping has never seemed like work to me, not unless the weather's really hot. I like the way I see instant results from my work."

Jeff snickered and shook his head. "'Mr. Glass is Half Full' again."

"Hey, there's nothing wrong with optimism. Plus, it's nice working alongside you; it reminds me of the day we demolished the lifeguard shed at the park. Remember?"

Jeff grinned. "What I recall best was the old guy in the golf cart bringing us sodas and telling us a joke about four gay men and a barstool."

After we'd finished spreading fertilizer, we toted several plastic sacks full of old mulch to the street curb for pickup by the garbage service. Then we commenced tearing open bags of fresh mulch and spreading the contents among the beds. The day was warm, and we both shed our shirts. When Jeff did so, I saw just how much weight he had lost since he'd visited Florida in March. His biceps and shoulder muscles weren't nearly as bulky, and I could easily count all his ribs.

I sliced open a mulch bag with an old steak knife we'd found in the garage. "So, I guess it'll just be you and me going to Indy Monday?"

Jeff nodded while he shook the contents of a mulch bag into the bed, making a chugging sound. "My folks offered to come with us, but I told them to stay in Peru and go to work. I don't need three people coming with me, plus they need to get used to the fact you're my main source of support."

"Am I?"

"Absolutely."

"Do you think they resent me for that?"

Jeff shook the last mulch from his bag and then knelt and spread the mound of eucalyptus shavings to a uniform depth, using his hands. "They probably do, and I guess it's understandable. After all, I'm the family prince, but now I've abdicated the throne and given myself to the guy who stole my virginity."

"You make me sound like I corrupted you."

Jeff looked at me and shook his head. "You only freed me so I could live as I ought to, and I'm very lucky you did."

Jeff's words caused a warm sensation inside my chest, like I'd swallowed a shot of bourbon. My thoughts spun while I shook the bag I held.

I guess he loves me as much as I do him, maybe even more than he loves his parents.

I glanced at my wristwatch. "You know, we haven't gone skin-to-skin since we arrived in Peru. Once we're done mulching, why don't you and I spend an hour in your bedroom?"

A smile crept across Jeff's lips.

"Okay, boyfriend, but only if you'll shower with me first. I'm not screwing a guy who smells like eucalyptus."

*

Saturday morning, I woke in my room at 6:00 a.m., and right away I knew I'd never go back to sleep. I could either lie in bed and stare at the ceiling or get up. So, I rose and shuffled into the bathroom, trying to be quiet so I wouldn't disturb Jeff.

Once dressed, I walked through the house and into the kitchen, where the aroma of freshly brewed coffee beckoned. I poured myself a glass of juice and drank it while gazing into the Brucellis' backyard. The sun had just risen, and dew glistened in the grass.

I filled a mug with coffee and wandered into the living room, where I found Mario reading the Fort Wayne newspaper in his easy chair. He wore boxer shorts and a T-shirt with an Indiana Pacers logo on the chest. Dark stubble blued his chin and cheeks.

"You're up early," he said.

I settled onto the sofa and plucked the sports section from the coffee table. "I couldn't sleep any longer," I said before studying the box score from last night's Tampa Bay Rays' contest with the Red Sox.

"I guess Jeff's still snoozing?"

I nodded. "He says the Hodgkin's makes him feel tired all the time. I guess he needs plenty of rest."

Mario took a sip from his coffee mug and swallowed. Then he set his newspaper section aside. "Have you read the materials they gave us at the cancer center yet?"

"Everything. Why?"

"It sounds like Jeff will spend a good deal of time in bed during chemotherapy. What'll you do with yourself when he's resting?"

I shrugged. "I'm taking an online course this summer. It's only three hours a week, but I'll need to study and watch the videos. And I plan to jog a few miles most days, down by the river."

"Ever done any house painting?"

"Plenty. During summers, my dad often hired me to paint restrooms and other buildings in the park. I'm pretty handy with a brush and roller."

Mario rubbed his chin with a knuckle. "The trim work, shutters, and exterior doors on this house need sanded and repainted. I'll pay you to do that, if you're interested."

"I can do the job, but you don't have to pay me. I'm living here for free, so it's the least I can do to help out."

Mario shook his head. "You're doing enough by helping Jeff get through his treatments, so if you do the painting, I'll insist on paying you a fair amount for your work. Plus, I have to confess, I absolutely detest painting. I'll do just about any type of work, but don't put sandpaper or a brush in my hand. In my book, it's the ultimate tedium."

I chuckled. "Painting doesn't bother me. I just put on my headphones and tune everything else out."

"What's your dad pay you for work at the park?"

"Minimum wage."

Mario extended his hand. "I'll increase that by another two bucks an hour. Deal?"

After we shook, I reached for my coffee while Mario continued.

"I'll have my wife visit the hardware store this weekend, to pick up paint chips. Once we've decided on a color, I'll bring home a few gallons, and you can get started whenever you please."

"Speaking of Catherine, where is she?"

Mario let out his breath. "She left the house for school an hour ago."

"But it's Saturday."

"True, but you have to understand, when she's feeling anxious—and she is right now—she likes to immerse herself in her job. It helps keep her worries at bay."

I thought back to the previous summer, when Jeff's grandmother's health had taken a turn for the worse, and how the Brucellis had abruptly returned to Indiana from Fort De Soto Park. Back then, Jeff had described his family as operating in "crisis mode," and now it seemed they were doing so again.

"I know she's worried about Jeff," I said. "And I suppose having me here isn't helping matters."

"What makes you say that?"

I shifted my weight in my chair. "I know the two of you aren't happy I'm Jeff's partner; I'm sure you'd prefer it were otherwise."

Mario moistened his lips. "We're trying our best to accept things, but you and Jeff will need to give us time to absorb the situation. We only learned you two were a couple recently. It's a bit difficult for us to envision what sort of future he'll have with you as his partner. And this business of him transferring to Florida State..."

"Jeff loves it down there, and FSU's a good school."

"But it's almost nine hundred miles from here. Our family's always been close, and we don't want that to change."

"It won't if I have any say in the matter. It's my hope you'll accept me as a part of your lives. We can spend holidays together. Jeff and I will visit during summer, and you can visit us in Florida too."

Mario lowered his gaze for a moment before returning it to mine. "What will you do if Jeff's cancer gets the best of him? Have you thought about it?"

"I won't even consider the possibility. I'm here to make sure Jeff wins the battle, and I believe he will, as long as we're here to support him. Honestly, you couldn't chase me out of this house with a shotgun."

A little smile crept onto Mario's lips. He reached across the coffee table and patted my wrist.

"You really *do* love him, don't you?"

A shiver ran down my spine from Mario's gentle touch, and I gazed into his dark brown eyes when I answered.

"I adore Jeff and always will."

*

The day preceding Jeff's first chemotherapy cycle, Mario, Catherine, Jeff, and I attended a potluck luncheon at a farmhouse where Jeff's paternal aunt and her husband lived with their three kids. There must have been forty people there, all folks from Mario's side of the family. The day was sunny and warm, and little kids played tag in a cornfield, while teenagers gathered at a picnic table, engrossed in their smartphones.

I stood alongside Jeff when people approached and wished him well with his cancer treatments, and each time this happened, Jeff introduced me as "my friend from Florida who'll help me get through this."

The introduction drew some curious stares, but folks were friendly enough, and I didn't feel uncomfortable.

"Ordinarily," Jeff told me, "during the upcoming months, you'd see these relatives, and many others from my mom's side of the family, on a regular basis. They're always visiting on weekends and evenings. But you know what the patient brochure says: I have to limit my contact with people while I'm going through chemo, to lessen my chances of getting infected with something."

The priest from the Brucellis' church, Father Laughlin, attended, and he looked a bit out of place in his black clothing and white collar. But he seemed kind when he spoke with Jeff and shook my hand. Just before we sat down to eat, Laughlin said a prayer, thanking God for the food and family fellowship, and also asking Him to watch over Jeff in the months ahead.

"Do you think it's true, what your mom said about Father Laughlin?" I whispered to Jeff.

"What's that?"

"That he wouldn't let you take communion if he knew about us."

Jeff rolled his eyes while he passed me a platter of biscuits. "Who knows? And it's not important to me anyway. I can do without the weekly wafer."

CHAPTER THIRTY-ONE

Monday morning's weather was damp and dreary when I drove Jeff to Indianapolis in the Impala. He wore jeans, sneakers, and a polo shirt, looking more like a prep school student than a cancer patient. We said little to each other during the trip. Instead we listened to a Fort Wayne country western radio station while rolling past cornfields and pastureland.

At the Simon Cancer Center, we rode the elevator to the fourth floor, where a receptionist recorded our arrival time and notified the chemotherapy clinic of our presence. Then she directed us to a hallway. The clinic was a brightly lit room with a semicircle of vinyl-upholstered chaises facing plate glass windows offering a pleasant view of the cityscape.

An aide clutching a clipboard greeted us with a smile before leading us to one of the chaises.

"Have a seat here," she said to Jeff, "and make yourself comfortable. In a few minutes, we'll draw blood from your arm to check your white cell and platelet counts. Assuming Dr. Mashburn finds them acceptable, we'll administer an anti-nausea medication, then your ABVD drip."

After Jeff reclined on the chaise, I took the chair next to it. Then I asked Jeff, "How are you feeling right now?"

"Nervous as hell."

I took Jeff's hand in mine and squeezed. "I am, too, but this place doesn't look scary at all. It's like a day spa."

Jeff scowled. "One where they feed you poison."

A phlebotomist in scrubs, a guy a little older than me and Jeff, appeared with a cart holding a variety of tubes, hypodermic needles, bandages and so forth. He drew several vials of blood from a vein in Jeff's forearm, and I winced while watching the Chianti-colored liquid bubble in the glass cylinders.

Jeff kept his gaze on the windows the entire time.

After the phlebotomist finished drawing blood, he attached bar-coded labels to each tube while speaking to Jeff. "I'll take these to the lab right away. Once they clear you for chemo, I'll be back to insert a catheter in your arm, to facilitate the IV drips you'll receive."

Jeff nodded.

A few minutes later, Dr. Mashburn appeared in his lab coat and necktie. He greeted me with a wave and patted Jeff's shoulder. "Feeling okay?"

When Jeff shrugged in response, the doctor turned down one corner of his mouth and shot me a glance before returning his gaze to Jeff.

"I know this process is unnerving, but we know what we're doing here. This is absolutely the best course of action to deal with your Hodgkin's, and like I said at our last meeting, I have every reason to believe we'll be successful."

Jeff gazed into his lap. "Tell me again—how soon before the side effects kick in?"

Mashburn crossed his arms at his chest. "An hour or two after we finish your ABVD drip. You should plan on taking it easy the rest of today—no physical exertion of any kind, understand?"

After Jeff gave Mashburn the okay sign, Mashburn looked at me.

"I guess you'll drive him home?"

I nodded.

"All right, then," Mashburn said, squeezing Jeff's shoulder. "I should hear from the lab shortly, then we'll proceed. Any questions, fellas?"

We both shook our heads. Mashburn cruised out of the room with the tail of his lab coat billowing behind him.

Jeff looked at me and rubbed his lips together. "During the drive down here, I kept thinking about our camping trip at Manatee Springs State Park. Remember?"

"Of course."

"I'd never felt happier. The sunshine, the spring, and the cypress trees. The canoe trip and those huge fish that kept jumping out of the water. What were they called?"

"Gulf sturgeons."

Jeff smiled and shook his head. "What a great experience, but then we came back to Fort De Soto, and an hour later I was off to Peru with my folks. Talk about a letdown; I walked around feeling depressed for weeks."

I stroked Jeff's wrist with a fingertip while he continued.

"Back then, who knew things would go from bad to worse, that I'd get cancer and end up in this place? Why me?"

Yeah, why?

"Look," I said, "the situation's not bleak. It's true you'll feel lousy many times in the months ahead. We both know that, and we'll deal with it. But at least you and I are together and living under the same roof. Your parents could have said no, but they didn't, and we should be grateful for that."

Jeff looked at me nodded. "I'm whining, aren't I?"

"A little."

"Sorry, I'll stop. And speaking of my folks, I think you're starting to win my dad over. On the way home from Sunday mass, he told Mom he's decided you're good for me. Plus, I think he's ecstatic he won't have to paint our house this summer."

We both chuckled while a nurse in scrubs and white lace-up shoes approached Jeff's chaise with a smile on her pretty face.

"Mr. Brucelli?"

"That's me, but call me Jeff."

"I'm Jennifer Frazier, I'll be your chemotherapy nurse for each of your four cycles."

Jeff pointed at me. "He's my partner, Jakub Mazur, and also my medical power of attorney."

Jennifer nodded. "I saw that in your chart earlier. The three of us will get closely acquainted in the weeks ahead, so let's go on a first-name basis. And if there are any questions or concerns about this process, don't either of you hesitate to ask. It's what I'm here for."

"Will the chemo drug burn when it enters my body?"

Jennifer shook her head. "The infusion is almost painless, trust me."

Jeff pointed to a backpack resting at my feet. "I brought a book to read while it takes place. The patient brochure recommended it."

"It's a good way to pass the time, or—" Jennifer pointed to a flat screen monitor mounted on an arm bolted to the ceiling. "—you can watch TV if you prefer. There's a remote on the table next to you."

Jeff frowned. "I'm not much of a daytime television fan."

"You don't like *Jerry Springer* reruns?"

"U-m-m, no. I think I'll stick with my book."

Fifteen or twenty minutes passed while Jeff and I talked about the e-mails we'd received from our respective universities, reporting our spring semester grades. Jeff had earned two Bs and two As, while I had received *all* As for the first time in my college career.

"My dad'll be pleased when I call him later today. Taking the apartment with Brian was the best thing I could have done for my schooling. I should have moved off campus my second year instead of living in the dorm again."

The same phlebotomist returned to insert a catheter into a vein in the back of Jeff's forearm, just above his wrist. The catheter wasn't much larger than a kitchen match. The phlebotomist secured it to Jeff's skin with clear medical tape.

"Your lab report came back fine," he told Jeff.

Moments later, Jennifer returned with an electronic pump on a pole with four wheels. The pump's face was a maze of buttons plus an LCD screen. This time, Jennifer wore latex gloves and plastic goggles. She placed the pole alongside Jeff's chaise and plugged the pump's power cord into a wall outlet. A plastic bag filled with a clear solution hung from the pole, with a tube extending from it.

"What's in the bag?" Jeff asked.

"Your anti-nausea medication."

Jennifer raised a hinged table on the side of Jeff's chaise to a horizontal position. Then she placed Jeff's arm on the table and inserted the end of the plastic tubing into his catheter.

"Doing okay?" she asked him.

"Yeah, I'm fine."

Jennifer glanced at her wristwatch. Then she made an entry on a clipboard hanging on the wall beside Jeff's bed. "I'll start the flow of the medication now. It will take about a half hour to drain the bag, so I'll come back then."

All around the room, chaises were filling up with patients dressed in street clothing, all with a companion in tow. Many were gray-haired, but a few were as young as Jeff, and while some appeared perfectly healthy, others looked like concentration camp survivors—gaunt, with dark circles under their eyes. The men wore ball caps, the women head scarves, to cover up their hairless scalps, and I couldn't help but shudder when gazing at them.

When I looked back at Jeff, he pointed his chin at a spindly man in a nearby chaise who looked like he'd been a participant in a hunger strike. His cheeks were hollow, the bones of his face prominent.

"I wonder if I'll look like that two months from now?"

The chemo clinic quickly turned into a beehive of activity while nurses and physicians scurried here and there, talking with patients, hooking them up to IV drips and making chart entries. I handed Jeff his book, *Camino Island* by John Grisham, and then I read from my own selection, a paperback edition of *To Kill a Mockingbird* by Harper Lee I had found on a bookshelf in the Brucellis' den. In high school, I'd read the novel and liked it okay. But I suspected I might find it more compelling, since I was older now.

Eventually, Jennifer returned, this time wearing a paper gown with full-length sleeves, in addition to latex gloves and goggles. She carried another plastic bag of ruby-colored solution with a tube extending from it. While she mounted the bag on the pole alongside Jeff's chaise, he looked her over from her forehead to her shoes.

"What's with the getup? You look like a member of a hazmat team."

"Safety precautions. ABVD is highly toxic, so I can't let it get in my eyes or even touch my skin."

"But you're pumping it into my bloodstream?"

"That's correct."

Jeff shook his head.

Jennifer patted his shoulder. "It's going to be okay, kiddo. Relax and let us do what we need to, okay?"

Jeff lowered his gaze and nodded.

After Jennifer detached the empty anti-nausea bag from Jeff's catheter, she hooked up the ABVD bag in its place. Then she flicked a button on the pole pump, and numbers blinked on the LCD screen.

"This will take about forty minutes," she said while glancing at her wristwatch. After she made another entry on the clipboard, she hung it on the wall beside Jeff's chaise. Then she turned back to Jeff. "You may feel a slight burning sensation in your arm, right around the edges of your catheter. Other than that, you won't experience any pain."

Jennifer's gaze traveled to me and back to Jeff. "Any questions?"

We both shook our heads; then she was gone.

Jeff drew a deep breath and puffed out his cheeks before exhaling. "Well, here we go—the poisoning begins..."

"Can I get you some water, or maybe a soda?"

"I'm not thirsty. In fact, I don't need anything right now. I just want to get this done so we can go home."

We both opened our books and I commenced reading Scout Finch's description of the "tired old town of Maycomb." Meanwhile, Jeff turned the pages of Grisham's novel, and I suppose both of us tried to forget where we were. But it was hard. I kept returning my gaze to the bag of ABVD, knowing its toxic contents were draining into Jeff's arm, drip by drip.

My thoughts turned to Fort De Soto Park, and I wondered what conditions were like down there that day. Early May in central Florida is particularly beautiful. The summer's heat and humidity have not yet arrived, and the Gulf water has a perfect temperature for bathing. Rain seldom falls. In the afternoon, a delightful sea breeze blows from the west. And fishing becomes productive at the park, when speckled trout, redfish, and flounder get more active on the grass flats.

But I would not taste of Fort De Soto's spring and summer bounties. Instead, I'd dwell in a prairie town, one with little to offer but boredom and blandness. I'd live among townsfolk who would most certainly disapprove of the acts Jeff and I enjoyed in private, the very things that meant so much to us. And not just intercourse, but simple acts like holding hands or snuggling under a blanket when Jeff's parents weren't around.

According to the brochure provided us by the cancer center, sexual activity was permissible while Jeff underwent chemotherapy, although we'd have to refrain from intimacies for seventy-two hours after each treatment, as Jeff's body fluids, during that period, could expose me to the toxin he'd been infused with. The brochure also said Jeff's interest in sex, and his ability to perform in bed, might be impaired or could disappear altogether, until he ended his treatments and his body recovered from the ravages wrought by the ABVD.

I reached for Jeff's hand and interwove my fingers with his.

"What is it?" he asked.

"I just felt like touching you."

Jeff made a little smile. "Remember last Wednesday afternoon?"

He referred to our lovemaking at the Brucellis' house, after we'd fertilized and mulched the tulip beds. We showered together, scrubbing each other with a washcloth in between slurpy kisses and groping. Then we moved to Jeff's room, where we writhed on the mattress like a pair of lovestruck teenagers.

Since then, we'd done little more than sneak a kiss or a pat on the ass when neither of Jeff's parents were around. There in the chemotherapy clinic, I yearned for another round of intimacy with Jeff, even though I knew it was unlikely my urges would be fulfilled in the days ahead.

Quit dwelling on your own selfish needs, Mazur. Focus on Jeff's.

I glanced at my wristwatch, then the ABVD bag. "A half hour's gone by since you started infusing that stuff. Jennifer said it would take forty minutes, right?"

Jeff nodded.

"Then we're almost done," I said, "and it hasn't been too bad, really."

Jeff turned down one corner of his mouth. "This is the easy part; we'll see how things are in a few hours."

"You read the brochure. Not everyone suffers from side effects, or if they do, the effects are often mild, especially with guys your age."

"Okay, Mr. Optimism, just don't expect me to do jumping jacks when we get home."

My cell phone chimed, and when I checked the screen, I saw my father was the caller.

"Hey, Dad. What's up?"

"Are you at the hospital?"

"Yeah, but we're almost done here."

"Put Jeff on for a moment, will you?"

Dad and Jeff conversed for a few minutes, and I was touched my father had taken time from his busy day to call my boyfriend. When they finished talking,

Jeff handed the phone back to me, just as Jennifer approached in her gown, gloves, and goggles.

"I have to go, Dad. The nurse is here, but thanks so much for calling. We'll talk again soon."

Jennifer studied the LCD screen on the IV pump and made a note in Jeff's chart. "Okay," she told him, "your first cycle's complete. How do you feel?"

Jeff shrugged while Jennifer detached the IV tube from Jeff's catheter. Then she removed the catheter from Jeff's forearm and dabbed his skin with disinfectant before applying a bandage to the insertion area.

"How long's the drive home?" she asked.

"About an hour," Jeff answered.

"When you get there, expect an upset stomach at the very least, and probably diarrhea as well. Don't be frightened; it's a normal reaction to the ABVD's presence in your body. You'll also suffer from fatigue because your red blood cell count will shrink. Get plenty of rest and drink fluids like fruit juice or soda. And I know food won't look very interesting, but it's important to eat. Understand?"

Jeff nodded.

"Have a safe trip home," Jennifer said. "I'll see you both in three weeks."

I clung to a hope Jeff might not suffer the typical side effects from his first cycle, but no. Halfway back to Peru, he asked me to pull the car onto the road shoulder. His face was as pale as an eggshell, and as soon as we came to a stop, he unclipped his seatbelt, flung his door open, and vomited, releasing a torrent of greenish liquid that looked nasty and smelled even worse.

He spat a few times while I patted his shoulder. "You okay?"

"Not really. Hand me a bottle of water, will you?"

Jeff swished his mouth out and spat again before closing his car door and sitting upright. "God, that was awful. My stomach felt like it was full of snakes."

"Is it better now?"

Jeff nodded. "But let's get moving. The sooner I'm near a toilet the better."

I trembled while steering onto the roadway and accelerating. The reality of Jeff's situation was settling over me like a lead blanket. The chemo would be hellish, and now there was no turning back. Already, the ABVD was taking effect, and Jeff was at its mercy while the stuff traveled through his body.

I felt frightened and utterly helpless, but did my best not to let it show. I kept my gaze fixed on the highway while flexing my fingers on the steering wheel.

"Well," Jeff said, "that was fun, wasn't it?"

I worked my jaw from side to side. "I'm sorry, I wish there was something I could do."

"You *are* doing something, Mazur: You're here."

CHAPTER THIRTY-TWO

My memories of events in the days following Jeff's first chemo cycle are vivid.

Once we arrived in Peru, Jeff bolted for the bathroom and drained his bowels. Then he vomited into the sink. After he'd cleaned himself up, he climbed into bed and pulled the covers up to his chin. I sat alongside him on a ladder-back chair, keeping one hand on Jeff's forearm and fingering the fine hairs growing there. When I asked if I could heat up a can of soup for his lunch , he shook his head.

"I'm not hungry."

"But Jennifer said it's important to eat."

"Maybe later. If I tried to swallow food right now—even soup—I'd only puke it back up."

I brought Jeff a can of ginger ale from the fridge. "The patient brochure says it's important to stay hydrated, especially when you have the shits. So, drink this."

"Yes, Nurse Nancy."

Jeff drank half the can's contents before placing it on his nightstand. His face remained as white as milk. "It's past noon," he said, "and you're probably hungry. Go fix yourself some lunch while I rest."

In the kitchen, while I made a ham and cheese sandwich, Catherine called me from work to see how things had gone. I described the chemotherapy session with Jennifer in detail and explained Jeff's reaction to it.

"Should I come home?" Catherine asked.

"I don't think it's necessary. He's resting right now, and if he needs anything, I'll take care of it."

Before I finished my sandwich, Mario phoned. I repeated what I'd told Catherine, and by the time I returned to Jeff's room, he was sleeping. I sat on the ladder-back chair, watching him breathe and recalling the mornings I had lain beside him in Florida, right after waking, when I listened to his soft snoring and admired his delicate facial features. I thought of our many conversations when we'd talked about spending our summer at Fort De Soto, and all the things we'd do for fun. Who knew we'd end up in Peru, or that Jeff would spend his summer having his system wrecked with poison?

Around two p.m., Jeff's IU roommate, Tyler, stopped by, with a backpack hanging from one of his shoulders. Jeff was still asleep, so I closed his bedroom door, and Tyler and I sat on the living room sofa while I described the morning's events for the third time that day.

Tyler made a face when I described Jeff's digestive issues. "Do you think his doctor's doing what's best?"

"I guess, but I wasn't expecting the side effects to appear so soon. We didn't even make it halfway home before Jeff lost his breakfast."

"I brought you guys something," Tyler said while unzipping one pocket of his backpack. He produced a small baggy of marijuana and a glass pipe. "These might help. I read on the Internet weed is good for controlling nausea from chemo. Just don't tell Jeff's parents you got it from me; I don't want my All-American Boy image tarnished."

For the first time that day, I laughed.

"Look," Tyler said, "like I told you back in Bloomington, there's not a lot to do in Peru. I'll be busy as hell with the dairy during daytime, but I'm free most evenings, so let's hang out and drink beer, or we can see a movie in Fort Wayne. Jeff won't mind if you leave him a few hours, I'm sure."

Jeff didn't wake up until his folks came home, around 4:00 p.m. By then, he'd regained color in his face and seemed in better spirits. His parents sat on his mattress, one on either side of him, while he talked about the day's events.

"The nausea was awful, but you don't have to worry, Jakub took good care of me."

Jeff joined me and his parents at the dinner table, but when he took a bite of beef stew, he made a face like he'd swallowed lemon juice. "I'm sorry," he said to Catherine, "but this food tastes nasty to me."

"Try to eat some anyway," I said.

Jeff nodded, and he *did* consume several spoonfuls, but that was it, and I wondered just how many pounds he might lose in the months ahead. He was skinny enough as it was, and I made myself a promise to do whatever I could to keep his weight up.

After dinner, Jeff and I sat at the picnic table in his backyard. The sun had set, and the western sky glowed in shades of pink, gold, and robin's-egg-blue. A light breeze stirred leaves on a neighbor's black ash tree.

Jeff chuckled when I spoke of Tyler's visit that afternoon and the marijuana he'd left with me.

"I'll have a smoke tomorrow, when my parents aren't home. Maybe it'll settle my stomach."

Later that evening, we sat in the Brucellis' den watching a film on cable TV with Jeff's parents. The movie, one from Tom Cruise's *Mission: Impossible* series, wasn't all that interesting, and my thoughts wandered back to the day's events, especially the moment when Jeff had asked me to stop the car so he could puke on the road shoulder.

In the months ahead, would I have the emotional strength to deal with Jeff's challenges?

*

Ten days passed, each pretty much the same as the one before. I normally woke around seven and often shared breakfast with Mario before he left for work. We took turns studying the sports page and talking baseball. I, of course, was a Tampa Bay Rays fan, while Mario favored the Chicago Cubs.

"Maybe one Saturday," he said, "if Jeff's feeling up to it, we'll drive up to Chicago and see a game at Wrigley Field. Ever been there?"

I shook my head.

"It's the prettiest park in the MLB, so much better than that Quonset hut the Rays play in."

Jeff usually woke around nine, and after a shower, he dressed and forced down a bowl of hot cereal, saying little and rarely smiling. I did my best to stimulate conversation by talking about items appearing in the Fort Wayne newspaper, but Jeff showed little interest in current events.

One morning, I noticed a bruise on Jeff's upper arm, and when I asked about it, he shrugged.

"Stupid me, I wasn't paying attention and banged into the bathroom door jamb last night. Remember what the patient brochure said? The chemo's destroying most of my blood platelets, so I'll bruise and bleed easily."

After the incident, Jeff used an electric razor so he wouldn't cut himself when he shaved.

To relieve his boredom, I tried to be creative. We played chess and gin rummy at the picnic table in the backyard. Jeff's parents had bought him a subscription to the *New York Times* online daily crossword puzzle, and we solved it together every morning. Jeff continued having bouts with diarrhea, so he had to be careful about leaving the house until he was sure his bowels were empty, but sometimes I drove us down one of Miami County's two-lane roads. We cruised past croplands and cow pastures while listening to wind rush through the Impala's interior.

Almost every day, Jeff accompanied me when I visited the Wabash River, where I took a three-mile run. While I jogged, Jeff sat on a park bench and read a magazine or a book, and he seemed to enjoy the fresh air and sunshine. I know I did, and running helped drain tension from my body when I cruised along a dirt path, listening to my breathing and checking out the river's muddy water through gaps between the trees lining its banks.

One morning, while I unloaded the dishwasher in the kitchen, Jeff hollered a few choice curse words, and when I found him in the bathroom we shared, he stood at the vanity, clutching a hairbrush and staring at his reflection in the medicine cabinet's mirror. When I asked what the problem was, he pointed to several tufts of dark hair resting in the sink.

"It's happening already—I'm going bald, and soon I'll look like one of the old guys at the chemo clinic."

One bright spot was marijuana's effect on Jeff's nausea. The weed settled his stomach and gave him welcome relief, but did nothing to improve his appetite, and I worried constantly about his weight.

Tyler came by the house a few times to check on Jeff's progress, and on a Friday evening, he suggested we—me, Jeff, and Tyler—drive to Fort Wayne to see a movie.

Jeff shook his head. "You guys go, but I'm too tired to make the trip. I'd probably fall asleep in the theater."

So, Tyler and I went to the film, but I had a hard time enjoying myself, because guilt dogged me about leaving Jeff behind. His parents were home to keep him company, but I still felt like I'd abandoned Jeff when I should have remained in Peru and passed the evening with him.

On the ride home, when I told Tyler about my guilt, he grimaced.

"My aunt—my dad's sister—became my grandmother's live-in caregiver when grandma couldn't stay alone anymore. Once or twice a week, Mom spent an evening there so Aunt Carol had time to herself, and it's important you do the same. You're entitled to a life outside of Jeff and his illness."

CHAPTER THIRTY-THREE

Jeff and I returned to Simon Cancer Center early on a Tuesday morning, just after Memorial Day weekend. Sunshine poured through the room's plate glass while a different phlebotomist, this one female, used a syringe to fill vials with blood as Jeff lay on the chaise and stared at the ceiling. By now, his hair had thinned, and he weighed 155 pounds, twenty less than he had back in December when he visited Florida. His skin was pale, due to lack of outdoor activity, and his cheekbones seemed more prominent.

While we waited for Jeff's lab results, Dr. Mashburn appeared, accompanied by ten or so medical students who didn't look a whole lot older than me or Jeff. After shaking Jeff's hand and mine, he introduced Jeff to the students before introducing me as Jeff's partner.

"This is a teaching hospital," Mashburn explained to Jeff, "and our students often accompany staff physicians on their rounds. With your permission, I'll discuss your HL and describe your course of treatment."

Jeff shrugged.

After Mashburn finished discussing Jeff's situation, the doctor looked at Jeff.

"I should have your lab results shortly, and assuming they're acceptable, we'll begin your second cycle. I'll be back later so we can talk. I want to hear how you've handled the ABVD so far."

Mashburn charged off with his students in tow, while Jeff scowled.

"What is it?" I asked.

"Those kids stared at me like I was some kind of ghoul. This whole chemo thing's making me look creepy."

Twenty minutes passed before the phlebotomist returned to insert a catheter in Jeff's forearm. "I'm sorry," she said, "but this will cause substantial bruising, due to your low platelet count. It's unavoidable, I'm afraid."

Jeff made a face, just when Jennifer, the chemo nurse, appeared wheeling her pump with a bag of anti-nausea medication dangling from it. She greeted us with a smile before attaching the IV drip to Jeff's catheter.

"Same procedure as before," she told Jeff. "This'll take a half hour, then you'll infuse the ABVD."

Mashburn returned, this time *sans* his student entourage. He studied Jeff's chart for a minute or so before returning it to a hook on the wall. Then he stood at the foot of Jeff's chaise while we talked.

"Tell me about the side effects from your first cycle. How bad have they been?"

"Pretty awful. The nausea hit me right away, then the diarrhea. I've dropped weight and don't have much energy. As you can see, I'm starting to lose my hair, and I have a nice collection of bruises on my limbs. It seems every day I earn myself another one."

Mashburn pursed his lips. "You're avoiding restaurant food?"

Jeff nodded.

"Any fevers?"

"Not so far."

"I'm concerned about your weight loss. I know food tastes terrible right now, but I want you to drink a few protein shakes, every day. You'll find them at the drug store."

I glanced here and there before lowering my voice.

"A friend gave us some marijuana; it controls Jeff's nausea pretty well."

Mashburn winked at me. "By law I can't recommend Jeff use it, but if the weed helps, I won't tell you to stop."

It wasn't long before Jennifer returned in her "hazmat" outfit, carrying a bag of ABVD she connected to Jeff's catheter and to the pump beside Jeff's bed.

"Feeling okay?" she asked him.

"Oh, just peachy, Jennifer—never better."

I handed Jeff his Grisham novel, and I read *To Kill a Mockingbird* while the red liquid on the pole slowly dripped into Jeff's vein. Nearly every chaise in the chemo center was occupied by a patient, many of whom I recognized from Jeff's previous cycle. Some looked okay, but most appeared like pale scarecrows.

Forty-five maddening minutes passed, and I might have read three pages from Harper Lee's novel. I simply couldn't concentrate, knowing the poison was coursing through Jeff's body, and dreading what lay ahead in the next hours and days.

As soon as the ABVD drip bag emptied, Jennifer detached the tube and removed Jeff's catheter. Already, the back of his hand and the lower part of his forearm had purpled, and while we walked to the parking garage, Jeff examined the bruising.

"Jesus Christ, I look like I was in a car wreck."

Before we left the garage, Jeff pulled a joint and butane lighter from the Impala's glove box and lit up. Thankfully, he didn't get sick to his stomach during the drive home, and we decided we would give Tyler money for more weed the next time we saw him.

Once we reached the Brucellis', Jeff headed for the bathroom while I heated up a can of soup and assembled a turkey sandwich in the kitchen. But when I offered Jeff lunch, he shook his head before undressing and climbing into bed.

"I'm feeling weak. Just let me sleep, okay?"

Of course, both Mario and Catherine phoned me to see how things had gone, and after I explained the morning's course of events to both of them, I sat at the kitchen table, sipping soup and staring out of the window above the sink. The day had warmed up, the sun shone, and I decided to spend some time outdoors.

After I finished my lunch, I checked on Jeff and found him asleep. I ran my fingers through his hair and kissed him on the cheek, but didn't wake him. Instead, I eased his bedroom door shut. In my room, I changed into gym shorts, a T-shirt, and sneakers. I grabbed a backpack and my cell phone and wheeled Jeff's Schwinn bicycle out of the garage. Then I cruised through the neighborhood, enjoying the sunshine on my shoulders.

I pedaled downtown to visit the Peru Public Library on Main Street, an impressive stone structure with an arched entryway, built in the early 1900s. Inside, the place was as quiet as an empty church, and not many people were present, just a staffer and a few older folks who sat at computer stations. I had Mario's library card with me, and once I found the Fiction section, I picked out three books: Kurt Vonnegut's *Slaughterhouse-Five*, *The Catcher in the Rye* by J. D. Salinger, and *Wonder Boys* by Michael Chabon.

At the checkout counter, a silver-haired man with skin as pale as cake flour scanned my books. "I read *The Catcher in the Rye* in high school," he said. "It was quite controversial at the time, with the salty language and all. But I doubt it is today."

"I read it during high school, too, and didn't really like the book—I found it depressing—but now I think I'll give it another try."

The man handed me back the books and library card.

"I know Mario Brucelli; he teaches my grandson's shop class. Mind if I ask why you have his card?"

After I explained, the old guy pursed his lips and shook his head. "I'm sorry to hear about Jeff. How's he feeling?"

"Not too well. He just went through his second chemotherapy cycle, and it's left him weak."

The man nodded. "My daughter was treated for breast cancer, about ten years ago. The chemo darned near killed her. She looked like a hobgoblin, and of course all her hair fell out. She wore a wig for a few months as I recall."

"Is she okay now?"

He lowered his gaze and rubbed his lips together. "I'm afraid we lost Paula; God rest her soul."

Shit...

Back at the Brucellis' house, Jeff still slept, so I brewed a cup of coffee and read Holden Caulfield's rambling narration about his troubles at Pencey Prep. I found Salinger's writing style mildly irritating, like I was stuck in a room with a snotty teenager who wouldn't ever shut up, but decided to stick with the book. What better did I have to do with my time?

Jeff finally woke around 3:00 p.m., and he joined me on the living room sofa. He wore sleep pants, a T-shirt, and house slippers. His hair was in tangles, his face pale, but when I asked how he felt, he shrugged.

"I have the shits again, but my stomach's calm at least. I may have a few more hits off that joint before my folks get home."

I scooted over to Jeff's side of the sofa and put my arm across his shoulders. Then I kissed his cheek. Jeff turned his face toward me, and we snogged like two kids in the back seat of a car.

I reached between Jeff's legs to caress his erection. "Wish I could pleasure you with my mouth," I said.

"You know the rules—no swapping fluids for a few days—but at least I can still get a stiffy, and that's *something* to be grateful for."

We kissed again, and I thought of the first time Jeff had penetrated me, when both of us were sheltered by my tent on the banks of the Peace River. I recalled how thrilling the experience was, and how satisfied I had been afterward, and now I longed to experience those emotions again. I considered asking Jeff to bone me using a condom, as suggested in his patient brochure, but I knew he was tired from the chemo cycle, and asking him to perform at that level might not be good for him.

"Just think," I said. "when you're healthy again and we're both in Tallahassee, we can do all the outdoor activities we love most. And every night, we'll fall asleep in each other's arms. It'll be amazing."

"You know," Jeff said, "my radiation therapy lasts seven weeks. I won't be able to leave Peru until late October at the earliest, and what'll you do when fall semester starts in August?"

"I'll take a leave of absence and stay in Peru. We can move to Tallahassee once you're done with your treatments and feeling okay again."

"I doubt your dad will be too happy about that."

I shrugged. "I'm not leaving here without you, so it's not up for discussion."

Jeff chuckled.

"What is it?" I asked.

"You're a persistent bastard, aren't you?"

I rearranged my limbs and fixed my gaze on Jeff's.

"I wasn't always. For the longest time, I accepted whatever life tossed my way, but not anymore. I won't let your cancer steal what we have between us—I couldn't stand losing you. So, if I have to miss fall semester, I will."

*

On Thursday morning, two days after Jeff's second chemo cycle, I woke to the sound of him vomiting. I found him squatting on the bathroom floor with his head hanging over the toilet bowl.

"Hey," I whispered, "are you okay?"

When Jeff looked up at me, his face was light green in color, his eyes bloodshot. He resembled a zombie in a horror film, but I did my best not to let him know how ghastly he appeared. He spat twice into the toilet and then flushed.

"Get me a bottle of cold water, will you?"

In the kitchen, Mario looked up from his newspaper to say good morning. The room smelled of freshly brewed coffee and fried bacon, but after what I'd just seen in the bathroom, the thought of eating breakfast made my guts churn.

"Jeff's sick to his stomach," I said.

Mario put down his paper. "Should I check on him?"

I shook my head. "He's a mess right now, and would only feel worse if you saw how bad he looks. Let me get him cleaned up first, then you can stop by his room before you leave for work. Give us twenty minutes."

Mario didn't argue with me.

Back in the bathroom, I turned on the shower and pulled Jeff to his feet. "Let's bathe; you'll feel better when you get yourself clean."

After he drank some water, Jeff slipped out of his underwear and climbed over the tub's rim, while I kept a firm grip on his upper arm so he wouldn't fall. Then we stood under the warm flow of water, and I soaped Jeff's limbs with a washcloth. He swayed while I scrubbed his armpits, buttocks, and back, but at least his eyes looked somewhat normal now, and the greenness in his face had faded.

"I guess the effect of the weed I smoked last night must've worn off," he said while I shampooed his hair and scrubbed his scalp with my fingertips. "My stomach was so jittery I barely made it in here."

When I looked down at the tub's floor, strands of Jeff's hair glided across the porcelain and cruised toward the drain.

Minutes later, Jeff wore sleep pants and a fresh T-shirt, and his hair was neatly combed. He sat up in bed when Mario knocked on the door jamb, and even did his best to smile.

"Hey, Dad."

Mario sat on the mattress beside Jeff. He was dressed in a Dickies work shirt and matching pants, along with steel-toed boots, and he smelled of aftershave lotion. He patted Jeff's thigh through the blanket.

"I understand your stomach's upset this morning?"

Jeff nodded. "But I'm feeling better now that I showered. Jakub's taking care of me, so everything's okay."

Mario glanced at me and smiled before returning his gaze to Jeff. "You're lucky to have Jakub around. In fact, we're *all* fortunate he's here."

"Does Mom feel that way?"

Mario drew a breath. "Your mother's having a tough time dealing with the fact you're seriously ill, so accepting Jakub into our family right now is difficult for her. Try to be patient."

"Jesus, Dad. Not only is Jakub taking care of me around the clock, he's helping with the daily chores *and* the yard. Hell, he's even painting the goddamned house; what more does she want?"

Mario gazed into his lap. "You have to understand; our archdiocese considers homosexual activity a sin."

Jeff scowled and shook his head. "She's not being fair to Jakub or me. I'm keeping up my end of the bargain we made. I go to Sunday mass with you and Mom. Jakub and I only get affectionate in private, at least when we're in Peru, and we sleep in separate bedrooms. In return, Mom needs to accept us for who we are."

"I'm working on it," Mario said, rising to his feet. "Anything I can do for you before I leave for work?"

Jeff shook his head. "Jakub has everything under control."

CHAPTER THIRTY-FOUR

A week after Jeff's third chemotherapy cycle, just when June ended, I stood on a six-foot aluminum ladder, scraping loose paint from a fascia board on the Brucellis' house, using a wire brush. I wore my headphones and listened to one of my favorite country western groups, Florida Georgia Line. I kept my phone on vibrate so Jeff could summon me if he needed something, and I rocked my hips to the beat of a number titled "Sun Daze."

The day was warm, and I had shed my shirt, so I wore only a ragged pair of khaki shorts and my oldest sneakers. The sun felt nice on my shoulders and arms while I worked. Earlier, Tyler had called from his family's dairy farm, to see if I'd spend the following afternoon with him, a Saturday.

"We'll buy beer at a sketchy convenience store where they're not careful about checking IDs. Tomorrow's supposed to be sunny, and I know a granite quarry where we can go for a swim. Then we'll cruise in my dad's truck."

I always looked forward to spending time with Tyler. In the two months I had lived in Peru, I'd grown to know him pretty well, and I valued his friendship. He was bright and sensitive, and he seemed to enjoy my company.

"I'm just a farm kid, really," he told me early on, when we shared a six-pack while lying on a blanket in a cornfield, gazing up at the starry sky. "I couldn't imagine growing up in an area like Tampa Bay, especially in the park where you live. What a lucky guy."

"Don't be too impressed. First of all, I didn't have any friends to speak of, and I *never* dated. Jeff was the first guy I ever got personal with, and that was only a year ago, so I wouldn't call my life all that exciting."

"But Peru *has* to make you feel restricted."

I rose to a sitting position. "Not really. I stay busy looking after Jeff and doing chores around his house, and I like taking runs along the Wabash. Plus, the weather's stinking hot in Florida this time of year, so I have no complaints."

Another evening, Tyler, Jeff, and I played Risk at the Brucellis' kitchen table, and I laughed like crazy at stories Tyler and Jeff shared from their high school days, tales of binge-drinking, pulling pranks on friends, and drag-racing on dirt roads outside of town.

"I'm surprised we didn't get ourselves killed or seriously injured," Jeff said.

"Remember prom our junior year?" Tyler said. "I was buzzed on weed and got so warm from dancing,

I tore off my shirt and ran around bare-chested till the Dean of Men, old man Mumbles, chased me out of the gymnasium and told me not to come back."

Jeff giggled. "Your poor date... What was her name?"

"Angela."

"She spent the rest of the evening by herself. No *wonder* you guys never went out again."

Now, on my ladder, I descended and relocated to a separate section of fascia, and while I scraped loose paint, I tried to imagine what it must have been like for a gay boy like Jeff to grow up in a conservative place like Peru. He had probably felt lonely and isolated, much as I did during high school. But at least we had each other now, and hopefully solitude was something we'd both put behind us for good.

*

Tyler and I lay on bath towels spread on a granite slab, fifteen feet above a shimmering pool of turquoise water. The sky was cloudless, the air still and warm, and the croaky voices of a group of nearby teenage boys echoed off the quarry walls. We both wore swim trunks and our hair was damp from the swim we'd taken minutes before. We had dived from a cliff high above the chilly water and then spent ten minutes treading before scaling up a series of ledges to reach our towels.

The slab we lay on absorbed the sun's heat and warmed us while beads of water evaporated on our skins. I lay on my back, wearing sunglasses so the afternoon sunlight wouldn't sear my eyeballs, while Tyler lay on his stomach with his cheek resting on his crossed forearms.

An hour before, when Tyler had picked me up at the Brucellis', we tried talking Jeff into joining us, but he only waved us off.

"You guys go ahead. To be honest, right now I'm too tired to climb ledges."

"You'll be okay here by yourself?" I asked.

"Mom will be home in an hour; it's fine."

Now, at the quarry, Tyler knitted his eyebrows. "Jeff's looking pretty run down these days. And what's with the bruises on his arms? He looks like he fell down a flight of stairs."

"His blood platelets got wiped out by the chemo cycles. All he has to do is bump into a chair, and another bruise pops up."

"Do you think he'll be okay?"

I scratched my stubbly chin. "I sure hope so, but that stuff they pump into his body at the cancer center really tears him up."

While marijuana helped with Jeff's nausea, other side effects of the ABVD had appeared. By now, about half of Jeff's hair had fallen out. He suffered from bouts of diarrhea, and sores had erupted on the inside of his mouth; they made eating uncomfortable. Most days he felt too tired to take a walk around the block, and his weight was now at a hundred and forty pounds, thirty-five less than back in December.

About the only outdoor activity he enjoyed was riding around in the Impala with me at the wheel, so I took him for an hour's drive each day, if his digestive system allowed him to stray from the toilet for that length of time.

"I have nightmares in the wee hours," Jeff told me one morning while we showered together. "I wake up trembling like a kid in a spook house. My sheets are tangled, and I've drooled all over my pillow."

Now, Tyler rose to a sitting position facing the quarry. He raised his knees and rested his forearms on them. Sunlight reflected in gold streaks weaving through his hair.

"You know," he said, "sometimes I feel guilty when I think about Jeff's cancer. Here I am, as healthy as a colt and sitting in the sunshine, while he's probably lying on the sofa and feeling like shit. I wish there was something I could do to help."

I rose to a sitting position myself. "You're helping a lot by coming to the house and spending time with Jeff. It means so much to him, just to play cards or watch a baseball game with you. It helps him feel somewhat normal."

Tyler cleared his throat. "Mind if I ask a personal question?"

"What's that?"

"Are you guys still having sex?"

I winced while recalling an episode occurring the week before. Jeff and I had tried to get passionate while his folks were at work, but he couldn't even maintain an erection.

"I'm as limp as a dishrag," he blurted while tears rolled down his cheeks.

"We *were* for a while there," I told Tyler, "but lately it's less and less. Jeff's so weak he doesn't have enough energy to do much, and it's frustrating for him."

"And for you, I'm sure."

I nodded.

"Wish I could help you out there," Tyler said, "but I play for the wrong team."

I smiled at him. "I'm fine, really. If I get horny, I go to my room and grab the jelly tube from my nightstand. Ten minutes later, I'm good, so it's not a problem. And Jeff and I still get affectionate when his parents aren't around. We hold each other while we watch TV."

When Tyler rose, his knees crackled.

"Why don't we take another swim? Then we'll get in the truck and ride around. Those beers in the cooler are calling us."

*

On a Thursday afternoon during the second week of July, I had just finished mowing the Brucellis' lawn when an afternoon rainstorm blew into town and chased me inside the house. Shirtless and sweaty, I joined Jeff on the loveseat in the den, where he watched *Jeopardy* on the flat-screen television. As soon as I sat down, Jeff turned the TV off and sniffed the air.

"You smell like sweat and grass clippings."

"Guess I'll grab a shower," I said, but when I tried rising, Jeff grabbed my forearm.

"You don't smell *that* bad. Just stay here and hold me."

I wrapped both arms around Jeff's shoulders and nuzzled his ear. I smooched his cheek but didn't try doing more because if I had tongue-kissed Jeff, I would have irritated the sores in his mouth. Still, being close to him made my pulse accelerate, and I grew stiff.

Jeff looked down at the bulge in my shorts and snickered. Then he poked it with a fingertip. "Want me to take care of that for you?"

Moments later, my shorts were open, and Jeff stroked me with his hand while I licked his neck and twirled my tongue in his ear. We hadn't been intimate in many days, and Jeff's gentle touch had my heart pounding like a pile driver. Jeff, of course, didn't get hard, but his breathing quickened, and his face turned pink. We both grew so excited, we didn't realize Catherine had come home, not until she walked into the den, just when I groaned and shot my load all over my chest and belly.

Her voice sounded as sharp as a whip crack.

"What do you two think you're doing?"

My cheeks burned while I shoved my erection down one leg of my shorts and pulled up the zipper.

Catherine stood with her hands on her hips, staring at the cluster of pearls dotting my torso. I was embarrassed as hell, since I didn't have anything to wipe myself with, but Jeff didn't seem the least bit concerned about the situation.

"We were having sex, Mom, as best I'm able these days."

"I thought we agreed you wouldn't do it under our roof."

"I never said that; I only agreed we wouldn't in your presence, and I wasn't expecting you home so early today."

I cleared my throat and looked at Jeff. "I should clean myself up."

Jeff shook his head. "I'll do it for you."

He lowered his face to my torso and lapped at my semen.

"Stop that," Catherine cried. "Don't you have any respect for yourself? Do you know how disgusting I find your behavior?"

Jeff looked up from his work and licked his lips.

"*Do* I disgust you, Mom? Is my love for Jakub wrong in your view? Well, I'm sorry, but the fact you or the Catholic church disapproves of what we do isn't going to change a goddamned thing, and the sooner you understand that the better."

"You're acting selfishly, Jeff."

"No, I'm just being me, and I'll tell you something. Despite how shitty I look and how tired I am, right before you walked into the room, I felt human for a change—like a person loved and desired—and there is nothing wrong with that."

Catherine's hands hung at her hips while she flexed her fingers. "Jakub, why don't you leave the room? I need to talk with my son."

"He's going nowhere. Whatever you have to tell me, you can say in Jakub's presence."

Catherine's gaze traveled from Jeff to me and back. Then she sat in Mario's recliner, and the vinyl creaked beneath her weight. Her chin quivered when she spoke to Jeff.

"Summer semester ends in mid-August, and I'll be available to take care of you full time. I can drive you to and from the cancer center, and do whatever else is necessary. Meanwhile, Jakub can go back to Florida."

"That's *not* going to happen, Mom. Jakub won't leave until I'm healthy enough to go with him—end of story."

By now, the puddles of come remaining on my skin had gelled, and the situation seemed terribly awkward, with me sitting there shirtless, sticky, and smelling bad, while my presence in the Brucellis' home was debated. But right then, I knew Jeff expected me to stay put, so I made no attempt to depart the room.

Catherine's eyes glistened when she turned her gaze to me.

"You probably think I'm a witch—in fact I'm sure you do—but I'm only trying to be the best mother I can. And I fear God may take Jeff from me permanently if he continues down the path you've led him. Father Laughlin—"

Jeff leaped to his feet.

"Wait a minute. First of all, I've been queer since I hit puberty, long before I met Jakub. So, he hasn't *led* me anywhere. And maybe Father Laughlin runs your life, but not mine. I need Jakub here while I try to get through this misery. Mom, I'm going to tell you something important, so please listen. I won't make it without Jakub; I can't. If you truly care about me—and I know you do—then drop the idea of him leaving."

Catherine looked up at Jeff for a long moment and then she thrust her face into her hands and sobbed.

Jeff sat down on the recliner's arm; he embraced Catherine's shoulders. "Don't cry; it'll be okay. Jakub will make sure I survive this. Just let him do his job, will you?"

Catherine spoke through her fingers. "I'm only trying to do what's right; it's what a mother should do."

"You and Dad *are* doing what's right by letting Jakub live with us. And there's something more..."

"What?"

"Jakub has to sleep in my room from now on. Many evenings, I have nightmares, and they frighten the hell out of me. I shouldn't go to bed alone right now; I need Jakub there so he can hold me whenever I'm scared. Can you understand that?"

Catherine wiped tears from her face with the back of her wrist.

"I can't make that decision on my own; I'll need to speak with your father when he gets home from work."

"That's fine, but I want Jakub with me tonight. I can't wake up to an empty room again; it's too damned spooky."

No one talked for a minute or so, not until I coughed.

"Um, if we're done here, can I take a shower?"

*

Mario, as I expected, had no problem with me sharing Jeff's bed each night, and Catherine seemed resigned to the situation, even though I knew she didn't like it. Thereafter, Jeff and I slept spoon-style, and gradually the nightmares receded.

Even though I woke earlier than Jeff most days, I never left the bed until he did. Instead, I lay there and held him while trying to think pleasant thoughts. I recalled the days Jeff and I had spent at Fort De Soto. Back then, Jeff had been so vibrant and beautiful, and it was hard to believe the ravaged body next to me belonged to the same guy.

Jeff's hair had thinned to the point where I saw all of his pale and bumpy scalp. The hair on his legs and under his arms was gone, and so were his eyebrows. His cheeks were hollow. Whenever we rode in the car, Jeff wore a ball cap, a long-sleeved T-shirt, and blue jeans, to mask his gaunt appearance and the bruises on his limbs. He refused to accompany me when I shopped at the drug store for his protein shakes and ceased joining me on my daily visits to the Wabash River. He quit attending mass on Sundays too, much to his parents' dismay.

"I'm sorry, but I don't want anyone seeing me like this. Once the chemo's done and I look better, I'll go to church again."

When June passed, I dreaded Jeff's final chemo cycle, scheduled for July 9.

So did Jeff.

"I wish we could stop at three cycles," he said one afternoon while we drove on an unpaved road, kicking up dust clouds behind the Impala. "I'm certain the last one will come close to killing me. The side effects are always worst in the days right afterward, and I don't know if I'll have the strength to handle them."

I squeezed Jeff's nape. "We'll get you through it, and then you'll be done with this crap."

One night, Jeff stood naked before his bedroom's full-length mirror, studying his reflection in the glass. "I look like a twelve-year-old—no pubic hair."

Jeff had to be careful what kinds of liquids and solid foods he consumed, due to the sores in his mouth. Orange juice and coffee were out of the question, as were most fruits, excepting bananas. The rest were too acidic. The same was true of tomato-based products like pasta sauce.

"It sets my mouth on fire," Jeff told his mother when he tried to eat lasagna she'd prepared. Of course, he couldn't eat anything warm, not even soup. Everything he ingested had to cool before it reached his lips.

Jeff rested far more frequently now, and while he did so, I kept myself busy with my runs at the river, my online course and household chores, and working on my house painting project. By now, I had applied two coats of latex to all the roof fascia and window shutters, and I was halfway done with the exterior and garage doors. The place looked pretty sharp, I thought, and Mario agreed.

"It'll seem like a brand-new home when you're finished," he told me one day while I cleaned a paint brush in the garage's utility sink. "I appreciate the thorough job you're doing."

Evening meals continued to be tense. Of course, Catherine and Mario were accomplished cooks, and the food was always stellar, but conversation never flowed smoothly. Catherine spoke of her students, Mario of his work at the hardware store, and I talked about whatever book I was reading or something I'd seen in the newspaper.

Jeff often said little or nothing, I suppose because eating was such a distasteful activity for him, no matter how tasty the meal was. When he chewed his food, a pained expression often crossed his pale face, and I could tell swallowing required great effort on his part.

A few times, Jeff fell asleep at the table, and I had to rouse him before escorting him to his bedroom and tucking him under the covers. The second time this occurred, after I returned to the dining room, Catherine lowered her voice.

"I'm worried. Do you think we should phone Dr. Mashburn?"

I hunched my shoulders. "If you want, I'll do that tomorrow morning."

The next day, I placed the call, and about an hour later, Mashburn returned it. I talked with him where Jeff wouldn't hear me, pacing back and forth while describing Jeff's present condition.

"He's not sure he'll have the strength to handle the fourth cycle, and neither am I. Can we postpone it a few weeks while I try to get his energy level restored?"

"I wouldn't recommend that," Mashburn said, "not unless his lab work's unacceptable on the ninth. If his white blood cell and platelet counts are okay, we should proceed. I know it'll be hard on Jeff, but it's important to treat Hodgkin's aggressively, in order to get the result we want."

When I relayed the conversation to Catherine, she cursed for the first time since I'd met her. "Shit, sometimes I think they're *trying* to kill him."

And when I shared Mashburn's advice with Mario, he let out his breath. "I sure hope the doctor knows what he's doing, but I guess we'll have to trust him. What other choice do we have?"

The Fourth of July was a Wednesday, and five of us gathered at the Brucellis' backyard picnic table— Jeff, Tyler, Catherine, Mario, and me. Mario grilled burgers and hot dogs over charcoal, and the table groaned with food: potato salad, coleslaw, baskets of chips, a jar of dill pickles, and two kinds of layer cake.

Everyone gobbled the food except Jeff, who only ate half a hot dog and a spoonful of potato salad.

When the sun dipped below the western horizon, Mario lit a propane lantern. Then we all relaxed in folding lawn chairs, watching fireworks ignite over the river. When a particularly bright rocket exploded, I turned my gaze to Jeff and looked at him in profile. His clothes hung on his frame like a starving man's. His face looked angular, and I shivered in the warm night air.

Was it possible I might lose him?

CHAPTER THIRTY-FIVE

July 9 arrived far too quickly.

Jeff and I rose around 6:30; we showered together before getting dressed. In the kitchen, where we dined on oatmeal studded with raisins and dusted with wheat germ, Mario studied his newspaper while Catherine reviewed her lesson plans for the day. No one seemed in the mood to talk, and when Jeff's parents left for work, they only wished him well and gave him a hug before departing.

The sky was overcast, and a scent of rain hung in the air when we climbed into the Impala. Jeff slumped in the passenger seat while I maneuvered through Peru's suburban streets and entered the highway heading south. Traffic was light. We cruised at a steady sixty-five miles per hour with the radio playing Fort Wayne's country western station.

A car dealership's jingle played when Jeff switched off the radio and slumped back into his seat.

"I want to talk."

"Okay."

"Have you ever thought about death, and what happens to our thoughts and memories after our bodies perish?"

I flexed my fingers against the steering wheel when I answered.

"After Brian died, yeah. For a while there, I actually thought I might hear from him, if there *is* such a thing as an afterlife. I even tried talking to him when I was alone, thinking maybe he could hear me. But nothing ever happened."

Jeff rubbed his chin with a knuckle. "I worry if I die, there won't be anything left of me. I'll just disappear, and after a while people won't even think of me anymore. If that's the case, what's the point of life?"

"Maybe the object is to enjoy it while you're here."

No apprehension arose in me when Jeff and I signed in at the chemotherapy clinic. We picked out a chaise with a nice view of the city, and soon the phlebotomist arrived with his needles and vials. When Jeff rolled up his shirt sleeve, he had so many bruises on his forearm, he looked like a dalmatian. He winced when the phlebotomist pricked him.

"We should have your lab results within a half hour," the phlebotomist said. "Then Dr. Mashburn will decide how he wants to proceed."

"This ain't my first rodeo," Jeff said. "I know the drill."

"Think I'll get some coffee," I told Jeff. "Want anything?"

He shook his head and pointed at the newspaper we'd brought from Peru. "Hand me the sports section, okay?"

But five minutes later, when I returned with my coffee, the newspaper rested on his lap, and Jeff was fast asleep with his head turned to one side and his mouth gaping.

All around us, patients settled into chaises while aides and phlebotomists scurried here and there. Nurse Jennifer gave me a wave while she passed by in her gloves and goggles, wheeling a pump through the room.

I took the sports section from Jeff's lap and studied the box score from the previous night's Rays game with Baltimore. At this point in the season, if I were home at Fort De Soto, my dad and I would likely have attended at least a half dozen home games, and I wondered to myself if Dad had gone to a few by himself. But he hadn't mentioned anything about baseball during our infrequent phone calls we'd shared since my arrival in Peru. In fact, he'd said very little during our talks, mostly asking questions about Jeff, or talking about events in the park.

Was he lonely living in the ranger's residence by himself? Or had he grown accustomed to his solitary evenings? Maybe after spending all day with park guests and staff, he was grateful to be alone for a few hours.

I roused Jeff when Dr. Mashburn arrived in his lab coat with his usual entourage of medical students, and when the doctor asked Jeff how he was feeling, Jeff yawned before doffing his ball cap to display his nearly bald head.

"Just grand, doc; I couldn't be better."

Mashburn lowered his chin and pursed his lips. "I know this has been rough, but medically you're doing just fine. Your platelet and white cell counts have rebounded quite well from your last cycle, so you're good to go today."

"All right, then," Jeff said. "Let the poisoning proceed."

As soon as Mashburn departed, I looked at Jeff and frowned. "I don't think the doctor appreciates your gallows humor."

"He's not the one going through this shit. If he were in my shoes, I doubt he'd be laughing it up either. And those kids, his students? They need to know just how miserable this process is before they put some poor patient through it."

The phlebotomist returned to insert Jeff's catheter. Then Jennifer appeared, wheeling her pump with a bag of anti-nausea medication dangling from it, and while she hooked it up to Jeff's catheter, he told her, "I don't know why you bother giving me that stuff because it doesn't do any good. I'd be better off puffing on a joint."

"I'm sorry," Jennifer said, "but it's clinic protocol."

"Okay, but I'll be toking in the parking garage, as soon as we're done here."

Time seemed to stand still while the bag's contents dripped into Jeff's bloodstream. At his request, I handed him his headphones and MP3 player from my backpack, then I read from *The Catcher in the Rye*. Back in May, I had finished half the book, but found it mildly depressing, so I set it aside and read my other two selections, Chabon's *Wonder Boys* and Vonnegut's *Slaughterhouse-Five*, finding both more satisfying. Still, I felt an obligation to finish Salinger's novel, and now I was almost done with it.

There in the chemo clinic, I read the part where Caulfield's in New York City, late at night. He visits the Antolinis, friends of his parents, and decides to sleep on their sofa. When he wakes up in the dark, during the wee hours, Mr. Antolini is sitting on the floor next to the sofa, petting Caulfield's head. Caulfield gets highly agitated because he thinks Antolini has made a "perverty" pass at him. He gets dressed and leaves, all the while sweating heavily because he's so upset.

While I studied the prose, I recalled reading the scene in high school. At the time, I didn't consider myself gay, and back then I wondered how *I* would have reacted if one of my parents' male friends had put the moves on me. Would I have sweated too?

Jennifer reappeared in her gown, goggles, and gloves, toting a bag of ABVD, and minutes later the cursed red chemical dripped its way into Jeff's system.

When I closed my eyes, I visualized the stuff encountering Jeff's white cells in his bloodstream and obliterating them before they even had a chance to do their job defending Jeff's health. From what I'd read, much of the ABVD cocktail drugs had been in use by oncologists for almost fifty years. Couldn't medical science have come up with something less devastating to Jeff's immune and digestive systems? The stuff seemed almost barbaric.

Anger bubbled inside me because I knew what lay in store for Jeff in the days ahead, but I made a promise to myself: I would maintain a positive attitude. I would stay strong for Jeff, and do whatever was necessary to get him through this final cycle. No matter how bad things might get, I would not lose faith, because if I did, I knew Jeff would too.

It's show time, Mazur.

*

I sat on the rim of the tub in the bathroom I shared with Jeff, watching him vomit into the toilet. Again, his face had turned that ghastly olive-green shade, and I had to fight the urge to puke myself.

After we had left the cancer center that morning, we didn't make it halfway back to Peru before Jeff asked me to pull into a truck stop so he could drain his bowels in the men's room. I went in there with him and stood outside the toilet stall, listening to him squirt and hoping no one would enter until Jeff was finished.

When he flushed, I asked if he was okay.

"Oh, yeah, I'm *great*. Just give me a minute to wipe my ass, will you?"

Now, in the bathroom at the Brucellis', Jeff rinsed his mouth out with water from the basin tap, while I kept a hand on his shoulder to steady him. His face was slowly returning to its normal color. After he'd washed up, we went to his room and both of us undressed. Then we climbed under the covers, and I held Jeff in my arms.

"Stomach better?"

"I guess. I really hoped the weed I smoked in the garage would keep this from happening, but not this time."

"You know the next few days will be the worst—it's always the same after a cycle. But things will settle down. Just be strong and we'll get through it."

Jeff kissed my collarbone. "You're an angel, Jakub."

I nuzzled his bumpy scalp, and before five minutes had passed, Jeff snored. But I continued to hold him while gazing through his bedroom windows.

Outside, the sky had cleared and the sun shone. A neighbor's kid, a little boy of seven or so, played with a border collie in his backyard, tossing a ball so the dog could retrieve it. I suspected the boy didn't have a care in the world. What did he know of disappearing moms, or suicides, or chemotherapy's miseries?

I tried to recall what my life had been like when I was seven, but couldn't. My earliest memories dated to the last year my mother had lived at Fort De Soto, and even those were hazy. Was I a happy child before she vanished? I certainly wasn't afterward. Until the day Jeff first took me into his arms, I'd sort of sleepwalked through life. But after Jeff claimed me as his lover, it seemed as if the clouds in my personal sky had parted, and a ray of sunshine had appeared, one so bright it thawed my frozen heart.

Now, those clouds threatened to return. If Jeff didn't make it, what would become of me? I'd return to Tallahassee and resume my life there, of course. But what kind of a world would it be without Jeff? And without Brian?

Okay, Mazur, you're thinking too much. Get moving.

I slipped from underneath the covers and tucked them around Jeff's shoulders. Then I dressed and went to the kitchen, and while I opened a can of soup, Catherine arrived, dressed in her usual work attire—nice blouse, skirt, and leather pumps.

"I'm on lunch break," she told me while she reached into a cupboard for a protein bar. "How did Jeff's chemo go?"

I poured the soup into a saucepan and put it on a range burner to simmer.

"It's been a rough morning," I said before describing Jeff's digestive upsets. "I got him into bed, and he's asleep right now. He's worn out, I think."

Catherine toyed with the wrapper on the protein bar, flicking the edges back and forth. "I know how much it means to Jeff to have you here while he goes through this. Mario and I are grateful for all you've done."

"Are you?"

Catherine lowered her gaze and nodded. "I know it may not seem that way at times, and I'll admit I didn't want you here at first. I thought you were a bad influence on Jeff. But now I see he was right—you're giving him the strength he needs to fight. I'm afraid if he didn't have you here, he'd have given up long ago."

I stirred my soup while I spoke.

"Please know I'm in Peru because I love Jeff more than anyone else in the world, and he loves me as well. I know it may sound strange to you, how we could have those kinds of feelings for each other. But it's real, and isn't going away. You know that, right?"

Catherine set her protein bar aside, unopened. Then she folded her hands in her lap and looked up at me.

"I don't understand homosexuality. As a girl, I was taught love between two men was a sin, something shameful. And that's tough for me to unlearn, but I'm trying. You see, when Jeff was growing up, Mario and I had a vision of how Jeff's life would unfold. We thought he'd marry and raise children. We believed he would follow the teachings of the church and lead a righteous life. We never dreamed..."

I kept stirring my soup. "Life's funny, isn't it? You think you have everything figured out, and you know exactly what lies ahead. Then it all blows up in your face, and you realize all your plans and expectations were just an illusion."

Catherine nodded. "Everything's unpredictable. I never thought I'd lose my mother so early in life. Her health declined rapidly last summer, and then she was gone, just like that."

"Has Jeff told you about *my* mother?"

"Yes, and I'm so sorry. No child should have to deal with a loss like that."

I poured my soup into a bowl and sat down across the table from Catherine.

"When Jeff told me he had cancer, I made myself a promise I wasn't going to be a passive bystander in the situation. I decided to put my life on hold so I could help save Jeff's, and I'm doing that as best I can."

Catherine patted my forearm. "You've done amazingly well, both Mario and I see that. You're a good person, Jakub, and if I have said or done anything to offend you, I apologize."

"It's okay, we've all been under a lot of stress, and—"

"No, it's *not* okay. I was wrong, and I hope you'll believe me when I say I'm sorry."

I lowered my gaze and nodded.

Catherine rose and returned the unopened protein bar to the cupboard. Then she lifted her purse from the drainboard. "I need to get back to school. But before I leave, can we agree on something?"

"What's that?"

"Why don't you and I start out fresh? From now on, as far as I am concerned, you're part of our family and always will be. And if you and Jeff want to show affection to each other in our home, I won't mind and neither will Mario. You boys do as you damned well please."

CHAPTER THIRTY-SIX

The week following Jeff's fourth chemo cycle was nothing short of harrowing.

No matter how much marijuana he smoked, the nausea wouldn't quit, nor would the diarrhea. Jeff's mouth grew so inflamed he could barely ingest food or drink. At best, he consumed protein shakes and occasionally downed a bowl of cooled oatmeal. He spent most of each day in bed, propped up against a stack of pillows, while I read to him from a magazine or the newspaper.

Jeff was too wobbly on his feet to shower, so every morning I bathed him in the tub, scrubbing his emaciated and hairless limbs with a washcloth while he fought to keep his chin raised and his eyes open. I helped him dress in clean sleep pants and a T-shirt before he crawled back into bed, exhausted from his efforts.

Mario came down with a head cold and could not be in the same room with Jeff, for fear Jeff would catch whatever he had. I decided to avoid Mario as well, so I wouldn't get sick myself. I ate my evening meals in Jeff's room and made sure to wash my hands at least once an hour, to cleanse myself of any germs I may have been exposed to in the house.

When Tyler asked me to visit Fort Wayne for a movie, I declined. "Jeff's going through a rough patch, and I can't leave here for that long. Maybe in a week or two, but not now."

I still allowed myself an hour each afternoon, right after Catherine arrived home from work, to visit the river for a three-mile run. The jogging helped ease my anxieties.

Jeff's nightmares returned with a vengeance. Three or four times, he woke me when he thrashed around under the covers and babbled nonsense. Each time, after I'd calmed him down, he described his dreams.

"I was in the bottom of a dry well, maybe twenty feet beneath ground level. The well was full of these big hairy spiders; they kept crawling on me and gnawing my skin, and the bites stung like hell. I heard people up above, walking around, but when I called for help, they couldn't hear me. It was awful."

In another dream, Jeff was chased naked by a pack of wolves through a forest of twisted trees and thorny shrubs that tore at his flesh and caused him to bleed. The animals got so close he heard their panting and smelled their fetid breaths.

"They kept snarling and yelping; they wanted to tear me to pieces," Jeff said while I held him in the darkness and he trembled. "I've never been so scared in my life."

By the end of the week, Jeff had lost the remaining hairs from his scalp, and when he looked at his reflection in his bureau mirror, he broke down and blubbered like a child.

"I don't know how you stand looking at me anymore."

What should I say?

"I don't give a shit about your appearance. You're my boyfriend, and that's what matters."

Jeff looked over his shoulder at me.

"You're a fucking *saint*, Mazur. You know that?"

*

On a sunny Friday afternoon, after Jeff drank his protein shake and swallowed a multivitamin, I insisted he join me at the picnic table in the backyard.

"The fresh air will do you some good."

Of course, I had to keep a hand in Jeff's armpit while I led him outside, to make sure he didn't falter, but he made it. His long-sleeved T-shirt and blue jeans hung from his frame like a scarecrow's garb, and his face was eggshell pale. He wore a Chicago Cubs ball cap turned backward. I had a deck of cards with me, but when I suggested we play a round of gin rummy, Jeff demurred.

"I can't concentrate too well right now; maybe next week I'll be able to."

"We could play rock/paper/scissors instead."

A smile crossed Jeff's lips while he shook his head. "You're a nut sometimes."

"I'm crazy about *you*, that's for certain."

"Even now?"

"What do you mean?"

"You know what I'm talking about. Who knows if I'll be alive in six months? You'd be wise to put some of your eggs in another basket."

"Don't say that."

"Why not?"

I rose and placed my hands on my hips. "Because I'm not letting you die. I know you're going through hell right now, but you shouldn't think negative thoughts."

Jeff laid his cheek against the table top; he drew a deep breath and let it out. "I'm sorry, but walking out here took every bit of energy I had. I'm as weak as a kitten right now."

I stood behind Jeff and rubbed his shoulders while I talked.

"I had a dream about us last night. We stood atop the fortress at Fort De Soto Park, looking at Fort Dade and the lighthouse on Egmont Key. It was one of those pretty winter days we have there in February, when the air is cool and dry, and the sky's cloudless. We kissed each other, right out in the open."

"Sounds nice."

"It was, and one day, maybe next February, you and I will realize that dream. We'll make it happen."

Jeff swallowed, and his Adam's apple bobbed. "I'll bet you'd like to be home right now, doing something like fishing or swimming in the Gulf."

I kept rubbing Jeff's bony shoulders.

"Honestly, I'm fine with living in Peru at the moment. The weather's nice, and I get to spend every day with you. And things are getting better between me and your mom."

"Really?"

I described my conversation with Catherine in the kitchen, two days before.

"Well, that's a minor miracle," Jeff said. "So, we can snuggle in the den when we watch TV?"

"It seems so."

I sat down next to Jeff, so close our hips and knees touched. Then I placed my hand on his thigh. I knew the neighbors might see us, but didn't care.

"When you're feeling a little better, we'll get out of the house and take a drive each day. I looked at a map. I've always wanted to see the Notre Dame campus, and it's only about an hour from here. What do you think?"

"If my guts settle down, sure, it's a pretty place. When I was in high school, Dad took me up there for a visit. He and Mom wanted me to apply, but I said, 'No freakin' way I'm going to a school run by the Catholic church; I'll attend IU instead.'"

I turned down one corner of my mouth. "Do you think it worries them you're not a believer?"

"I'm sure it does, especially with what I'm going through right now. If I die, they probably think I won't go to heaven, that my soul will end up in purgatory or worse."

"Purgatory?"

A pained expression crossed Jeff's face. "It's supposedly a place halfway between Earth and Heaven; that's the best I can explain it. But I don't think it exists. In fact, I don't believe in anything spiritual."

"Let's stop talking about death," I said. "We need to focus on something else."

"Such as?"

"Let's talk about love instead."

Chapter Thirty-Seven

A week after Jeff's fourth chemotherapy cycle, his digestive system had calmed. His diarrhea went away, and the marijuana kept his nausea in check. Of course, he still felt weak and spent a good deal of time in bed, but he had enough energy to play cards or chess. Tyler came over one night, and the three of us played Monopoly in a game that lasted till midnight. Jeff won and seemed buoyed by his ability to concentrate.

On a Wednesday afternoon, Tyler joined me on my run at the river. The day was warm and sunny, and we both worked up a sweat. Our T-shirts darkened in the armpits and stuck to our backs. At the end of the run, we both guzzled from a water fountain in a city park and then we sat on a bench and enjoyed the greenery surrounding us.

"Jeff seemed a little better when I was over last," Tyler said, referring to the night we'd played Monopoly.

I nodded. "I'm hoping the worst is behind him, since his chemo cycles are complete."

But I was wrong.

Two days later, on a Friday morning, Jeff woke with a raging fever. His T-shirt and sleep pants were soaked with sweat, his eyes were glassy and his face flushed. I drove him to the local hospital, Dukes Memorial, where they admitted Jeff and put him under the care of an internist.

After conferring by phone with Dr. Mashburn, the internist put Jeff on an antibiotic IV drip in one arm, and a saline solution drip in the other, to keep him hydrated. A nurse gave Jeff liquid acetaminophen in a little cup to help lower his body temperature.

Jeff shivered when an aide gave him a sponge bath, and as soon as he was clean, the aide covered him with three blankets to keep him warm. She also placed a surgical mask on Jeff's face, to prevent inhalation of any more infectious agents. A vital signs monitor on a rolling stand kept track of Jeff's pulse rate, body temperature, and blood pressure.

Both Mario and Catherine left work to join us at the hospital, but by the time they arrived, Jeff was asleep. The three of us sat in Jeff's private, second-floor room, listening to his shallow breathing, and I held one of his hands while I talked with his parents.

"What do you suppose happened?" Catherine asked.

I shrugged and shook my head. "The only person he's been around, other than us, was Tyler, and he's not sick. But there could have been germs on a magazine we got through the mail, something as simple as that. The patient brochure said it might happen."

Mario rose and walked to the room's only window. He jingled the keys in his pocket while staring into the hospital's parking lot. "Why can't the poor kid get a break? God knows how far this will set his recovery back."

I left the room to phone Mashburn myself, and after I waited on hold for fifteen minutes, the doctor came on the line, sounding slightly agitated.

"Would Jeff be better off at your hospital?" I asked. "We could have him transported there by ambulance."

"I'd counsel against that. We can't do anything more over here than they're doing in Peru. We'll keep up the IV drips and acetaminophen doses until his fever subsides. Then he'll need complete bed rest until he rebounds, hopefully in several days."

"Will he have to stay in the hospital till he does?"

"Absolutely; I want him under medical supervision around the clock—it's imperative."

I raked my fingers through my hair while I paced in the hallway outside Jeff's room, and my voice sounded funny when I spoke.

"How serious is this situation? Is Jeff's life in danger?"

"I'm sorry to tell you so, but it could be. This is exactly what we *don't* want to happen in the weeks following a chemo cycle. He doesn't have many white blood cells to fight the infection attacking his body. According to the internist, Jeff's temperature was 106 when he was admitted, and that's concerning. He could experience convulsions. The acetaminophen he received and the IV drips will hopefully get that under control, but everything's dicey at this moment."

Holy shit.

After Mashburn rang off, I returned to Jeff's room, but I didn't share Mashburn's concerns with Jeff's parents. I knew they'd worry themselves to death if I did, so I sat at Jeff's bedside and held his hand while Mario paced the room and Catherine sat in a corner, cross-stitching. Outside, the shadows had grown long, and my head ached. My stomach growled because I hadn't eaten a thing all day.

"Do you think they have a cafeteria here?" I asked. "I'm starving."

Catherine looked up from her work. "It's on the first floor."

I hated to leave Jeff, but figured I'd need nourishment for the hours ahead, so I found the cafeteria. I bought myself a roast beef sandwich and wolfed it down at a table. Then I drank a carton of milk, and my headache quickly subsided. Meanwhile, my thoughts spun when I thought of my conversation with Mashburn. How had Jeff's condition gone to hell so quickly? Only the day before he'd seemed on the rebound, but now...

Don't even think about it, Mazur—stay positive.

I seethed when I recalled my phone conversation with Mashburn, days before Jeff's fourth chemo cycle, when I'd suggested we postpone things until Jeff's strength improved. Why didn't I *insist* on it? After all, I was with Jeff every day and certainly had a better feel for what he could tolerate. I wasn't just his medical power of attorney, I was his lover, but to Mashburn, Jeff was only one of many patients and little more than a number.

Still, ruing my failure to stand my ground with Mashburn wasn't helping matters was it? I'd have to deal with things as they presently stood, and that meant being strong and doing whatever I could to get Jeff through his infection.

Move it.

At the nurse's station on Jeff's floor, I spoke to a woman in scrubs behind the desk.

"I'm Jeff Brucelli's partner. He's quite sick, and I need to be with him 24/7, so I'll have to sleep in his room. Any problem with that?"

The nurse lowered her gaze. "Normally, we don't allow visitors to stay overnight. Hospital policy—"

"I don't care about hospital policy. Jeff's fighting for his life, and I have to help him; it's my responsibility."

She looked up at me and let out her breath. "I'll have a gurney with a pillow and blanket brought to his room. You won't be too comfortable but..."

"I only need a place to lie down."

Back at Jeff's room, Mario sat in the chair next the bed, perusing a *Sports Illustrated*, while Catherine continued to cross-stitch as before.

"I'm going to spend the night here," I told them, "and I'll need things from home—my shaving kit and a change of clothing, and maybe a book to read. Will you bring those to me?"

Mario closed his magazine and rose. "Of course," he said before turning to Catherine. "Come on, darling, let's go."

Catherine knitted her eyebrows, looking first at me, then Mario.

"I'm not sure we should leave right now."

"Jakub has things under control here. If we're needed, he can call us. In the meantime, I'm as hungry as a bear, and I'm sure you are too."

Catherine approached Jeff and kissed his fevered brow. Then she looked at me.

"Don't let him leave us, please."

*

"Jakub?"

My eyelids fluttered open, and for a moment I didn't know where I was. I lay on the gurney in Jeff's darkened room, wearing a T-shirt and boxer shorts. Weak light entered from the hallway, enough so I could see.

I tossed my blanket aside and went to Jeff. His eyes were open, but he looked disoriented, so I sat beside him on his bed and stroked his cheek.

"You're in the hospital. How are you feeling?"

Jeff pulled his surgical mask aside. "Thirsty. Can you get me something to drink?"

After I poured him a glass of water, he propped himself up on an elbow and guzzled the entire thing in seconds.

"More, please."

I poured another glass, and when he'd finished it, he lay back down and gazed at the ceiling.

I stared at the blinking numbers on the vital signs monitor. Jeff's temperature was down to 102—not good but certainly better than before.

"What time is it?" he asked.

I picked up my cell phone. "A little past three."

"You're sleeping here?"

"Of course. I wasn't going to leave you by yourself."

A nurse, this one a middle-aged guy, entered the room, and I stepped aside while he studied the vital signs monitor and made notations on Jeff's chart. Then he dosed Jeff with acetaminophen.

"Why am I so thirsty?" Jeff asked him.

"You had an extremely high fever, and your body's dehydrated. It's important you drink as much fluid as possible, to get your temperature down. How about a can of ginger ale and a cup of crushed ice?"

Jeff nodded, and minutes later he sipped from a straw, making gurgling sounds in the semidarkness while I sat beside him on his mattress.

"I guess my folks went home?"

"I told them to. Mario works at the hardware store this morning, and your mom has exams to grade. There's no sense in three of us crowding this room day and night."

"Thanks for staying. It felt great to wake up and see you here, but that stretcher thingy doesn't look too comfortable."

I shrugged.

Jeff laid his hand on my forearm, and his touch on my skin sent a shiver up my spine. I slipped his surgical mask back into place. Then I palmed his bumpy scalp while a mild sense of relief washed over me. Okay, he looked like hell and still ran a fever, but at least he was conscious and aware of his surroundings. He could converse with me, and that was certainly an improvement over his condition the previous day.

"How long was I asleep?" he asked, his voice muffled by the mask.

"At least fifteen hours. You were in rough shape, and I was worried as hell."

"I can't remember much about yesterday, just you getting me out of bed and into the car. The rest is kind of a blur."

I nodded. "I spoke on the phone with Mashburn. I'm so pissed at myself for not postponing your last chemo cycle. If we'd done that, I'm sure this wouldn't have happened."

"You're not to blame. We knew infections were a risk we'd face. I should get some more sleep now, and you ought to also. Go back to bed, Nurse Mazur."

I kissed Jeff's forehead and then I lay down. Moments before I fell asleep, Jeff spoke in a hoarse whisper.

"Jakub?"

"Yeah?"

"I love you."

*

The next several days were ones I'd like to forget but never will. Jeff's condition seesawed between somewhat stable and downright awful. His body temperature dropped to 102, then spiked to 105 or 106. One day, the nurse's aide had to change Jeff's sheets three times because they grew so damp with his sweat. And at times, Jeff's brain became so addled, he didn't even know who I was.

I refused to leave Jeff's room, except to visit the hospital cafeteria for something to eat. Catherine and Mario brought me a suitcase full of my clothing, so I could change into clean clothes after showering in Jeff's bathroom.

The internist kept switching antibiotic drips, trying new types and hoping one might prove more effective, but nothing seemed to improve the situation. So, whenever Jeff had moments of lucidity, I made him drink as much ginger ale as his stomach would hold, to keep him hydrated.

After day four, when the internist stopped by Jeff's room, I asked why he couldn't get Jeff's fevers under control.

"I suspect his infection is viral, so antibiotics aren't helping. Our best hope is Jeff's body will generate enough white blood cells to fight the virus, but he's not eating, and that isn't good. He needs nutrition in order to create leukocytes, so I'm ordering installation of a feeding tube."

Shit.

After sedating him, a nurse inserted one end of the tube in Jeff's nostril. Then she worked it all the way down to his stomach while I cringed. When the process was completed, the nurse hooked the other end of the tube up to a bagful of liquid nutrients hanging from yet another rack at Jeff's bedside.

Jeff shook his head while his gaze traveled over all the equipment surrounding him. "I feel like a cyborg," he told me through the surgical mask he continued to wear.

Of course, Jeff couldn't get out of bed to use the toilet in his bathroom, so during rare times when he needed to pee, he used a bedpan I'd empty and clean after he did his business. I always wore latex gloves when I did this sort of thing, to avoid any exposure to whatever ABVD remained in Jeff's system.

By now, I was on a first-name basis with all the staff on Jeff's floor—nurses, aides, and even the guy who mopped the floors. I knew many of the folks working in the cafeteria too. But if anyone objected to my constant presence at the hospital, they didn't say so, and no one seemed to care that Jeff and I were a couple.

Catherine and Mario visited often, but I sensed they felt confident in my ability to look after Jeff's needs and communicate those to his doctor and the hospital personnel. Mario stayed busy at the hardware store, and Catherine consumed herself with winding down summer semester at the high school.

Whenever I shaved in Jeff's bathroom, after my morning shower, I'd look at my reflection in the mirror and shake my head. I didn't look a whole lot better than Jeff. My face and limbs were as pale as milk. Dark crescents appeared beneath my eyes, and several zits dotted my cheeks. I'd lost weight too.

The second night I slept in Jeff's room, the nursing staff ordered a real hospital bed brought in to replace the gurney. The bed was far more comfortable, and thereafter I slept a lot better, despite the constant foot traffic passing by Jeff's door throughout the night.

A few evenings, Tyler stopped by to keep me company, and to say hi to Jeff if he were awake and coherent. I'd play chess or gin rummy with Tyler while he spoke of his work at his parents' dairy farm.

"Those damned cows need more attention than children. And regulations require us to sanitize the milk processing equipment daily. It's a lot of work, and we're short-handed right now. With the economy chugging like it is, finding reliable labor is tough. There aren't many folks looking for the kinds of jobs we offer."

Mario and Catherine supplied me with a steady stream of books from their home or the public library. I'd developed a liking for the novels of John Irving, and I plowed through *The Cider House Rules, The World According to Garp,* and *The Hotel New Hampshire.* Reading those books helped pass the time I spent idly at Jeff's bedside, and I even sent Irving an e-mail via his website, thanking him for writing his stories. I explained how much they were helping me get through Jeff's ordeal.

Finally, on day six of Jeff's hospital stay, I woke to find him sitting up with the part of his bed behind his back raised. His surgical mask was turned to the side and he sipped from a cup of ginger ale and ice. Color had returned to his face. He wore his IU ball cap, and a *National Geographic* magazine rested on his lap.

My eyebrows jumped when I saw him. "You're up?"

"I have been for an hour or so, but I kept quiet so I wouldn't wake you."

I reached for my jeans and slipped into them. Then I padded barefoot over to Jeff's bed to kiss his cheek. "You look better than you have in a while," I said before checking the vital signs monitor. Jeff's body temperature was down to 101.

Just after I showered and dressed, the internist came by in his lab coat. He perused Jeff's chart while sunlight streaming into the room reflected off the stethoscope hanging from his shoulder.

"I know that feeding tube's uncomfortable," he told Jeff. "Think you could swallow protein shakes now?"

Jeff nodded and pointed to his nose. "Anything to get rid of this bastard."

The doctor scribbled something on Jeff's chart with a ballpoint pen. "I'll have the lab check your white cell count this morning. If it's improved, we can take you off the IV drips and get rid of that surgical mask as well."

"That'd be nice, doc."

I phoned Catherine, then Mario, to let them know what was going on, and both sounded relieved.

"It's the first good news we've had in two weeks," Catherine said. "Thank you, Jakub, for all you've done. I know it's made a huge difference in Jeff's recovery."

It wasn't long before Jeff's IVs and feeding tube were disconnected, and once I was sure he was able to stand up, I took him into the bathroom for a warm shower, his first since arriving at the hospital. I scrubbed him from his feet to the top of his hairless head.

"God, this feels good," he told me while I soaped his stringy arm.

We stayed at the hospital three more nights before the internist authorized Jeff's release, and when time came for us to leave, I spent an hour thanking all of the hospital staff for their kindnesses during our stay, even the folks in the cafeteria and the cleaning people.

Of course, hospital policy required Jeff be transported to the Impala in a wheelchair, and staff along our way kept waving and wishing Jeff the best of luck in the days ahead. Jeff wore street clothes and his ball cap and he smiled at them all, looking happier than I'd seen him since the day before his fourth chemo cycle.

Once in the car, he slumped against the passenger's door while I steered us through downtown Peru, past the boarded-up storefronts.

"I feel like I've been released from prison."

I rubbed his thigh while steering with one hand. "You were awfully brave; I don't know where you found the strength."

Jeff hissed. "I got it from you, stupid."

Chapter Thirty-Eight

Jeff's health improved in the weeks after his release from Dukes Memorial. His appetite returned, and the sores in his mouth faded, so he was able to eat solid food again. No more diarrhea, nausea, or nightmares. I continued to share Jeff's bed with him each night, and we showered together every morning. Little wisps of hair appeared on Jeff's head, as well as in his armpits, his pubic area, and on his arms and legs. Whiskers sprouted on his chin and cheeks, and one morning he shaved for the first time in months.

"I'm an adult again," he told me while he dragged a razor across his face.

We resumed our car rides through corn country, and Jeff often accompanied me to the river to watch me take my runs. The August weather was so unlike Florida's mugginess. Most days, the temperature peaked around eighty, humidity was low, and the skies were clear.

On a Saturday morning, I drove us to South Bend, to visit University of Notre Dame's campus.

The day was sunny, and warm wind rushed through the Impala's interior while we cruised northward on US Highway 31, passing by croplands. Jeff still looked gaunt, but the hollowness in his cheeks had lessened.

The leafy Notre Dame campus and its neo-Gothic architecture awed me when Jeff and I strode its sidewalks. I marveled at the gold-domed Main Building, the Basilica of the Sacred Heart, and the "touchdown Jesus" mural at the library. Of course, we *had* to visit the football stadium, a mammoth bowl seating eighty thousand for Fighting Irish contests.

Classes were not in session, so we encountered few people during our visit, mostly maintenance crews and tourists like ourselves. We probably walked for ninety minutes before Jeff said he needed to rest. From Peru, we'd brought a cooler packed with sandwiches and sodas, and now we dined in the shade of an elm tree at the edge of the north quad.

"This place is beautiful," I told Jeff. "I can't believe you passed up a chance to attend."

Jeff made a face as if he'd swallowed something bitter.

"You don't understand, the Roman Catholic subculture can be suffocating. I wasn't willing to subject myself to four years of religious nonsense— it's not what a college education is about."

I lowered my gaze and then returned it to Jeff's.

"Will you attend church with your folks again?"

Jeff rocked his head from side to side. "In a couple of months, maybe, once I don't look like a cadaver. I don't *want* to go, but I made a deal with them, and I intend to keep it as long as we're living with them."

I told Jeff about a phone conversation I'd held with my academic adviser at FSU, two days before. "He obtained permission to grant me a leave of absence for fall semester. I won't need to return until January."

"What about your apartment?"

"I'll let Mason stay there. He already told me he would, and that way I won't have to put my stuff in storage."

We both worked on our sandwiches, remaining silent for a bit, until Jeff cleared his throat.

"You know, I think the worst of this shit is behind me, now chemo's done. I wouldn't mind if you went back to Tallahassee for fall classes. I can drive myself to the radiation treatments, the patient brochure from the cancer center says so."

I shook my head. "I'm not leaving here without you."

*

Jeff's radiation treatments commenced on the second Monday in August, and when we arrived at Simon Cancer Center, we went to the building's fifth floor, where we met with Janet Horowitz, MD, Jeff's radiation oncologist, a raven-haired woman in a lab coat. We sat in her office while she discussed the course of Jeff's radiation therapy. Her speech was laced with an upper Midwestern accent.

"We'll focus on the lymph nodes in Jeff's armpits and the sides of his neck, and those areas will be marked with small tattoos he'll receive once this meeting ends. The tattoos ensure our radiation therapist targets the exact areas we need to treat, nothing more.

"We will administer therapy five days per week, Monday through Friday, for seven weeks. Each session will take less than thirty minutes. The three of us will meet each Monday morning, prior to that day's session, so I can monitor how you're handling the therapy."

"Is it painful?" Jeff asked.

Horowitz shook her head. "Aside from minor burns on your skin, you won't feel much of anything."

"What about side effects?" I asked.

"Some patients experience radiation fatigue—a lack of energy—but that's about it."

Next, we met with a male nurse in a private examination room, where Jeff's chart rested on a table, opened to photos of Jeff's neck and armpits, each with small circles drawn on them.

"This is the center's tattoo parlor," the nurse told us.

Jeff removed his shirt. He lay on the examination table, and joined his hands behind his neck while the nurse shaved what little hair grew in Jeff's armpits with a dry razor.

Jeff shook his head while he watched. "I'm back to looking like a twelve-year-old."

After shaving Jeff, the nurse used a needle and ink to make little dots in a circular pattern inside each of Jeff's armpits. Jeff winced and chewed his lips while he was pricked, but he kept still. The nurse made similar markings on Jeff's neck, beneath each of his ears.

"My mother never wanted me to get tats," Jeff told the nurse. "I wonder what she'll say when she sees what you've done here."

The nurse snickered. "The ones in your armpits won't be visible, and as for these on your neck... they're barely noticeable."

When Jeff glanced at me, I nodded. "Plus, you can always pop your shirt collars."

Jeff flicked me the bird.

Once the tattoos were finished, the nurse applied protective skin cream to the marked areas. "You'll take this home with you today," he said, handing Jeff the jar. "Apply more to all four areas early this evening, and do the same every time you're treated. It'll lessen your burns."

Jeff rose and tossed his shirt over his shoulder. Then the nurse led us into a brightly lit room where a bulky machine loomed over a padded table. He handed Jeff's chart to a stout, red-haired woman in scrubs and white leather lace-ups.

"This is Melanie Sturdevant," the nurse said. "She's your radiation therapist."

After we introduced ourselves, the therapist had Jeff lie on the table on his back.

"This won't take long; you'll be on your way in no time."

Before the procedure commenced, I had to move to an adjacent control room so I wouldn't be exposed to any radiation, but I could still see Jeff lying under the monstrous machine and looking terribly vulnerable. I crossed my arms at my chest and worked my jaw from side to side while the process unfolded.

Jeff gathered his fingers behind his neck. Then the therapist flicked a switch on the machine, and a thin beam of bright green light shone down on Jeff. The therapist adjusted the machine's positioning so the beam focused on one of Jeff's armpits. She said something to Jeff I couldn't hear, and Jeff nodded in response.

After the therapist joined me in the control room, she turned a dial.

"Jeff's receiving his first dose right now."

After a few minutes, she turned the dial off and returned to Jeff, to reposition the radiation machine before coming back to the control room and repeating the process with Jeff's other armpit. She zapped either side of his neck in similar fashion.

Minutes later, she told Jeff, "You can put your shirt on now."

"That's all there is to it?"

Melanie nodded while she made notations in Jeff's chart. "Any questions?"

Jeff and I looked at each other, then at Melanie.

"I guess we thought this would be more complicated," I said. "Is there anything we should expect to happen later today? Will Jeff get sick to his stomach?"

Melanie shook her head. "He may feel listless, some patients do. And he might experience minor burning in the areas I treated, but that's about it."

*

The treatments unfolded like clockwork. Every weekday morning, Jeff and I rose at 7:30 and showered. Jeff's appetite had returned, and the sores in his mouth were gone, so now he could drink orange juice and eat corn flakes. He handled hot coffee too. At quarter till nine, each treatment day, we climbed into the Impala to make the hourlong drive to Indianapolis.

I had purchased a book of *L.A. Times* crossword puzzles, and we often solved one or two in the car, to help pass the time while we cruised through farm country.

Jeff looked better than he had in months, but the hair on his head had not grown out yet, and he continued to wear his ball cap in public. He'd put on six pounds since his stay at Dukes Memorial, and the bruises on his limbs had faded.

Each Monday, prior to Jeff's radiation treatment, we met with Dr. Horowitz so she could examine Jeff's skin and see how he was tolerating his therapy.

"I'm feeling okay," Jeff told her, two weeks into his treatments. "Compared to chemo, this is a piece of cake."

But one afternoon in Peru, when I suggested we take a bike ride, Jeff declined.

"Not sure I'm strong enough for that yet. Give me another couple of weeks, then we'll see."

I had finished my house painting project at the Brucellis', leaving me with more time on my hands than I knew what to do with. I continued checking books out of the public library, and kept up my daily runs at the river, usually accompanied by Jeff. While I ran, he sat on a park bench and savored the warm August sunshine.

Classes would commence at Miami County schools the last week of August, and both Mario and Catherine returned to work several days before that, leaving Jeff and me alone at the house. We hung out in our boxer shorts and even got affectionate from time to time, though Jeff didn't have enough energy for full-fledged intercourse. Still, it was nice feeling the touch of his lips on my skin.

Tyler spent an evening with us before he returned to IU for fall semester. He told Jeff, "It'll feel weird without you in Bloomington. Why don't you guys pay us a visit one weekend? I'll get football tickets if you do."

Jeff puckered one side of his face. "Maybe when my hair grows out, and I put on more weight."

Labor Day weekend, one of Catherine's sisters hosted an extended family gathering at her farm outside of Peru. But when Catherine asked us to attend, Jeff said no.

"I can't mingle with that multitude. I look like hell, plus I don't want everyone fawning over me because of my illness."

So, Jeff and I stayed home, and I made grilled cheese sandwiches with tomato slices for our lunch. Then we took an afternoon drive.

Jeff fingered the dashboard. "I hope I didn't sound like a whiny bitch when I refused to go to the party. I know Mom was disappointed."

"You had a right to say no, if you weren't up for it. But honestly, you don't look all that bad."

After Jeff lowered his sun visor, he removed his ball cap and studied his reflection in the little mirror.

"Are you kidding? I would have scared small children if I'd gone."

"Look, if your baldness bothers you so much, why don't you get a hairpiece from the cancer center? I'm sure they have one that'll work."

Jeff slammed the ball cap back onto his head. "I am *not* wearing a fucking wig. No way; you can forget it."

"It was just an idea, so don't get crabby with me."

Jeff shook his head. "You don't understand what it's like to look as ugly as I do."

I squeezed Jeff's nape and rocked him from side to side while I sang the words to Joe Cocker's corny song from the 1970s, "You Are So Beautiful."

At first, Jeff scowled and shook his head, as if I were acting stupidly. But halfway through the song, he thrust his face into his hands and wept.

"What is it?" I asked.

"I'm so lucky to have you. Most guys in your shoes would have bailed on this situation long ago. How will I ever repay you for what you've done?"

I kept my hand on the back of Jeff's neck while he whimpered.

"You don't *owe* me anything. I'm here because I want to be, and I don't expect any kind of reward. I already told you at the picnic table in your folks' backyard—it's my job to do whatever I can to get you healthy."

Jeff sniffled while he wiped his dripping eyes with the sleeve of his T-shirt. "I feel so tense right now, like I have squirrels in my belly."

I let go of Jeff's neck and returned my hand to the steering wheel.

"Let's do something about that, shall we?"

Minutes later, I pulled into a convenience store, where I bought a six-pack of beer and a bag of chips. After I placed those on the Impala's back seat, I drove us to the quarry where I'd swum with Tyler. Jeff and I found a ledge overlooking the water; we sat with our legs dangling while we sipped from our beers and snacked on the chips. The day was warm and sunny, but no bathers were present, so we had the quarry to ourselves.

Jeff studied his beer can after he took a swig and burped. "I haven't drunk alcohol since I started chemotherapy. Don't let me get too buzzed, or I'll topple into the water and won't be able to climb back up here."

"Your limit is two cans, lightweight."

I told Jeff about the day I'd visited the quarry with Tyler, and how Tyler apologized for being straight and unable to satisfy my sexual needs while Jeff went through chemo. "What a sweet guy," I said. "You'll miss him when you move to Florida, won't you?"

Jeff nodded. "He's a good friend, and always has been."

"We should accept his invitation and pay a visit to Bloomington one weekend. A Hoosiers football game sounds like fun."

Jeff licked his lips while he studied the placid water before us.

"It would be, and I'd enjoy seeing both Tyler and Craig, but not anytime soon. Maybe in October, if I'm looking better."

CHAPTER THIRTY-NINE

Mid-September arrived, and with it, cooler temperatures. At night, I needed a sweater or light jacket when leaving the house, and I wore a sweatshirt for my runs at the river. Leaves on certain trees turned from green to gold, and when I drove Jeff to Indianapolis, farmers harvested their crops using massive equipment to collect the corn and soybeans.

Jeff had completed five weeks of radiation therapy and suffered no side effects other than slight fatigue. Most days, he took a nap after lunch, but he always woke refreshed. I finally coaxed him into taking a daily bicycle ride to the river when I went there for a run. The round trip was a distance of seven miles, and he tolerated the effort without difficulty.

Jeff had gained twelve pounds since his release from Dukes Memorial, all of it muscle tissue in his arms, legs, and buttocks, and now he was eating as much as I. His body hair was returning and so was the hair on his scalp, but the latter didn't look or feel like Jeff's had in the past. Instead of soft and wavy, it felt coarse and grew in tight curls, but at least he had hair.

Since I had so much time on my hands, I volunteered to cook dinner for our household on weekdays.

"You guys are busy with teaching," I told Mario and Catherine at the table one night. "Just buy the food and give me the recipes; I'll take care of everything else."

Truthfully, I enjoyed the cooking and learned a lot about the use of herbs and spices to flavor dishes I cooked. I found garlic, especially, improved the taste of most any main course I prepared. I made veal scaloppini and mussels in clam sauce. One night I served calamari marinara, another night shrimp over vermicelli. I prepared fresh spinach salads jazzed up with parmesan cheese and extra-virgin olive oil. And we always shared a bottle of red or white wine with our meals.

One night, over a plate of ravioli, Mario looked at me and shook his head. "This is delicious. You'd better be careful or we won't *let* you go back to Florida."

Jeff's gaze flitted between his parents. "Speaking of Florida, my application for transfer to FSU's been granted. Assuming Mashburn says I'm healthy, I plan to start school down there in January."

After Jeff's parents exchanged glances, Catherine put her fork on her plate.

"I'm not sure you'll be ready for a move like that so soon."

"So *soon*? That's ten weeks from now. I'm done with radiation therapy at the end of this month, and then what'll I do with my time in Peru, play tiddlywinks?"

Catherine shifted her weight in her chair. "I'm only saying you should focus on your recovery. Stress won't be good for you, and—"

"Mom, if my cancer's gone—and we should know real soon—Jakub and I will leave for Florida after Christmas. You and Dad need to accept that."

Mario cleared his throat. "We know you're eager to get on with your life, and we understand you and Jakub want to be together. But let's discuss the whole thing with the medical folks. Your health comes first, that's all we're saying."

I patted Jeff's forearm. "Let's see what Dr. Mashburn says."

Jeff shook off my hand. He tossed his napkin on the table and rose. "I'm *not* staying in Peru; I'll go crazy if I do. No matter what anyone says, I'm out of here in December."

Jeff strode from the room while his parents and I remained at the table, gazing at each other and not saying anything for several seconds, until Catherine spoke to me.

"We're not trying to keep Jeff from going with you. We only want to be sure he's healthy before he leaves; I hope you understand that."

Mario chimed in, "We know you want what's best for Jeff, and that might mean delaying his move to Florida."

I lowered my chin and nodded. "I'll talk with him about it."

Minutes later, I went to Jeff's room. He lay on his bed with one arm crooked behind his head. His cheeks were flushed, and his chest rose and fell with his breathing. He gazed at the ceiling when he spoke.

"I know what my parents are up to; it's *so* transparent. They're looking for excuses to keep me here, and it won't surprise me if they lobby Mashburn behind my back, so he'll tell us I should stay in Indiana."

I sat on the mattress next to Jeff.

"I think we're getting ahead of ourselves here. First, let's finish the radiation treatments. After that, according to the patient brochure, Mashburn will take biopsies to see if your cancer's gone. If it is, fine, but if not..."

"Then what? I can't ask you to skip another semester at school; it wouldn't be fair. And I meant what I said in the dining room: I'll go nuts if I have to stay here past December, especially without you around."

"And *I* was serious about what I told you up at Notre Dame—I'm not leaving Peru without you. One way or another, we're living together from now on. And I don't care if I miss another semester, I'll do it if I have to."

"But—"

I placed my hand over Jeff's mouth to silence him.

"I won't go through one more day without you; it's more important to me than anything, even school. So, forget about sending me back to Tallahassee alone."

*

Jeff's final radiation treatment took place on the last Friday in September, and after he dressed, we thanked Melanie for all she'd done. Then we met with Mashburn in his office. Sunlight poured through the plate glass windows while the doctor sat in a swivel chair behind his desk, leafing through Jeff's chart and fingering his lips.

"You've been a brave patient," he told Jeff. "I know the chemotherapy was rough, and your hospital admission was especially scary."

"Doc, there ought to be a gentler method of treating cancer."

"I wish there were," Mashburn said, "but..."

"Where do we go from here? I need to get on with my life."

The doctor closed Jeff's chart and rested his hands on it. "We'll schedule you for biopsies next week. I'll take several from your armpits and neck, in the areas we radiated. If no cancer cells are found in those, you're good to go."

"What if you *do* find cancer cells?"

Mashburn rubbed his chin with a knuckle. "Let's just hope we don't."

CHAPTER FORTY

The days leading up to Jeff's appointment for biopsies were torturous for all four members of our household. No one seemed able to sit still. Whenever he was home, Mario busied himself in the garage, building a new bookcase for the den, while Catherine rearranged her kitchen cabinets and pantry, banging pots and pans and moving bags of pasta from one shelf to another. Meanwhile, Jeff played video games on the console in his room.

I spent hours walking the streets of Peru with my hands shoved into the hip pockets of my blue jeans and my gaze fixed on the pavement before me while my thoughts swirled. Our lives—mine and Jeff's— were beyond our control, just as Patricia Bigelow had told me in my counseling sessions. I had done all I could do, and now we had to sit and wait.

A few times, I dragged Jeff away from his console, to take drives past the harvested cornfields. They had once looked so vibrant and green, but now were simply flat, brown, and forlorn.

I still looked forward to my runs at the river, when my cardiovascular system pumped and my brain shifted into a semi-hypnotic state. And, of course, I spent much time in the kitchen, preparing our evening meals. I did whatever I could to keep my mind off Jeff's upcoming appointment and whatever results it would generate.

Certain nights, I found it hard to sleep. I lay beside Jeff in the darkness, listening to him breathe and feeling the warmth of his skin touching mine, and I tried to imagine what my life might be like without Jeff in it. How could I possibly go on without him?

Jeff's appointment was set for Tuesday morning, and the Sunday preceding it, at Catherine and Mario's insistence, Jeff attended mass at St. Charles. Afterward, the three met with Father Laughlin for a private prayer session. I was invited to join them but declined.

Tuesday, when I drove Jeff to the cancer center, a light rain fell, and the sky looked like dirty dishwater. Jeff and I said little to each other, nor did we switch on the radio. Instead, we both stared out of the windshield and listened to the wipers clack.

At the center, an aide escorted us to a windowless surgical room, where Jeff lay on a padded table with his shirt removed. A bright surgical lamp beamed down on him. I sat in a vinyl-upholstered chair, wearing a surgical mask and wincing while I watched Mashburn inject Jeff's neck and armpits with local anesthetic. Using a scalpel, Mashburn made small incisions at the sites of Jeff's tattoos, and from inside each incision, Mashburn collected what looked like little pearls, using his scalpel and a pair of tweezers. The pearls went into four vials the aide labeled with bar-coded stickers. Then, after Mashburn dabbed the incisions with disinfectant, he closed them with a few stitches.

My belly twitched and my hands trembled while I watched the procedure. Jeff kept his gaze on the ceiling, and I tried to imagine what kind of thoughts might dwell inside his head. The entire procedure took less than thirty minutes, and afterward, while Jeff buttoned his shirt, Mashburn talked to him.

"I'll send these biopsies to the lab, and we should have your results by midday tomorrow. I'll phone you as soon as I receive them, but in the meantime, try not to worry. The odds are very good we'll have a successful outcome."

While we walked back to the parking garage, Jeff spat on the sidewalk. "After what I've been through, we damned sure *better* have a 'successful outcome.'"

That night, when Jeff and I crawled into bed, we arranged ourselves in the spoon position, with Jeff's back to me and my arm draping his chest. Jeff fell asleep within minutes, but not me. All I could think about were Jeff's biopsies, and depending on their outcome, where our lives would go from there. If the lab found cancer cells in Jeff's lymph nodes, would he undergo more cycles of chemotherapy and radiation treatments? If so, could Jeff tolerate the procedures? Could I? And if no cancer cells were found, would Jeff and I leave for Florida after Christmas, or would his parents convince him to stay longer in Peru?

I looked back on the five long months I'd spent in Indiana, and wondered if I might have to live there longer. If so, what would I do with myself, especially when cold weather came, and I couldn't do much of anything outdoors? I'd probably go stir-crazy, cooped up in the house all day while Jeff spent most of his time in bed or in the bathroom.

Somewhere in the bowels of Simon Cancer Center, a lab technician likely examined Jeff's biopsies under a high-powered microscope. What was he seeing?

I closed my eyes and asked myself if I ought to say a sort of prayer, asking whatever deity might rule our universe for help. Of course, I didn't believe in the God they'd taught me about in Sunday school when I was a kid. That all struck me as little more than a fairy tale. But I believed in the concept of karma. If we behaved badly, life eventually punished us. But if we treated others well, and took care of our responsibilities, we got rewarded for it. And hadn't Jeff and I done everything right since my arrival in Bloomington, back in May? Hadn't we *earned* a positive outcome?

Oh, deity, oh, karma, cast your blessing upon this man I lie with, this good and decent guy I love so dearly. Cleanse his body of disease and make him whole. Let him live for many decades, so I can bask in his love and beauty. You gave him to me for a reason, I know you did. You brought him into my life so he could lift me from the misery of my youth. Don't take him from me now, please.

Karma, I'm offering you a bargain. You know how badly my mother hurt me, and you know the hate and anger I feel inside me whenever I think of her. But I promise you this: If you spare Jeff's life, I'll surrender my grudge. I will forgive my mother, sincerely and completely and for all time.

So...do we have a deal?

Wednesday, both Catherine and Mario took the day off from work, and the four of us lurked about the house, trying to keep ourselves busy and doing our best not to think about the call we knew was coming. Catherine graded student essays while Mario focused on his bookcase project, applying a coat of stain to the wood with a bristle brush.

I thought about going for a walk or a bike ride—anything to break the tension—but I couldn't make myself open the front door. I needed to be present when Mashburn broke the news, whatever it might be.

Jeff couldn't sit still. He kept pacing from room to room, chewing hangnails and running his fingers through the woolly hair on his scalp. His cheeks were flushed, and his eyes wiggled in their sockets.

To me, the wall clock in the living room sounded like a sledgehammer busting concrete each time it ticked. I tried to read a new John Irving novel I'd checked out from the library, but the words on the pages turned into pinwheels whenever I looked at them. So, I sat in my room and stared into my laptop computer's screen, surfing my favorite websites and social media outlets, but finding none of them the least bit interesting.

Around noon, when I offered to fix sandwiches for everyone, Jeff and his parents said they weren't hungry, and truthfully, I wasn't either. I forced myself to eat a slice of whole wheat bread slathered in peanut butter, but found it tough to swallow each bite, as if the food were paste.

I sat in the den with Jeff, watching stupid daytime TV, when Mashburn's call came around 1:30, and as soon as Jeff's phone chimed, he looked at the screen and hollered, "It's him."

Jeff switched off the television while Mario and Catherine joined us. I held Jeff's hand in mine and squeezed his fingers, while his parents stood together with Mario's arm draped across Catherine's shoulders. Jeff drew a deep breath before he accepted the call. His face remained expressionless while he listened to Mashburn. A time or two he said, "All right, okay," but otherwise Mashburn did all the talking.

The conversation lasted only a few minutes before Jeff said, "I understand, and thanks, doc, I appreciate all you've done. The same goes for the other folks at the cancer center; they've been great."

After Mashburn rang off, Jeff stared at his cell phone and massaged it with a fingertip.

"Well?" I said.

Jeff looked at me, and a lovely smile spread across his face.

*

Mother, if you can hear me, we need to talk.

I sat alone at the picnic table in the Brucellis' backyard. The sun shone, but a cool breeze blew from the north, and I wore a hoodie and jeans to keep myself warm. I stared into space while speaking to Mom inside my head.

I made a deal with karma, or whomever runs this crazy world we live in. I said if Jeff—he's my partner—were cured of cancer I would, in return, offer you my full and complete forgiveness for all the pain and sorrow you caused me by your disappearance.

Jeff's healthy, so I am keeping my promise.

I don't know where you are today or if you are even alive. But should you hear me, please listen. I don't understand why you left me and Dad, but I suppose you had your reasons, whatever they were. And I am forgiving you for what you did, I mean it. I'm surrendering my bitterness, once and for all, and walking away from it.

I wish you all the best, Mom.

I truly do.

*

Forgiving my mother caused a tectonic shift in my outlook on life. Suddenly, I was almost carefree, and I smiled and laughed more often. When I ran along the banks of the Wabash, I felt weightless.

One afternoon, I thought about the Paul Boese quote Patricia Bigelow had shared with me—*Forgiveness does not change the past, but it does enlarge the future*—and I knew Patricia was right. By forgiving my mother, I had released myself from the shackles I'd burdened myself with for so many years.

Mom couldn't hurt me anymore.

CHAPTER FORTY-ONE

We moved through the month of October, and Jeff's condition improved dramatically. He regained much of the weight he'd lost during chemotherapy, the hair on his head grew more densely, and his body hair fully returned.

When Tyler invited us to the IU/Penn State football game in Bloomington, Jeff agreed to go. We drove down on Friday afternoon and stayed until Sunday. And though the Hoosiers lost a close game, I still enjoyed myself immensely. It felt special to mingle with a huge crowd of spirited people, especially after the months of grim tension we'd endured in Peru. Tyler, Craig, Jeff, and I tailgated near the stadium, guzzling beers and tossing back shots of tequila so we'd have a good buzz going when game time arrived. The day was crisp and sunny, and we all wore hoodies and blue jeans.

I grilled steaks for our dinner Saturday night, and after we dined, we watched a little more football on TV. Then Jeff and I went to bed in his old room and held each other in the darkness. Jeff's skin felt warm and his leg fuzz tickled mine pleasantly when he brought his lips to my ear and whispered.

"God, it feels good to be healthy again."

*

The first Monday in November, Jeff and I paid a follow-up visit to Dr. Mashburn at the cancer center, and when we discussed Jeff's moving to Florida in January, the doctor only shrugged.

"Unless something unforeseen comes up, I see no reason for Jeff to stay in Indiana. And I hear winter's a nice time of year down south—no shoveling snow."

When I came down with a nasty head cold, just before Thanksgiving, Jeff babied me like I was six years old, dosing me with cold remedies and homemade chicken soup. He sat at my bedside and played cards with me, or we watched movies on his laptop computer. Sometimes, he wrapped me in a blanket, and we watched football on TV in the den with our arms around each other's shoulders.

"You're spoiling me," I told him.

"Considering how you took care of me, it's the least I can do. Shut up, and let me play nurse for a change."

So, I did.

Outdoors, the late November conditions were cold and dreary. The sun almost never shone, and sometimes we experienced what the Brucellis called "freezing rain." Looking out of the windows at the bleak weather, I found myself pining for Florida's clear skies and moderate temperatures.

One evening, I spoke on the phone with Mason, to let him know Jeff and I would take over the Tallahassee apartment in January, and he would need to find some other living situation.

"It's not a problem. I think I've finally convinced Jessica to share a place with me."

"You're kidding."

"Nope, I'm simply irresistible."

When I phoned my dad on Thanksgiving Day, we discussed Christmas plans.

"If you'd like, I can ride a bus down to Florida so you're not alone for the holidays."

"I appreciate the offer, but please don't do that. Stay up there with Jeff and his folks. We'll have other chances to celebrate down here."

As Christmas gifts to each other, Jeff and I visited a jewelry store in Fort Wayne, where we bought matching gold signet rings. The jeweler engraved Jeff's initials on my ring and my initials on the ring Jeff would wear, and I was proud to walk around with the glittering band on my finger. To me, the rings were totems of our commitment to each other and also our vows of monogamy we'd exchanged down in Florida months before.

We belong to each other.

Jeff's sex drive returned with a vengeance. It seemed he couldn't get enough physical attention from me. Weekdays, as soon as Mario and Catherine left the house for work, Jeff seized my hand and pulled me into his bedroom while I laughed like an idiot.

Jeff and I attended several holiday parties hosted by relatives on both sides of Jeff's family, and I met so many people I couldn't possibly remember all their names. More than once, women studied the rings Jeff and I wore, but no comments were made, no questions asked.

Christmas Eve, Jeff attended midnight mass with his parents, while I stayed home and built a blaze in the living room fireplace. The Brucellis' tree glittered with lights and shiny bulbs, and a jumble of gifts rested beneath its lower boughs. I sipped from a mug of eggnog spiked with bourbon while I thought of all that had transpired during the year—Jeff's two visits to Florida, Brian's death and his funeral in Fort Lauderdale, my counseling sessions, and my move to Indiana. I thought of the miseries Jeff had endured during chemotherapy, of his hospitalization and the nights I lay in his room at Dukes Memorial, terrified I might lose him.

I knew I had changed a good deal in the past eighteen months. I wasn't a loner, brooding over my mother's disappearance anymore. I had Jeff as my companion in life and believed I always would. And when Jeff's cancer struck, I didn't behave like a helpless bystander. Instead, I put my life on hold and thrust myself into Jeff's family, even though his parents didn't approve of my presence. I made their home mine and did whatever was necessary to help Jeff survive his cancer.

And through it all, I never once apologized for being queer. I insisted on respect for my relationship with Jeff, not only from his parents but from the health care people. I did so because I knew the love Jeff and I shared was a gift I rightfully took pride in.

You made it all happen, Mazur.

Well...you and karma.

CHAPTER FORTY-TWO

Two days after Christmas, late in the afternoon, Jeff and I loaded our belongings into the Impala's trunk and rear seat. The day was dreary. Snow carpeted the ground, and aside from a few blue spruces, trees in the neighborhood were barren.

We would leave for Florida early the next morning.

Jeff had already registered for his classes at FSU—I had as well—and school would start January 7. Our plan was to unload most everything from the Impala into my Tallahassee apartment. We would spend one night there, then drive down to Fort De Soto to pick up a few more of my possessions and spend New Year's Eve with my dad.

"I can't wait to get away from this lousy Indiana weather," Jeff groused. "Think it'll be sunny in St. Pete?"

"It usually is. Two days from now, you'll probably walk around in shorts and a T-shirt."

Due to the poor weather we'd endured in Peru since mid-November, I had ceased running altogether at the river. Conditions were too cold. But one of the first things I planned to do at Fort De Soto was to run three miles on the park's bicycle path.

Jeff's parents were both on Christmas break from their respective schools, and Mario busied himself with refinishing a pair of antique rocking chairs, while Catherine sewed new drapes for the living room. Both had been abnormally quiet since Christmas morning, and I knew why: they dreaded Jeff's departure for Florida.

For our final dinner in Peru, I prepared lasagna, along with a Caesar salad. Scents of garlic and oregano wafted from the cooktop, where a red meat sauce simmered and curly noodles the size of roof shingles bubbled in a pot.

At the dining table, when I served the meal, Mario uncorked a bottle of Chianti, and after he poured a glassful for each of us, he looked from face to face.

"I want to make a holiday toast, but before we raise our glasses, I have some things to say. The past seven months have been tough, especially for Jeff. Each of us has suffered in his or her own way, but we made it through this ordeal as a family."

Mario turned to me. "Our family includes you now, Jakub. I can't tell you how grateful we are for all you've done since you arrived in Peru. No one else could have taken better care of Jeff, and you've been a tremendous help around the house too."

"Yes," Catherine interjected, looking at me. "Mario and I consider you a blessing from God to our family."

Mario swung his gaze to Jeff.

"Your mother and I are proud of you for the courage you displayed in fighting your cancer. At times, I feared you might give up; I know *I* might have had I been in your shoes. But you never quit, even when they put you in the hospital."

Jeff cleared his throat. He took my hand in his and kissed the back of my wrist while his parents watched without even flinching.

"I wouldn't be here today if Jakub hadn't come to Indiana. *He* deserves more of the credit than I do."

*

Jeff and I rose when daylight emerged beyond the bedroom windows. We showered together and shaved side by side at the bathroom sink before dressing. In the kitchen, we found Catherine preparing a breakfast of waffles and Canadian bacon.

Mario looked up from his newspaper, still dressed in his flannel robe and fleece-lined house slippers. When we sat beside him at the kitchen table, he asked, "What time do you fellas think you'll reach Tallahassee?"

Jeff glanced at his wristwatch. "If we don't hit many slowdowns, I'm guessing around nine this evening. We'll switch drivers every few hours, so it's not such an ordeal for either of us."

Forty-five minutes later, Jeff and I hugged his parents at their front door. Catherine kissed Jeff's cheek and mine as well. Then we were off, with Jeff behind the wheel.

I studied the modest homes and commercial buildings we passed on our way to US 31. They were all familiar to me now because I'd walked or bicycled by them countless times—the library and courthouse, the boarded-up storefronts downtown, St. Charles Catholic Church, and the hospital. Of course, I gazed at the frozen Wabash River and recalled the many runs I'd taken along its banks during warmer weather.

For a moment, sadness crept into my heart because, in truth, I had taken a liking to Peru and its people.

But would I ever see the place again?

*

To avoid the inevitable traffic congestion in the Atlanta area, we took I-65 southward, passing through Louisville, Nashville, and Birmingham. Much of the drive was picturesque, because the land rolled and was often forested. We did two-hour shifts behind the wheel, and after my second one, I napped in the passenger seat for well over an hour. We sometimes listened to the sound system—Kenny Chesney, Luke Bryan, and The Chainsmokers. We solved crossword puzzles too. But a lot of the time, we simply held hands and kept quiet.

The sun had already set when we reached Montgomery, where we dined on fried chicken at a truck stop, alongside guys in flannel shirts and ball caps, and by the time we reached the Florida state line, the time was close to 9:30. In Tallahassee, we stopped at a convenience store to buy a twelve-pack of beer before curb-parking the Impala in front of my apartment building. The air temperature was cool, but nothing like Peru's. Our breaths did not steam when we climbed the stairs, clutching our overnight bags and the twelve-pack.

Mason answered when I knocked, and after I set down my things, we embraced. I felt the power of his body and smelled his gamey scent while he patted my back and smooched my cheek. His stubble scratched against mine.

"You fellas must be dog tired," he told us while he shook Jeff's hand.

I handed out beers, and when I stashed the rest in the fridge, I shook my head in dismay. The glass shelves were sticky with food spills, and other than a bottle of ketchup and a container of margarine, the box was barren, save for two pizza slices covered in green mold.

Jeff and I sat on the sofa with our knees touching, while Mason took the easy chair and caught us up on things.

"I found a place for me and Jessica, a two-bedroom house with shade trees and a carport, right off Jackson Bluff Road. We move in New Year's Day."

"It sounds so *domestic*," I said.

Mason shrugged. "I can't be a wild man forever, plus she's good for me. She makes me take life a bit more seriously. And she's made it clear once we're living together, I'll have to take a shower and wash my hair every day. How about that?"

"It's certainly a step toward civility."

Mason swung his gaze to Jeff. "How're you feeling? Jakub's told me about what you went through; it must've been rough."

"The chemo wasn't fun, but I survived with his help."

After another round of beers, we all took turns in the bathroom, and when I used the toilet, it looked like it hadn't been cleaned a single time since I'd left for Bloomington. The sink was caked in soap scum—so was the tub—and mildew grew in the shower's grout.

We killed the lights, and Jeff and I climbed into my bed. Mason scooted into his and, within five minutes, his snores reverberated off the walls. I had forgotten how loud they could be at times, and the din he raised made it hard for me to go to sleep.

Jeff, on the other hand, drifted off in a matter of minutes.

I lay on my back, blinking at the ceiling with my fingers weaved behind my neck and my elbows jutting. It had been seven months since I'd slept in the apartment, and now I realized how noisy Tallahassee was compared to Peru. Even though the windows were closed, I heard roars of transfer trucks on Tennessee Street.

After living in the Brucellis' spacious home, the apartment seemed as cramped as an elevator car. And Mason clearly wasn't a housekeeper. Glow from a nearby streetlamp revealed a cobweb as broad as a catcher's mitt in one corner of the ceiling.

Every time I moved, the bedsprings beneath me creaked, and I thought of the comfortable bed Jeff and I had shared in Peru for so many months. I recalled my runs along the banks of the Wabash River. Then I snickered when I remembered swimming at the quarry with Tyler and how he'd apologized to me for being *straight*.

Would I ever see Tyler again?

I don't believe this, Mazur, you only left Peru fourteen hours ago, and already you're nostalgic about the place. Cut it out and get some sleep. You have a long day ahead of you tomorrow.

I wrapped my arm around Jeff's waist and kissed his nape.

Good night, baby. I love you.

*

I woke to the sound of Mason singing in the shower. He belted Johnny Cash's "Folsom Prison Blues," and did the song justice. Sunlight poured into the bedroom, reflecting off the ring on Jeff's left hand, while beyond the windows, dew glistened my building's Bahia grass lawn.

Jeff had shifted position in the night, and now he lay on his back, while I still lay on my side, facing him. I studied the radiation tattoo beneath his ear and fingered his tightly coiled hair. The patient brochure from the cancer center said Jeff's hair would eventually return to its previous, wavy texture, maybe six months from now. Otherwise, he looked much as he had when we'd canoed the Suwanee River, nearly a year before—lean, with sleek muscles and good color in his face.

I kissed his cheek. "Hey, wake up."

Jeff's eyelids fluttered open. His gaze traveled about the room for a few moments, as if he wasn't sure where he was.

I tapped his forehead with a fingertip. "We're in Tallahassee. Remember?"

He nodded and winced. "This bed's kind of lumpy."

I turned down one corner of my mouth. "I wish it were comfortable like yours in Peru. But I have money saved from what your folks paid me to paint their house. I'll get us a better mattress real soon, I promise."

A cloud of steam billowed from the bathroom when Mason emerged in his birthday suit. Water droplets glistened on his shoulders when he ambled to his bureau and fished out a pair of jeans.

"You fellas sleep okay?"

I cleared my throat. "I'll have to adjust this place; it's noisier than I remembered. And your snoring…"

*

Because Mason's cupboards were barren and his fridge empty, Jeff and I ate western omelets at a diner on Monroe Street. Then we hit the road for St. Petersburg, heading southward on US 19 with Jeff behind the wheel. Traffic was sparse; we encountered only a few transfer trucks and a car or two. The sun shone, and Spanish moss beards swayed in a light breeze while we passed by forests and pasturelands.

We hadn't bothered to shave. Sunlight reflected in the dark stubble dusting Jeff's chin and cheeks and his curly hair glistened. I couldn't help myself; I leaned toward him and kissed his temple.

"You're looking awfully sexy this morning," I said.

He turned his gaze from the windshield to look at me. "Much better than a few months ago, I hope. I resembled a goddamned spook back then."

"Well, you don't now, and it's all that matters."

Jeff returned his gaze to the highway, but he patted my thigh and squeezed it. "I'll never forget the morning I woke up in the hospital and saw you lying on that stupid gurney. It meant so much to know you were there."

Jeff left his right hand on my thigh and steered with his left. We rode in silence until we reached the town of Perry, where we stopped at McDonald's to buy coffee and use the men's room.

"Do you mind driving for a while?" Jeff asked when we returned to the Impala. "I'm still tired from yesterday, and I might take a nap if that's okay with you."

"No *problema.*"

I really *didn't* mind. I wanted time to think about the days we'd spend in Fort De Soto and how the dynamics of my family home would work, now my dad knew Jeff and I were a couple. How would Dad react if Jeff and I showed physical affection to each other? Would he care if I put my arm around Jeff's shoulders while we watched TV? Might he feel squeamish, knowing what Jeff and I would do after we switched off my bedroom lights each evening?

Jeff snored softly, with his cheek resting against a balled-up jacket he'd stuffed between his head and the passenger window. His face bore a contented expression, as if he dreamed of something pleasant.

I thought of when I'd first met him in the Fort De Soto campground. Before that, I had never known the simple joy of *belonging* to someone completely. But Jeff had steadily chipped away at the mantle of loneliness and sorrow I'd borne for so many years. He introduced me to the beauty of life and the wonder of romantic love.

And I believed Jeff's fight with cancer had only strengthened our bond. It cemented our feelings for each other. If our love could survive the horrors of chemotherapy, Jeff's hospitalization, and our claustrophobic days in Peru, it would surely endure any challenge we might face in the years ahead.

I thought about Brian's death, and I knew I still carried a good measure of guilt inside me. But I couldn't change the past, could I? And both Patricia and Mason had told me the same thing—Brian's suicide was an inevitability, and maybe they were right.

Patricia had also told me I needed to forgive *myself* when it came to Brian's death, but how could I go about doing that?

*

By the time we reached Fort De Soto, the time was a little past 2:00 p.m. We stopped at the ranger's station to greet my dad, and when he saw us, a smile spread across his face. He hugged me and then turned to Jeff and looked him over.

"You seem pretty healthy," Dad said.

"I was well taken care of."

"Any food in the house?" I asked. "We haven't eaten lunch, and I'm starving."

"I hit the supermarket yesterday evening. Help yourselves to anything you'd like, but I'm grilling pork chops and baking sweet potatoes for dinner tonight, so don't get too full."

At the house, we made turkey and cheese sandwiches and devoured them on the back porch, seated on the glider sofa. A great white heron perched on a mangrove limb, and sunlight glittered on the bayou's placid surface. The sky was cloudless, the air cool and dry.

"God, I love this place," Jeff told me, in between bites from his sandwich.

"It seems like forever since I've been here," I said.

And it had been, actually—about nine months, the longest period of time I'd been absent from Fort De Soto since my family moved into the ranger's residence, when I was eight. But nothing seemed to have changed, not our household furnishings nor the natural beauty surrounding us. The place had a timeless feel to it.

Once we'd finished our lunch, we went to my bedroom and undressed. We lay naked in each other's arms while our tongues dueled and our lips smacked, and it wasn't long before the bedsprings sang.

Afterward, I rested my cheek on Jeff's sternum and listened to his heart beat. I recalled the day when Jeff had left Fort De Soto for Indiana, at the end of our spring break, the previous March, and I remembered crying my eyes out on the bed we lay in now.

Jeff toyed with my ear while, somewhere in the distance, an osprey chattered away.

"I could lie here like this forever."

"We have a whole week to enjoy Florida," I said. "Anything you'd particularly like to do?"

Jeff drew a breath and let it out. "Honestly, I don't care *what* we do. I'm just happy to be healthy and doing things with you. If all we do is hang out in the park, I'm fine. And I want to get some sun on this pale body of mine."

"Then let's get ourselves cleaned up and dressed. You can borrow my dad's bike, and we'll go for a ride to the fort. Sound good?"

Twenty minutes later, our tires ground against the crushed shell road while we pedaled through the campground, passing tents and camper vehicles. The place seemed filled to capacity with folks from up north who'd left the dismal climate up there in search of warmth.

Jeff and I were shirtless, wearing only shorts and sneakers, and the sun's rays felt delicious on my skin. I let my gaze travel over Jeff's lean physique. He hadn't gained all the muscle back he'd lost since contracting Hodgkin's lymphoma, but he wasn't skinny anymore either. He looked...normal.

At the fort, we ascended a metal staircase to the summit, where we stood side by side, gazing at a freighter plowing through the Tampa Bay shipping channel. The lighthouse on Egmont Key winked at us, and a flock of pelicans passed overhead in a V-formation, looking like warplanes in flight.

"Hey," I said. "I'll bet you've forgotten that dream I had one night in Peru, right after your fourth chemo cycle. I told you about it at the picnic table in your backyard."

Jeff looked at me and grinned. "I *do* remember, and how you said we'd make it happen, next time we visited here."

I glanced about. We had the summit to ourselves.

"I'll do it if you will, lover boy."

Jeff stepped to me and seized the back of my neck. Our lips smacked, and our tongues rubbed while I traced Jeff's bumpy spine with my fingertips. The kiss lasted a couple of minutes, ending only when a group of children came bounding up the metal staircase, chattering away and laughing.

When we parted, Jeff kept his gaze locked onto mine while he wiped spittle from his lips with the back of his hand.

"*That* was pretty cool, Mazur. I'd call it a dream come true."

CHAPTER FORTY-THREE

Our week at Fort De Soto flew by so quickly, it was over before I knew it. But perhaps that's because Jeff and I had so much fun each day. Of course, the Gulf water was too chilly for swimming, but every afternoon, we walked barefoot and shirtless on the beach, and our skins quickly gained color. We fished from the bay and Gulf piers for speckled trout. Every evening, we shared dinner with my dad, who seemed to enjoy the company and the meals I cooked for us.

A couple of nights, Jeff and I drove to downtown St. Petersburg, to attend movies at the cineplex near Beach Drive, and it was nice to hold Jeff's hand in the darkened theaters.

We still had a baggy of weed purchased through Tyler, back in Peru, and twice we smoked up in the picnic area at North Beach, at night when no one but us was around. Then we slobbered like kids at a prom party.

On New Year's Eve, my dad, Jeff, and I took folding lawn chairs to the Arrowhead picnic area at the park's northwestern corner, where we watched the fireworks display put on by the City of St. Pete Beach. The night was cool, and we all wore sweaters and light jackets to stay warm.

About halfway through the display, a sudden urge hit me, a desire to put my arm around Jeff's shoulders, and when I did so, I glanced over at my dad.

"Do you mind what I'm doing with Jeff right now? Does it make you uncomfortable?"

Dad looked at us for a long moment before he shrugged. "It's fine."

Jeff placed his hand on my thigh and squeezed, and then I looked at him when a rocket exploded, illuminating his handsome face. He had never looked so beautiful to me as he did right then. I so badly wanted to kiss him but didn't, not wanting to push the envelope *too* far with my father.

Two days later, Jeff and I tossed our belongings into the Impala's trunk. My dad handed me a check for a thousand dollars, for upcoming rent and other living expenses, and after he hugged both of us, Jeff and I hit the road, heading for Tallahassee. A cold front approached from the north, and the sky was gunmetal gray. Rain fell intermittently while the windshield wipers flipped back and forth.

Jeff steered, and while we crossed Tampa Bay via the Howard Frankland Bridge, he shook his head. "I sure hated leaving Fort De Soto, and I don't think your dad was happy about our departure either."

"I know, and I feel guilty about it. I'm sure he likes our company more than he lets on."

It was midafternoon by the time we reached Tallahassee, where the sky was gray, the air chilly and damp. We visited a supermarket to stock our fridge and cupboards, since I knew they'd be barren after Mason's departure.

He had moved out on New Year's Day, and when we arrived at the apartment, it seemed strange with his belongings gone—his bed and dresser, and his clothing and shoes that seemed to strew the place no matter how much I complained. His pungent body odor wasn't scenting the air anymore, but a tinge of sadness arose within me at his absence.

Good old Mason.

A manila envelope addressed to me, with a Fort Lauderdale return address, rested on the dining table. Mason had pasted a sticky note to it.

> *This came from Aunt Laura a few days ago. I can't imagine what it is.*

A sense of unease crept through me when I fingered the envelope's edge. After all this time, why would Brian's mom write me?

I waited to open the envelope until Jeff climbed into the shower. Inside were a single sheet of Laura's personal stationery, and a smaller envelope with my name inscribed on it in Brian's blocky handwriting.

First, I read Laura's note.

Dear Jakub:

It has been nearly a year since Brian left us, and last week I decided the time had finally come to dispose of his belongings—his clothing and shoes and other personal items someone else might put to use. While going through his things, I found this envelope in a jacket pocket. Because it's sealed, I did not open the envelope, so I don't know what's inside, but I thought you'd want to have it.

I hope you and Mason are well.

Sincerely,

Laura Keene.

My hands shook when I tore open the smaller envelope. Inside were two sheets of lined paper torn from a spiral notebook.

Dear Jakub:

By the time you find this, I'll be gone, a fate of my own choosing. I didn't make this decision lightly. For a long time now, I've known it's what's best for me, so try to understand, and please don't be sad. I'm in a better place now.

Your companionship over the past two years has meant everything to me. I couldn't have asked for a better friend. And please don't think what I've done is your fault in any way, because it isn't.

I had a terrible childhood. My parents had no business bringing a kid into the world. I never felt loved by them. They only admired my achievements, so I tried my best to please them, but my efforts were never enough.

I've led a lonely life. I always did my best to hide my sadness from people—even from you—but it's been there every day, dragging me down, and I am worn out from fighting my sorrow.

I need a rest.

I'm so happy you found Jeff. You deserve the happiness he brings to you because you're a good guy, Jakub, and don't ever think otherwise.

Goodbye and good luck. I will miss you.

Much love,

Brian.

Tears flowed down my cheeks when I reached into my bureau drawer to retrieve Brian's Eagle Scout photo. I sat on my mattress, gazing into Brian's cobalt eyes, and I sensed the pain lurking behind them.

Oh, buddy...

I was wiping my eyes with my wrist and sniffling when Jeff entered the bedroom with a towel wrapped about his waist. He sat beside me on the bed and put his arm around my shoulders.

"What is it? What's wrong?"

I handed Brian's note to Jeff.

"I had no idea he was so unhappy," I finally managed to say, after Jeff finished reading. "I guess I never really knew him."

Jeff brought me a wad of toilet paper from the bathroom and told me to blow my nose. While I honked, he slipped into a fresh pair of briefs.

"I never met Brian, but he clearly was a guy who never let his true feelings show, maybe because they were too hurtful to express. I think that's true for many men. They walk through life hiding who they really are."

"But you're not that way," I said. "You always say exactly what's on your mind, even when you know it's embarrassing or maybe it'll piss somebody off."

"True, but I'm the exception, not the rule."

I recalled the time Brian had wept when telling me about his sister's death. At least he trusted me enough the show his feelings that one time. And maybe if I had tried to get him to open up more often...

Stop it, Mazur. Brian said it right there in the note—his death was not your fault. He killed himself because he wanted to. He couldn't go on living with his pain.

Forgive yourself, and let Brian go.

CHAPTER FORTY-FOUR

Late on a Saturday afternoon in early May, Jeff and I sat on a bench in Maclay Gardens State Park, a beautiful property north of Tallahassee, located on Thomasville Road. Azaleas, camellias, and carnations bloomed; the air was fragrant with their scents. A mockingbird tootled on a live oak's limb while a breeze stirred fronds on a nearby sabal palm.

A half hour before, we had attended Mason and Jessica's wedding ceremony, along with forty other guests, and a now a reception was underway in the park's social hall, but Jeff had asked me to slip away with him to a secluded area.

Sunshine reflected in his dark and wavy hair. By now, it looked as it had when I first met him, nearly two years before. We both wore starched oxford cloth shirts and dress slacks, and our leather slip-ons gleamed from the polishing we'd given them the night before.

I glanced here and there, then took Jeff's hand in mine. "You're looking very handsome. When we go back to the reception, I may ask you to dance."

Jeff looked at me and grinned. "Hey, why not?"

I kissed his cheek and nuzzled his ear. "Or maybe we should stay here and smooch for a while. It's such a pretty spot."

"We might give some squirrel a heart attack. Let's save that for later, but in the meantime, I was thinking..."

"What?"

"Mason's ceremony was nice. I think we should have one of our own, maybe this summer."

My vision blurred. "Are you asking me to marry you?"

Jeff snickered. "Why do you think I wanted to go for a walk?"

I lowered my chin and licked my lips before returning my gaze to Jeff's. "Where would we hold the wedding? Peru?"

"Uh-h-h, I'm not sure my Indiana relatives are ready for that. So, I'm thinking your father's home at Fort De Soto instead. After all, it's where we first..."

My thoughts turned back to the day when we sat on the glider sofa on Dad's back porch. A thunderstorm raged, and rain stippled the surface of the bayou. Jeff touched my cheek, and that was all it took—I was in love and had been ever since.

Even when he stood at death's door, looking like a wraith, my love for Jeff never faltered. And now he was healed and offering himself to me, completely and for all time. What more could I ask for?

Say something, idiot.

I cleared my throat and tried my best not to cry.

"Oh, Brucelli, my darling, I'll be proud to be your husband. You can count on that."

About the Author

Jere' M. Fishback is a former journalist and trial attorney. He lives on a barrier island on Florida's Gulf coast, where he enjoys watching sunsets with a glass of wine in his hand and a grin on his face.

Website: www.jeremfishback.com/blog1

Other books by this author

I Love You Johnny Darling

On The Way to San Jose

Becoming Andy Hunsinger

Kevin Corrigan and Me

Tyler Buckspan

Also Available from NineStar Press

Connect with NineStar Press

www.ninestarpress.com

www.facebook.com/ninestarpress

www.facebook.com/groups/NineStarNiche

www.twitter.com/ninestarpress

www.tumblr.com/blog/ninestarpress